Beach
House
Summer

Beach House Summer

SARAH MORGAN

HQN

HQN®

ISBN-13: 978-1-335-42752-6

Beach House Summer

Copyright © 2022 by Sarah Morgan

For questions and comments about the quality of this book, please contact us
at CustomerService@Harlequin.com.

HQN
22 Adelaide St. West, 41st Floor
Toronto, Ontario M5H 4E3, Canada
www.Harlequin.com

Printed in U.S.A.

Recycling programs
for this product may
not exist in your area.

To Britt, with love

Beach House Summer

1

Ashley

She slid into his car, hoping this wasn't a mistake. It hadn't been her first choice of plan, but the others had failed and she was desperate.

He smiled at her, and there was so much charm in that smile that she forgot everything around her. The way he looked at her made her feel as if she was the only woman in the world.

To add to the charm he had the car, a high-performance convertible, low, sleek and expensive. It shrieked, *Look at me*, in case the other trappings of wealth and power hadn't already drawn your attention.

Her mother would have warned her not to get in the car with him, but her mother was gone now and Ashley was making the best decisions she could with no one close to offer her advice or caution. She remembered the first time she'd ridden a bike on her own, unsteady, unbalanced, hands sweating on the handlebars, her mother shouting, *Keep peddling!* She remembered her first swimming lesson where she'd slid under the surface and gulped down so much water she'd thought she was going to empty the pool. She'd been sure she was going to drown but then she felt hands lifting her to the surface and a voice cutting through water-clogged ears: *Keep kicking!*

She was on her own now. There was no one to tug her to the surface if she was drowning. No one to steady the wheels of her bike when she wobbled. Her mother had been the safety net in her life and they'd grown even closer after her father died. But now if she fell she'd hit the ground with nothing and no one to cushion her fall.

He turned onto Mulholland Drive and picked up speed. The engine gave a throaty roar and the wind played with her hair as they sped upward through the Hollywood Hills. She'd never been in a car like this before. Never met a man like him.

They climbed higher and higher, passing luxury mansions, catching glimpses of a lifestyle beyond the reach of even her imagination. Envy slid through her. Did problems go away when you had so much? Did the people living here experience the same anxieties as normal people or did those high walls and security cameras insulate them from life? Could you buy happiness?

No, but money could make life easier, which was why she was here.

Spread beneath them were views of downtown, Hollywood and the San Fernando Valley.

Stay focused.

"I know the best place to see the sunset." His warm, deep voice had helped propel him from yet another TV personality to a megastar. "You're never going to forget it."

She was sure of it. This moment was significant for so many reasons.

What would happen to that confidence when she told him her news?

Nausea rolled in her stomach and she was relieved she'd been unable to eat breakfast or lunch.

"You're quiet." He drove with one hand on the wheel, supremely confident. One hand, his eyes mostly on her. She wanted to tell him to keep his attention on the road.

"I'm a little nervous."

"Are you intimidated? Don't be. I'm just a normal, regular guy."

Yeah, right.

He was driving fast now, enjoying the car, the moment, *his life.* She knew that was about to change. She'd rehearsed a speech. Practiced a hundred times in front of the mirror.

I've got something to tell you.

"Could you slow down?"

"You prefer slow?" His hand caressed the wheel. "I can go slow when I need to. What did you say your name was?"

He didn't recognize her. He didn't have a clue who she was. How could he not know?

She sat rigid in her seat. Was she really that forgettable and unimportant?

In this part of town, where everyone was someone, she was no one.

She fought the disillusion and the humiliation.

"I'm Mandy. I'm from Connecticut."

Her name wasn't Mandy. She'd never been to Connecticut. Couldn't even put it on a map.

He should know that. *She wanted him to know that.* She wanted him to say, *I know you're not Mandy,* but he didn't, of course, because women came and went from his life and he was already moving on to the next one.

"And you're sure we've met before? I wouldn't have forgotten someone as pretty as you."

She'd had dreams about him. Fantasies. She'd thought about him day and night for the past couple of months, ever since she'd first laid eyes on him.

But he didn't know her. There was no recognition.

Her eyes stung. She told herself it was the wind in her face because her mother had drummed into her that life was too short to cry over a man. She wouldn't be here at all except that she'd felt alone and scared and needed to do something to help herself.

She was afraid she couldn't do this on her own, and he had to take some responsibility, surely? He shouldn't be allowed to just walk away. That wasn't right. Like it or not, they were bonded.

"We've met." She rested her hand on her abdomen. Blinked away the tears. The time to wish she'd been more careful was long gone. She had to look forward. Had to do the right thing, but it wasn't easy.

Her body told her she was an adult, but inside she still felt like the child who had wobbled on that bike with her ponytail flying.

He glanced at her again, curious. "Now I think about it, you do look familiar. Can't place you, though. Don't be offended." He gave her another flash of those perfect white teeth. "I meet a lot of women."

She knew that. She knew his reputation, and yet still she was here. What did that say about her? She should have more pride, but pride and desperation didn't fit comfortably together.

"I'm not offended." Under the fear she was furious. And fiercely determined.

She wasn't going to let this guy ruin her life. That wasn't going to happen.

They were climbing now. Climbing, climbing, the road winding upward into the hills while the city lay beneath them like a glittering carpet. She felt like Peter Pan, flying over rooftops.

Should she tell him now? Was this a good moment?

Her heart started to pound, heavy beats thudding a warning against her ribs. She hadn't thought he'd bring her somewhere this remote. She shouldn't have climbed into his car. Another bad decision to add to the ones she'd already made. The longer she waited to tell him, the farther they were from civilization and people. People who could help her. But who would help? Who was there?

She had no one. Just herself, which was why she was here now, doing what needed to be done regardless of the consequences.

Thinking of consequences made her palms grow damp. She should do it right now, while half his attention was on the road.

She waited as he waltzed the car around another bend and hit another straight stretch of road. She could already see the next bend up ahead.

"Mr. Whitman? Cliff? There's something I need to tell you."

2

Joanna

Joanna Whitman learned of her ex-husband's death while she was eating breakfast. She was on her second cup of strong espresso when his face popped up on her TV screen. She grabbed the remote, intending to do what she always did these days when he appeared in her life—turn him off—when she realized that behind that standard head and shoulders shot wasn't a sea of adoring fans, or one of his exclusive restaurants, but the mangled wreckage of a car in a ravine.

She saw the words *Breaking News* appear on the screen and turned up the sound in time to hear the newsreader telling the world that celebrity chef Cliff Whitman had been killed in an accident and that they would be giving more information as they had it. Currently all they knew was that his car had gone off the road. He'd been pronounced dead at the scene. His passenger, a young woman as yet unnamed, had been flown to the hospital, her condition unknown.

A young woman.

Joanna tightened her fingers on the remote. Of course she'd be young. Cliff had a pattern, and that pattern hadn't changed as he aged. He was the most competitive person she'd ever met, driven by an insecurity that went bone deep. He wanted the highest TV ratings, the biggest crowds for public appearances, the longest waiting lists for his restaurants. When it came to women he wanted them younger and thinner, choosing them as carefully as he chose the ingredients he used in his kitchens. *Fresh and seasonal.*

On most days Joanna felt like someone past her sell-by date. She was forty. Were you supposed to feel like this at forty? She'd wasted half her life on a man who had repeatedly let her down.

She stared at the TV, her gaze fixed on the smoking wreckage. Hadn't she always said his libido would be the death of him?

Her phone rang and she checked the screen.

Not a friend (did she have any true friends? It was something she often wondered), but Rita, Cliff's personal assistant and his lover for the past six months.

Joanna didn't want to talk to Rita. She didn't want to talk to anyone. She knew from painful experience that anything she said would find its way into the media and be used to construct an image of her as a pathetic creature, worthy of pity. Whatever Cliff did, she somehow became the story. And no matter how much she told herself that it didn't matter because *they* didn't matter, and that the woman they wrote about wasn't really her, she still found it distressing. Not only the intrusion and the inaccuracies, and there were many of those, but the constant reminder of her biggest mistake—not leaving him sooner.

She'd stayed ridiculously loyal to him for two decades, and yes, she regretted it now. He'd made her extravagant promises and told her she was the best thing in his life and that this time things were going to be different, and naively she'd believed him. And she hadn't just done it once. She'd done it repeatedly. She'd thought, *This time he means it and things will be different,* but things never were different and he hadn't meant it. And now she felt stupid for believing he'd ever change, and that the things he said would ever be anything other than empty words spoken to induce her to stay, but she'd so badly wanted to believe him because the alternative was to accept that under the charm and the warmth Cliff Whitman was a cheat and a liar, and that she'd stayed with him far too long.

She'd finally left him, but the news stories never went away, which meant that even though she'd finally divorced him she still sometimes felt as if they were together. Her mistake was an anchor that held her fast. Whatever she did in the future, she'd be dragging her past with Cliff along with her.

She rejected the call, muted the sound on the TV, but continued to stare at the words scrolling along the bottom of the screen.

Celebrity chef Cliff Whitman killed in car accident.

Dead at the scene.

Well, damn.

She'd spent the last year wanting to kill him herself and she didn't know whether to feel elated or cheated. After everything he'd done, everything he'd put her through, it seemed unfair of the universe to have deprived her of the chance to play at least a small part in his demise.

A hysterical laugh burst from her and she slapped her hand over her mouth, shocked. Had she really just thought that? She was a compassionate human being. She valued kindness above almost all other qualities, possibly because her encounters with it had been rare. And yet here she was thinking that if she'd seen his car hovering on the edge of a ravine she might have given it a hard push.

What did that say about her?

Her legs were shaking. Why were her legs shaking? She sat down hard on the nearest chair. *Dead.* Her journey with Cliff had been bumpy, but she'd known him for half her life. She should be sad, shouldn't she? She should feel something? Yes, Cliff Whitman was a liar and a cheat who had almost broken her, but he was still a person. And there had been a time when they'd loved each other, even if that love had been complicated. There had been good parts. At the beginning of their marriage he'd brought her breakfast in bed on Sunday mornings, flaky, buttery croissants he'd baked himself and juice freshly squeezed from the citrus fruit that grew in their home orchard. He'd listened to her. He'd made her laugh. She'd organized his chaotic life, leaving him free to play the part he enjoyed most—being Cliff. He'd said they were a perfect team.

She stood up abruptly and fetched a glass of ice water. She drank it quickly, trying to cool the hot burn of emotion.

Whatever had happened between them, death was always a tragedy. *Was it? Was she being hypocritical?* She should probably cry, if not for him, then for the woman who'd made the bad decision to get into the car with him. Joanna sympathized. She was never one to judge the bad decisions of another. She'd made so many bad decisions in her life she could no longer count them.

She thought about Rita. Would she be shocked to discover she hadn't been the only woman in Cliff's life? Why was it that a woman so rarely believed that a serial cheater would cheat on them? They all thought they were different. That they were special. That they would be the one to tame him. When he said, *You're the one*, they believed him.

Joanna had believed that, too. She'd needed to believe that. When she'd met him she'd been vulnerable and heartbroken. She'd wanted so badly to be special to someone. To have someone whose love she could rely on. She'd thought love meant security, and it had taken a long time—too long—for her to understand that they were different things.

Putting the empty glass down, she took a deep breath and forced herself to think. She and Cliff were no longer married, but they still shared the business. Cliff's was a brand, but now the figurehead was gone. What did that mean for the company they'd built together? She'd invested more than twenty years of her life into its growth and success, which was why she hadn't walked away from it at the same time as her marriage. It had represented the only consistency and security she had left. Also Cliff's gave her a focus, and she needed that. The media didn't understand, of course. They didn't understand how she could still work alongside a man who had repeatedly humiliated her.

She closed her eyes. *Forget that. Don't think about that.*

Right now the worst part was that there would be a funeral, and she hated funerals. No matter whose funeral it was, it was always her father's funeral. Again and again, like some kind of cruel time-travel trick. And she was always ten years old, shivering as the cool Californian rain blended with her tears. This was different, of course. She'd adored her father, and her father had adored her back. He was the only man whose love she'd been sure of. But even with him love hadn't meant security because he'd left her, felled by a heart attack in the middle of the living room with her as a witness. She could still hear the sickening thud as his body had hit the floor.

And now there would be Cliff's funeral. Did she have to go? The thought of it made her want to reach for a drink, even though she wasn't much of a drinker.

Yes, she had to go. Divorce or no divorce, it was the respectful thing to do. People would be watching. Everyone would want to know how she felt, not that she would tell them. She never spoke to the press.

How did she feel?

She heard sounds in the distance and then the insistent buzz of her gate intercom. Without thinking she stepped to the window and looked down the sweep of the drive to the large iron gates that protected her from the outside world.

A camera flashed and she gasped and quickly closed the shutters. No!

Unlike Cliff, she'd never sought fame or celebrity but she'd been caught in his spotlight, anyway. It was one of the reasons she'd moved to a different neighborhood after the divorce. She'd hoped to be able to slide away from the dazzling beam of attention that always landed on him. She'd chosen to live in a small, discreet community, rather than up among the flashy mansions in Bel Air where Cliff entertained lavishly on his verdant terrace with views of mountains and ocean. They'd found her, of course, because the media could find anyone, but she'd hoped that by living a quiet, low-key, non-newsworthy, Cliff-free life she'd become less interesting to them.

She'd been wrong. They continued to write about her, exposing all her secrets for the public to enjoy. They knew about her father's death. They knew she was estranged from her stepmother, Denise. They'd tracked her down and predictably, Denise had been only too happy to voice her opinion. *She's no daughter of mine. Always was a difficult child.*

Her phone rang, dragging her back from a downward spiral into the past. This time it was her assistant, Nessa.

Joanna answered it, grateful for the distraction. "Hi."

"Can you let me in, boss? I'm outside the garden room. I used the back entrance."

"I don't have a back entrance."

"I took a secret route."

Joanna walked to the back of the house, mystified and alarmed.

She'd chosen the house because it was secure. When she'd first viewed it, instead of admiring kitchen appliances and ceiling height, she'd been checking areas of vulnerability. The dense woodland at the back had been a plus. This was an unfashionable area. There was no road, and no running trails. Her property was protected by a high wall and tall, mature trees that concealed the back of the house from view.

It had been a carefully considered purchase, but when she walked through the door she never once thought, *I love this house*, or even, *I'm home*. She didn't think of it as home. Home was a place where you felt safe and could relax. Neither of those things could happen when you were an object of public interest.

She walked through the garden room and saw Nessa standing on her deck, glancing furtively over her shoulder. Normally impeccably groomed, she had twigs stuck in her hair and her shoes were muddied and scuffed.

Shaken by the discovery that her home wasn't as secure as she'd thought, Joanna opened the door and Nessa virtually fell inside.

"What is *wrong* with people? I tried coming in the conventional way, actually through the front door, you know, like a normal person? But there are a million people with cameras and two TV vans, which, frankly, I don't get because why are *you* news? You're not the one who was trying to have sex in a moving vehicle. I'm all for multitasking, but it depends on the task, doesn't it? Sex and driving—call me boring, but those two things do *not* go together."

"Nessa, breathe—"

"So I've been thinking about this." Nessa shrugged off her backpack and toed off her shoes. "I've ruined my shoes by the way. I was thinking maybe we can charge them to Cliff as this was all his fault. Do you have any antiseptic? I scratched myself coming through the woods. I don't want to die of some vile disease because you need me right now."

Joanna's head was spinning. "You came through the woods at the back of the house?"

"Yes. I remembered you telling me the woods were one of your reasons for picking this place. They can't get to you from the back, only the front. That's what you said. You only have to watch one direction. So I thought, *Right, I'll get to her from the back*, but it's not pedestrian friendly. Do I have mud on my cheek? I bet I do." She scrubbed randomly at her face and then adjusted her glasses, which had settled at a strange angle on her nose. "I am not cut out for wilderness adventures. Give me California sunshine and beaches and I'm there, but a dark forest full of insects, snakes, bears and coyotes? That's me out. Can you check me for spiders?" She spun and showed her back to Joanna, who dutifully checked.

"You're spider free. But even if you made it through the woods, how did you get over the wall?"

"I climbed. Don't ask for details." Nessa tugged at a twig that was tangled in her curls. "I grew up with three brothers. I have skills that would make your eyes pop. And don't worry, no one followed me. No one is that stupid. Also, there were no humans in that woods. At least no live ones. Willing to bet there are a few dead ones, though. Bodies undiscovered." She grinned. "Spooky."

"Nessa..." Joanna brushed a leaf from Nessa's shoulder. "What are you *doing* here?"

"I'm your assistant, and I figured you'd need assistance."

"I—I'm not really thinking about work right now."

"Of course you're not. I'm here for more than work. I'm your right-hand woman. The dragon at your gate." Nessa polished a smudge from her glasses. "When you employed me, you said I had to be there for you in both calm and crisis, so here I am. I assume this is the crisis part. We're in this together. Bring it on."

Together.

Joanna felt a pressure in her chest. Someone had thought of her. Someone wanted to help her. Yes, she paid Nessa, but she was going to ignore that part.

"You don't want to be exposed to this circus."

Nessa tilted her head. "You are."

"I have no choice. You do."

"And I choose being here with you, so that's decided."

The strange feeling in her chest spread to her throat. People generally distanced themselves from her, afraid of being tainted by association. They didn't want to find themselves in that spotlight. "Have you really thought this through?"

"What is there to think through? We're a team. In my interview you said I'd need to be versatile. I hope you'll remember the whole climbing the wall thing when you give me a reference, not that I'm planning on leaving you any time soon because this is my dream job and you're an inspirational boss. Now what can I do? We can make a statement."

"I never make a statement. I never say anything."

"In that case I can call the cops and get them to move that mob with cameras at the end of your drive."

Joanna looked at her assistant's flushed, earnest face and suddenly didn't feel quite so alone.

She wasn't alone. She had Nessa.

Hiring Nessa as her assistant two years earlier had been one of the better decisions she'd made in her life. Her team had lined up a selection of experienced candidates for her to interview but then Nessa had bounced into the room, fresh out of college, vibrating with energy and enthusiasm and popping with ideas. Ignoring the disapproval of her colleagues, Joanna had given her the job and had never regretted that decision. Nessa had proved herself to be discreet, reliable and sharp as the business end of a razor blade.

Not all my decisions are bad, Joanna thought as she locked the back door.

"I'm glad you're here, but I don't want you to do anything about the cameras. Leave them."

"Nothing?" Nessa gaped at her and then looked guilty. "I'm so thoughtless. Here I am worrying about spiders and press statements, and you've just lost the man you were married to for two decades. I know you were divorced, and that he wasn't exactly..." Her voice trailed off as she studied Joanna's face. "I mean, twenty years is a long time, even if he was a—" She gave a helpless shrug. "Give me some clues here. I want to say the right thing, but I don't know what that is. How *do* you feel? Are you sad or mad? Do I get you tissues or a punching bag?"

"I don't know how I feel." Joanna decided not to mention her less than charitable thoughts. "I feel…strange."

"Yeah, well, strange about covers it. Can I grab a glass of water? Turns out covert operations in dense woodland is thirsty work. Then I'll brush my hair, work magic with makeup so that I don't look as if I'm dressed for Halloween and get to work."

"Go through to the kitchen. Help yourself. I'll join you in a minute."

Joanna went through the whole of the ground floor at the front of the house making sure all the blinds were closed before returning to the kitchen. They could stay there with their cameras, but she'd give them nothing to photograph. And if someone was brazen enough to breach her gates, they wouldn't be rewarded for it.

Nessa had settled herself at the kitchen island. She had a glass of water in one hand and her phone in the other. She was scrolling through social media. "We're trending, no surprise there. Interesting hashtags. Lots of speculation about what they were doing when the car went off the road—" she sent Joanna a sideways glance "—sorry. This is…awkward."

"It's fine."

"Some people are saying it's a shame because it was his recipe for citrus salmon that made them realize good food wasn't just for restaurants."

He created that recipe for me, Joanna thought. *He was trying to teach me to cook. I ruined the salmon and he laughed at me and said some people couldn't be taught.* That was the day she'd given up cooking.

"Others are saying he was a sleaze, good riddance, yada yada," Nessa continued, scrolling. "They've managed to get a comment from two of the women he—*what?* No way." She stared at the screen.

"What?"

"You don't want to know. If you want my advice, delete all your personal social media accounts."

"I don't have social media accounts."

"Good decision." Nessa carried on scrolling, her expression alternating between disgust and surprise.

Joanna sighed. "That bad?"

Nessa hesitated. "There are a few decent people out there. People saying a death is always sad. Some of the comments are pretty neutral, some wondering who the woman was…" She sneaked a look at Joanna.

"I don't know."

"Of course you don't. Why would you? You're divorced from him. Whoever she is, I bet she's wishing now she got into a car with a different guy. I mean, we've all had bad dates, but *that*—" Nessa shrugged, took a gulp of water and continued scrolling. "Some people are wondering if this will mean the end of the business. Will it?" She glanced up. "The business is called Cliff's. And Chef Cliff is—" She stopped.

Joanna sat down opposite her.

"Dead. You can say it."

And Nessa was right. It would affect the business. The business they'd built together. She'd given up on their marriage, but she hadn't given up on that. She'd spent the past twenty years nurturing it, watching it grow. It was her baby.

She felt a pang, thinking of the actual baby she'd lost. One minute she'd been eleven weeks pregnant, excited about her future as a mother, the next she'd been sitting in the bathroom sobbing. Her son. She'd buried that pain deep, but that didn't mean it had gone away. Sometimes she'd wake up and think, *My boy would be ten years old today*, and she'd imagine the gift she would have bought, and the adventures they would have had together and how much she would have loved him. Would her priorities have been different if she'd had a child? Her marriage?

Her phone rang again and Nessa glanced at her.

"Do you want me to answer that?"

"No."

"It might be a friend."

If she said, *I don't have any real friends*, Nessa would feel sorry for her and Joanna didn't want anyone feeling sorry for her. She wanted to protect the last fragile strands of her pride.

"If it is, then I'll call them back."

Of all the bad things about being married to Cliff, and there had been many, the media attention had been among the worst. Cliff himself had been emotionally bulletproof. Whatever they accused him of he'd laugh, wink, give them a *"No comment"* or a *"Let's focus on what happens in my kitchen, not my bedroom."* For some reason Joanna had never understood, his bad behavior had increased his appeal. He was shocking, but supremely watchable. His TV ratings rose, no matter what he did. He was unapologetic about his colorful personal life, so sure that his charm would ultimately guarantee him forgiveness for all his misdeeds that it was impossible to shame or embarrass him.

Oh, how she loathed being the subject of attention and gossip. Cliff hadn't understood her aversion. He'd hungered for the limelight, and not only because it was essential to building his brand. If attention was a large pie, he would have greedily devoured the whole thing without offering her a sliver. But perhaps precisely because she wasn't interested, the media chose to focus on her. How did she feel about his latest affair? Why didn't she leave? Had she no self-respect? She became a case study in humiliation, although she'd never understood why the shame should be hers when he was the one who was cheating. They photographed her from every angle, commented on the weight she'd lost, how haggard she looked, their speculation cruel and deeply personal. *If he cheats, it must be her fault.* They'd speculated on whether in marrying a man fourteen years her senior she'd somehow been trying to replace her father. That suggestion had offended her more than any of them. Cliff was nothing like her father. Hearing the two of them mentioned in the same breath had made her want to lash out.

Why did they hate her so much? It was a question she'd often pondered, and the only explanation that made sense was that they envied her. They envied her going to bed with Cliff, waking up next to Cliff, wearing his ring on her finger. And the only way to handle that envy was to convince themselves that she was having a miserable life.

They might have felt better had they known that most of the time she was.

The buzzer rang again and Nessa sent an angry look in the direction of the door.

"They're like hyenas, ready to chomp down on a carcass."

"Yes." Given that she was the carcass, the analogy wasn't comfortable.

"The stuff they say about you is all total crap. Aren't you ever tempted to give your side of things?"

What would be the point? *He said, she said…* "They don't want the truth."

"Surprising they don't get bored, as you never give them a response. I guess they need to milk the story, and they hope that if they're persistent you might eventually say something. Cliff's dead, so he's not going to be saying anything, the girl is in the hospital—that leaves you. They'll want your reaction."

What was her reaction? What *did* she feel?

"Dead." She said the word aloud again, trying to make it real. Testing herself. Pressing, to see if it hurt.

Nessa eyed her. "Can I pour you a drink? A real drink?"

"No, thank you." Her thoughts were complicated enough without clouding them with alcohol. Untangling her emotions was complicated. Was she feeling humiliated? Cliff's behavior had continually embarrassed her, even after they were divorced. Was she prostrate with grief? Angry at the impact his actions might have on the business and the people they employed?

Joanna finished her coffee. It was cold, but she didn't care. She felt oddly detached. She felt grief, yes, but was it grief for Cliff or grief for the life she'd wanted that had never turned out the way she'd hoped?

She wasn't sure what she felt. It couldn't be relief, because that would make her hard-hearted. *Would it? Or would it make her human?*

The buzzer sounded again. Annoying. Persistent.

Nessa slid off the stool and refilled her glass. "I'll tell people in the office you won't be in for a few days. Give it time to calm down. They'll soon move on to something, or someone, else." She added ice to the glass, splashing droplets of water onto smooth Italian tiles. "Anyway, unless you're going to wear a disguise and shimmy over the wall like I did, your only way out of this place is through the front entrance. You can drive over the photographers, but then you'd be arrested and I don't have enough money in my account to bail you out. I suppose they'll go away eventually."

"They won't go away."

She knew how this worked. There would be endless gossip. In the past she'd even been the subject of a women's daytime chat show. *Successful women who stay with men who cheat.*

Joanna had watched it, appalled but also fascinated by this external analysis of her life. Was that really who they thought she was? Apparently she was a doormat, a coward, a disgrace to women. Where was her strength? Her dignity?

To them she wasn't a person, she was a story. She was ratings, sales, a commercial opportunity, a talking point. They weren't interested in the truth.

They didn't know anything about her relationship. They

didn't know anything about her life before she'd met Cliff. They weren't interested in who she was or what she felt. They didn't know that although Cliff was the face of the business, it was her hard work that had made him famous. There was a popular TV show, a chain of expensive restaurants, branded cookware, cookbooks—the franchise had grown like a monster.

Please, Joanna, I can't do this without you.

He was the face of the company, but she was the engine. She kept everything going, and he knew it.

He'd known it, she reminded herself. It was all in the past now. There was no more Cliff.

Why did you crash, Cliff? Were you driving too fast?

Nessa put a glass of water in front of her. "It's a crappy situation, boss, no doubt about that. But as my mom always says, no matter how bad things get there's always someone worse off than you. I hate it when she says that. Seriously annoying actually, but I have to admit that mostly she is right. Although it's true that right now I wouldn't want to be you—"

"Thank you, Nessa,"

"Do you know who I *definitely* wouldn't want to be?" She pushed her glasses up her nose and gave Joanna a meaningful look. "That girl in the car. Don't know who she is or what she was doing, but I would *not* want her life."

The girl in the car. Joanna didn't know who she was or what she'd been doing, either.

The one thing she *did* know was that even though he was dead, Cliff Whitman had still managed to ruin her day.

3

Ashley

Ashley lay in the hospital bed, listening to the beep of machines. There wasn't a single part of her that didn't ache. She felt as if someone had pushed a knife into her side. Her head was foggy, but her brain was clear. She remembered everything. She wished she didn't.

"You're awake. That's good." A woman wearing a white coat stepped closer. "I'm Dr. Ramirez. How are you feeling?"

Like roadkill. Which was almost how she'd ended up. She was reliving it over and over again. The flashbacks were almost as scary as the real thing.

She tried to speak but her mouth was dry and a nurse stepped forward and gave her a sip of water.

"You were in an accident." The doctor spoke carefully. "You were a passenger. Your car went off the road. Do you remember what happened?"

A weightless moment of horror. A scream. Hers? His? Rolling, rolling, not knowing which way was up. An explosion of pain. *I'm going to die here. We're both going to die here.*

They couldn't find out the truth, could they? They couldn't know what she'd said to Cliff in the moments before he'd crashed? Now he was dead, she just wanted the whole thing to go away. She wanted to forget she'd ever come here. Forget she'd ever climbed into his car.

"Ashley? Do you remember anything at all?"

"No." She remembered making a bad decision. A series of bad decisions. Her mother had raised her not to lie but all her instincts told her that this was one of those occasions when the truth was best withheld, at least until she'd had time to think things through. The way she felt, that moment might not be coming quickly. "My side hurts."

Ashley tuned out as the doctor listed her injuries. There were lots of them, and that wasn't counting the stuff they couldn't see.

She felt a flash of anxiety. Would it be okay? Would everything be okay?

"I hurt everywhere."

"We can increase your pain relief. As well as your more serious injuries, you have a cracked rib and severe bruising. We'll be watching you carefully over the next few days. You're lucky to be alive." The doctor hesitated. "Is there someone we can contact? Family? Friends? We didn't find any emergency contact details when you were brought in."

No emergency contact. That said everything about her life, didn't it? There was no one she could call.

She was alone in the world, apart from the medical team who were paid to care for her.

She felt an emptiness and then a flash of panic. *Keep peddling, Ashley! Keep kicking.* She had to figure out what to do next, but her brain was blurred by pain and the remnants of anesthetic. She didn't want to be here, but what choice did she have? She couldn't even sit up without help. And even if she could, where would she go? She hadn't anticipated this outcome. She didn't have any sort of backup plan, not even a bad one.

The doctor exchanged glances with the nurse.

"The man you were with—"

"Cliff." There was no reason to pretend she hadn't known his name. "He's dead. I know." She knew he was dead, and yet the memory uppermost in her mind wasn't the crash, but the look in his eyes in that split second before he'd lost control.

Shock. Disbelief. Anger.

She shivered. It hadn't gone the way she'd expected it to. None of it had. Even if he'd lived, the outcome would have been bad.

The doctor frowned. "You know he's dead? I thought you didn't remember—?"

Ashley gestured to the TV screen visible in the waiting area beyond the glass windows of the ward. There was no sound, but the rolling news at the bottom confirmed that celebrity chef Cliff Whitman had been killed in an accident on Mulholland Drive. An unknown woman had been removed from the wreckage and taken to the hospital.

That was her. She was an unknown woman.

The irony didn't escape her. Despite their history she'd been unknown to Cliff, too.

Right now she was relieved to be unknown, and she wanted to stay that way. She wanted to wind the clock back, slide back into her old life and somehow forget this horrible mistake.

Another image flashed up on the screen. A slim woman wearing jeans and a simple white shirt, holding her hand up to ward off photographers. Her sunglasses were so huge they obscured most of her face. She looked haunted. Hunted.

Joanna Whitman.

Ashley's stomach rebelled. "I'm going to be sick."

The nurse handed her a bowl and she retched miserably even though there was nothing in her stomach.

I'm sorry, I'm sorry.

Was she a bad person? She didn't dare ask herself that question.

"Close the blinds and turn that TV off." The doctor scowled

at the flustered nurse and Ashley lay still, exhausted. She could have told them not to bother because the news images weren't showing her anything she hadn't already seen up close. When the car had eventually stopped rolling she'd registered two things. Firstly, that somehow she was still alive and all her limbs appeared to still be attached to her body. Secondly, that Cliff Whitman hadn't been so lucky.

She'd never seen a dead body before but she hadn't been in any doubt that she was looking at one.

And it was all her fault.

Would the outcome have been different if she'd picked another moment to tell him what she needed to tell him?

She could still hear his voice saying, *That isn't possible*, and remembered her high-pitched reply, *If you have sex, then it's always a possibility!*

In that moment she'd had his full attention, which was why he'd driven off the road.

Did that make her a murderer?

You are in deep trouble, Ashley.

She wanted to run, but she couldn't even sit up let alone move from the bed.

The doctor adjusted the drip running into her arm. "Do you remember anything at all?"

"I remember climbing into his car." She could imagine what they thought of her. What was going through their heads.

But whatever they were imagining, the truth was probably far juicier.

She felt hot and then cold. She thought about Joanna Whitman and squirmed. The woman had looked awful.

"When you're feeling strong enough, the police want to talk to you. They want to know if you have an idea what might have caused the accident. It wasn't raining. Visibility was good."

"I don't know. I don't remember much. One minute we were

driving and the next we were flying over the edge." She didn't want to talk to the police. She didn't want questions. *How much could they find out?*

Could you be locked up for telling someone something they didn't want to hear?

She saw the nurse turn to look at the machine and hoped they didn't have a lie detector rigged alongside all the other medical equipment.

The doctor gave a reassuring smile. "Try not to worry. Short-term amnesia isn't uncommon after an accident like yours. You were lucky. But you might as well settle in because we won't be discharging you for a while. The good news is that the baby is fine."

Ashley stared at her. "Baby?"

"Yes. Your baby. You're pregnant. Around ten weeks." Dr. Ramirez paused. "You didn't know?"

Yes, she'd known. *Of course* she'd known. That was why she'd been in the car with Cliff.

But she hadn't wanted anyone else to know. Not until she'd figured out what to do next.

Oh, Ashley.

She was in even bigger trouble than she'd thought.

4

Melanie

Melanie Miller bit into a slice of toast to stop herself engaging with her daughter. There was a time when she might have let her temper fly, but that was before she'd had her own child and learned to hold it back. But she didn't pretend it was easy. It didn't help that she wasn't a morning person. If Greg hadn't pulled the covers off her that morning, she would have stayed asleep.

"You *never* listen to me!" Eden stood, arms folded, a defiant look on her pretty face. "I'm not going to college. Ever. What's the point?"

Do not answer that.

Mel took another bite of toast. This encounter was going to cost her an extra run on the beach to burn off the calories, but better that than an emotional collision with Eden that might take days to mend.

"Mom! Why aren't you saying anything? I'm tired of studying. It's a waste of a life. And what does college give you, anyway, except massive debt? I don't want a 'career.' I want to do something with art or photography. Something creative that's fun and leaves me with loads of time to surf. And maybe I won't earn masses of money, but I want more from life than a paycheck. I want to stay true to my authentic self. I want to follow my dreams. I don't want to settle, like you did."

Mel choked on her toast. Right now her authentic self wanted to give her daughter a piece of her mind.

She reminded herself that the world looked different when you were a teenager. You saw possibility, untainted by reality. A road with no obstacles. Choices that were simple.

I don't want to settle, like you did.

The words woke up a part of her she mostly ignored. She tried to put it to sleep again, reminding herself that there was more than one reason to do a job and they were all valid. Some people went after the money, and there was nothing wrong with that. Some people wanted to do something worthwhile that would give them a sense of purpose. Mel had followed tradition and joined the family business. The Surf Café overlooked the beach and had been established by her grandparents as somewhere the local community could gather to eat and drink. These days there were twice as many tourists as locals at any given time, but it was still a popular haunt for the inhabitants of Silver Point, almost all of who Mel knew well. At least once a week when she was growing up her parents had said, *This place will be yours and Nate's one day.* Mel had occasionally thought, *But what if I don't want it?*

She pushed that thought aside. The café was part of her life. She'd been helping out there since she could walk. In her time she'd done all of it, but now she handled the administrative side, which, if she was honest, wasn't particularly exciting, but the business was her family's pride and joy and she and her twin brother, Nate, had a duty to keep the place going.

Occasionally, when they were exceptionally busy, she helped out with the customers but only when they were desperate. She didn't have Nate's charm and easygoing manner. She was too impatient. If she was left in charge they probably would have gone out of business. She preferred managing the books. At least numbers didn't complain and tell you that you'd brought the wrong food, or that the hamburger wasn't quite cooked as they liked it even though you'd delivered exactly what they'd ordered.

The job gave her flexibility, which she was grateful for as a working parent, and she enjoyed working with her brother, although she wouldn't in a million years admit that to him. And the job came with other advantages. Mel couldn't make it through the week without indulging in at least one of Nate's pecan chocolate brownies. Eden was addicted to his white chocolate and macadamia cookies, and even Greg, who tried to avoid sugar, had been known to lose all willpower when confronted by a slice of apple and cinnamon tart. If you were feeling virtuous there was always the Bay Shrimp salad, and if you had time to sit and savor the moment, then you could settle at one of the tables in the outdoor seating area, sheltered by cypress trees, and watch the Pacific crash onto a sweep of soft white sand.

Eden was frowning at her. "Mom?"

"Yes, I heard you." She couldn't do this now. Reinforcements were called for. "Greg! Coffee is ready."

"I'm here." Greg strolled into the room and Eden immediately shifted from combative to cheerful.

"Hi, Dad."

"Hi yourself." He greeted his daughter with a swift kiss on the top of her head, which Eden still tolerated as long as no one she knew was around to witness it. "How's my family this morning?"

Tired, Mel thought as she stood up and handed him the flask of coffee she'd made. Eden had been a feisty toddler, with firm opinions on everything from clothes to food. Mel had told herself that things would get easier when she was a teenager. She'd been wrong. Maybe she should stop fighting with her. Stop trying to steer her decisions in a more sensible direction. At what point should you step back and let them live their lives, mistakes and all?

The question nagged at her and she was relieved when Eden and Greg departed, one to school and one to work.

Mel wasn't needed in the café for a few hours and she decided to use the time to find a book to replace the one she'd finished in the bath the night before.

She grabbed her purse and her keys and headed out of the house. It was a five-minute stroll to Main Street, and she lifted her face to the sun in an attempt to lower her stress levels.

It was early, but already the streets were buzzing with summer visitors.

Mel pushed open the door of the Beach Bookstore and the bell clanged in that pleasing, familiar way that reminded her why she'd chosen to work in the family business and stay in her hometown of Silver Point, California.

Silver Point, with its cobbled streets and glorious beaches, was a much-photographed section of the Californian coastline to the annoyance of the police department, who were tired of people almost killing themselves while posing for the perfect selfie. The small ocean-side town nestled between the Pacific Ocean and the Santa Lucia Mountains. In the peak summer months people often drove right past it on their way to the tourist hotspots of Carmel and Monterey.

That suited Mel. She loved her home, where mountains met the ocean, and would happily have kept it all to herself. This was her place and she belonged here, with these people she'd known all her life. She ran on the numerous hiking trails that crisscrossed the mountains, through forests of Monterey pine, cyprus and cedar trees. She surfed and swam in the ocean under skies so blue it seemed unreal.

Still, Eden's words dug at her. It was like walking with a stone in her shoe.

I don't want to settle, like you did.

She had a brief vision of high heels and city life, the busy buzz of crowded streets and the glint of sunshine on glass skyscrapers.

She hadn't settled. She absolutely hadn't settled, and it was because she loved this part of the Californian coastline that she could understand Eden's reluctance to leave it, but having fun wasn't a job. And if it was fun she wanted, why reject college? Mel had *loved* college. She'd had her first legal drink, smoked pot and done a ton of things you were supposed to do when you were young, danced until her feet hurt, talked until her jaw hurt, had lots of sex with Greg (although to be fair she'd been doing that since she was sixteen so that was more of the same, although the same was *good*), and then she'd trained as a CPA, and started work in the café using her business skills. And maybe that wasn't exactly *fun*, but it was a stable job and that was something to be grateful for. Having fun didn't pay the rent. Having fun didn't guarantee you a secure future, and surely wanting that for her only child didn't make her a bad mother?

Maybe instead of a novel, she should buy a book on parenting.

"Got anything on managing difficult teenagers?" She peered over the counter where Mary-Lou was retrieving books from a box.

"Mel!" Mary-Lou scrambled to her feet, red-faced from exertion. "Eden again?"

"If you feel the ground shaking around here folks assume it's an earthquake, but not in my house. At home we call it an Eden-quake. I had to call in the police."

"That bad?" Mary-Lou grinned. "And did the officer involved make an arrest?"

"Fortunately Greg's an expert on de-escalation tactics in crisis situations, which is the reason we're all still alive and none of the hostages were harmed. I married him for his negotiation skills. He's the most reasonable, patient man I've ever met."

Mary-Lou straightened her dress. "Who was the hostage?"

"Depends who's asking." Mel picked up a leaflet from the counter and then put it back. "I finished that thriller you recommended. It was good, although Greg tells me there is no way they could have discovered all that from a corpse that old."

"That's what you talk about over dinner? Corpses? Romantic. I guess you've run out of things to talk about after all these years."

"We're keeping it real." Mel grinned. "And we can't flirt or talk sexy with Eden there, although now I think of it that's a perfect way to clear the room." She filed that idea away for later use and Mary-Lou shook her head.

"He's a keeper, that's for sure. The community is lucky to have him looking out for us. And so are you."

"I know." Mel glanced at the shelves. "So what do I read next? What have you got for me?"

"Something better than fiction." Mary-Lou leaned closer, a reliable sign that she was about to impart a priceless nugget of gossip.

Because she didn't have anywhere to be for the next hour, Melanie leaned in, although why they were whispering she had no idea. There were three other people browsing the shelves, all of them tourists who weren't likely to be the slightest bit interested in the antics of the locals.

"Is this about Mrs. Highgate's poodle? Because I already heard all about it." The much-pampered pooch had escaped the day before and dug up all the neighbor's newly planted begonias. The neighbor being Edna Casey, that little adventure had resulted in a visit from the police. Mel had heard about it from Greg, who had taken the call before breakfast.

"This is bigger than Mrs. Highgate's poodle. Don't you watch the news?" Mary-Lou beamed at the tourist hovering behind Melanie. "How can I help you?"

"I'll take these two, thank you." The woman handed over two paperbacks.

News?

Melanie waited, foot tapping, while Mary-Lou rang up the purchases and made small talk about the weather and the various attractions that the woman should see while she was in town and, by the way, had she read the next three books in the series she was buying?

As a result of that exchange the woman left the store carrying five books, rather than the two she'd originally intended to purchase, and Mel glanced at her friend in admiration.

"Choose two, get sold three more?"

"It's a solid sales strategy and a guaranteed way to stay in business." Mary-Lou leaned forward again. "Have you really not seen the news this morning?"

"I told you, I was handling a major domestic incident." Mel grabbed a thriller from the shelf closest to the desk. "How about this one? Any good?"

"Yes. Don't you watch TV?"

"The news creates tension. I've been listening to Mozart. Supposed to be good for stress levels. I'm the mother of a teenager. My stress levels are always high, without making things worse. I doubt even Mozart is going to crack it but I'm willing to give it a try if he is. If that fails I'm probably turning to alcohol." Mel flipped the book over and read the back. She took her time because she knew Mary-Lou was burning to share whatever news Mel had missed and she didn't see why she shouldn't have a little fun once in a while. "So what's happening?"

"Cliff Whitman?"

Mel's good mood drained away. She slapped the book down on the counter. "What about Cliff Whitman?"

Mary-Lou drew her finger across her throat and Mel frowned, confused.

"He had an accident with one of his own kitchen knives? Someone slit his throat?" It wouldn't have surprised her. If she'd been married to Cliff she would have murdered him before they'd reached their first anniversary. She would have tossed him into the ocean where, no doubt, his body would have sunk without trace, dragged to the bottom by the weight of his ego.

Greg, steady, reasonable and unflappable at all times, would have pointed out that there were different sides to a person, but the only side of Cliff Whitman that Mel wanted to see was the back of him.

"Not his throat—" Mary-Lou was eager to share the details "—but he's dead. I guess that's what happens when you get into your flashy sports car—such a cliché for a man of his age—and show off in the Hollywood Hills."

"Dead?" Mel felt a twinge of guilt. She'd been maligning a dead guy, which made her a little uncomfortable. On the other hand she hadn't known he was dead when she maligned him, and also this was Cliff Whitman. It was hard to have generous thoughts about someone who had destroyed the relationship of two people she loved (she heaped most of the blame on Cliff) and ruined their perfect unit of four. And yes, she was emotionally involved because one of those people had been her best friend and the other her brother, and yes, two decades had passed, but Mel hadn't forgotten. But still… "Dead how? He crashed?"

Did Nate know? Had he heard?

"Car went off the road into a ravine. And get this…" Mary-Lou lowered her voice, which somehow made it even louder. "He had a woman with him."

Mel's stomach dropped as if she'd been pushed into the ravine with him. *Joanna.* "No." She couldn't breathe. The sense of loss was crushing, and then came the guilt. Guilt that she hadn't tried harder to mend the rift while she'd had a chance.

"Mel? You're white as paper. Sit down! Don't you pass out on my floor." Mary-Lou fussed over her. Pulled out a chair. "Are you sick? What's wrong?"

"Joanna—" Mel thumped onto the chair and managed to choke out the word. "It's just a shock, that's all. I can't believe she's gone."

"Gone?" Mary-Lou was looking at her strangely. "She hasn't gone anywhere. Are you thinking—? It wasn't Joanna in the car."

"You—what?" Mel grasped the seat of the chair. "Why did you tell me it was?"

"I didn't. I said he had a woman in the car. No one knows who, but it wasn't Joanna." Mary-Lou patted her shoulder. "Sorry to give you a fright. The news report said 'unknown woman.' She's been taken to the hospital. No more details have been released."

Unknown woman.

Still recovering from the shock of thinking Joanna was dead, Mel pushed her hair out of her eyes and tried to imagine what she'd do if Greg was speeding around picking up unknown women.

"Joanna isn't a girl. She's forty this year." How had that happened? It seemed only yesterday they were blowing out fourteen candles on a cake. *I've made a wish.*

Mel hadn't asked what the wish was. She hadn't needed to. They'd been at that stage of their friendship where they'd known every single thing about each other.

"I still remember the day she set fire to the kitchen in the Surf Café and put your brother in the hospital. Hard to forget a sight like that."

Mel hadn't forgotten it, either. Flashing blue lights. Her mother crying. Joanna crying, too, tears smearing soot across her cheeks.

"She didn't burn the place on purpose, Mary-Lou. It was an

accident. She was cooking a romantic meal for Nate. She was flaming the pancakes—"

"And there was just a little too much flame." Mary-Lou shook her head. "Your brother was lucky he didn't lose more than his eyebrows. Those two were inseparable. I was shocked when they broke up and she left town so suddenly. Felt sorry for him. I'd pictured them together forever, you know?"

Mel did know, because she'd pictured the same thing. It had been a sharp and painful lesson that life didn't always turn out the way you thought it would. "History."

"Couldn't believe she went off with that chef when she'd only known him five minutes. Although she was such a terrible cook, maybe it wasn't such a bad choice. That girl would have starved or blown herself up if she'd been left to feed herself. Still, she certainly got more than she bargained for with Cliff Whitman."

That was true.

How had Joanna put up with it? The girl Mel had grown up with had been loyal and loving. Yes, trouble had followed her around like a puppy, but that wasn't all Joanna's fault and she did plenty of good things alongside the bad. She never forgot a birthday. She baked cookies for people when they'd had a bad day (and some said Joanna's cookies were guaranteed to make a bad day worse). All she'd wanted growing up was Nate, so how had she ended up with Chef Sleaze?

And what was Nate going to think about this latest development?

"You haven't heard from her, then?" Mary-Lou picked up the book Mel had been considering and placed it back on the shelf. "I thought she might have reached out."

"No." Mel's mouth felt dry. "She hasn't reached out. Why would she?"

She'd thought she'd put it behind her, but the shock of thinking it was Joanna in that accident had ripped away the shield she'd built and now she realized the hurt was still there, raw and real.

She told herself it was because Joanna had punched a hole in her brother's heart and of course that was going to make her angry and defensive, but it was more than that.

Right at the start when it first happened Mel had swallowed her pride and tried contacting her, but Joanna had ghosted her. Joanna, who she'd loved like a sister. They'd learned to swim together, worn each other's clothes, pierced each other's ears using a needle from her mother's sewing box (the *blood*!), shared everything from makeup to chocolate. They'd been inseparable, until Joanna had chosen to separate them. She'd left Silver Point without a backward glance, and she'd left Mel and their friendship, too.

Nate had refused to discuss it. He'd drowned his sorrows with Greg, leaving Mel to stew and simmer on her own.

The next time she saw Joanna had been in the press. After the first affair, Mel had seen pictures of her looking haggard and awful, hand over her face as she tried to avoid the media. It had only been a few years at that point, maybe less, and Mel had picked up the phone and called her even though doing so made her feel disloyal to Nate. Joanna had changed her number.

Mel had thought, *At least I tried*, and given up. And too much time had passed for her to rethink that decision.

Even if Mel had found a way to reach out past the hurt and awkwardness, and Joanna took her call, what would they talk about? What did they have in common? Mel was small town and Joanna was big city. Mel spent her time working in the café, hanging out with her family and the people she'd grown up with, eating barbecue and walking on the beach. Joanna went to opening nights, award ceremonies and walked on red carpets.

"I'm sure she has plenty of people who can help her." She'd seen the evidence. Photographs of Joanna Whitman shopping with girlfriends, Joanna Whitman playing tennis, Joanna Whitman at the theater. It had fascinated her, seeing Joanna looking styled and groomed because growing up that had never been her priority, although that could have been because nature had already been generous. Thick eyelashes, green eyes and hair the color of fall foliage had been a striking combination, although Joanna hadn't seemed to care. Mel remembered her doing cartwheels on the beach, sand dusting the ends of her hair and her bare legs. Her looks were part of her, along with her generous nature and her inability to cook anything without burning it to a crisp.

She'd changed, but maybe that was what happened when the man you married always had his eye on the woman waiting behind you.

If the pictures told the truth, then Joanna led a glittering life. But the price she paid for that life was Cliff, and that price, Mel thought, was too high. Presumably Joanna had come to the same conclusion because she'd finally divorced him a year ago.

And now he was dead.

Mary-Lou put a fresh stack of bookmarks on the counter. "I always do a double take when I see her walking the red carpet at some event or other looking all fancy. I think to myself, that's Joanna, who used to come in here and borrow books when my mother was running the store."

Mel tilted her head. "She loved reading, but her stepmother thought books were a waste of money."

"Don't talk to me about that woman. I swear Denise modeled herself on all those wicked stepmothers we saw in the movies when we were kids. She was the reason my mother used to lend Joanna the books, even though there was no hope of selling them after. She used to say, *That poor girl needs some escape from living with that woman.* It used to bother her something awful, the thought of little Joanna being alone with her."

It was an uncomfortable memory. Mel had tried to avoid spending time in Joanna's house. They'd usually met at the beach, or Joanna had come and spent time with Mel in her home. When Mel had visited Otter's Nest, she'd counted the hours until she could leave. It wasn't that she was *scared* of Joanna's stepmother exactly, but Denise certainly wasn't a comfortable woman to be around. She'd mentioned it to her friend once.

Your stepmom doesn't like me.

My stepmom doesn't like anyone.

Mel had only good memories of Joanna's father. She remembered him as a warm, fun-loving man who had adored Joanna. Widowed when Joanna was born, he'd finally remarried when Joanna was eight years old. "She used to tell Joanna she'd never wanted kids."

"Can you imagine anyone saying that to a child?" Mary-Lou's mouth tightened. "And if you feel that way, fine, but you don't marry a man with a child."

"I guess she never thought he'd die and leave her with sole charge. Anyway, it's all in the past now."

She'd once asked Joanna what was wrong with her stepmother and she could still remember her reply. *Her life didn't turn out the way she expected.*

Did anyone's life turn out the way they expected?

Mel wasn't sure. If someone had asked her when she was sixteen what she'd be doing in ten years she would have assumed Nate would have married Joanna, making her officially a relative of Mel's and not just a best friend. She would have imagined they would have had a couple of kids, cousins to the bunch of kids Mel planned to have with Greg. She'd pictured long blissful summers punctuated by family barbecues, and noisy Thanksgivings.

All of which went to prove that planning was a waste of time.

Mel and Greg had Eden, but nature had dictated no more

children. Joanna had married Cliff Whitman, and Nate's significant other was currently his rescue dog, Bess.

"Your mom was kind to her. Joanna adored her. How is she doing by the way?"

"Her arthritis is worse. I'd like to be around more for her, but finding someone to help out in this place isn't easy," Mary-Lou said. "Do you think your brother has seen the news? I wonder if he still thinks about her. Took him five years before he'd risk getting tangled up with another woman after she walked out."

"This is all history, Mary-Lou. Nate did fall in love again and he did marry." She hated talking about her brother with anyone, but she knew he wouldn't want to hear himself painted as a victim.

"And divorced a few years later."

"You can't blame Joanna for that." Although for a while, she blamed Joanna for a lot of things. Why wouldn't she? Joanna had left Nate. Nate, who she'd always said was her soul mate. Nate wasn't just Mel's brother, he was her *twin*. When he hurt, she hurt. He was older by four minutes and he'd always defended her. She did the same for him. She'd had a right to be angry, and an equal right to be angry that Joanna had turned her back on their friendship so easily.

Mary-Lou tilted her head. "Reckon she'll come back?"

"Back here? No. Why would she? She hasn't been back in twenty years."

"True, but sometimes when bad things happen it's a wakeup call. You realize what's important. What you turned your back on. You want home."

"Silver Point isn't her home. Hasn't been her home for two decades." And none of us were important, Mel thought. *I wasn't important.*

"She still owns Otter's Nest." Mary-Lou gave her a meaningful look, which Mel understood.

Joanna's father, perhaps with some prescience, had left Otter's Nest to Joanna and not his second wife.

Maybe he'd known, Mel thought. *Maybe he'd known deep down what Denise was like, and that one day Joanna might need somewhere that was hers.*

How would he have felt to know Joanna wasn't living there?

"Her stepmother hated the place. She hated the fact that it was isolated, that she had to climb in the car to get to town." Mel could still remember her complaining.

"Still, her husband leaving the place to Joanna? That had to sting."

Mel knew things about Joanna's life that other people in town didn't, but even though they hadn't spoken for twenty years that didn't mean she was about to reveal a secret.

"Well, the woman is living up the coast in Carmel now, so I guess she's happy."

"Nothing is ever going to make that woman happy. She wouldn't recognize Otter's Nest if she visited. It's so fancy." Mary-Lou reshelved a book that had been put back in the wrong place. "It won some architectural award."

"You've never seen it. None of us have."

"I've seen pictures. It's all eco this, and sustainable that. All that money and fuss knocking down the old place and rebuilding. Why hire some fancy architect from San Francisco to turn Otter's Nest into a coastal paradise if you're never going to use it?"

"Prime real estate? An investment?"

Mel remembered the long summer days they'd spent on the small curve of sand in front of Otter's Nest. The beach house itself was perched just above the cove, with a sandy path leading to the beach. The first time Greg had kissed her they'd been sitting on the sand, watching the sun go down. They'd been fourteen years old.

I'm going to marry you, Melanie.

"She doesn't exactly need the income. Not that I'd swap places. All the money in the world wouldn't tempt me to be with a man like Cliff Whitman," Mary-Lou said. "What self-respecting woman stays married to a man like that for two decades?"

That, Mel couldn't answer and she knew Mary-Lou wasn't the only one to speculate on that topic.

"I guess none of us really knows what goes on inside another couple's relationship."

How was Joanna feeling right now? She'd divorced the man, but Mel knew nothing in life was that simple. Was she heartbroken? Was she opening champagne?

The old Joanna, the Joanna she'd giggled with, surfed with, dreamed about boys with, would have hated the attention. The old Joanna had the kindest, biggest heart. But the person Joanna had become—

Mel didn't know her.

"I feel for her," Mary-Lou said. "And even though I wouldn't say no to the money, I would say no to her life. She can't even go to the store without having her picture taken. Can you imagine? They showed pictures of her home on the news this morning. Fancy mansion. Press and photographers crawling all over it. What use is a house like that if you're afraid to leave it? Might as well be a prison. She'd have more privacy in Otter's Nest, but I'm sure you're right." She waved her hand. "Joanna hasn't shown her face around here in twenty years. Why would she come now?"

5

Joanna

Joanna lay on her back in the middle of her bed, feeling no inclination at all to leave it. She savored those blissful few seconds before she was properly awake, before her brain cleared itself of sleep and reminded her that she was living the life she'd chosen.

A life paved with bad choices.

Sometimes she imagined how her life would look if she'd made different decisions. If she'd paused, instead of rushing forward. If she'd taken one route instead of another. It was easy to judge yourself harshly when you glanced back down the road you'd traveled. Decisions that had seemed clear at the time were harder to understand with distance. You made a wrong turn, and then another and another, and before you knew it you were hopelessly lost and there was no going back so you kept moving forward. You stuck with something you knew was bad because at least it was familiar and, anyway, you no longer knew what good looked like, or how to find it.

She heard clattering in the kitchen and froze. And then she remembered. Nessa. Not some random member of the press who had somehow forced their way into her home. Nessa, her loyal assistant, who had insisted on staying and had moved into Joanna's guest room. *I can't run the gauntlet by going through those gates every day, and I'm not taking any chances in the wild woods, so for now I'm your lodger.*

Joanna had readily agreed. Having Nessa around forced her into action and stopped her overthinking. Right now, Nessa was the closest thing she had to a friend.

What did that say about her?

Joanna pushed back the covers and forced herself to start the day. She looked wistfully at the towering stack of books on her nightstand and fought the impulse to lock the door and spend the day lost in someone else's world.

Instead, she walked to the bathroom, showered, cleaned her teeth and dressed in her habitual work outfit of jeans and a white shirt. She spent less than five minutes on her makeup because that was the maximum time she could stand staring at her pale face. She looked deader than Cliff.

Why did you crash, Cliff? Had you been drinking?

She was asking the same questions as everyone else.

She didn't need to look through her windows to know that the photographers were still outside her gate, parked in their vans, watching the house through long lenses.

She'd let two days pass and when they showed no signs of losing interest she'd hired security in order to be able to safely drive to her office. Two burly, unsmiling men with muscular shoulders and no sense of humor. They'd called her Mrs Whitman, which she hated.

She didn't want to be Mrs. Whitman. She didn't want to spend the rest of her days as one of Cliff's accessories.

Their head office had been surrounded, too, so she'd said reassuring words to the team, grabbed what she needed and tried not to see the relief on their faces when she said she'd be working from home. They didn't want her there, taking focus away from the company, but at the same time work didn't stop because Cliff was no longer alive.

Cliff had spent as little time as possible in the office. Partly because he was usually busy filming a project, visiting one of the restaurants, promoting one of his books and generally keeping his profile high in the media, but also because Cliff had been severely dyslexic and part of his strategy to conceal that fact was to never be in a position where he was expected to read something or sign something without Joanna by his side. Joanna didn't understand why he hid it. She'd suggested many times that his success might inspire other people with dyslexia, but Cliff wasn't interested in inspiring or helping anyone else. His focus was on maintaining the image he'd created for himself. He wanted to believe he was the person he'd created. He wanted the public to believe that, too.

The reality was that Cliff had little involvement with the work that went on behind the scenes. The company was run by an efficient management team, but it was Joanna who had managed Cliff. Even after the divorce, that hadn't changed. She managed his diary, his transport, his media commitments and his insecurities.

It was Joanna who compiled all the recipes for Cliff's books, painstakingly weighing and measuring all the ingredients that Cliff threw together by instinct and noting them down. He'd never followed a recipe in his life, but he knew what flavors worked together.

In the early days it had been fun. Exciting even. But that had gradually changed. The more the public expected of him, the more pressure he'd felt and the more his insecurities grew. He became a victim of his own creation.

Why did you crash, Cliff? Were you showing off?

She headed downstairs and found Nessa in the kitchen acquainting herself with the coffee machine.

She handed Joanna a cup. "So is the business going to go down, boss? Because there are rumors."

"The business is fine." For now. She'd talked briefly to Michael, their CEO, who was in charge of operations. He'd assured her that despite having lost their figurehead, there was no reason why the business would suffer in the short term. "Bookings are up in all the restaurants, the latest book is done and with the publisher—" She didn't want to think about this now. For once in her life, she wanted to think about herself and not Cliff.

Was she wrong to have stayed with the business? Should she have extracted herself completely when she divorced him? Maybe, but at the time she was throwing out most of her life, and adding the job to it had seemed too huge. Cliff had begged her not to divorce him, and then begged her not to leave the business. He'd been afraid that without her as his right-hand woman the whole thing would fall apart and he'd be in the wrong place at the wrong time.

She'd agreed to continue working with him, which was why she still had to think of the business.

Why did you crash, Cliff? Who was that woman?

"The press are still out there. I made you breakfast. Hope that's okay." Nessa tipped scrambled eggs onto toast and put the plate in front of Joanna, who looked at it without enthusiasm.

"I'm not hungry."

"Try a mouthful. I'm a good cook. Not Cliff good, obviously, but good enough. My mother taught me."

Joanna felt a pang. Maybe if she'd had a mother to teach her, she wouldn't be such a disaster in the kitchen.

She picked up the fork, not because she liked the idea of food, but because she liked Nessa. "Maybe you should offer those photographers a drink or a sandwich."

"You're kidding."

Joanna sliced off a small piece of toast. "They're just doing their job."

"Yeah, well, we don't have to help them by keeping them fed and watered. Haven't you ever seen those signs at the zoo? Don't feed the animals? Same thing applies here." Nessa looked pointedly at her. "You're not eating. My mom always says you can't handle a crisis on an empty stomach."

To appease her, Joanna ate a mouthful. "Tastes good. And you're right that you probably shouldn't take them food. I don't want to encourage them." She was tired of trying to evade them. Tired of not being able to leave her house without having a camera thrust in her face. The fact that she and Cliff were no longer married didn't seem to worry them. In their eyes no one knew Cliff better than she did, and they were determined to go to any lengths to uncover the truth.

Did she know the identity of the young woman?

Did she think he'd been drinking the night of the accident?

She stuck to her usual approach and said nothing. She and Michael had sent a statement to all their employees, reassuring them. They'd focused on the business, not the personal.

But it was the personal that interested the media.

"I've been through your inbox." Nessa put a cup of coffee in front of her. "Mostly it's all the usual stuff. Nothing urgent. And the producer of *Cliff Cooks* called. They've put the filming on hold, obviously. She wants to talk to you."

"Why? I can't do anything about the fact they've lost their star presenter." One of Cliff's affairs when they were still married had been with Cally Martin, the producer. Joanna pushed the plate away, her appetite gone. "I'll call her." But not yet. When she was ready. Cally, presumably, was in a panic knowing that her golden goose had flown over a cliff.

Why did you crash, Cliff? Were you distracted? What were you doing with that girl?

"You need to eat more. If you lose weight, it will give them something to write about." Nessa pushed the plate back toward her. "Do you know what you need? A spa day or something. You need to get away. You need to relax."

"Leaving this house means looking over my shoulder the

whole time. It's not relaxing." Technically she wasn't trapped, but it felt that way. She was trapped by the choices she'd made. "Maybe I should climb over the wall, as you did, and disappear."

"Not the worst idea in the world, apart from the spiders." Nessa buttered toast for herself. "I feel self-conscious making you food when you're probably used to creating restaurant-worthy dishes."

"I'm not. I'm a terrible cook." She used Cliff's own words, because she knew they were true. *You're a terrible cook, Joanna.*

Nessa stared at her, toast halfway to her mouth. "I don't believe you."

"Why not?"

"Because Cliff must have taught you."

It showed how little Nessa had known about Cliff. Even if Joanna had shown talent, he wouldn't have wanted her to be a good cook. He needed to be the best. The most popular. He didn't want competition. He couldn't handle it.

"Cliff cooked when we were together, and after the divorce I either ordered in or ate something simple." Fruit and cheese. Salads that required washing and not much else. "I'm good at opening containers."

She could have told Nessa that elaborate food reminded her of Cliff, so her favorite dishes were all things he would never have touched. Mac and cheese that she bought from the deli and reheated. Cold cuts and raw vegetables.

Simple food became an act of rebellion, a way of distancing herself from her past life.

She hadn't only divorced Cliff, she'd divorced that side of her life that ate lobster ravioli.

"Maybe you should stay with a friend for a while." Nessa stabbed at some crumbs with her fingertip. "I mean, just until things calm down."

Friends?

Since the news had broken, two "friends" had messaged her to cancel arrangements for lunch the following week.

She'd had a wide circle of acquaintances when she was married to Cliff. People she'd meet socially, people she ate lunch with, and drank wine with and shopped with, but she'd mostly distanced herself when she'd ended her marriage. Were they really friends? A friend should be someone who cared about you, who you trusted, and she didn't have anyone in her life who fitted that description.

She felt an urge to test her theory.

Picking up her phone, she scrolled through her contacts and called Heather, who was probably the person she saw most frequently. Heather ran the communications company that Cliff had used on occasion for various campaigns, which was how they'd met. Cliff had put a lot of business her way. Since then she and Heather had played tennis regularly. Three times a week, slamming a ball across a net. Three times a week of forehands, backhands and polite conversation. Three times a week of wondering if this was really how she wanted to spend her time.

Heather answered immediately. "Joanna! I've been so worried about you. If there's anything you need… I've been meaning to call."

But she hadn't called.

"Hi, Heather—"

"I was sorry to hear about Cliff." The woman's voice tailed off, as if she wasn't sure whether she was supposed to be sorry or not. "What exactly happened, do you know?"

Was she supposed to be clairvoyant? "I have no idea."

"Who is that young woman? They say she's alive, so surely she must have spoken to someone by now? Was it a one-night thing do you think? One wonders if she was—" Heather lowered her voice. "Do you think he *paid* her?"

"I know nothing about her, or her relationship with Cliff. We're divorced, Heather." Why did she need to remind people of that fact?

"But you were married to him for two decades—I mean, you deserve a medal frankly—and you knew him better than anyone. It must be hard on you."

"The hardest part right now is that the press has surrounded my house and don't seem in a hurry to leave." And friends who asked the same questions as journalists. Friends who talked to journalists.

A source close to Joanna said...

"Is that so surprising? This is juicy," Heather said, "and it's a little light relief from all the bad news out there. People would rather read about Cliff's colorful sex life than read serious stuff. Not me, of course," she added hastily. "I barely read any of that."

Joanna was sure she salivated over every word. "I can't leave my house without them following me."

"Oh, poor you. I wish I could help." They were empty words, delivered as a platitude.

Joanna knew that, but decided to test her theory, anyway.

"You could help." She stared at the remains of her egg, congealing on her plate. "Could I stay with you for a few days?"

There was a pause. "Stay? You mean overnight? With us?"

"If the media know I'm not here, they might lose interest and move on to something else."

"Or they might follow you here. I'm sorry, Joanna, but Bryan has a lot of things going on at work and cannot afford to have a whiff of scandal at the moment. Plus Jilly is home from college, so we don't have much room."

Seven bedrooms, Joanna thought. Heather had seven bedrooms. How much room did they need?

"I understand." She understood that it was nothing to do with room, and everything to do with the baggage Joanna brought with her. She could pull together enough people for a charity ball if she needed to, but she didn't have anyone who loved her enough to care about her welfare.

She felt a heaviness in her chest. The outcome of the call wasn't a surprise, so why did she feel so disappointed?

"Goodbye, Heather." She ended the call and Nessa pulled a face.

"I'm guessing that was a no."

"No one wants a guest who comes with their own press pack."

"Yeah, well, you don't want to stay with her, anyway. You need to get out of the city. Go somewhere remote." Nessa finished her breakfast. "Maybe you should book a hotel."

The idea held no appeal. She'd been alone for years, both within her marriage and outside it, but she'd never felt more alone than she did at that moment. And vulnerable. Unfamiliar surroundings where she couldn't properly protect herself wouldn't help that.

"Have you checked the news sites today? What are they saying?"

"Nothing."

"I know that isn't true."

Nessa sighed. "Nothing you want to know about. Nothing new. Nothing you haven't seen before, I'm sure."

"Pass me my laptop."

"I need it. I'm working."

"Nessa—"

"If I say no will you fire me?" Nessa hesitated and then pushed it across the kitchen island to Joanna. "You honestly shouldn't look."

She looked, and saw that Nessa was right. Because they didn't have anything new to say, they'd dredged up the old stories of Cliff's transgressions over the years. To add visual impact they'd published an old photo of Joanna, taken in about the fifth year of their marriage.

She remembered that night clearly. They'd had a terrible fight an hour before they were due to leave the house. She'd refused to attend the event, afraid she'd be unable to stand on that carpet and smile and not reveal all their dirty secrets to the public. But Cliff had insisted. He'd persuaded her that not to go would attract even more attention. He'd told her that he loved her, that the whole thing was a mistake, that everything was going to be different moving forward. And what people didn't understand was how convincing Cliff could be, to the point that she actually believed that this time would be different. *You fool, Joanna.*

The other thing that people didn't understand was that he was a showman. A performer. Anyone looking at him or talking to him would assume he was a man in control of his life, and at the very top of his game. She was the only one who knew the real Cliff. She was the only one who saw the insecurity, the desperate need for validation and reassurance, the fear.

The first time Cliff's affairs had been made public, she'd locked herself in the bathroom of the huge house they shared together. She'd sat on the floor for hours at a time, afraid to leave her home, trapped by the enormity of her humiliation. The thought that everyone was talking about her was paralyzing. They were unpicking every small detail of her looks and personality in their attempts to justify why Cliff might stray. The fault wasn't his, apparently, it was hers. She'd even started to wonder if they were right. She'd felt like a failure.

Unlovable.

When she looked back at photographs from that time, she barely recognized herself. She looked gaunt and thin, her face so pale she could have successfully auditioned for a vampire movie and not needed makeup.

She closed the laptop. "You're right. I shouldn't have looked."

How long would this continue? How many times would she have to say "no comment"?

Presumably until the woman who had been with Cliff in the car was discharged from the hospital and could answer some questions.

"Er, Joanna…" Nessa pointed a remote at the TV. "They're filming from the hospital. Maybe there's some real news for a change."

A picture of a young woman appeared on the screen.

She had blonde hair and a wild, terrified expression on her face. The photo was slightly blurred, as if it had been snapped in a hurry.

The news presenter announced in a grave voice that photos had emerged of the unknown woman who had been rescued from the crash. Unnamed sources had revealed that she was pregnant, but no one knew more than that. Her name had yet to be revealed. The hospital team was refusing to comment. Everyone was asking the same question. Was the baby Cliff's?

Joanna felt as if she was watching in slow motion.

Baby?

Nessa made a sound. "Pregnant?"

Breathing rapidly, Joanna dragged a stool from beneath the kitchen island and sat down hard.

Why did you crash, Cliff? Did she tell you she was pregnant?

"How can no one know who she is? Does she have amnesia or something?" Nessa put the remote down. "Even if she's lost her purse, surely someone is missing her by now? I can't go a day without someone in my family checking on me. If it's not my mom, it's my brothers. That's a blurry photo, but she looks pretty young. Someone out there must recognize her."

Joanna picked up the remote, paused the image and stared.

Her heart started to pound.

No. It couldn't be. Could it?

The remote slipped from her fingers and landed on the countertop with a clatter but she didn't notice.

She stood up and walked to the screen so she could take a closer look.

It was hard to tell. She could be wrong. She *had* to be wrong, surely? Not possible. It didn't make sense. Unless—

She sat back down, legs shaking.

There was only one way to find out, and that was to see the woman in person.

And if she was right, if her suspicions proved to be correct, then this woman wasn't "unknown." Joanna knew exactly who she was.

She knew everything. She even knew why Cliff had crashed the car.

"Nessa—" Her voice was croaky. "I need to drive to the hospital."

6

Ashley

How had they managed to take her photo? And how had they found out she was pregnant?

No one knew exactly how, but somehow it had leaked.

And that was bad, so bad.

The hospital had expressed their deep dismay, offered an apology and assured her that there would be an investigation. They suspected another patient was responsible, but how it had happened hardly mattered. What mattered was that it had, and the invasion of privacy was a shock.

Ashley had always lived a quiet, low-key, ordinary life. Her father had died when she was twelve and her mother had worked hard in two jobs to keep them solvent. Ashley had excelled at math and had wanted to study computer engineering, but then life had changed in an instant and college was no longer an option. If her mother hadn't died, she probably wouldn't be in the position she was in now. But she had, and here she was, angry at the world, angry at her mother for leaving her like this when she needed her more than ever, guilty for feeling angry. Most of all she was scared because now she had to figure out life by herself. She didn't know how, and so far her attempts to solve her problems had been spectacularly unsuccessful.

She wanted to slide quietly back into what was left of her old life, but that door was closed. There was no "quietly." Everyone wanted to know who she was and what she'd been doing in the car with Cliff.

No one had ever been interested in her, but suddenly everyone was interested.

The doctors, the police, the media—

She felt the beginnings of panic and concentrated on her breathing while she stared at the pictures of Joanna Whitman. How did she stand having cameras pushed in her face? How did she survive it?

Ashley knew everything there was to know about Cliff's exwife. Thanks to the internet, she'd searched, read, filed away the information until she felt she knew Joanna Whitman personally. She knew that she'd grown up in a small town on the Californian coast, that her mother had died when Joanna was born and that her father had remarried when Joanna was eight. She'd lost her father two years later and, according to gossip, she and her stepmother were estranged. It all seemed horribly sad to Ashley, who had enjoyed a very happy, uncomplicated childhood until her father's death.

How had Joanna coped? Ashley had read about every one of Cliff's infidelities, scrutinized the pictures of the women he'd had affairs with. She knew about Joanna's miscarriage, and how heartbroken she'd been. She'd read about it, along with the rest of the world, and seen the pictures of her looking thin and strained. Life happened to people, Ashley knew that now, and often you had no control over the bad things. But life had happened to Joanna Whitman in full view of the public gaze, which must have made everything so much worse. Ashley wouldn't have wanted anyone to witness the state she'd been in when her mother had died. Emotions that raw weren't for public consumption.

How was Joanna reacting to Cliff's death? Had she seen the latest story on the news? Did she know Ashley was pregnant?

Ashley felt her face burn with shame at the thought of adding more crap to Joanna's already crappy life. Joanna probably wished that Ashley had been killed in that crash, too.

Feeling guilty, she hauled herself to the bathroom and then limped back to the bed. Her side was killing her. It hurt to breathe. The bruise on her head still throbbed. Exhausted from the effort required to simply walk across the room, she sank onto the edge of the bed, legs shaking. They'd taken out the drips and drains, but she felt ridiculously weak. She worried endlessly about the baby even though the doctors had assured her everything was fine.

She wanted to get out of here. She wanted to leave the hospital and go back to a life of anonymity. She wanted to put this whole episode behind her, but she had more than herself to worry about.

A baby.

She rested her hand on her abdomen, even though there was nothing to feel yet. She imagined it, nestled inside her, relying on her for everything.

What was she going to do?

How could she leave the hospital when she was so weak she could barely cross the room without needing help? There was no way she could travel, and the nurse had told her that a group of reporters and photographers had been watching the entrance of the hospital for days, waiting for her to emerge. One had been caught prowling the corridors and been forcibly ejected by security.

The police had interviewed her again, and she'd told them what she could. She told them that she'd met Cliff before, that he'd asked her to take a drive with him, that her name was Ashley Blake and that she'd recently arrived in LA looking for a fresh start after the death of her mother. All of it was true.

She'd described the moments before the crash. The police had asked her to recall the conversation and she'd told them that she couldn't remember exactly. They'd been chatting about nothing in particular, which was definitely untrue but she didn't see how the truth was going to help Cliff now. He was gone, and she needed to protect herself and her baby. She didn't want the media delving into her life. She needed to lie low while she made a new plan. So far she was out of inspiration.

Gingerly, treating her body like a fragile object that could break any moment, she slid back into bed and closed her eyes.

She opened them an hour later to find a nurse hovering over her.

"Ashley? You have a visitor."

Her heart plummeted. "Not the police again? There's nothing more I can tell them."

"Not the police. A friend."

Friend? Her friends didn't even know where she was and since she'd lost her phone in the accident she hadn't been able to contact them.

Ashley was about to tell the nurse that she didn't want to talk to anyone when a figure appeared in the doorway. She wore a large sun hat and her hair, blonde, poured over her shoulders. She looked as if she was ready for the beach.

Ashley stared, her mind blank. She didn't know this person. Was she a photographer? No, there was no sign of a camera or even a phone. A reporter, muscling her way into the hospital by claiming to be Ashley's friend? She looked more closely and decided there was something familiar about the woman's face.

The nurse smiled at her. "I'll leave you to it. I'll be right outside if you need anything." She smiled at the woman on her way past and closed the door behind her.

Ashley felt her heart start to pound because now she realized why the woman seemed familiar.

It was Joanna Whitman, although it wasn't surprising she hadn't recognized her at first because everything about her was different.

Her heart hammered a warning. Her skin turned clammy. She tried to speak but her mouth was so dry she couldn't produce any saliva.

What was Joanna doing here? What possible reason would she have for turning up at the hospital? Was she angry because Ashley had been in the car with Cliff? Was this about the baby?

This was getting worse and worse.

What was she supposed to say? *I'm sorry for your loss. I'm sorry if I was the cause of your loss. I'm sorry for ever getting into your husband's car.* Ex-husband, she reminded herself. Joanna had divorced Cliff. In theory she shouldn't care who climbed into his car. But you couldn't be married to the same person for twenty years and not feel something, surely?

The woman sat down in the chair next to the bed. "I'm—"

"I know who you are." Ashley was suddenly desperate for a drink of water. "You look different."

"Looking different is the only way to avoid attention. There's a great deal of interest in you." She removed the hat and Ashley thought that Joanna Whitman looked as good as a blonde as she did as a redhead.

She tugged the covers higher, conscious of how bad she must look. "It's not my fault. Someone took my photograph. They think it might have been a patient. I don't even know why they'd be interested in me." *Don't be naive, Ashley. Of course you know.*

"They're interested because you were in the car with Cliff when he died." Joanna's voice was calm. "Because you're young and pretty, and they know there has to be a story here. They won't stop digging until they find it."

She didn't want them to find it. She didn't want any of this, but she didn't know how to make it go away.

What was she supposed to say? Should she apologize? But for what exactly?

"I don't understand why you're here." She forced herself to look at Joanna, and she thought about what she knew. She'd married Cliff when she was eighteen. Everyone knew the story because Cliff had recounted it often enough over the years in various interviews. *I stopped at a little beach restaurant and there she was, my beautiful Joanna, eighteen years old, waiting tables. When I finished my meal I asked for two things. The check and her number.*

He made it sound like the love story of the century, except that everyone knew what had happened after that. Anyone hoping for Cinderella vibes and happy endings was going to be seriously disappointed by the story of Cliff and Joanna, which came closer to Shakespearean tragedy.

"I'm here," Joanna said, "because I wanted to talk to you."

About what? Suspicious and scared, Ashley studied her face, searching for clues, but Joanna revealed nothing. Married to Cliff, she'd probably had plenty of practice at hiding her emotions.

"I was in the car with your husband." She started to cough and clutched her stomach because coughing was agony.

"Ex-husband." Joanna stood up and poured her a glass of water. "How bad are your injuries? Have they told you when you'll be able to leave the hospital?"

Ashley took the water. "Thank you. I can't leave for a while." And she wasn't sure what she felt about that. She was relieved she wasn't dead, obviously, but she was scared of the medical bills. But at least this hospital was a comparatively safe place. Outside the hospital walls that wouldn't be the case. Presumably Joanna knew that, and her next question confirmed it.

"What will you do when you leave here? Do you have plans?"

No, she didn't have plans. Her plans were lying in the bottom of a ravine.

"I'll figure something out."

"Do you have family? Is your mother coming?"

"My mother is dead." Ashley felt her insides lurch. "It's just me."

Joanna looked at her for a long moment. "And it's true that you're pregnant?"

"Yes." She slammed into a brick wall of reality. Right now she didn't feel capable of looking after herself, let alone another person.

"Do you have someone to go to?" Joanna persisted. "Somewhere you can lie low for a while? Where is your home?"

"Why do you care?" Presumably she was afraid that Ashley was going to talk to one of the journalists who were hovering around the hospital. She was protecting her interests, but Ashley had no intention of talking to anyone. "I'm not going to say anything, if that's what you're worried about. I just want to be left alone."

"Good luck with that." Joanna gave a faint smile, but it wasn't mocking. There was kindness there and also sympathy.

Ashley handed the glass back and slumped back against the pillows. "They're not going to leave me alone, are they? I guess if you have any tips, then I'm ready to hear them." Desperation trumped pride. Few people had as much experience dealing with intrusive questions as Joanna.

"I don't have any tips, but I do have a proposition."

Ashley's stomach lurched.

What could Joanna Whitman possibly have to say to her?

Whatever it was, it couldn't be good.

7

Melanie

Mel jogged along the beach, past the surfers and the girls in bikinis, and the families who were busy building sand sculptures. She'd done the same with Eden, years ago before their relationship had become complicated.

This morning she'd been sipping her coffee in the kitchen when she'd heard sounds from upstairs. She'd known it wasn't Greg, because he'd left earlier to investigate reports of a noisy party at one of the rental properties at the far end of Silver Point. Which meant Eden was awake early.

Her stomach had knotted and she'd felt a rush of sudden dread because any moment now her daughter would appear. Mel hadn't slept well and she didn't want to start her day in combat mode. She missed those simple days when Eden was little and had bounced across the room to greet her with a hug.

When had she last heard the words *I love you, Mom*?

It had been a long time.

Mel had tipped her coffee away, scribbled a note saying, *Gone to work, have a good day* and quietly let herself out of the house. Then she'd felt like the worst mother in the world so she'd tiptoed back in and added *Love you* to the note. It was true, she did love Eden, although right now she didn't like her very much.

Would her anxiety and attention have been diluted had she had more than one child? Was that how it worked?

Either way, it was a sad state of affairs when going into work early was more appealing than staying home. When running was less about fitness and more about reducing stress. But Eden wasn't entirely responsible for the tight feeling in her stomach and the tension in her muscles. She'd been stressed ever since Mary-Lou had told her about the accident. She knew Joanna hadn't been in the car. She knew Joanna hadn't died. But the thought of it had shaken her up and made her think.

What if she had died? What if it had been Joanna's body they'd dragged from the wreckage? How would Mel have felt? What would she have felt?

Regret, for not having tried harder to make contact. For giving up so easily. Mel had been offended, deeply hurt, more than a little angry. And her damn temper had put a flaming barrier between her and rational thought.

She stopped running, bent over and tried to catch her breath.

She couldn't stop thinking that it could have been Joanna in that car.

Was she a bad person? What was friendship if it wasn't standing firm when someone tried to push you away? At the very least she should have made it clear to Joanna that when she was ready to talk, Mel would be here waiting. But she'd taken her hurt feelings and nurtured them while she'd waited for Joanna to call. And time had passed, and then the gap between them had widened until it seemed impassable.

She waved a greeting to a couple of locals and then headed to the Surf Café.

It was early but the deck was already busy, which didn't surprise her because the café was everyone's favorite place to be. For a start it occupied possibly the best position on this stretch of coastline, right in front of the beach with a view of the ocean and the surfers. Waves crashed onto the sand just yards away and if you closed your eyes you could almost feel the spray. Often in the mornings the beach was blanketed in sea mist, but this morning the skies were clear. And if the views and the position weren't enough to tempt you, then there was the food and the atmosphere.

Their parents and grandparents had focused on providing food and drink, and Nate, sociable and easygoing by nature, had expanded on that. Two nights a week he arranged entertainment, tapping into the community and supporting local artists. He held painting classes and cookery classes. Earlier that month he'd found a local jeweler willing to give a demonstration. But most popular of all were the evenings when he invited musicians, when the soft sounds of music tangled with the sounds of the ocean and people nursed their drinks and watched the sun set over the water and created memories that would last forever. Everyone agreed that the reason they loved the Surf Café wasn't the position, although that was unbeatable, or the food, which was delicious. The best thing about the place was the atmosphere that somehow left you feeling as if you'd had a two-week vacation.

"Hey, Mel." Rhonda waved at her from her table at the front of the deck, then snapped a photo of her coffee. "Everything your brother makes is a work of art."

"Hey yourself." Mel could never understand why people wanted to take photos of their food instead of just enjoying it, but she paused by the table, happy to chat. She and Rhonda had been in school together, a label that applied to most people of her age in Silver Point.

The doors to the café were open and she could see Nate handing over a breakfast order to a girl in a pair of surf shorts.

They were both laughing.

Rhonda glanced at them and sighed. "He laughs, he flirts, but he never dates."

"He dates plenty."

"But nothing serious, not since his divorce. I have been in love with him since high school, did you know that?"

Mel did know that. And so did Nate. "Rhonda, you've been married twice."

Mention of high school tugged her mind back to Joanna again. It had been over a week since the story broke, Cliff Whitman's death was still all over the news and Nate hadn't mentioned it once. It was almost killing her not to raise it.

Rhonda sipped her coffee. "I should have married your brother. That's where I went wrong."

Did Rhonda see her wince? She hoped not.

"You don't want to be married to my brother, Rhonda." *You don't want me as a sister-in-law.*

"No? Look at him." Rhonda sat back in her chair and gazed toward Nate, who was now crouched down having a serious conversation with Jack Townsend's four-year-old daughter. "He always has time for people. He's the best listener, and that body of his—do you know that sometimes I just sit on my deck and watch him surf?"

No, she didn't know that. She didn't want to know that, but Rhonda had obviously decided that it was confession time. "Rhonda—"

"Those shoulders. The way his muscles—"

"Whoa." Mel held up a hand. "Thanks, but I really don't want to think about my brother in that way, if it's okay with you. And thinking about you watching him? It's bordering on creepy."

"All I'm saying is that he's about as close to perfect as a man can be."

Mel let her hand drop. "Have you been drinking? He's not perfect, Rhonda. Far from it." In fact, she did think her brother was pretty close to perfect, annoyingly so, but to admit that would be to encourage Rhonda.

Rhonda took another sip of coffee. "So tell me one thing that's wrong with him."

One thing? She could have made a list. That was a sister's job, wasn't it? Top of that list would have been the fact that Nate was stubborn. Once he had an idea in his head, he wouldn't shift no matter how much you pushed and argued the point. And he kept his thoughts to himself far too much for her liking. He worked things out on his own, whereas she liked to voice everything going on in her head. They were close, always had been, and most of the time she knew what he was thinking even when he didn't tell her, but the fact that he didn't tell her things exasperated her.

He'd never once talked to her about what had happened with Joanna all those years before. Joanna breaking up with him and leaving with Cliff was the single biggest emotional blow they'd suffered in the first two decades of their lives, and yet Nate had never once discussed it with her. He'd spent a lot of time surfing, then headed off to college and traveled a bit before returning home and taking over the café.

Whenever Mel had tried to raise the subject of Joanna, he'd shut her down, and then time had passed and eventually she'd stopped asking.

But then Cliff Whitman had driven into a ravine.

And still Nate hadn't mentioned it.

"You see?" Rhonda took her silence to mean a win. "You know him better than anyone, and you can't find anything wrong with him."

Mel decided the conversation needed to end. "If I started on all the things wrong with him, I'd still be going at lunchtime and I have work to do. Have a great day, Rhonda." She flashed a smile and wound her way through the other tables, throwing out greetings like confetti but not pausing long enough for anyone to engage in conversation.

Nate saw her approach and lifted an eyebrow. "You're early. Who are you and what have you done with my sister?"

"She's gone, replaced with a better version. Do you think I should have studied psychology?"

"You?" Nate laughed. "Since when did you become interested in the workings of the human mind?"

"Since I don't understand humans. Are you going to take pity on me and feed me coffee?" Mel waved a hand toward the machine that looked more like a space station than a device for producing her favorite beverage. "I need strong coffee before I switch on the computer and see how much money you've been spending."

"Make it yourself."

"You want to spend the rest of the day fixing what I've broken?"

Nate sighed, relented and stepped toward the coffee machine. "So why do you need to understand humans? Whose behavior is leaving you baffled today?"

Mel thought about Eden. She thought about Joanna. "I'm not great at reading people, that's all." She watched as he produced a perfect espresso. "I prefer people to say what they're thinking and feeling and save me doing all the work. Take Rhonda for example. She never makes any secret of the fact she wants to marry you. She just puts it right out there for everyone to see."

Nate almost dropped the cup he was holding. "What?"

"I'll take that, thank you." She removed it from his hand before it could hit the floor along with his jaw. "She thinks you're perfect. I, of course, was tempted to list all the ways in which you are far from perfect, but in the end I didn't. But you might be interested to know you're the only man she has ever loved."

Nate looked startled. "What about the guys she married?"

"I made the same point. You don't want to know what her answer was."

"I'll make a point not to ask. So why are you here so early? What's wrong?"

"Why does something have to be wrong for me to arrive at the family business that I've been frequenting since before I could walk?" She eyed the freshly baked croissants, tempted. "Maybe I just felt like coming to help my brother."

He intercepted her look, put a croissant onto a plate and pushed it toward her. "Things rough with Eden again?"

"What makes you say that?"

"The fact that you'd rather be here than in your own house."

Should she be annoyed or pleased that he knew her as well as she knew him?

"You're right, things are rough. I'm the worst mother in the world and I don't understand her."

Nate looked sympathetic. "This is why you wish you'd studied psychology?"

Her shoulders sagged. The air around her felt heavy. "She doesn't want to go to college. She wants to stay here and surf, hang out on the beach with her friends and maybe volunteer at the marine sanctuary, take photographs, make jewelry, paint pictures—I don't know. And I don't know what to do about it. She's old enough to take responsibility for her own choices, but what if I can see her choices are wrong? You can't undo big mistakes, can you? Is there a sanctuary for anxious mothers? Because I might need to check myself in there. I hope they have a plentiful supply of alcohol."

Nate walked around the counter and pulled her into a hug. "You're a great mother, Mel. And everything will work out fine."

She couldn't see how it would, but she was grateful to him for trying to make her feel better and she was grateful for the hug.

Her heart softened. He was stubborn and annoying, but he was also kind and generous and probably a much better person than she was. Also, he was her twin and she loved him.

How Joanna could have chosen Cliff over him, she didn't know. It was one of the many mysteries of life she'd never understand.

She'd taken it personally, that was the truth. Reject Nate?

Affronted all over again she gave a sniff and pulled away. "The person who counts doesn't think I'm a great mother, but thanks. I appreciate the vote of confidence." She pulled off a corner of warm, flaky croissant and ate it. "You might not be perfect, but your baking is and so is your coffee." She glanced around. "Where's Shannon? Why are you on your own here?"

"Shannon left on Friday. Took a job in Monterey. Fancy place with linen napkins and silverware. She thinks the tips will be better." Nate took her empty cup. "I did tell you."

"Did you?" Mel remembered the conversation vaguely. "You're in charge of hiring and firing and you have astonishing gifts of persuasion, so I guess I thought you'd talk her out of it."

"Well, I didn't. And no, so far I haven't found a replacement. If you know anyone looking to work here over the summer, let me know."

"You still have Don and Nicky. And I can help out front if I have to."

Nate raised an eyebrow. "You'd do that for me?"

"Only because you hugged me when I needed it most. Don't read too much into it. It would be a temporary thing."

"Too right it would be temporary. The business would never survive your plain speaking."

"I believe in calling a burger a burger."

"You believe the customer is always wrong."

"Only when they don't know what they want, or change their mind about what they ordered and then complain about it." Mel ate another mouthful of croissant and shrugged. "But for a short time I'm prepared to smile and suck it up."

Nate looked unconvinced. "You can do that?"

"I guess we'll find out." She put the plate down. "You won't be able to manage without me, will you?"

"It will be fine." As usual he was laid-back and relaxed. She would have given anything to be half as relaxed as he was.

"What if it isn't fine?"

"Then we'll deal with it." He frowned. "Is there something else bothering you? You seem agitated."

"I don't know, it's just—" She wanted to ask if he'd seen the news reports about Cliff Whitman, but she knew he had. It had been splashed everywhere. He couldn't have missed it, and yet he hadn't mentioned it. She didn't want to raise something that might open old wounds.

Did he think about it? Did he think about Joanna and wonder what she was doing? Damn it, this was her brother and she should be able to talk about anything she wanted to talk about with him. "You've seen the news?"

"The news?"

Was he being intentionally annoying? "Cliff Whitman. Joanna."

He sighed. "I wondered how long it would take you to ask."

"If you knew I was waiting for you to tell me, why didn't you mention it? Talk about it?"

"Because there's nothing to talk about. Have I seen the news about Cliff Whitman? Yes. Have I seen the pictures of Joanna? Another yes. Do I lie in bed thinking of her at night? No. Does my heart ache? Only if I eat a huge meal really late at night, but then again that might be an ulcer."

"You have an ulcer?"

"Not yet, but with a sister like you I'm braced for it."

"How did you know I've been dying to ask you about Joanna?"

"Because I've known you my whole life. You were the same when you were six years old. You wanted to know what I was thinking about everything."

"I did not."

"You did. It's the reason I let Greg marry you, so you'd ask him that question instead of me for the next sixty years."

"Sixty? Why only sixty?" Mel kept it light. "We married at twenty and we have good genes on both sides of the family, so according to a very complex mathematical model that I just this moment invented, I'm expecting at least seventy years together." She expected her brother to tease her about that but he didn't.

His gaze softened. "You're lucky, you and Greg."

Mel felt a pang of guilt. Had she been tactless? Whatever he said to the contrary, she knew how much he'd loved Joanna. He'd probably imagined spending the rest of his life with her.

Perhaps she needed to push him a little harder. "I still think about Joanna. I miss her. When I first heard about it I thought she was in the car. I thought she was dead alongside him and I felt this massive sense of shock, then sadness and regret that we didn't stay in touch. I was so angry with her for having hurt you, and angry that she'd ended the relationship with me, too. She was my best friend."

Nate turned away and focused on the coffee machine. "Let it go, Mel."

"Easy to say. Don't you ever think about her?"

Nate's hesitation confirmed her suspicion that yes, he did sometimes think about Joanna, but she knew he wouldn't admit it and sure enough he shook his head.

"It was another life. Another time. We were both kids. I've moved on and so has she. She was married to another man for two decades."

"And I have a question about that." It was something that had been on her mind. "Why does a woman stay with a man for twenty years, put up with all that crap and then suddenly divorce him. I mean, if you've stayed for twenty years, why not stay another ten? What made her suddenly snap?"

"Why are you asking me?" He moved to the counter and wiped the coffee machine. "I'm no expert on relationships."

"But you're good with people. You understand people. And you always say you've got to look for the reason people do things. So why did she divorce him after two decades?"

Nate stacked clean cups. "Probably one affair too many."

"That was my first assumption, but then I started thinking. She'd already put up with countless affairs, so it can't have been that. It must have been something else."

Nate sighed. "Do you want to tell me what you think it was, so that we can end this conversation?"

"I don't know. That's the thing." She frowned. "I can't figure it out. I looked at all the news stuff again, tried to figure out what happened a year ago, but there's nothing."

"Maybe she'd just had enough." Nate smiled over her shoulder to a customer and Mel knew the conversation was over.

There would be no more talk about Joanna, not with Nate at least.

As usual they'd had one of those conversation where she did all the talking, and he listened but gave very little in the way of a response.

She was still no closer to knowing what he was thinking.

She headed to the office, sat down at the desk and flicked to the news. There were pictures of the press outside of Joanna's house, and speculation that she was no longer even staying there.

No one seemed to know where she was.

Mel sighed, switched to the spreadsheet she'd been working on the day before and tried to ignore the pull of regret that tugged at her insides.

Wherever Joanna was, she hoped she was doing okay.

8

Joanna

Joanna gripped the wheel of the unfamiliar vehicle.

She was going back. Having said she'd never do it, having put the past behind her, she was going back. It was a logical decision. She owned a house in Silver Point. There was no reason why she shouldn't stay there for a while.

She felt a moment of sick dread and reasoned with herself. How could the memories of her old life possibly be worse than the realities of her current one?

And she wasn't going back to the past, not really. For a start, her stepmother wasn't there. Neither was the old Otter's Nest. The rotten planks and the corners, cracks and creaks of the original beach house were gone. Now, there were only the memories and she wasn't going to think about those.

Never call me "Mom." I'm not your mom.

Joanna had only made that mistake once, in the early days. Denise had made it clear that although she was married to Joanna's father, she wasn't, and never would be, Joanna's mother. She'd never wanted maternal responsibility. She'd wanted Joanna's father, and Joanna had been an unwanted added extra.

Her last encounter with Denise had been one of the worst moments of her life.

Joanna registered pain in her hands and realized she was gripping the wheel so tightly she was restricting blood flow.

Releasing the wheel with one hand and then the other, she flexed her fingers.

How would the inhabitants of Silver Point feel about her return? No doubt there would be a ripple of trepidation, but since Joanna had no intention of mixing with the local community that didn't matter.

She would do what she did best. Lie low. She'd live the way she'd been living in LA, only this time she had the view, the beach that nestled at the foot of her property and a higher chance of privacy.

And she was going to need privacy, thanks to her most recent decision. *You think I made bad decisions in the past, Denise? Wait until you see what I've done this time.*

In the passenger seat next to her, the girl shifted. "I still can't believe you're doing this."

Joanna couldn't believe she was doing it, either. "Well, I am."

"I keep waiting for you to throw me out on a street corner."

"I'm not throwing you anywhere, Ashley." It was too late for that. She'd made her decision and now she had to live with it.

"I don't know why you're being nice to me. I was in the car with your husband."

"Ex-husband." *Damn you, Cliff.* Suppressing her anger, Joanna kept her eyes fixed on the road.

"But you have no reason to help me."

Joanna wished she'd stop talking. "Do you have anyone else who could help you?"

There was a long silence. "No." Ashley's voice sounded smaller. "I was trying to help myself. That's what adults do, isn't it?" She made it sound as if she'd recently accepted a new role and was trying it on for size.

"There's nothing wrong with accepting help, Ashley."

"So you're doing this because—why?"

Why was she doing this? "I feel sympathy for your situation. I know what it's like to have your privacy invaded. And I know what it's like to feel alone. I want you to know you're not alone." Joanna wasn't sure that was the whole reason, but it was enough for now. The moment she'd seen Ashley's face on the TV she'd known that they were going to have to somehow disappear. Even if it was only temporary, and she was realistic about their chances of evading the press for long, then it would at least give them time to breathe, think and plan.

Ashley wriggled, trying to get comfortable. "You're nothing like I thought you'd be. Did you really climb over the wall at the back of your house?"

"Yes." It was past midnight and she wasn't in her own car, but still Joanna checked her mirror. Traffic out of the city was heavy, even in the early hours of the morning, but it didn't seem that anyone was following her. She allowed herself a fleeting moment of triumph. This time she'd beaten them. The knowledge made her feel a little more in control.

Joanna silently thanked Nessa and her mechanic brother for their generosity. Hiring a car would have created a trail. Borrowing one from Nessa's brother seemed like the best option.

"No hurry to return it," Nessa had said as she'd handed over the keys. "But I want to hear from you regularly, otherwise I'll worry."

Joanna planned to speak to her frequently. She still had a job to do, but for the foreseeable future she'd be doing it remotely.

"So you borrowed a car from a colleague and parked it away from your house so no one saw it, dressed all in black, climbed over a wall, left the lights burning in your house so they'd think you were still in it and then you sneaked through the woods behind your house with just a flashlight. This is like being in an action movie."

"Not really." It was her life. *Her life.* How had she been reduced to climbing over walls and hiding? "I almost broke my ankle twice trying to navigate my way through the trees in the dark."

"Weren't you scared?"

"A little." Should she admit that the alternative, staying, had scared her more?

"But you did it, anyway. That's brave. Doing all that in the dark on your own. You're like—like—an assassin or something."

It sounded so ridiculous Joanna almost smiled. "Are you always this dramatic?"

"No. But I've never played a starring role in an escape movie before. I was dreading having to confront those photographers. I did exactly what you told me to do. I told the nurses my friend was picking me up. I took the elevator to the first floor, changed in that bathroom you found. My heart was going crazy the whole time. The wig was a good idea, although I kept waiting for someone to put a hand on my shoulder and say, *Ashley, why do you suddenly have brown hair?*"

Joanna's heart was going crazy, too. When was the girl going to stop talking?

"It worked out fine."

"Thanks to you. Can I take the wig off now?"

"Yes." Joanna knew Ashley was chattering because she was nervous and she sympathized. She was nervous, too. Nervous about going back to Silver Point. Nervous that bringing Ashley with her on this trip might turn out to be another bad decision among the many she'd made in her life.

But what choice had she had?

She discovered that she was gripping the wheel again. *Pregnant.*

The girl hardly seemed able to care for herself, let alone another person, but she wasn't going to think about that now. Her head was so full of things she wasn't going to think about it was a wonder it didn't explode.

She glanced at Ashley and saw curly blonde hair and big blue eyes. *Oh, Cliff.* "Is there someone you'd like to call? I forgot to ask whether you have your phone or whether it was lost in the accident."

"I lost it, but then someone found it and the police returned it to me. But there's no one I need to call."

"Are you comfortable? There's a pillow on the back seat if you want to close your eyes for a while. You should sleep." *Please sleep.* She needed thinking time. This was the first opportunity she'd had to focus on herself without worrying who was watching her.

At some point, of course, she was going to have to think about Ashley. Figure out what to do next. But that wasn't her priority.

"I'm not tired. Also, I hurt all over, so sleeping isn't easy." Ashley shifted in her seat, trying to get comfortable.

Sleeping hadn't been easy for Joanna, either. The moment she lay down, the past played out in front of her. She couldn't stop thinking about the choices she'd made and berating herself.

The past few weeks had been the most emotionally exhausting of her life. And the loneliest. Not one person in her social circle had reached out to her. Acquaintances—she would never again refer to them as friends—people who had enjoyed her company in happier times, didn't want to come near her now and risk finding themselves in the spotlight, or worse, having to defend her against the judgment brigade.

She'd thought that getting away from the city would help, but now she was doubting that decision. She could leave the media behind, but not her emotions.

Silver Point? *Really, Joanna?*

She was gripped by a moment of extreme doubt and had an uncharacteristic urge to seek reassurance from someone. Anyone. She opened her mouth, glanced at Ashley and then closed it again. She'd climbed into Cliff's car, which didn't say much for her judgment.

Technically she should hate this girl. Her presence was yet another slap in the face, a reminder of Cliff's transgressions. There was a child. *What were you thinking, Cliff?*

And what was *she* thinking? Cliff's mistakes weren't hers. Even if they were still married—even thinking of that made her clench her jaw—his mistake wouldn't have been hers. She was not responsible for his actions.

But a child didn't deserve to suffer because of Cliff. And she had the means to offer support. Financially, she could help.

Emotionally?

She felt something tear open inside her. She thought back to the baby she'd lost. She'd wanted a child so badly, and to think that Cliff—

She closed her mind down. She wasn't going to think about that now. She didn't need another assault on her emotional resources. She needed to hold it together.

Ashley turned her head. "Do you think they're looking for me? Those reporters?"

"Yes." She saw no reason to lie or soften the truth.

"You were smart to tell me to wait by the entrance to the ER. That place was heaving with people. No one was paying any attention to me. And there were no photographers or anything, I checked. It helped that the staff kept moving me. I didn't know where I was half the time, so why would anyone else? I still don't know why you're doing this for me—" Ashley glanced at her "—but I figured even if you're kidnapping me, at least it's a place to stay, right?"

Joanna's head started to throb. "I'm not kidnapping you, Ashley."

"You think I'm being dramatic, but from where I'm sitting you're helping the woman who was in the car with your man. And that's kind of…unexpected. People don't do things like that."

She gripped the wheel tightly. "He wasn't my man. He hadn't been my man in a long time."

She kept her eyes forward.

It had been years since she'd traveled this road. Years since she'd ventured north.

She'd spent most of her adult life moving forward, but now she was going back.

How would it feel being there? Not like going home, because the central Californian coast hadn't been her home in two decades. Nor like being a tourist, because a tourist would freely explore the area. Walk into local stores, buy an ice cream without looking over her shoulder, offer cheerful greetings to the locals.

Joanna wouldn't be doing any of that, even though her family had been part of Silver Point for more than three generations.

Otter's Nest had originally belonged to her grandfather, Walter Rafferty. A moderately successful artist, Walter had inherited a small amount of money from a source that had never been confirmed. Rumor had it that he'd saved someone's life, but Joanna's father had said that given that the man never did anything for anyone, that was unlikely. Whatever the origin of the money, he'd bought a tired, weather-beaten beach house with stunning views over the deep blue Pacific Ocean. The place was shielded by forest, which had suited Walter, who was, by all accounts, an antisocial, moody individual. He'd chosen the place because it was just far enough out of town to deter casual visitors, because it had a spectacular garden with a proliferation of roses and fruit trees and he preferred plants to people, and because it had direct access to a stretch of beach that was otherwise inaccessible. He spent most of his time outdoors and had almost no interest in the house itself, which explained its gradual deterioration. Joanna's father had once told her that Walter had married his wife, Joanna's grandmother, not because he fell in love, but because he needed a woman to rescue Otter's Nest before it crumbled into the ocean.

Her grandmother had set about scrubbing, cleaning, fixing and generally making the place more habitable, not because she was keen to obey her grumpy spouse, but because she refused to live somewhere that looked as if it might fall down at any moment.

As a child Joanna had been unaware of how valuable this parcel of land was. To her it was home, and the home wasn't fancy. It had been left to her when her father died, a generous gesture that had extinguished any last hope she had of one day building a relationship with her stepmother.

Even after she'd left, she hadn't had the option to sell the place because Denise was still living in it. Would she have sold it right away if that hadn't been the case? Maybe. The house was layered with memories. The distant ones were good, but they'd been overshadowed by what came after. She'd ignored the problem, and then five years earlier her stepmother had announced that she'd had enough of living somewhere so far from town. She'd moved into a small house near Carmel-by-the-Sea, leaving Otter's Nest uninhabited.

Joanna had received numerous offers from people hungry to exploit the advantages of that particular piece of land, but she didn't want to sell. She'd thought about Walter, pruning his fruit trees, and her father starting every day with a swim in the ocean.

Instead of selling, she'd hired an architect. The development had been costly in both money and time but eventually a new beach house was completed, a contemporary masterpiece, blending sympathetically with its surroundings, exploiting all that was special about the landscape. She knew instinctively that her father would have approved, even though all that was left of the original Otter's Nest was the name.

For all its appeal, Joanna had never stayed there herself. She'd employed a company to manage it, and occasionally to rent it out. It was a business decision.

But coming back now wasn't business. It was personal.

She'd sleep in the bedroom with its wall of floor-to-ceiling glass overlooking the ocean. She'd sip her morning coffee on the terrace sheltered from the outside world by towering trees. She'd walk barefoot on the heated stone floors, relax in the tub with its view over the garden and follow the narrow sandy path that led the short distance to the beach. Otter's Nest was far from the worn and weathered bungalow that had been her home growing up. Now it was a premium property on a coastline known for premium properties. But it was still a beach house, and in huge demand despite the eye-watering rental costs.

She'd called the agent a few days earlier and asked them to cancel all reservations and make the place ready because she was loaning it to a friend. They'd probably figure out that she was intending to use it herself, which was another reason she wasn't confident that their whereabouts would remain a secret for long.

Cliff would have laughed at her attempts to regain a degree of privacy. Privacy, anonymity, had been his idea of hell.

She was one of the few people, perhaps the only person, who had understood the depths of Cliff's insecurity.

He needed five portions of praise a day to survive, and more to truly thrive. When things were going well he bounced through the door with a megawatt smile, energized by the positive attention. He was his own weather system—on a high one minute and in a depression the next. If ratings of his show were down, or the restaurants weren't booked out weeks in advance, his mood would change from sunny to volcanic. She'd been drawn to the sunny, and then learned to live with the other side of him. No one was perfect, were they? She definitely wasn't perfect, as her stepmother had frequently pointed out.

"This place we're going..." Ashley turned her head and looked at her. "You own it?"

"Yes. I grew up there." Why had she told her that? Now there would be questions, and she didn't want to answer questions.

"You have family there?"

Denise? "No." Her hands were hurting again and she released her grip on the wheel slightly. "No family."

"So it will be just us?"

"Yes. Just us." How was she going to handle that? She wasn't going to be alone, was she? She had Ashley. Ashley, who couldn't stop talking. Ashley, who had been in the car with Cliff. Ashley, who was a complication Joanna had yet to address.

Ashley, who was pregnant.

The sharp rip had become an ache in the center of her chest but it clearly wasn't visible because Ashley kept talking.

"Is it in the middle of nowhere?"

"I wouldn't describe it as nowhere. We don't have immediate neighbors." Joanna turned off the main highway and headed toward the coast.

The road curved alongside the ocean and through the darkness she could pick out the shadow of jagged rock, the flash of white as the waves rolled in and the spray as it erupted onto the shore.

She stopped in Santa Barbara just long enough to breathe in the salt air and stretch her tired limbs.

When she returned to the car she saw that Ashley was finally asleep, her head nestled deep in the pillow.

Relieved, Joanna reached into the back of the car and grabbed the blanket she'd packed. Careful not to wake her, she tucked it around the sleeping girl and then reached into her backpack and pulled out a flask. She poured herself a cup of the strong coffee she'd made earlier.

There was no one else around. In this moment it was just her, the darkness, the whip of the wind and the crash of the wild ocean.

The sound made her think of her father and it comforted her. Denise hadn't been a swimmer. She'd complained about the salt in her hair and the sand on her skin. The sea had been the one place Joanna had her father to herself. It had been just the two of them, laughing, splashing.

She'd spent more time on the small beach below Otter's Nest than she had in the house. She loved to swim, to feel the cold ocean close over her sun-warmed skin and stiffen her hair with salt. Even now, to plunge into the water was to plunge into happiness.

She stared at the water now, remembering.

Once, she'd had a life here. This had been her place, and then she'd tossed it to the wind and taken off without looking back. She'd been running away. And she was doing the same now, wasn't she? Running from the press. Running from Cliff's memory. Running from her life.

Was she ever going to live a life where she wasn't running?

Her eyes pricked with tiredness. Despite the coffee, her head felt foggy. It had been a long couple of weeks, and then there had been the funeral a few days before. More cameras. More questions. The exhausting, never-ending attention from people who didn't know her or care about her.

But now she could put that behind her.

Soon she'd be safe behind the gates of Otter's Nest.

How many memories would be waiting for her? That was something else she hadn't allowed herself to think about.

Mel and Greg.

Nate.

No. She couldn't, *wouldn't*, think about Nate. Not yet.

She swallowed the last mouthful of her coffee and tucked the flask back into her backpack.

With a last look at the ocean, she slid back into the car and continued north, winding her way up the coast until dawn sent spikes of color across the darkened sky.

It had been years, and yet she knew this last stretch of the journey so well. Each curve in the road, the sight of towering redwoods, the dramatic plunge of steep cliffs.

And then there it was, the turning to Otter's Nest, concealed from view between tall trees. There was no sign, nothing to indicate the presence of such an extraordinary property, an intentional security measure rather than an oversight, and if you didn't already know exactly where it was you'd miss the turning.

Joanna knew.

She turned onto the private access road, following it until she reached a set of large gates. They added another layer of privacy. From this angle you still couldn't see the beach house.

She pressed the button and the gates swung open, revealing another sweep of driveway studded by small solar lights.

The gates closed behind her and she parked in front of the house.

Ashley was still asleep so Joanna took advantage of the moment to take her first proper look at Otter's Nest.

From here the place looked unassuming, but that didn't concern her. She knew that all the wow factor would be at the front. The house was built into the slope, the design making the most of space, light and the incredible ocean views.

She unlocked the door, turned off the alarm and slid off her shoes.

She stood for a moment, braced and wary. She waited for the memories to come for her, like an intruder lying in wait. Waited for the past to slide stealthily back into her present.

But there was nothing. She felt nothing.

Flooded with relief, she felt her muscles relax. She'd been dreading this moment, but it was obvious to her now that painful memories had been destroyed along with the original home. Rotten wood, cracked glass, bitter memories. Everything had been removed. There were no reminders. Not a trace of familiarity, except for the land itself and the beach, of course. Always the beach.

She walked into the living room, saw the glint of sunlight on the ocean through the expanse of glass and gave a sigh of pleasure because the new building was every bit as spectacular as she'd known it would be. The room curved a full one hundred and eighty degrees, and floor-to-ceiling windows ensured a ringside seat for sunrise and sunset. Huge sliding doors opened onto the terrace and the garden and there, right in front of her, was the path that led to the beach. It was far enough away to protect the house from the lick and surge of the tide, but close enough to make you feel as if you could reach out and touch it.

The crescent beach at Otter's Nest was protected on both sides by the curve of the land and rocks.

She'd be able to sit there without being seen. She'd be able to swim in the sea. Watch whales and dolphins. And yes, there would definitely be memories there. Her father. *Nate.*

"Joanna?" Ashley's voice came from the doorway. "I didn't know where you were, so—"

"I didn't want to wake you." Enough of the past. She had the present to think about. "We should go straight to bed and get some proper sleep. We can talk in the morning."

"But it's morning now. The sun is coming up."

Joanna had been driving for half the night. She was emotionally and physically exhausted. She needed to close a door between her and Ashley, this problem she'd chosen to bring home with her. She needed space.

"I'll show you to your room. The bathroom should be stocked with everything you need. I hope you'll be comfortable."

Even though she'd never stayed here she knew the house, and she led Ashley up the curved staircase to the guest suite.

"This place is like a five-star hotel," Ashley muttered as she followed her into the bedroom.

Joanna pressed a button next to the bed and closed the blinds and flicked on the bedside light. "The bathroom is through that door, and my bedroom is across the hallway."

"Sure. Thanks." Ashley hesitated. "You seem really stressed. Are you okay?"

The fact that she'd noticed told Joanna that she was losing her usually firm grip on control. "I'm fine. I hope you sleep well. Call me if you need anything."

"Joanna—"

"I'm fine." Joanna backed away. "Get some rest. There will be plenty of time to talk." She urged the girl into the room and closed the door quietly.

Instead of going to the master suite she walked back down to the kitchen and opened the fridge. It was fully stocked, as she'd requested. She opened cupboards, checking that they'd delivered what she'd asked. There was enough food to ensure she wouldn't have to leave this place for at least a week, maybe two. After that—well, she'd face that problem later.

Exhaustion made her feel shivery and cold, but she knew she wouldn't be able to sleep. Her mind was like a drone, gliding over two decades of her life and more, sending inconvenient snapshots.

She grabbed a sweater and stepped out onto the terrace. The house might have changed, but the view hadn't and neither had the scents. Lavender and rose, the sharp hint of pine mingling with salt spray from the ocean below.

She followed the path to the beach, but instead of walking onto the sand she scrambled up onto one of the rocks that sheltered the bay. It was still early. No one would see her, because no one would be looking for her here. Not yet.

She hugged her knees against her chest and gazed at the water. Beyond the level of the rocks the swirl of currents made the water dangerous. Guests using the place were advised to sunbathe only and use the pool or the main beach at Silver Point for swimming and water fun, but Joanna had no intention of doing that. She'd grown up here. She knew the risks and she was a strong swimmer.

She stretched out her legs, enjoying the early-morning sun. At this time of day she didn't have to worry about burning.

At school she'd been teased for her freckles, but she'd never cared because her dad had always told her they were fairy dust, and only given to special people. He'd had the same dusting, as faint as a sprinkling of sand, and after he died she used to look in the mirror and imagine that a part of him had landed on her. It made her feel closer to him, knowing she was carrying them around.

She stared down at the white-capped ocean that swirled and smashed against the rocks, sending spray flying high. Often the view was blurred by the milky layer of marine fog that blanketed the California coastline in the early summer mornings, but today was clear and sunny.

She glanced behind her toward the main beach that stretched the length of Silver Point and saw a small figure far in the distance, running on the beach. *Mel?*

Her heart thumped and she slid down from the rock, scraping her leg in the process. What had she done? Had she just given herself away? No. No one would have recognized her from that distance, particularly when they weren't expecting her to be here. She was just a woman sitting on the rock. She could be anyone. Joanna tried to calm the panic that churned inside her.

Just because she and Mel had run on the beach together almost every morning didn't mean her old friend still kept to the same routine.

She felt a pang of nostalgia.

Mel had been her best friend. The person she trusted most in the world. But Mel was Nate's twin sister, which had made everything impossible.

Joanna had looked her up the week before, unable to resist the pull from the past.

She'd found out that Mel still lived here, which hadn't come as a surprise. She was now married to Greg, which wasn't a surprise, either. They had a daughter, Eden, and Joanna had felt a pang remembering the times they'd talked about raising their families together. They'd be in and out of each other's gardens, enjoying backyard barbecues and beach picnics. Mel and Greg. Joanna and Nate.

Nate.

She felt a sting of sadness and headed back up the path to the beach house.

She wasn't going to think about Nate, and she didn't need to worry about bumping into him because she had no intention of strolling into town or eating on the deck of the Surf Café.

She'd keep her life small and quiet, because she'd learned that it was better that way.

In all the words that had been written about her, there was one thing the press had missed.

She was, quite possibly, the loneliest woman in the world.

9

Ashley

Ashley woke to the sound of waves breaking on rock. A cool breeze wafted through the window. She lay there, groggy and disorientated, and then remembered where she was. Joanna Whitman's beach house. The bed was ridiculously comfortable and the pillows so soft it was like sleeping on a cloud. After nights of shifting restlessly on a hard, unyielding hospital bed, her skin irritated by rough sheets, this bed felt like something out of a fantasy. But the rest of it?

That was more like a horror movie and the big twist was yet to come.

She wanted to postpone the moment. She wanted to stay right here, cocooned in luxury, and pretend she was on vacation. She didn't want to have to wake up properly and face her problems.

She wished she'd never come to LA. She wished she'd never met Cliff. She wished she'd never climbed into his car or said what she'd said.

But as her mother had always taught her, there was no point in wishing for things you couldn't change. You just had to get on with it and make the best choice you could.

Ashley's current best choice would have been to stick her head under the pillow and stay there, but that would be cowardly, wouldn't it? Also rude.

What would her mother have said if she could see her now? With Joanna Whitman?

"You were sleeping so deeply I didn't want to wake you, but I thought you should probably get back to some sort of normal sleep pattern." Joanna placed a tray on the table by the open doors.

Ashley saw now why she'd heard the ocean and felt the breeze. While she'd been sleeping, Joanna had lifted the blinds and opened the doors. Those doors led directly onto a terrace bordered by a profusion of colorful plants and flowers.

How great would it be to be able to enjoy this without feeling guilty and anxious about everything?

She had so many decisions to make. So many pieces of information to process.

She'd had one plan. Talk to Cliff. That hadn't gone the way she'd hoped it would.

Of all the scenarios she'd imagined in her head, the one that had never featured was that she might actually kill him. Not that she'd tugged the wheel and landed them in that ravine or anything, but if she'd never met him, been more careful, hadn't chosen that exact moment to tell him about the pregnancy...

Cliff Whitman was dead because of her.

The thought left her feeling weak and shaky. The police had questioned her and been satisfied with her answers. Cliff was single. She wasn't underage. There was no reason why she shouldn't have been in his car. Her choices might be questionable, but they weren't illegal. It was ruled to be an unfortunate accident.

Ashley forced herself to sit up. Her life had been full of unfortunate accidents.

"I made you something to eat." Joanna picked up the tray

and put it on the bed next to Ashley. "You look pale. Are you feeling terrible?"

Joanna stacked pillows behind her as if she was a child and the unexpected kindness brought a lump to her throat. She felt horribly undeserving of such generosity from this woman.

"Why are you being so nice to me? You must hate me."

Joanna straightened the bedcovers. "I don't hate you."

She would, Ashley thought, if she knew the details. And it made her feel bad because she knew so much more about Joanna than Joanna knew about her.

Guilt gnawed at her insides. She didn't like holding all these secrets inside her. Could the baby sense them? Was it having a dose of anguish along with its mother?

She wanted to relax. She wanted to be calm. She wanted to tell Joanna everything, but how could she?

If she'd known that being an adult was this hard, she wouldn't have been in such a hurry to grow up. And now she had no choice.

She pressed her hand to her flat belly and mentally promised her baby that although she hadn't been the best mother up to this point, she was going to do better.

"You should eat something. There's fresh melon, berries and—" Joanna settled the tray on Ashley's legs. "What's wrong?"

"Nothing." Ashley forced the word from her thickened throat. Why was she so emotional? She had to stop. She had to think about the baby.

She felt the bed shift as Joanna sat down.

"Are you feeling unwell? I can call a doctor."

"No." Ashley didn't want a doctor. She wanted to start her life over, without all the lies and mistakes. And because the guilt and anxiety was too huge to contain, it finally spilled over. "I wish I'd never got into his car. I wish I'd never met him."

Joanna reached across and pulled a tissue from the box by the bed. "You're not the first woman to feel that way about

Cliff, I assure you." She handed Ashley the tissue and she took it, mortified.

"Did you?"

"About a million times." Joanna gave a wry smile. "Try and forget it for now. I suspect you're very tired, and being tired always makes things seem worse."

"My mom used to say that. She used to tell me that good sleep was one of the most important things a person could do for themselves. She was always telling me to stop looking at my phone, stop messaging friends in the middle of the night." Thinking about her mother made Ashley feel worse so she tried to stop that, too. There were so many things she couldn't think about, she was struggling to find a safe topic.

Joanna hesitated. "I'm sorry you lost her."

Ashley was sorry, too. She was sorry about a lot of things.

"It's been tough. Not that I'm making excuses or anything, but I've had a totally crap year."

Joanna said nothing and Ashley felt mortified. Joanna's year had been crap, too. In fact, much of her life had been crap. How must she be feeling? She'd seemed really stressed on the drive. Ashley had seen her gripping the steering wheel until her fingers went white and exhaling slowly as if she was having to work hard to keep herself under control.

Was she still grieving for Cliff? The whole divorce thing had to make it complicated, didn't it? And the affairs. Still, twenty years—Ashley couldn't get her head around all the emotions that could be locked inside Joanna.

Joanna stood up. "Why don't you stop thinking for a while, eat some breakfast and then join me on the terrace."

"I—yes, sure." She wanted to say the right thing, but she didn't know what that was. It was impossible to know what Joanna was thinking.

"Do you read?"

"Read? You mean books?"

Joanna smiled. "Yes, books. There's a library downstairs. It's the door next to the kitchen."

"You have your own library?"

"Yes. I love books. Reading them, and looking at them."

They were dealing with huge issues, and they were talking about books?

"I read. Used to read. Not so much lately." Her concentration was shot. She was having a baby. Cliff wasn't going to help her. "So are we going to talk?"

"Eventually, but I think what we both need more than anything right now is a rest, don't you? Eat something, and then join me by the pool."

"There's a pool? With the ocean a few steps away?"

Joanna smiled. "The ocean is cold. Not everyone likes that."

Library. Pool. Terrace. Beach. Ashley hadn't dipped her toe in water yet, but already she felt out of her depth.

"I don't have that many clothes."

"You won't need many. We won't be entertaining. My plan is that we stay here for the next couple of weeks to give us both time to breathe and figure out what to do next. Come and find me when you're ready."

Next? She was making it sound as if they were a team, bonded by their situation, but Ashley knew the only thing holding them together was Cliff. Cliff was dead, so where did that leave her?

Joanna left the room and Ashley stared at the rest of the breakfast without enthusiasm. She wasn't hungry, but she needed to eat because of the baby.

She forced down a single mouthful and then gave up and headed to the bathroom. There was a large bath positioned in front of a large window with a view of the garden, but Ashley opted instead for the shower. It took her a few minutes to figure out the controls, and then she stood under the hot spray for a long time, washing away the reminders of her hospital stay. Her bruises were fading and she ached a little less every day.

She lathered her hair, soaped her skin from head to foot and rested her hand on her abdomen. Did she feel a little bump or was that her imagination? How soon would she start to show?

Her head was full of questions. She was horrified and embarrassed by how ignorant she was.

"I'm sorry to be clueless." She talked to the baby, although if it could hear her, then that would mean it had heard other things and was probably already scarred by the world awaiting it outside the protection of her body. "I'll do better, I promise."

And she meant it. She was all the baby had. She was everything, so she had to *be* everything, and she would. She'd be loving but she'd also be truthful, no matter how hard it was. She wasn't going to let this baby down.

She needed a plan, but that started with Joanna. She didn't understand why Joanna was helping her, but Cliff was gone so there would be no help coming from that direction. Right now she'd take anything she could get.

For a split second she was back in the car, in those few moments between her telling him and him reacting to the news. She knew she'd never forget the look in his eyes or the words he'd spoken.

Ashley turned off the shower and forced herself to push the memory away. This wasn't the time to relive the trauma of the accident. She needed to focus on now, this moment, and the future.

She wrapped herself in one of the large, soft towels stacked on the glass shelf and dried her hair.

She delved into her bag to find clean clothes and saw her phone. She hadn't touched it since the police had handed it over.

Heart thudding, she switched it on.

Ten voice-mail messages.

She swallowed and turned the phone off again. She wasn't ready for that yet. One step at a time.

Burying the phone under a shirt, she pulled out jeans and a clean top. Both still fitted her, although she wasn't sure how long that would last.

Feeling self-conscious, she left the bedroom and headed downstairs. It was impossible not to look around, and what struck her wasn't the jaw-dropping design, or the luxury touches, but the fact that there was nothing personal on show. It was like staying in a hotel, not that Ashley would know because they'd never had the money for hotels. Part of her wanted to sneak a look into some of the other rooms, including the master bedroom and the library Joanna had mentioned, but she had a feeling they wouldn't tell her anything about the owner.

Like most people who read the popular press, she'd thought she knew Joanna Whitman, but it turned out she was a bit of a mystery. She owned this incredible place, and yet she'd never stayed here. In her position, Ashley would never have left. She would have spent every night in that delicious cocoon of a bed, and all her daylight hours ravenously devouring the view.

She passed the living room and saw deep, comfortable sofas and a large fireplace. A low table was stacked with art books and a sculpture. It was sophisticated. Grown up.

Ashley thought about the sofa at home, with its worn patches that her mother had mended and mended and then given up mending. She thought about how hard her mother had struggled to keep everything together after her dad had died. The hours on her feet. The snatched meals eaten standing up. The permanent frown. The falling asleep on the sofa.

Can we go and play, Mommy?

Not now, I have to work.

At sixteen, Ashley had worked, too. She'd got a job in the local pizza restaurant, waiting tables. She'd learned to ignore the complainers, the diners who ordered and then changed their minds and blamed her, the mean tippers and the men who hit on her. She ignored the long hours, the way her legs ached after a long day standing, the way her cheeks hurt from smiling when she didn't want to smile. She was working for a purpose, and that purpose was money. She gave most of her earnings to her mother, and put the rest into her college fund. It was depressingly small, but it was hers and it was something. When she wasn't working, she was studying. She didn't have a dollar to her name that she hadn't earned by being on her feet.

She thought about Cliff, but thinking of him made her feel as if someone had her heart in a vise so she stopped.

She decided that one day she wanted to live in a place like this, in a home that she actually owned, a place that didn't constantly show you its shortcomings. Most of all she wanted to have enough money so she didn't have to work every hour of every day. So she didn't have to constantly tell her child she was too busy.

The glass doors were open onto the terrace and Ashley could see Joanna sitting on one of the loungers by the pool. She was wearing shorts, and oversize sunglasses, and her hair fell loose over her shoulders like flames. She looked like a rare, exotic bird and Ashley wished she had half her quiet elegance.

Joanna had a book on her lap, but she wasn't reading. She appeared to be staring out across the ocean and Ashley couldn't blame her for that because she'd never seen a view like it. If she owned this place she would never have left it but maybe when you were rich fancy properties and incredible views were something you took for granted.

Or maybe there were other reasons Joanna wasn't reading. Was it being back here? Or was it because Ashley was with her? She strolled onto the terrace. "It's stunning here." There. She sounded confident. Not at all as if her insides were quaking with nerves. "Thank you for breakfast. Did you cook the pastries?"

"No, I don't cook. I arranged for the place to be stocked with food before our arrival."

"Well, they were delicious." Why didn't Joanna cook? Presumably because Cliff had done all the cooking for her.

"Did you find everything you needed? Was your room comfortable?"

"It was perfect. The shower was great. A bit like getting caught in a heavy rainstorm. At home I have to stand there while it tries to choke out a few drops."

It felt surreal, standing here by an idyllic pool, surrounded by the scents of summer with the vivid blue of the Pacific Ocean just steps away, and only Joanna Whitman for company.

What was she supposed to do? Should she stand up? Sit down?

In the end she sat on the lounger next to Joanna's. She'd perched on the edge, which gave her the option of standing suddenly if she needed to.

She had no idea how this conversation was going to go.

Once she told Joanna the truth, she'd probably be on the next bus back to the city. Or maybe she'd be walking.

She eyed the pool. It would have been great to swim, but maybe the people who used this place didn't actually get wet. Maybe the pool was an accessory, something to admire while they basked in the Californian sunshine, sipped margaritas and kept their hair dry.

Sunlight glinted on the water and the breeze sent a ripple of movement across the surface.

It looked tranquil and inviting. She had to keep reminding herself that she wasn't on vacation.

Joanna lowered her book. "You're welcome to swim if you'd like to."

Was she that obvious? "I'm fine."

"I'm sure I can find you a swimsuit. There's a closet on the first floor full of new clothes and equipment. If something fits, use it."

Ashley stared longingly at the water, and then shook her head. "Maybe later. Thanks."

Did Joanna not think this was weird? She was treating Ashley like a guest, when she should be treating her like the enemy.

Joanna was watching her through those large sunglasses that hid most of her face. "You said you'd had a bad year. You must miss your mother. Were you close?"

"Yes." Was that true? A year ago Ashley would have said that yes, they were close, but that was before. Could you consider yourself close to someone who kept things from you? What other bombshells would have emerged if her mother was still alive? Ashley had a whole lot of questions and no way of getting the answers. "My dad died when I was twelve so it's been the two of us since then." There was no reason not to tell Joanna that.

"Tell me about your dad. What did he do?"

It always struck Ashley as a strange question, as if what you did for a living defined who you were as a person. If you were what you did, then right now she was no one.

"His name was David. He was a mechanic. He could fix pretty much anything." But that wasn't who he was to Ashley. To her he was the man who taught her to change a tire and grow tomatoes in the backyard. He'd been obsessed with the outdoors and taken her hiking every weekend. They'd hiked long distances, and she'd sometimes struggled to keep up with him. Whenever she thought she couldn't do something he'd pushed her harder. *"Don't you quit, Ashley Blake,"* he'd yelled when she'd sat down on the edge of the trail, too tired to carry on. *"Don't you ever give up. Even if your feet are tired and your legs are aching, you keep going. One step at a time."* She wondered now if he'd really been talking about hiking or if he'd been showing her a way forward through the tough parts of life.

One step at a time.

He'd also taught her to always tell the truth, and never borrow money.

What he hadn't taught her was what to do when her back was against the wall. What happened to morality when you were desperate? What would he say if he could see her now? If he'd seen her climbing into the car with Cliff?

I'm sorry, Dad.

"Do you have any other family?"

"No." So that was it. Joanna wanted to get rid of her. "Don't worry. As soon as I can, I'll be out of your hair."

"You shouldn't rush anywhere. Let the interest in you die down."

Would that happen?

"I still don't know how those photographers found out I was pregnant. Do you think they'll come here?"

Joanna slid a bookmark into the book and closed it carefully. "Almost certainly," she said. "But hopefully it will take them a little while to figure out where you are."

Because the last place anyone would look for her was with Joanna Whitman.

"So you grew up here, and then you built this amazing place, but you never came back until now?"

"That's right."

"If I owned it, I'd never leave." She tilted her head and felt the hot sun on her face. "All you can hear is the sea and the birds. And it's private. From the road, you wouldn't even guess there was a beach house here."

She'd never been to a place like this before. It was as if they were removed from the world outside, which, given everything that had happened, was a good thing.

She should have felt relaxed, but she wasn't. There were too many issues unresolved, too many problems and no solutions. And the biggest mystery of all was Joanna herself.

She wasn't the way the media portrayed her. On TV she rarely spoke, which made her seem like a doormat, but Ashley knew now that she wasn't a doormat. Joanna Whitman wasn't weak, she was private. She was strong and in control, but she did it in a quiet way so that no one really noticed. Take now, for example.

"You beat them." Ashley watched as a tiny bird swooped down and skimmed the surface of the pool. "All those photographers. Reporters. People asking questions. You beat them."

"I've had experience."

It was sobering to think that this thing that was happening to her, this interest in her life, had been happening to Joanna for decades.

"They write stuff that isn't even true. Stuff about you. I don't know how you stand it."

"It was hard, particularly at the beginning." Joanna picked up a tube of sunscreen and squeezed some into her palm. "I was about your age. I'd grown up here, in a small town among people I'd known all my life. Funnily enough I thought I was used to gossip, but it turned out I hadn't even dipped my toe in the water. I suppose the difference was that here people actually knew me, whereas most people just know what they've read online."

Ashley hadn't expected her to be so honest. She felt a little uncomfortable, because it wasn't as if they knew each other. Still, she was too fascinated not to probe for more. Maybe if she knew more, she might understand why Joanna had brought her here.

"Did you like it at the beginning? I mean, fame and everything. Some people want that, don't they? Celebrity?" She'd seen pictures on the internet. Studied them. Cliff and Joanna. It was always Cliff and Joanna, never Joanna and Cliff, as if she was second in a hierarchy.

Joanna hesitated. "I hated it." Something about the way she said the words made Ashley think she'd never spoken them aloud before.

"Because you're a private person?"

"Yes. I wanted to live my life in private, make my mistakes in private."

Did she consider Cliff to be a mistake?

Ashley tried to imagine him with Joanna. She wouldn't have put the two of them together, but what did she know? On the other hand Joanna had divorced him, so maybe she knew more than she thought.

"Whenever I saw him on TV he seemed like someone who liked the attention."

"You watched his shows?" Joanna glanced at her and Ashley felt her heart beat faster.

Were they approaching confession time?

"Sometimes." She'd watched every single one. She'd studied him. Paused the recording. "He had this way of drawing people in."

"Yes." Joanna gave her a long look, as if she was figuring something out.

Ashley squirmed. "So if you grew up here, you must still know people who live here. You'll want to see them."

"No." Joanna looked away. "There's no one I want to see."

"Why? Are we hiding?"

"You can come and go as you please. You're not a prisoner, Ashley, but I assumed you'd prefer some privacy while you rest and recuperate and figure out a plan."

It sounded good, except she didn't have a plan. She didn't have a clue what to do next.

Joanna poured a glass of water from a jug by her side. "Do you have a job? Are you in college?"

"I've had a job since I was sixteen." She thought about Luigi, the owner of the pizza restaurant. He'd always been kind to her. "The plan was to go to college, but my mom's medical bills were huge. And that's fine," she added quickly, "because that was the priority, obviously. I worked when I could, and a neighbor came and sat with her."

"Was her illness sudden?"

"Yes. She had pneumonia and then it turned to septicemia." It still didn't seem real to her. How could someone be fine one minute and then dead the next? "To begin with they thought she'd recover. We talked about things we'd never talked about before..." And she knew she'd never, ever forget that conversation. She had so many questions. So much still unresolved. "And then she got worse. She was in intensive care for a few weeks and then she died." It was a relief to finally talk about it to someone. There was only so much a person could hold inside and she was already holding far too much.

"That's so tough." Joanna's voice was gentle.

"They said she should have recovered, but she didn't. The infection was too much and her body couldn't handle it." It was the thing she'd struggled with the most. The randomness of life. The fact that you could be doing fine one minute, and then dead the next. The shock had been disorientating. "It made me wonder what the point of planning is. I mean, my mom had plans. There was stuff she was going to do when I went off to college. We had our life all worked out, and it was nothing earthshaking—small things, you know?—but I was excited and she was excited."

She probably shouldn't say any of these things to Joanna but she needed to say them to someone. She'd been alone with her thoughts for too long and Joanna was a good listener. Or maybe it was because she understood how it felt to have life turned upside down.

"What were you hoping to study?"

"Excuse me?" Ashley's head was still stuck in the past. She could smell the hospital room, hear the sounds of the machines and see her mother's pale face.

"Which program did you choose?"

"Oh." She forced herself back to the present. "Computer science. I've always been good at it. My dad always joked that he was too old to understand it, so I needed to learn everything so that I could teach him. He'd fix my car, I'd fix his laptop, that kind of thing. After he died I went on a summer program. I hoped he would have been proud that I did that."

"I'm sure he would. And you enjoyed it?"

"Yes. They taught me some HTML, CSS, some JavaScript. It was great. They had these really cool people talk to us, and they'd done interesting stuff. It was probably a good thing to do because I got my first choice of college—" She shrugged, embarrassed by how much she'd told Joanna, who was a stranger. "But that might have been because I'm a girl."

"Why would you say that?"

Ashley picked at the corner of her fingernail. "Because there aren't enough girls doing STEM subjects."

"I'm sure that's not why you got a place. I'm sure it's because you're smart, and they were smart enough to see that. They saw potential." Joanna paused. "There are plenty of people out there who will make you think you're not good enough. That you should think small. Play it safe. Be less than you're capable of being. The important thing is not to believe them. If there's something you badly want to do, if you have a dream, you owe it to yourself to give it a try." Something in the way she said it made Ashley wonder if someone, at some point, had made Joanna feel she wasn't good enough.

"Did you have a dream?"

"At your age?" Joanna gave a quiet smile. "Yes. I wanted to work in a bookstore. I wanted to spend my days helping people choose exactly the right book for their mood. I found books such a comfort when I was growing up, and I wanted to help other people find that."

Ashley thought about the bookshelves she'd seen. "But you never did work in a bookstore?"

"No. And I regret that. I should have worked in a bookstore instead of waiting tables."

Because then she would never have met Cliff? Was that what she was saying?

She thought about Joanna's life. She'd been married to a celebrity, and her days and nights had seemed to be an endless round of red carpet events. For many people, that would be the dream. But not Joanna. She'd wanted to work in a bookstore, which just went to prove that one person's dream was another's nightmare.

Ashley shifted uncomfortably. She felt as if she'd peeped through a gap in the curtains into Joanna's real world. "I suppose life happens, and then we end up taking a different path. That's what has happened to me. My mom died, I couldn't get my head around college even if I could have afforded it and then I got—"

"Pregnant."

Ashley felt her face grow hot. This was the moment she'd been dreading. Joanna was going to ask her about the baby. And if she told her the truth, the whole unvarnished truth, Joanna would throw her out.

She felt a sense of desolation, followed by panic. She didn't want Joanna to throw her out. She wanted to stay here with the pool and the privacy and Joanna's quiet, calming company until she'd figured out what to do.

But that wasn't the adult thing to do, was it? No one was going to come along and fix things for her. She was going to have to fix things herself.

Feeling sick, hands shaking, she took a deep breath.

"Joanna, there's something I need to—"

"Not now." Joanna lay back against the lounger and picked up her book again. "We'll talk about it another time."

"But—"

"I know we need to talk, but it can wait."

Could it?

She'd braced herself, finally, to tell Joanna the truth. Was this a reprieve, or an extension of torture?

She wasn't sure.

10

Melanie

Mel waited until Greg's car pulled out of the drive, and then pulled a basket from the cupboard in the kitchen. She knew that if she'd told Greg what she was planning to do, he would have tried to stop her. *If she wanted to see you, she would have called.* He'd loved Joanna, too, of course. They'd all grown up together. But Greg was more accepting of the fact that life was complicated and people changed. He didn't need an explanation for everything, but he didn't understand how it felt to lose a friendship that she'd thought would last forever.

Mel wanted an explanation.

Even after so many years, she wanted one, which was why she was going to see Joanna. And yes, the thought of it made her feel sick and light-headed, but she needed to *know*.

She'd been planning it all week, since she'd first seen that tiny figure sitting up on the rock in the far distance. She'd known, even without being able to make out the features, that it was Joanna. She'd felt it.

And she'd waited. She'd waited for Joanna to call her, or show up at her door, or *something*. She hadn't been able to think about anything else. She'd missed most of the conversation at dinner, been too distracted to even think about fighting with Eden and lain awake until the early hours every night playing out every scenario in her head, working out what she'd say, what she'd do if she opened her door and found Joanna standing there, or bumped into her in the Beach Bookstore. In the end it had all been wasted because Joanna didn't make contact. She didn't appear in town. She was invisible. There was nothing. Not even a handwritten note pushed into her mailbox.

Joanna didn't want to talk to Mel and that hurt more than she could have imagined.

It felt as if Joanna had rejected her twice.

She'd been staying here for a whole week and hadn't reached out (as if they were strangers! As if they hadn't shared every single minute of their lives up until the age of eighteen), so Mel decided that she would go to Joanna. Confronting her face-to-face couldn't possibly make her feel worse. She needed answers. She wanted to know what had happened. She wanted to know what she'd done.

Because she must have done something, surely? She could no longer pretend that Joanna had simply been too busy or wrapped up in her new exciting life, or distracted by her love for Cliff (although that part had never made sense), or preoccupied by a wide circle of new friends. The painful truth was that she'd cut Mel out of her life without an explanation, as if she was a wasp in an apple. She hadn't given Mel a chance to have her say.

But she was going to have her say now, and if this turned out to be a mistake, then it was a mistake. Better to do something and be wrong than do nothing.

And whatever happened, at least she'd have closure of sorts.

Mel put the basket in the car and drove to the farmers market that popped up on the far section of Main Street once a week.

She was feeling nervous and wanted to avoid conversation, so she was brisk and businesslike as she swept up plump tomatoes, a fresh sourdough loaf, cheese, a jar of local honey and some ripe peaches. On impulse, she nipped into the Surf Café and bagged up some of Nate's macadamia and white chocolate cookies while he was busy serving a customer.

It was a short drive along the coast road to Otter's Nest, but long enough for her to almost change her mind.

Why was she doing this? It had been twenty years. She should have put it behind her. What did she think the outcome would be? What could possibly be fixed after twenty years?

Joanna probably wouldn't even answer the door to her.

And that would make Mel feel awful, but at least she'd know that she'd tried.

It was easy to miss the turnoff if you didn't know where it was, but Mel had taken this road so many times she could have found it with her eyes shut. In fact, she had once found it with her eyes shut, as part of a bet with Nate. When she thought back to some of the things they'd done as teenagers she wondered how they were still alive.

She took the turning, noticing that there was no sign. Nothing to tell the visitor that a property lay at the end of this track. The road wound through the forest, shaded by a canopy of Monterey pine and coast live oak. Occasionally she caught a glimpse of the tempting sparkle of the ocean through the trees.

Mel slowed down to take the first bend, and then the second. After the third bend she saw gates.

She pulled up and contemplated this new barrier. When they were growing up Otter's Nest didn't have gates. In fact, looking back on it, it didn't have much of anything except one of the best views on this stretch of coastline. And her best friend.

Mel walked over to the gates and hesitated. You couldn't see the house from here, and it was all so anonymous that she wondered for a moment if she was even in the right place. If she was wrong, and the place was rented out to some rich tycoon trying to escape Silicon Valley, then she was going to look pretty stupid.

With a shrug, she pressed the buzzer. She'd looked stupid before and survived.

She waited. And waited.

There was no answer.

She was about to give up and head back to her car when a voice came through the intercom.

"Hello?"

Mel's heart gave a little thump. "Joanna? It's me, Mel. Mel Monroe."

There was a long pause. Silence. Mel thought, *This was a mistake. I shouldn't have come. I'm setting myself up to be hurt again.*

And she couldn't quite believe that she, Mel, was standing outside Joanna's house, begging to be let in when once they'd been as close as sisters.

They'd done everything together, Mel and Joanna, Nate and Greg, the four friends inseparable. And then at some point the balance had shifted and the four of them had become Mel and Greg and Nate and Joanna.

It had happened on Mel and Nate's sixteenth birthday. They'd had a party on the beach and Joanna had found her halfway through the evening, eyes shining, expression dreamy.

I kissed your brother.

Mel had been shocked, which was hypocritical because she'd been kissing Greg for months. But this was different. Joanna and Nate? She'd been full of doubt and full of questions. Had it been just one kiss? More than a kiss? Was it the start of something? What happened when they broke up? If it got messy? Mostly, if she was honest, she'd been thinking about herself. What it would mean for her. She didn't want to lose her best friend to her brother. She didn't want to have to choose between her best friend and her brother. She and Joanna shared everything, but that wouldn't happen if she was with Nate.

It had been a complicated time, hovering as they were on

the cusp of adulthood but still clinging to their childhood friendship.

Turned out her fears had foundation. They did break up. It had turned messy. Maybe it had been inevitable. It had been inevitable from the moment the four of them had ceased to be the four of them and begun to be two plus two. Mel and Greg. Joanna and Nate.

What happened, Joanna? Why did you leave like that?

Mel stepped away from the gate. She shouldn't have come.

She was about to slide back into her car and make a rapid exit when the gates swung open.

Was that an invitation?

Presumably, yes.

Leaving the car where she'd parked it, Mel walked through the gates, committed to this plan whether it turned out to be a mistake or not. The drive curved, just as she remembered, and then opened up and there was the house, Otter's Nest, except that this version was nothing like the original.

She stared openmouthed at the smooth, contemporary lines of the structure and then the door opened and Joanna stepped out.

Mel felt a powerful rush of emotion and almost went toward her but then she saw Joanna pause, as if she was deciding whether this was a good idea or not, and that pause hurt Mel's feelings all over again.

A tiny optimistic part of her had imagined them running toward each other like a scene from the movies, the twenty years of silence forgotten in their joy at seeing each other again. It was all a mistake. There was a simple explanation…

Her practical side tugged her back to earth again.

She told herself that maybe if she'd been through what Joanna had, she'd be cautious, too.

She stopped a safe distance away and they both stared at each other, unsure. Once, they'd spent almost every waking minute in each other's company, but it had been more than two decades since they'd seen each other in person. There had been no goodbye. No hugs and promises. One day Joanna had been there, and the next she'd been gone.

There had been so many things Mel had wanted to say, but she'd never had the chance to say them.

You left without telling me you were going.

You broke my brother's heart.

She'd called and left messages. There had been no response, which had upset Mel even more. Why couldn't Joanna at least have given a reason so that Mel could try and understand?

Technically Joanna had dumped her the way she'd dumped Nate.

Mel had been traumatized. She'd been ghosted by her best friend. After almost two decades of friendship with all the highs and lows, all she'd been left with were questions.

Joanna had married Cliff (bad decision in Mel's opinion) and five years later Nate had married Phoebe (equally bad decision). Four years after that Nate and Phoebe had divorced, and this time Mel hadn't bothered asking what had happened because she knew. You couldn't marry one person while you were still in love with another and she was sure Nate had never stopped loving Joanna. How he felt about her now, she had no idea because he was more likely to share his beer with her than his thoughts.

Joanna spoke first. "How did you find out I was here?"

It had been years, Mel thought, and that was the first thing she was going to say?

"I saw you on the rock. You're the only person who ever sits on that rock."

"In two decades?"

"Yes. I knew it was you." She didn't even ask herself why.

"If you know I'm here, then I guess everyone does."

"No. And I'm sure no one else would have been able to recognize you. Except maybe if they had binoculars."

Joanna didn't smile. "They often do. And long lenses and, occasionally, drones, although fortunately they no longer fly those over the house."

Mel couldn't imagine it, but she believed it because she saw the change in her old friend. The wariness. The suspicion. Even the way she held herself suggested that she was braced to retreat in an instant if the need arose. "It must be hell."

"It's life."

Joanna's life. Not Mel's.

"Trust me, no one knows you're here. If they did, I would have heard the gossip. You know what this place is like." She paused. "When I saw you on that rock I thought you might contact me."

"I haven't been in touch with anyone."

Anyone? Since when had Mel been "anyone"?

"So you came here for what? To hide?"

Joanna gave a quick shake of her head. "What are you doing here, Mel?"

Mel was asking herself the same question. Why was she here? What exactly did she think was going to happen? What did she *want* to happen? She was about to get rejected a second time, so maybe it was time to say what needed to be said.

"I thought it was time to apologize."

Joanna stiffened. "You don't have anything to apologize for."

"Not me. You." Was that too direct? No. "It's time you apologized to me."

"For what?"

"Are you kidding? You just left! Without saying anything. Without giving me a reason."

Joanna was breathing fast. "It's been more than twenty years, Mel—"

"Yes, I admit the apology is long overdue but that doesn't make it any less necessary." She realized that all the emotion she'd felt hadn't gone anywhere. It was still there, stored away for a time just like this. "We were best friends, Joanna! We did everything together. You were like a sister to me. There wasn't a thought either of us had that we didn't share. And then you fell in love with my brother, and yes, that made things a bit more complicated and it didn't turn out the way any of us would have wanted it to, but I don't understand why that had to take our friendship down, too. I don't see why I had to be collateral damage. Was it because you thought I wouldn't forgive you for ditching my brother?"

The silence was long.

Eventually Joanna spoke. "That's why you came here? To yell at me? Dredge up the past?"

"I didn't mean to yell, but this was huge for me. I thought it would be huge for you, too." She was embarrassed by her own lack of control and the contrast between her emotional response and Joanna's composure. "You ghosted me. Who the hell does that—?" She choked on the words, drowning under the tide of emotion. "How could you just walk away? Didn't you miss me? I missed you. I hurt. Badly. And it's never gone away, Joanna. Not for me. And maybe it's because I don't understand what happened. And yes, it's been a long time, but if I did something or said something that made you want to cut me from your life, then I want to know. Even after all this time, I want to know. It would help." Would it help? She had no idea.

"It wasn't about you."

"If that's true, then why didn't we stay in touch?"

Joanna straightened her shoulders. "Because I couldn't."

"What do you mean you couldn't?" Mel had waited too long for this conversation to leave it at that. "You physically couldn't? Someone stole your phone? You lost my number? Cliff wouldn't let you? *What?*" She was shouting. What was *wrong* with her? She was standing in a driveway, screaming at someone she hadn't seen in years. It was inappropriate. Disproportionate. But she couldn't help it. It was how she felt. The emotional side of her was having a party and she couldn't stop it.

It made it worse that Joanna was keeping all her emotions locked inside.

She used to show her feelings. Love, laughter, pain, grief. Joanna had expressed them all freely. On the day of her father's funeral she'd howled. She'd screamed. She'd dropped to her knees and tried to climb into the grave with him. She'd been oblivious to her stepmother's horrified demand that she pull herself together. Joanna hadn't been able to pull herself together. The damage was too great. She was like a vase that had been dropped onto concrete. Shattered. She was no longer whole, and she didn't care who witnessed her break into pieces. Her father was dead and she wanted him back, *she wanted him back*, and if she couldn't have him back, then she wanted to die, too. That was her goal. Her stepmother had offered her no comfort. It was Mel who had pushed her way through the adults who were standing by awkwardly. Mel who had hugged her. Mel who had rocked her, cried with her, held her as she'd sobbed and tried to tear out her own hair. It was Mel who had pulled her back from the edge. Mel who had understood that she hadn't just lost her father, but she'd lost the one person in the world who put her above everything and everyone else. She'd lost that most precious gift of all. Unconditional love. It was gone forever.

Except it wasn't, because she'd had Mel, and they'd sworn when they were four years old that nothing would ever come between them. Mel had honored that promise. Believed in it.

But somehow Joanna had forgotten it.

Where was that girl now? Where were those emotions?

Joanna was watching her. "I couldn't stay in touch. It would have been too hard."

"You mean because of Nate? We were friends before you and my brother were lovers." She saw color bloom on Joanna's cheeks.

"That was a long time ago."

Was she going to ask about Nate? Did she ever wonder about him? Did she regret ending it?

Mel decided to focus on the present. "You've had a tough time. You look thin." She remembered their teenage years, the pair of them dieting and standing in front of mirrors and being horribly self-conscious about their appearance every summer when it was swimsuits and beach barbecues and midnight swims and *boys*. They'd worried about thighs and boobs and stomachs and— *God, they'd been young*, she thought. All the things that had mattered to them back then didn't matter at all compared to the real stuff. She wished she could have told her teenage self that one day she'd be grateful to have a body that just worked and allowed her to run on the beach, and swim in the sea, make love with Greg and give birth to her daughter. Her anxieties had been nothing, but back then they'd seemed like everything.

"It hasn't been the easiest time."

It was such a ridiculous understatement that Mel laughed and to her relief Joanna laughed, too, and that laughter warmed the atmosphere.

They'd always had the ability to make each other laugh. One look was often all it had taken. A shared thought. Reading each other's minds. There had been times when they'd choked at the dinner table, and times when they'd been thrown out of class. Mel missed that. She had plenty of friends she laughed with, but nothing that came close to that rib-aching, agonizing laughter that had come from being with Joanna.

"Do you want to come in?" Finally Joanna smiled, and in that moment Mel caught a glimpse of the girl who had once been her best friend.

"Do you want me to come in?"

"Yes."

"Why?"

"Because it would be better than yelling at me outside?"

"No more yelling, I promise." Mel shrugged. "I think I might have been bottling that up."

Joanna's eyes gleamed. "Seemed like it."

"But hey, if yelling gets me a tour of the new place, then I can yell some more."

"You want a tour? As long as you're prepared. It's nothing like the old place."

Was she expecting judgment? "I wouldn't need a tour if it was still the old place, would I?" Mel remembered the basket in the car. "Wait just a moment." She sprinted back to the car. She wished now she'd added one of Rhonda's chicken pot pies. She tried to resist them, but Joanna looked like she needed the calories.

"I picked up a few things from the farmers market." She handed the basket to Joanna. "I didn't know what you wanted. Or if I'd get to talk to you. You probably already have all the food you need. Or maybe this isn't gourmet enough for you. You probably cook everything from scratch."

"It was thoughtful of you to bring something." Joanna looked inside the basket. "Cookies!"

"Nate made them. He runs the Surf Café now. We took over from our parents." She waited for Joanna's reaction at the mention of her brother but she saw nothing.

The composure that had slipped for a moment when Mel let rip was back. "Of course. Family business. I'm sure it's successful. So you didn't jet off and get a job in the Big Apple? I imagined you sitting in a glass corner office barking out orders."

So Joanna had thought about her. "No. I chose to stay here. You didn't get a job in a bookstore."

"No. Childish dreams." Joanna looked at her and they shared a smile of understanding.

"I suppose life doesn't always turn out the way you plan."

"That's true. How are your parents?"

"They're well, thanks. They decided to make the most of their retirement, hired a van and they're touring South America." There was more to it than that, of course, but this wasn't the time to share it. "Dad's developed an interest in photography so we get a burst of photos most days."

"And your mom?"

"She wanted to try writing a book, although I'm not sure she's ever going to finish it." Was Joanna going to ask about Nate? No personal questions about him? Wasn't she even going to ask if he was married?

Why not tell her, anyway? "Nate divides his time between the restaurant and the adaptive surf program. The kids love him."

See what a good person he is? Why did you leave him, Joanna?

"And you?" Joanna seemed determined to talk about everything except Nate. "You work in the café, too?"

"Yes. I do all the admin. The ordering, the accounts. Everything that isn't cooking or customers basically." It sounded boring, even to her. "I got pregnant with Eden pretty quickly and our parents needed help in the café, so that's where I ended up." Had she sold out? Ever since Eden had made that accusation she'd been unable to get the words out of her head. But Nate needed her, the café had needed her and she and Greg needed the salary she drew from it. "I still run, though. And I do yoga on the beach every Tuesday and Thursday. If you're hanging around for a bit, you could join me."

"Maybe. So far I haven't left the beach house." Joanna transferred the basket onto her arm. "Come in. You won't recognize Otter's Nest."

"You have no idea how many times I've wanted to peek inside this place." Mel stepped inside. Curiosity overwhelmed all other emotions. "Clever design. No glass at all by the entrance so nowhere a photographer can get a sneaky shot."

"We've had some high-profile people using the place. The position and security is always a draw." Joanna showed her the kitchen, the study, a downstairs bedroom with doors opening onto the garden, and all Mel could think as she peeped and peered and gazed was that Joanna had erased the past. There was nothing of the old Otter's Nest here. No memories. The old building with its cracked walls, peeling paintwork and broken shutters that didn't quite close, the ugly cushions favored by Joanna's stepmother—all gone, to be replaced by this sophisticated, stylish beach house.

Mel thought of her own home, crammed with memories of their life together as a family. Photos, awards, souvenirs they'd picked up on various vacations over the years. Eden's early attempts at pottery that she couldn't bring herself to throw away or even put in storage. Everything in the place told a story of the past.

Joanna's house had no past. Joanna had basically wiped history.

She followed Joanna through the spacious living room and out onto the terrace.

The surroundings were more sophisticated, the garden welltended and stocked with a profusion of colorful plants, but the view hadn't changed.

Mel gazed at the ocean, just a few steps away. "The view is the same, obviously, but nothing else. There's nothing of the old Otter's Nest left."

Joanna stiffened. "I don't expect you to understand—"

"I understand. Just because we haven't spoken for ages doesn't mean I don't understand. I don't know who you are now, but I knew who you were then. And the old Otter's Nest was part of then." Mel walked to the edge of the terrace and looked back at the beach house nestling in lush gardens and framed by tall trees. "It's stunning."

"My stepmother thinks I butchered the place. She came out to look at it when the building was completed. She wrote to me and said my father would be turning in his grave."

Horrible woman, Mel thought. "For what it's worth, she's wrong. Your father would have loved it."

"You think so?"

"Yes. He was an enthusiast, and always chasing the next adventure. I can hear his voice now. He would have said, *What a brilliant, exciting idea. Do it.*"

"That's exactly what he would have said. Thank you for that." Joanna voice sounded scratchy and Mel glanced at her.

"He'd be pleased that you're back."

"Yes, I think he would."

Mel frowned. "Are you all right?"

Joanna paused. "I haven't talked about my father in years. It feels strange."

Why wouldn't she have talked about him?

"Have you seen your stepmother?"

"No." Joanna straightened her shoulders. "I'm sure rumors say otherwise, but it was her choice to move. She wanted something small, easy to maintain and close to town. Not Silver Point, obviously, because apparently my 'antics' made it difficult for her to show her face in town. I embarrassed her. She said the locals were hostile and suspicious of her."

Mel felt anger rumble. "She should be embarrassed, all right, but not because of anything you did. And if any of us were hostile, which I doubt because we're mostly a friendly bunch as you know, then it would have been because of the way she treated you. Are you going to see her while you're here?"

"I don't know." Joanna turned. "Coming here was a sponta-neous decision. I don't plan on leaving the beach house."

"How did you leave LA without anyone following you?"

"I left in the middle of the night. I needed to get away." Her gaze darted to the beach and Mel had a feeling there was some-thing Joanna wasn't telling her.

"Well, if you're looking for privacy and space to think, then you chose well."

"Space to think. That's it." Joanna's gaze was back on her. "I haven't decided what happens next."

Mel frowned. "But if you're not leaving the house, then all you've done is swap one trap for another. Although admittedly this one has a truly great view. You should come into town, Joanna. Even if the press discover you're here, the locals would protect you."

Joanna stooped to pull a dead flower from its stem. "That's a romantic fantasy. We both know that's not true."

It hurt, the lack of trust, but maybe that was what two de-cades with Cliff Whitman did for you.

"How long will you stay?"

"I don't know. Until the press figure out I'm here. Then I suppose I'll have to move on."

Mel tried to imagine her movements being dictated by any-thing other than her own wishes.

"You shouldn't have to leave unless you want to. That's not fair."

Joanna stared out over the ocean. "Life isn't always fair."

"I know. I found that out that time I was grounded for doing your homework. Or maybe you don't remember—"

"I remember." Joanna laughed and Mel laughed, too, the two of them connecting over that shared memory.

And just like that her anger dissolved.

"This is still your home, Joanna. You're still one of us. Plenty of folks had a problem with Denise, but never you. There are no journalists or photographers snooping around in town. If there were, I'd know about it. And I'm not going to tell anyone you're here. Obviously." Was it obvious? "You should come into town and have a look around. The place hasn't changed much. Your favorite Beach Bookstore is still there, still run by Mary-Lou although she's always torn between the store and caring for her mother."

"Care for her? What's wrong with Vivian?"

"Arthritis. Can't get around too well. Mary-Lou goes home a few times a day and closes the store."

"I'm sorry to hear that."

"Life sucks sometimes." She tried to think of places from their past. "Remember every Friday we stopped at Frozen Flavor for ice cream? You always chose double chocolate, and I—"

"Mint chocolate chip." Joanna finished her sentence. "It's still there?"

"Exactly the same. Had a few makeovers, and a few extra fancy flavors, but basically the same. Jane took over from her mother. Put all the prices up. Eden and her friends hang out there after school, just as we did." She felt a little pang. "I miss the days when we thought an ice cream solved everything."

"Me, too."

"Maybe we could—" Mel broke off midsentence as Joanna shook her head.

"I can't do things like that without attracting attention. It would turn into a circus."

"But you can't stay locked away up here forever."

"There are worse places to be locked away." Joanna walked to the kitchen. "Do you want a drink? Something to eat?"

"Are you offering to cook me something?"

"I don't cook." Joanna pushed the basket toward her. "Choose something."

Mel took a cookie. Joanna had been married to a top chef

for two decades. How could she possibly still not cook? "Nate makes the best cookies. He's not married. Nate, I mean. He was married, for a while, but it didn't work out."

Joanna poured lemonade into tall glasses. "It happens."

That was it? That was all she was going to say? "Don't you care?"

"It was a long time ago. Another life. He probably barely remembers me." Joanna took a sip of lemonade and Mel saw the slight shake of her hand and knew that no matter what she said, she did care.

"Of course he remembers you. He was a total mess after you left."

Joanna put the glass down slowly. "A mess?"

"Yes. I wanted to kill you for a while, for leaving like that with no warning. You broke his heart." She saw Joanna's expression change. "I'm sorry. I shouldn't have said that, but I'm his twin and I'm overprotective, you know that. I'm not trying to make you feel guilty. It was a long time ago."

Joanna stared at her for a long moment and then picked a slice of lemon out of her drink. "What exactly did he tell you?"

"Nothing. You know Nate. He doesn't talk about his feelings, particularly not with me. But he was heartbroken. For a long time."

How could Joanna not have known that?

Joanna rolled the glass in her hand, sliding her thumb over the frosted surface. "Now I understand why you think I owe you an apology."

"What's that supposed to mean?" Confused, Mel was about to push her harder when she saw movement on the beach. She grabbed Joanna's arm and propelled her toward the house. "There's someone down there. They must have come by boat or something. I didn't even think that was possible. *Go, go, go!* I'll handle this. I'll get rid of them."

Joanna put the glass down. "Get rid of them?"

"Yes. I'm married to an officer of the law, remember? One phone call is all it's going to take and Greg will be here to defend you." Why was Joanna looking at her like that? "Go! I've got this."

Joanna seemed to rouse herself. "Don't call Greg. It's okay. It's just Ashley. She's doing yoga. It helps her relax." She extracted herself from Mel's grip and gave her a curious look. "You were going to protect me from an intruder?"

"Of course. You deserve privacy. I was going to use my outdoor voice, as Eden calls it. Terrifying. Wait—" Mel paused. "You said Ashley. *The* Ashley? The girl who was in the car with Cliff?"

"Yes."

That couldn't be right. "You're kidding me, Joanna."

"I'm not kidding you."

"The girl who is having Cliff's baby? You *have* to be kidding me."

Joanna tensed. "Can you stop saying that?"

How could she, when the whole thing was so unbelievable. Ashley, here? Why would someone in Joanna's position do a thing like that?

What would happen when the press got hold of *that* story?

No wonder Joanna didn't plan on leaving Otter's Nest.

She floundered, hunting for the right words. She'd questioned many of Joanna's decisions, but this one was off the scale. "You're giving houseroom to the girl Cliff made pregnant?"

Joanna's expression was blank. "It's complicated."

"No kidding. Sorry—" Mel raised her hands in apology. "I didn't mean to say it again. Truly. That's the last time those words are going to pass my lips, but what's going on, Joanna?"

"She had nowhere else to go."

Mel was about to say, *So what?* But then she finally saw something familiar in Joanna's eyes, a flash of determination, and she realized that although it seemed that her old friend had changed in some way, fundamentally she hadn't changed at all. Joanna Rafferty had always found it impossible to walk past anything lost and vulnerable, maybe because she had felt that way herself. Abandoned animals, kids at school who were bullied, Joanna had taken them all under her wing. And sometimes that had turned out okay, and sometimes it hadn't.

And now she'd taken in Ashley. And there was only one way *that* was going to turn out.

"What's going to happen when the press find out?"

"I don't know," Joanna said. "Are you going to tell them?"

"Ouch." Mel was affronted. "No, of course I'm not going to tell them. But they're going to find out eventually. They're all wondering where you've gone. It won't take them long to track you here."

"You're probably right. And you should leave now. I'm sure you're busy." Joanna walked back through the beach house to the front door, leaving Mel with no choice but to follow.

She was virtually being ejected, and she still didn't really have any answers as to why Joanna had ended their friendship so abruptly.

"Joanna, I don't have to leave. I'm not going to—"

"Thanks for visiting, and for bringing the basket. I appreciate it."

And without exactly knowing how it had happened, Mel found herself standing in front of a closed door. What had she expected? That they'd put the past behind them and pick up where they'd left off? That Joanna would meet Mel's emotional honesty with a few confessions of her own?

Neither of those things had happened. She hadn't explained, and she hadn't apologized.

She'd thought that seeing Joanna would make her feel better, but it hadn't made her feel better at all.

It had made her want to bawl her eyes out.

11

Joanna

Joanna paced the kitchen and then poured herself a glass of water.

What had she been *thinking*?

What was the point of having gone to all this trouble to disappear for a while, only to open the door to someone who was the heart and soul of Silver Point? No doubt it would take all of five minutes for the locals to discover that Joanna was giving houseroom to the "unknown" woman who had been in Cliff's car. She might as well have called the press herself and declared open house.

But she'd been taken by surprise.

Not for one moment had she thought Mel might actually show up at her door. She'd been thrown to see her standing there, then flooded with memories of the past and their friendship, and Nate. It had unsettled her to the point that she couldn't think.

And now she'd potentially exposed Ashley to unwanted attention.

Would Mel say something?

She'd learned to trust no one and yet for some reason she still trusted Mel.

She drank the water and put the glass down.

Mel had been shocked that Joanna had brought Ashley here.

She probably thought it was a mistake, but Joanna knew now that it wasn't a mistake. Yes, she'd had her own doubts in the beginning, but every second she spent with Ashley made her more convinced she'd done the right thing.

Ashley was scared, and Joanna knew how that felt.

Ashley was alone, and Joanna knew how that felt, too.

Ashley was trying to hide how scared and alone she was, and Joanna had more experience of that than anyone.

Bringing her here might just be the best choice she'd made in a long time, not just for Ashley but also for herself.

Despite her initial trepidation, being back at Otter's Nest had been calming. At night she lay on the huge bed in the master bedroom, listening to the sound of the surf on the beach and breathing in the fresh ocean air. She hadn't closed the doors once and it felt as if she was sleeping on the sand. Her dreams were vivid. Her father teaching her to swim and surf. Reading to her on their perch on the rocks. There were no dreams of Cliff, perhaps because he had made no imprint on this part of her life. He'd never visited Otter's Nest. It was as if the last twenty years had been wiped away.

But as for the years before that—

Joanna stared at the basket that Mel had brought.

Seeing her old friend had brought back so many memories, some sweet, some sour, and also some confusion because Mel had been upset—angry?—and thought Joanna owed her an apology. Which meant Nate hadn't told her what had happened.

She reached into the basket.

Nate makes the best cookies.

She removed the bag with the jaunty Surf Café logo. It was strange to think of him running the café as his parents had done before him. And Mel working there, too.

She opened another bag and found tomatoes, jewel red and still on the vine. She pulled one out and sniffed it. It was impossible to live with a chef for twenty years and not appreciate good food, even if she wasn't capable of producing it herself.

Fresh is always best, Joanna. Breathe in. What can you smell?

Joanna put the tomatoes down. Right now she could smell the sea, and the flowers in the garden. Summer. *She could smell summer.*

She was forty years old and she had no idea what she wanted to do with her life, but she wanted to stop running. Every decision she'd made in her life—leaving Silver Point, marrying Cliff—had been driven from a desire to escape the situation she was in.

She was about to call Ashley when the girl appeared, out of breath, in the doorway. She was wearing a spotted bikini and a wrap from the selection Joanna had given her. Her feet were bare and dusted with sand from the beach. Her hair was loose over her shoulders and her cheeks were pink from the Californian sun. She looked a thousand times healthier and more relaxed than the girl Joanna had rescued from the hospital.

"I saw someone! How did they find us? How did they get in?"

I let her in, Joanna thought.

She felt the same unease Ashley was feeling, but she didn't show it.

"It was Mel. She was a friend of mine when I was growing up." She grabbed plates from the cupboard. "You should eat. You're not eating enough."

"I'm not hungry." Ashley slid her feet into flip-flops and grabbed a towel that she'd left on the side. "If she was a friend, she won't tell people we're here, right?"

She saw no reason not to be honest. "I don't think she'd do it on purpose, but this is a small town. It's impossible to keep secrets in a small town."

Ashley rubbed at the edges of her hair with the towel. "So do we have to leave?"

We.

The word tugged them close. They were in this together.

Joanna put a cookie in front of Ashley. Better junk food than no food. "Do you want to leave?"

"No. This place is like paradise. Also, you like it. I can tell. You're more relaxed, and that's good."

"Then we won't leave."

"And if the press show up?"

When, Joanna thought. When, not if. "It's not easy to get access. We'll be safe here."

"Maybe they won't be interested. Maybe they're bored with the whole story by now." Ashley looked far more relaxed about it than Joanna felt, but that might have been because she had no idea what was coming.

"Let's hope so." She was sure, absolutely sure, that once the true story emerged they were going to be anything but bored.

Ashley draped the towel over the back of the chair. "How good a friend was she?"

The best. "We were close."

"But you didn't stay in touch?"

"No." If Mel hadn't been Nate's twin, would it have been different? "Until today, I hadn't seen her for two decades."

"So you've not spoken to her for longer than I've been alive."

"Yes. I suppose that's right."

Why had Mel come to see her now? Curiosity? Surely she hadn't taken such a big step just because she wanted an apology?

"Why did you lose touch?" Ashley poured herself some orange juice from the jug Joanna had put on the table.

Joanna thought about Nate. "It's complicated."

Ashley, who clearly had no trouble delving for truths, opened her mouth to press further and Joanna was relieved when her phone rang.

"I have to take this. It's Nessa, my assistant. You should eat something. The cookies are good." Cookies by Nate. *She wasn't going to think about Nate.*

She wandered out onto the terrace and felt the breeze lift her hair.

She'd been anxious about coming back here, but now she was here she didn't want to leave.

She answered the call. "Nessa. Is everything okay?"

"Depends how you define okay, boss. Okay is subjective, isn't it? I mean, one person can—" She broke off. "Forget it. Things are not okay. I've had a call from a journalist."

Joanna picked a dead flower from a geranium. "You don't have to take their calls."

"I know, but this one left a message telling me she had the biggest scoop of the century and if I didn't answer, then you'd probably fire me."

"I am never firing you, Nessa, you know that." Joanna snapped another head off the plant, this time a perfectly healthy one. Had Mel called the press? No, she wouldn't do that. Would she? "What does she think she knows?" She listened while Nessa told her and at some point her legs turned as liquid as melted butter and she sat down hard on the lounger.

So they knew the truth. How had they found out?

It couldn't have been Mel. Mel didn't have access to the information the journalist had.

And that was a relief, but it didn't change the fact they had a problem.

It had been inevitable, of course. She'd known that. And she'd done what she always did. She'd chosen to run from it. Her strategy had been avoidance. She'd hidden, because that was how she lived her life.

"Boss? Joanna? Are you there?"

"Yes."

"I told her it was a load of lies, and—"

"It's not lies."

There was silence. "It's not? You…knew?"

"Yes, I knew." Joanna took a long, slow breath, trying to think. "Do you have her number?"

"Yes." Nessa sounded unsure now. "She says the story is going live at midnight and if you want to give some sort of comment you have to call her by this afternoon. I can't believe… What can I do?"

"Nothing. Send over the details and I'll get back to you later. Thanks, Nessa."

"Of course. And, Joanna—" Nessa paused "—for what it's worth, I think you're an incredible person. Doing what you did, knowing…"

Incredible person? Hardly.

Joanna ended the call and sat for a moment. Now what? The press had been hungry for a story from the moment they'd discovered there was a woman in Cliff's car. They were going to get more than even they had hoped for.

"Is everything all right?" Ashley stood in the doorway, a frown on her forehead and anxiety in her eyes.

Joanna felt the weight of responsibility. "Come and sit down. There's something I need to say to you."

"There's something I want to say, too." Ashley sat on the lounger next to her. "It's great here. And I know you love it. I've seen you swimming in the mornings in the sea and reading your book on the lounger. I don't think we should leave."

"Things have changed. That was my assistant. She had a call from a journalist who is working on an exclusive." The sun was blazing and Joanna wondered how life could feel so difficult on such a glorious day. It felt wrong somehow. "They're publishing the story tomorrow, which means that everyone will know."

"A journalist? So your friend did say something? Call someone?"

"No, it wasn't her."

"How do you know that?"

"Because she wouldn't." Deep down, she'd known that. No matter how angry or upset Mel was, she wouldn't betray their friendship. "And because this journalist has information that Mel couldn't possibly have known. She's been digging around in the past, researching her story." And it was going to be bad. She'd lived through this often enough to know that.

Ashley was still in a state of blissful ignorance. "Story? What story?"

Joanna rubbed her palms over her legs. Why was it that the two innocent parties in all this, the two people who had the least reason to feel awkward or embarrassed, were the ones having this conversation? "We both know which story. I know the truth, Ashley. I've known who you were from the moment they showed your picture on the TV. I recognized you."

"I don't know what you mean. We've never met. You couldn't possibly have recognized me." She looked young, and scared, and Joanna felt old and tired.

"I recognized you," she said, "because you look exactly like your mother, although I had no idea what you were doing in Cliff's car. That part confused me at first."

Ashley's lips parted as she sucked in air. "You knew my mother? You met her?"

"No. I've seen photographs." What would she have done if she'd met her? Would she have slapped her? No, Joanna had never hit anyone. Would she have shouted at her? *Do you know what you did?* There was no point in even wondering because Ashley's mother was dead, and Joanna was never going to meet her. It felt weird to have never met the person who had changed her life so profoundly.

Ashley licked her lips. "I don't understand."

Joanna didn't understand, either, she never had, but she knew the facts.

"I don't know what your mother told you, but she was Cliff's first affair."

Ashley stared at her. Swallowed. "Joanna—"

"And now a journalist who is slightly sharper than the others has somehow managed to figure it out. She probably found that old photograph, read about the suggestion of an affair, or maybe she noticed the resemblance as I did. I don't know the details, but however it happened, she knows the truth."

"The truth?"

Joanna stared at the pool, focused on the glistening discs of sunlight playing across the surface of the water.

"She knows that you weren't Cliff's lover," she said. "You're his daughter. And the story will be live tomorrow."

12

Ashley

Story? How had her life turned into someone else's story?

She felt shaky and also scared, because this whole thing was spiraling out of her control.

Ever since she'd first found out the truth about who her real father was, a part of her had been screaming inside. *No, no, no.* It was horrible. *He* was horrible. He'd actually flirted with her. Thinking about it made her feel sick. And now Joanna was telling her that the whole world was about to find out. Her private humiliation was about to be made public.

And Joanna had known who she was the whole time.

Ever since that moment in the hospital she'd been going over and over it in her mind, trying to figure out exactly when to tell Joanna the truth. It had never seemed like the right moment, but now she realized that the right moment would have been when Joanna had sat down next to her.

Hi, I'm Ashley and I'm your ex-husband's daughter. You should probably leave now.

She was so angry with her mother for not being honest, but hadn't she just done the same thing? She'd been planning to tell the truth at a time convenient to her, but Joanna had known the truth all along.

She'd known, but she'd brought her here, anyway. She'd taken care of her, even though Ashley was the living, breathing embodiment of Cliff's transgressions.

"How did you find out? You said you noticed the resemblance—it was the photo?" Her teeth were chattering. She had to pull herself together. It didn't matter how bad the truth made her feel, she had to deal with it. She had to deal with the fact that she was Cliff Whitman's daughter, that there was a hell of a lot her mother hadn't told her, that she was now sitting in front of his ex-wife and that she was pregnant. It was enough to make her want to crawl back under the covers and never come out.

If Joanna felt a fraction of what she was feeling, it was no wonder she preferred to live a low-key life.

"Ashley, take a breath." Joanna's voice was kind.

How could she be kind, knowing who Ashley was?

"I feel—" Her breath hitched and she felt Joanna's hand close over hers.

"I can imagine how you feel, but you need to take a breath. You need to stay calm. Think about the baby. It's going to be all right. We're going to figure this out together."

Together.

Ashley felt the pressure of Joanna's hand on hers and her eyes filled. If she'd admired Joanna before, then she loved her a little at that point. Loved her not only for her kindness, but also for her calm and generosity. She was drowning and the firm pressure of Joanna's hand on hers was the only thing preventing her from sliding under the surface.

But Joanna was right. She had to stay calm for the baby.

"I'm okay." She took another breath, clung to Joanna's hand. "Thank you."

"It's a shock, I know. The first time I read a story about myself in the press I felt as if a bunch of people were crowded in my bathroom watching me take a shower."

"That's not—it's not just about what they're going to write. It's the whole thing. The whole story. How long have you known about my mother and Cliff?"

"I had my suspicions right back when it happened. Cliff and I had been married two years. He was filming in San Diego. Normally I would have gone with him, but that particular time I didn't because I was pregnant and couldn't stop being sick." She paused. "I didn't even mind not going. I was so excited and thrilled to be pregnant, and if being sick every morning was the price I had to pay to have our baby, then I was willing to pay it. I told Cliff he should go without me. I didn't want to cramp his style. Afterward, of course, I wondered what would have happened if I'd gone."

Ashley had no idea what to say. She felt sick, too, but this time it was nothing to do with her pregnancy. "I'm sorry."

"The truth is that Cliff probably would have slept with your mother, anyway. But that's beside the point." Joanna paused again, as if recounting the story was a challenge she wasn't quite up to. "A sharp-eyed journalist saw the two of them out together, having dinner in a place they probably thought was sufficiently out of the way and unfashionable that they wouldn't be noticed or recognized. But someone, somewhere, always recognized Cliff. It was something he enjoyed. He expected it. He believed recognition to be a mark of success. But it had its downsides, one of which was his inability to blend in. It was almost impossible for him to keep a low profile."

Cliff. Her father. This was her real father they were talking about and she couldn't get her head around it.

Joanna carried on talking. "The publication that ran the story rang me for a comment. Cliff denied it. Said it was work. A business meeting. The woman—your mother—worked at a venue they were using as a location for filming. I didn't believe him."

Ashley had a clear image of how that encounter might have played out.

Are you having an affair?

No, of course not.

"My mother told me that back then she sometimes worked freelance for an events company. Waitressing, that kind of thing. It was extra money."

Joanna barely reacted. "A few days later I lost the baby."

Without thinking Ashley pressed her palm to her flat belly. She hadn't thought the story could make her feel worse. She'd been wrong. "I'm sorry." Already she felt fiercely protective toward the baby she was carrying. "I read about your miscarriage." But she hadn't understood until now how awful it must be to have the most personal details of your life made public.

Joanna stared at the calm water of the pool. "It was my darkest, lowest moment. Cliff was wonderful and I stopped caring whether that rumor was true or not because I needed him badly. Nothing mattered to me except the baby. I couldn't get out of bed. I couldn't stop crying. People kept telling me that miscarriages were common, but I'd lost a child. I was bereft. Cliff was there for me. He didn't leave my side." Joanna gave a wan smile. "And now, looking back, I wonder how much of it was guilt, but at the time I needed him too much to question his motives. I ignored the rumors. I ignored the stories about your mother, and the photos. Even if it was true, it was over, that's what I told myself. Except it wasn't over. Because she was pregnant, too, only I didn't know that at the time."

"That was me. She was pregnant with me." Ashley felt as if her heart was being squeezed. "I feel guilty for existing."

Joanna rubbed her hand. "Don't. However emotional and difficult this is, let's not lose sight of the truth here. The whole thing was a mess, but the one person who was blameless was you."

"And you." Ashley's throat felt tight. "You were blameless, too. I should have told you the truth about being his daughter right away. I wanted to. Not saying anything has been making me feel sick. And I hate myself for not doing it sooner."

"I've avoided the conversation, too. Don't feel bad. I can see it was a horribly difficult thing to tell me. That's why you've not been eating?" Joanna frowned. "Can I fetch you something now?"

"I couldn't eat. I just want us to talk. I want you to tell me everything. I don't want us to have secrets. Don't keep anything back from me, however bad it is. You haven't told me how you found out I existed."

"It was about a year ago. I overheard a phone call. Cliff was in his study and he left the door open, something he never did. He was talking to someone." Joanna paused, remembering. "Shouting, not talking. He yelled, *I told you never to call me,* and I couldn't hear what she said—I assumed it was a woman—but whatever it was made him even more angry. I was still outside the door, but I would have heard him from almost anywhere in the house. He said, *I can't help, and it's no good begging. It's not my responsibility. You can't do this to me now.* He was furious, and... scared. I watched him through the crack in the door, and his face was red and he was sweating and I knew for sure that whatever it was they were talking about it definitely *was* his responsibility and he knew it."

Ashley's heart was pounding. "A year ago?" That would have been just after her mother had gotten sick. Just before she'd been taken into the hospital. And she remembered that call, because she remembered the words. She'd heard the other side of the conversation. The words Joanna wouldn't have heard. The words Cliff had been responding to. She remembered the tone as much as the content of the conversation. Her mother wasn't an emotional person. She never lost control, and yet she'd lost control that day. *You have to help. I'm begging you.* And Ashley had sat there frozen with shock, witnessing a side of her mother she'd never seen before. She'd wondered who she was talking to and how anyone could refuse to help someone who was so obviously desperate.

And now she knew.

Her mother had called Cliff Whitman. That was something she'd failed to mention to Ashley, along with many other things. It felt like another betrayal and it stung all the more because she had so many questions and no one she could ask. Her mother was dead. Cliff was dead.

But she had Joanna, and Joanna was still holding her hand. Joanna was telling her the truth and Ashley sensed it was as hard for Joanna to say it as it was for her to hear it.

"Yes, a year ago. That was when I finally decided to divorce him. You look pale. Wait there. I'm getting you some juice." Joanna stood up and returned a few moments later with freshly squeezed juice, cool from the fridge.

Ashley took a gulp and then another. She hadn't realized her mouth was so dry. "So you decided to divorce him because you discovered he'd cheated on you with my mother?" Had there ever been a more awkward conversation?

"No," Joanna said. "I divorced him because I discovered he had a child that he'd known about the whole time and refused to acknowledge. I'd forgiven him many things, but I couldn't forgive him that." She stood up quickly and paced across the terrace and back. "You'll have to excuse me. I'm not used to talking about this with anyone. I never have. It's…difficult."

Ashley almost wished she wasn't talking about it now, but there had been enough lies and cheating. She wanted the truth. But maybe that wasn't fair on Joanna. "If you're finding it too hard—"

"It's hard, but you deserve to know all of it." Joanna rubbed her fingers over her forehead, visibly stressed. "When your mother made that call, he panicked at the thought of it all coming out and what that would do to him. He never once thought about what you might need. He was thinking only of himself. I said to him, *You had a baby, Cliff. You have a child you've never met. A child who needs you, and you're worrying about yourself?* I told him he disgusted me."

Whoever thought Joanna was weak should see her now, Ashley thought. "What did he say?"

"He tried to deny it, but because I'd heard everything he had no choice but to confess the whole story. And it didn't make for happy listening. It turned out your mother told him she was pregnant as soon as she knew. He panicked and offered her money, but she told him she wasn't interested in his money if he wasn't prepared to be an active part of your life."

Ashley went hot and then cold.

"I didn't know that." Why didn't she? Why did she have to discover all these things when it was too late? There was no opportunity to discuss them now. No chance to ask her mother the questions that were crowding inside her. No chance to ask Cliff—*her father*—why he hadn't thought about what she might need. "I can imagine she would say a thing like that. She was proud. She always taught me the importance of self-reliance. Being able to support myself." And yet in that conversation Ashley had overheard, her mother had been yelling and desperate. "You found out for sure about the affair, and about me, at the same time?"

"Yes. He told me your mother had called him about eleven weeks after their affair. I'd just had a miscarriage." Joanna sat back down again. "It was the worst possible time to confess that he'd fathered a child with another woman."

"She raised me alone. And then she met my dad. At least, I always thought of him as my dad." Her view of everything had changed in the last few months. And her childhood had been happy. She hadn't had a clue about any of this in her mother's background. But her mother had known. She'd carried the truth with her for her whole life, and only revealed it at the end. And only because she sensed she wasn't going to recover. "I don't know if even my dad knew Cliff was my real father."

"I'm sure Cliff thought the whole thing was behind him. And he would have been relieved, because Cliff doesn't—didn't—like anything tarnishing his carefully constructed life. And then he took that phone call. Your mother was sick, and worried about how you'd manage when she was gone. That was why she reached out. She wanted him to agree to support you financially so that you could afford to go to college, but she also wanted him to take an active part in your life if something happened to her."

Ashley was shaking. "Why would she want that for me? This was a guy who pretended I didn't exist. He knew nothing about loyalty or responsibility. What was he ever going to bring to a relationship?"

"I'm guessing your mother was desperately worried about you. You have no other family?"

"No. My grandparents died when I was little and my mother was an only child."

"She was trying to look out for you. Doing what she thought was best. That was the phone call I overheard. I wanted him to step up and take responsibility." Joanna looked at her. "I wanted him to meet you and try and form some sort of relationship. He refused. Flimsy excuses to begin with—he didn't know where you were, he hadn't taken details." She pulled a face. "We had the biggest fight of our marriage."

Joanna had fought for her. Joanna Whitman, who owed her nothing, whose husband had cheated and humiliated her, had fought for what she believed to be right.

The last of Ashley's defenses slid down. "I always knew my dad wasn't my biological dad. She told me it was some random guy she'd met, and that he didn't matter. She'd been young and it had been a mistake, that's what she said. She met and married David when I was a baby. He was my dad. I called him that. I felt he was that." And she missed him. She missed his patience, and his kindness, and countless small things like the fact that he owned seven shirts exactly the same so that he didn't have to make a decision about what to wear in the morning. "She didn't tell me who my real dad was until right at the end, and I was shocked and I had a ton of questions but I didn't feel I could ask them because she was ill and nothing seemed to matter except that. And after she died I was—well, I wasn't in a good place. I held it together for a long time. I was like a robot to be honest, but then one day I just fell apart. That's when I got pregnant. Am I talking too much?"

"No." Joanna took the empty glass from her. "Talking is good. Do you want to tell me about him?"

Did she? Yes, she did. Joanna was a private person and yet she'd trusted Ashley with her secrets so why shouldn't Ashley do the same, even if it felt hard?

"I've known Jon forever. He's my best friend. Nothing romantic, but we hung out together." Maybe Joanna couldn't understand that. "I don't know when I first realized I had feelings for him that were more than friendship, but I didn't say anything. It was weird to be honest. I felt like I was breaking the rules. Crossing a boundary. I tried to ignore my feelings, pretend nothing had changed and carry on."

"That must have been hard."

"I valued our friendship too much to risk losing it. This was all before my mother died. We talked about everything from ice cream flavors to saving the planet. At school we used to message each other all the time. *Have you seen this*, and *Guess what just happened*. And then after my mother died there was a night when I was so scared of my own thoughts that I didn't want to be home on my own with them. I called him and he came right over, because that's the kind of person he is, and he stayed and one thing led to another. I guess my mother would have called it a mistake." It didn't feel hard at all to be saying this, but maybe that was because Joanna was one of those rare people who listened really carefully, actually hearing what you said rather than waiting for a gap to express an opinion.

"And did it feel like a mistake to you?"

"No." The worst night of her life had ended up feeling like the best. How could something that had felt so right possibly be wrong? She'd been at rock bottom, and he'd been there for her. "That was the night I knew for sure I loved him. I didn't say anything, though. I didn't have a clue how he felt. Still don't. Yeah, we spent the night together but I was a big emotional mess and it's not like he said *I love you* or anything. I didn't want to risk losing him as a friend, so I pretended nothing had changed." They'd been friends forever until that night, and now she wasn't sure what they were. "I didn't mean to get pregnant, though." When she'd first found out her reaction had been joy, then panic. But the joy had been there, even if only for a moment. She'd thought, *I'm not alone anymore*, and she'd also felt the pressure of responsibility, and a terrifying awareness that she was now an adult even though she'd had no training and felt unqualified.

"Jon doesn't know you're pregnant?"

"No." Ashley felt a twinge of guilt when she thought of the messages on her phone. She needed to listen to those messages. She needed to call him. But she didn't know what to say. "I will tell him, but I have to figure out the right time. I guess I'm scared. I don't want to lose my best friend. I grew up with him." She saw Joanna's expression change. "What? What did I say?"

"Nothing. Go on."

"Well, that's it, really. He was almost like a brother." Brother? Who was she kidding?

Joanna was obviously wondering the same thing. "Did he feel like a brother?"

"No." She hadn't let herself think about it, but now she did. His hands, his arms pulling her close, his mouth exploring hers, the way she'd felt. He'd murmured things, things she knew he probably didn't mean. Things that had been part of that night, and that night only. It had been the one blissfully perfect night in a series of awful ones and it hurt too much to remember it. How did they come to be talking about Jon? She already had a ton of other things she needed to focus on. "I don't want anything from him." She picked at the corner of her nail. "I guess I'm proud, too. I didn't want him to feel obligated. Anyway, I got to thinking about Cliff being my dad, and not wanting anything to do with me, and it really upset me."

"Yes." Joanna's voice was soft. "I can imagine it did."

"It doesn't make you feel good to know that you were that unimportant. And the fact that he hadn't helped my mother when she was desperate—"

"How did you end up in his car?"

"I decided I wanted to talk to him. I wanted answers—answers I hadn't managed to get from my mom. I wanted to see him face-to-face, just once. It wasn't about the money—" it was important to her that Joanna knew that "—but I suppose a part of me thought, well, he is my dad, and he's behaved badly and I want to understand why he did what he did. I wanted to challenge him and hear his side." She swallowed. "But he wouldn't take my calls." She saw Joanna's mouth tighten.

"You called him?"

"Yes. I didn't have his number so I called the studio, and head office. And used my real name. Probably a mistake, because he knew my name even though they didn't. He wouldn't take my calls. I guess he told his staff that I was an overzealous fan, or something. No way was I getting through on the phone. I just couldn't find a way to talk to him."

Joanna sat back with a sigh. "You should have called *me*. I would have put you straight through if that was truly what you wanted. Although I probably would have pointed out that if you were looking for emotional comfort or loyalty you'd be unlikely to get it from Cliff. When it came to relationships, he was a massive disappointment." That confession removed the last of the barriers between them.

"I believe you." Presumably no one knew better than Joanna, but it wouldn't have occurred to Ashley to contact Cliff's long-suffering wife. "I couldn't get through on the phone, so I waited outside the studio when he was recording the show and when he emerged I asked for his autograph. I didn't tell him who I was. I knew that if I did that he wouldn't even have the conversation and there were so many things I wanted to ask him. Things I deserved to know. I told him I'd watched all his shows, which was true. He seemed to like that."

"Yes, he would. You massaged his ego. Your mouth is dry, I can tell. Pause for a moment, and I'll fetch you water." Joanna stood up and fetched them both another drink. "Nothing pleased him more than flattery and being the center of attention."

Ashley sipped the water Joanna had handed her. "We chatted for a while about nothing."

"How did you get him to invite you for a drive?"

"It wasn't hard. I wore a short skirt and a low top. You know what he was like." Ashley felt herself blush. "Sorry. I didn't mean to offend you."

"Nothing could offend me after all these years. And yes, I do know what he was like."

"It worked. He asked me for an evening drive." Thinking about it now, it seemed a ridiculous thing to have done. How could she have been so reckless? "I said yes. I thought if I had him trapped in a car, he wouldn't be able to walk away or ignore me when I told him who I was."

"It was a bold and creative plan. He didn't recognize you?"

"No. He'd never met me, of course." She thought back and frowned. "But he did say that I looked familiar. I suspect he was thinking I was someone he—" She broke off and Joanna nodded.

"Someone he slept with. He was thinking lover. He wasn't thinking daughter."

It made her feel sick to think of it. Her father. Her hands were sweaty now. Shaking and sweaty. "And he drove fast up into the hills, and I kept wanting him to recognize me, and know who I was, but he didn't. And I realized that getting into that car was a mistake, and I wanted to get it over with so I blurted it out. I said, *I'm your daughter*, and he took his eyes off the road and stared at me for moment. It was just a few seconds, that's all, but we were near a bend and—" the memory came rushing at her like the road had "—I screamed. He tried to get control of the car but it was too late and I knew we were going over the edge and I just closed my eyes and got ready to die. And it was my fault. It was all my fault. If I hadn't told him that—"

"It wasn't your fault." Joanna took the glass from her before she could spill the contents. "You told him nothing he didn't already know."

"But he didn't know it was me. He'd done everything he could to avoid seeing me, or even talking to me." And she had no words to describe how that had made her feel. "I forced him to confront it. And we didn't even have a chance to talk at all, because the accident happened and I knew he was dead. And I as good as killed him." The guilt she'd been holding inside poured out of her, along with all the trauma of the past few weeks. She felt the hot sting of tears and this time she couldn't hold them back. She covered her face with her hands. "He's dead because of me. And to be honest I hated him by the time I got into the car. I hated him for the way he treated my mother, for the way he treated me, and if I'd known you then I would have hated him for the way he treated you, too—but I didn't want him to *die*."

"Of course you didn't."

"I feel so bad." She felt Joanna's arms come around her and then she was being hugged in a way she hadn't been hugged in months, since before her mother had died.

"It's not your fault." Joanna held her, stroked her hair, repeated those words again and again—*not your fault*—and Ashley sobbed into her shoulder and cried until there was nothing left inside her.

Finally she eased away, embarrassed. "Sorry..."

"Don't be sorry. I know exactly how it feels to be let down by Cliff, and that's what has happened to you. And I know how it feels to take the blame, to assume it's you, that it must be something you did or didn't do, but that isn't true." Joanna's voice shook. "You feel that way because you're a person who takes responsibility for her actions, but the responsibility in this case is not yours."

It was the first time Ashley had heard Joanna express this much emotion.

"You're speaking from experience."

"Yes. And that's why I'm telling you to put the blame where it belongs—squarely on him. If you're going to be upset, be upset about the decisions he made, not the decisions you made."

Ashley scrubbed at her face with her palm. "Do you think I'm upsetting the baby?"

"I think babies are tougher than that." Joanna handed her a tissue. "Which is a good thing, because life requires you to be resilient. And you're certainly that. Resilient and brave."

"I don't feel brave." Ashley blew her nose hard. "I don't feel brave at all."

"Ashley, you climbed into Cliff's car so that you could force him to account for his behavior. That's brave. And the way you've conducted yourself since—in the hospital and with me—I think you're incredible. The accident itself would have been enough to traumatize most people. You must have been terrified."

"I don't remember much. I remember a spinning feeling. I didn't know which way was up. My body was rattled and bashed. There was pain, and then it stopped and I lay there and realized I was still alive. And I was terrified the car was going to catch fire or something, because that's what happens in the movies. And then I looked at Cliff—" it was something she'd tried to block out, the sight of it "—and I knew he was dead." She felt Joanna's hand close over hers and wondered if she should stop talking. She knew she should probably tug her hand away because this was Cliff's wife and if it was hard for Ashley to think about how much harder must it be for her to hear about it, but she needed the comfort that was being offered.

"And then you were taken to the hospital."

"And they asked me a ton of questions, of course. I didn't want to tell them why I was in the car with Cliff. I didn't want it to come out that I was his daughter because it was too late for that to do any good, so I just said nothing and they assumed I was—" She shrugged. "I don't know. All this happened because I got into his car. That was stupid."

"No. You challenged Cliff. That was an incredibly brave thing to do. You didn't deserve what happened. You deserved answers. Later, when we've handled this latest story, I can try and give you some. I probably won't have all the ones you need, but I can do my best to fill in some of the gaps."

The story. For a moment she'd forgotten about it.

"What will the story say? How much do they know? I'm guessing it's all about Cliff and my mom, and me."

When she'd climbed into the car with Cliff she'd felt for-gettable and unimportant. She'd wanted his attention, she'd wanted her existence to be acknowledged, but that had never happened. Until now. Her existence was about to be publicly acknowledged.

The irony wasn't lost on her. This wasn't the attention she'd wanted.

Joanna nodded. "From what Nessa told me, the writer has pieced it all together. The timing of the affair with your mother, the fact that I was pregnant at the time—it's going to be a difficult piece to read."

"The story will be about you, too?" Ashley's despair was punctuated by a flash of anger. She sniffed, blew her nose and sat up a little straighter. It was bad enough that they were writing about her, but to write about Joanna, too, when none of this was her fault? Joanna had been kind. The only person who had been kind. She'd saved her from all the intrusive questions and press scrutiny, she'd brought her here and protected her, and now it was all going to start again and it was Ashley's fault. "Why write about you?" She clung to a last desperate hope that Joanna might be wrong about that part.

Joanna gave a faint smile. "Because our stories are linked."

The anger inside her grew. "I guess he'll say he's just doing his job, but why should people make a living out of exposing the worst moments of my life? What have I ever done to this reporter? What have you done to him?"

"Nessa tells me it's a her. And we've done nothing. We've never met, but that isn't relevant. It's not personal, although I understand that it feels personal when your most intimate secrets are revealed to everyone and anyone." Joanna sighed. "It always feels personal."

"I'd like to do the same back to him—I mean, her. I'd like to find what she's hiding and splash it out there for everyone to see." Ashley scowled. "See how she likes it."

"She's certainly tenacious. It must have taken an enormous

amount of digging to uncover the details she has." Joanna stared at the pool, lost in thought for a moment.

"Can we stop her writing it?"

Joanna stirred and glanced at her. "No. There were a few occasions when I tried, right back at the beginning. But it never works. Better to stay out of sight, lie low and wait for it to die down."

Ashley didn't want to lie low. The anger inside her had grown from a flicker to a flame. She wanted to snarl and fight back. "They shouldn't get to decide how we live. And I can't believe it's a woman. Whatever happened to sisterhood?"

"It's alive and well, which is why we're here for each other." Joanna gave her leg a reassuring squeeze. "I guess the reporter just didn't get the memo."

"Right." Was there really nothing they could do? "Should we give them an interview where we can put our side of things? Tell the truth. Then they might go away."

"They won't go away. And they don't want the truth. They want a story. It's not the same thing."

"So we let them say what they like and do nothing?"

"They can say what they like with or without our permission. We can talk to lawyers, but if what they're printing is fact, then there's little we can do, and to be honest once the article is out there the damage is done. Retaining lawyers just means we keep the story running. It stays high profile."

"So that's it?" Ashley was frustrated. "There's nothing we can do?"

"There's plenty we can do. We make ourselves invisible. We don't give them pictures or any kind of opportunity to describe how we're looking. If we don't feed it, the story will eventually die."

"You're saying we have to stay hidden in the beach house?"

"Why not?" Joanna glanced around and smiled. "It's not so bad here, after all."

It was idyllic, but that wasn't the point. They'd be hiding, as if they were guilty of something. She didn't like the idea of someone else making her hide, and dictating her choices. It was a form of bullying, wasn't it?

But this wasn't only about her, and just as she didn't want the reporters to dictate her choices, she didn't want to dictate to Joanna. Particularly as it was Ashley who had put Joanna in this position.

She had to respect what Joanna wanted. It was the least she could do.

The true impact of this on Joanna was gradually dawning on her.

"You came here to avoid attention. You wanted to escape them, and now they'll be coming here. And that's my fault." And Ashley was ready and willing to storm through Joanna's gate and tell them exactly what she thought of them, but Joanna didn't want that. Joanna had protected her, and now she had to protect Joanna.

"None of this is your fault, Ashley."

But that wasn't true, was it? It was easy enough to blame others but she'd played a part in everything that had happened. She was the one who had decided to speak to Cliff face-to-face. She was the one who had climbed into his car, and she was the one who had accepted Joanna's offer of help. If she hadn't come here, they probably would have tracked her down and left Joanna alone. But she had, and now there would be questions. The reporter would want to know why Joanna had brought Ashley here, and whether she'd known who she was all along. Whether Joanna had believed Ashley to be Cliff's lover or his daughter, there was a juicy story there. And Joanna would pay the price. Again.

It was wrong. So wrong.

"Why do we have to hide? Why can't we just stand up and tell them to mind their own business?" Could she make Joanna consider a different way? "We could make a statement of some sort. You wouldn't be on your own this time. I'd be with you. We could do it together."

Joanna stood up and scooped up the empty glasses. "No comment is better. Whatever you say, they have a way of twisting it. And they can make a story out of nothing. Your hair isn't perfect, so you've obviously not been taking care of yourself. You're wearing dark glasses, so you've obviously been crying." The words rushed out of her and she paused and took a couple of breaths. "It goes on. Don't worry. If we lie low and refuse to appear or answer their questions, then they will get bored eventually."

Ashley felt an ache of sympathy for Joanna, but also a sense of despair and frustration.

She didn't want to hide. She wanted to fight back. She didn't know how she was going to rebuild her life, or what her future looked like, but she knew she didn't want a bunch of nosy, news-hungry reporters to have a say in it.

She breathed slowly and ran through her options.

They were limited. Joanna didn't want to expose herself to scrutiny, even with Ashley there to offer a layer of protection. And the two of them together would simply make the story all the juicier.

Everyone would want to know why Joanna was caring for her ex-husband's child.

"Don't look so sick. It's going to be okay. I've dealt with this so many times, I'm an expert." Joanna gave her a quick smile. "I promise that whatever happens, I'm here for you. You're not on your own. I'm going to protect you."

Ashley felt a solid lump form in her throat. She was going to protect Joanna, too.

And there was only one way to do that.

13

Joanna

Joanna swam, feeling the chill of the ocean and the cool early-morning air.

This was her meditation, the single moment in her day when the world outside ceased to exist, but today she couldn't relax. She moved her arms and kicked her legs, feeling herself flow with the water, but her mind kept revolving through the events of the day before. That call from Nessa. The conversation she'd had with Ashley.

Joanna rolled onto her back.

Poor Ashley. She'd been so upset about it all, and that was understandable. She understood Ashley's outrage. She understood the desire to stand up and make your voice heard. Hadn't she felt the same way in the beginning? Experience had taught her it was the wrong thing to do, and she'd done her best to share that experience with Ashley.

The girl had been quiet and thoughtful for the rest of the evening, talking about anything except the forthcoming article, distracting them both with funny stories of her terrible ball skills and the time she'd hacked into the school computer and changed her teacher's photograph. She'd been caring and solicitous toward Joanna, constantly checking she was okay. It was Ashley who had made food for them both, although she'd eaten very little herself.

Joanna stared up at the sky and allowed the cold water to lap against her limbs.

This was her favorite time to swim, when most of the world was still asleep. There were no lifeguards on this private curve of sand by the beach house. No one who would see her if she found herself in trouble, and that was fine with her. She didn't want to be seen, and this wasn't the type of trouble that scared her. She'd learned to swim before she could walk, taught by her father, who had also taught her how to read the water. *Do you see that, Jo? The way the water looks darker right there? The calm water? That's a rip current. Don't go near it.* He'd taught her what to do if she did find herself caught in the current, taught her not to panic, to float and swim across the powerful pull of water instead of fighting it. *You can't swim against the rip, Jo.*

She floated now, feeling the sun on her face, enjoying the few moments of peace before a day of turmoil. Then she reluctantly swam back to shore, found the sand with her feet and eased out of the water.

She reached for the towel she'd left on the sand and dried the ends of her hair. Most of her life had felt as if she was caught in a strong current, pulled and tugged in a direction she didn't want to go. She'd been trapped by the force of it, flung around by Cliff and by the media, battered on the rocks of life. But she'd survived, and she'd survive this next crisis, whatever happened.

She hadn't read the article yet. She'd learned long ago that she couldn't control what they wrote, but she could control what she read and she'd chosen not to read it.

Usually she was protecting herself, but now she was protecting Ashley.

It was Cliff who should have been doing that, of course, but even if he hadn't driven himself into a ravine, he wouldn't have stepped up. Responsibility wasn't an ingredient he ever selected from life's menu.

He'd missed out by denying the existence of his daughter. Quite apart from the basic question of responsibility, Ashley was delightful. She was smart, funny and caring. And she was fierce in a way that Joanna had never been at the same age. She questioned, where Joanna had accepted.

She glanced up at the house, but there was no sign of life. Ashley was probably still sleeping, no doubt exhausted after the emotional confessions of the previous day. Hopefully she hadn't yet read what had been written about her.

Joanna walked barefoot back to the house, formulating a plan.

She and Ashley would stay home, and no matter how many journalists gathered at their gates, they wouldn't make a comment. She'd handled the fallout of Cliff's public indiscretions so many times before that she barely had to think it through.

She took her time in the shower, washing away salt and sea with her favorite citrus bodywash. Then she dried her hair and smoothed cream onto her face and her body. Despite sunscreen, she'd managed to burn a little and she spotted a few extra freckles when she studied herself in the mirror.

She dressed in jeans and a white shirt and then walked into the kitchen. Ignoring her laptop, she slid pastries into the oven and waited for them to warm.

She felt better than she'd thought she would.

Talking to Ashley had been cathartic. The facts remained the same but the painful emotions had lessened.

She squeezed juice, and piled everything onto a tray. She was going to persuade Ashley to eat. It was going to be a tough day and facing it on an empty stomach wouldn't help.

Joanna carried the tray through to the guest suite and tapped on the door.

There was no answer, but she opened the door quietly. If

Ashley was sleeping in, then she'd leave her, but it wouldn't hurt to check.

The room was dark, but even before she pressed the button to raise the blinds, Joanna could see the bed was empty.

She put the tray down on the table and felt a flicker of alarm. The bed wasn't just empty, it was made, as if no one had slept in it. And Ashley's small bag had gone. She checked the bathroom, and saw the towels neatly folded.

There was no sign of her.

It wasn't just Ashley's bag that had gone. Ashley had gone, too. Where? When? Why?

She was about to race from the room and start looking in the gardens when she saw the note propped by the lamp.

She opened it and sat down on the bed.

Joanna, I'm sorry I didn't tell you who I was. I'm sorry my mom had an affair with Cliff. Right now I'm sorry I exist, even though I know that's not my fault. Mostly I'm sorry that I let you bring me here. Because of me, the press will be at your door again. I know how much you hate that. I know you don't want to see them or talk to them and I understand why you feel that way.

If I'm not here, there will be less of a story for them so I'm leaving but I wanted to thank you for everything. You have less reason than anyone to be kind to me, and yet you're the kindest person I've met. I won't ever forget it. Don't worry about me. I'll be fine. Maybe we'll meet again one day. I'd like that.

Love, Ash

x

Joanna dropped the note. Left? Where had she gone?

She picked the note up and read it again.

The press will be at your door again. I know how much you hate that.

Ashley had left because of her. Because she didn't want to bring the press to Joanna.

Guilt rubbed alongside panic and anxiety. This was her fault. If she hadn't insisted that they hide away, this wouldn't have happened. If she hadn't been so honest about how much she hated facing the press, hated the intrusion, hated the things they wrote about her, maybe Ashley would still be here.

Why hadn't she sensed that Ashley was thinking of leaving? *Because she'd been focused on herself and avoiding publicity.* *Because she'd been sure that her way was the right way.* Joanna stuffed the note into her pocket.

She had to find her.

The possibility of bumping into a bunch of reporters seemed much less important than finding Ashley. This wasn't just about protecting her, it was about supporting a friend because that was what Ashley had become over the past days—a friend.

She raced to the front door and opened it, but her car was still sitting there. Ashley must have walked wherever she was going. Or had she called a cab?

Sweating now, Joanna headed back inside and went through her options. She could search for Ashley, but she had no idea where to start. Drive into town? Along the coast road?

She grabbed her keys, and the bag containing her wig, baseball cap and dark glasses, and was on her way to the door when her phone rang.

Number unknown.

She fumbled, almost dropped it. "Ashley?"

"No, it's Mel."

"Oh." Joanna was already heading toward the car. She put the phone on speaker, threw it onto the seat and stuffed her hair under the wig. The hat went on next, and then the glasses. "I can't talk now."

I'm sorry I exist.

What did that mean exactly? How sorry was she?

Joanna's mind flew to the worst possible scenario. What if something happened to her? This was Ashley, who had already been through so much. Ashley, who had been a stranger but now didn't feel like a stranger at all. Ashley, who felt as if she was somehow responsible for Joanna's situation.

Eighteen, pregnant and alone.

"Joanna?" Mel's voice was tinny and insistent. "Are you still there? I'm calling about Ashley—"

She snatched up the phone. "What about Ashley?"

"Greg picked her up in town. He has her safe."

Joanna's legs started to shake. *Thank you, thank you.* "Where?"

"He took her to the Surf Café. Nate's with her. They're in the back office, away from prying eyes. She didn't want us to call you, but I thought you'd want to know."

"I'll come right now. And thanks, Mel." She ended the call and headed through her gates.

Nate. Why did she have to be with Nate? Joanna didn't want to see Nate. Joanna didn't want to go into town, where there would be people who knew her. Joanna didn't want to risk facing reporters. If they weren't at Silver Point yet, they soon would be. And all the inhabitants of Silver Point knew the location of Otter's Nest.

It was okay. Everything was okay.

She would not abandon Ashley. She would not do what Cliff had done. And if the price for that was facing a bunch of reporters alongside her, then she'd do it. In fact, she'd do better than that. She'd make it clear that the press attention didn't bother her.

She jammed on the brakes at the junction of her road and paused. Her heart was hammering.

Enough!

She dragged off the hat and the wig and stuffed them back into her bag. Then she shook out her hair, and checked her reflection in the mirror.

Hi there, Joanna.

No more hiding. No more wigs, hats and dark glasses. If Ashley could show that much courage, then so could she.

She could not make up for Cliff's deficiencies, but she could make sure Ashley knew she wasn't alone. And if that meant walking through her own version of hell, then she'd do it. She'd see Nate, and handle her feelings whatever those were. She'd handle the locals, and the press, and anyone else who showed interest in her.

She turned onto the road and headed toward town.

So many of her childhood memories were wrapped up in the Surf Café. She and Nate would regularly raid the kitchen and then consume their spoils on the beach. Seafood rolls, chunky fries, perfect chewy cookies. Nate and Mel's parents had inherited the place from their own parents and it had always been a family-run concern. When she was growing up Joanna had occasionally served and cleared tables. The one thing she never did was cook, not since the day she'd cooked a romantic meal for Nate and almost burned the place to the ground.

Nate.

Nerves slithered in her stomach. Their relationship had been over for two decades. It felt like a lifetime ago. The special connection they'd once shared was long gone. Meeting him probably wouldn't even feel awkward. She'd be polite and friendly, and no doubt he would be the same. That last distressing encounter was so far behind them there was no point in even discussing it.

And anyway, this wasn't about her. All her focus was going to be on Ashley.

It was strange to think that only a short time before she'd

been panicking that having Ashley with her might be a mistake, and now she was panicking that Ashley might be leaving. She didn't want her to leave, and not just because she was worried about her.

She enjoyed Ashley's company. She enjoyed her sense of humor, and her frankness, and her way of looking at the world.

She drove into town and saw tourists with ice creams and cameras strolling down the pretty streets and snapping photos. No one paid her any attention. Their interest was in Silver Point, not her. There was no sign of reporters.

She kept her gaze fixed straight ahead and drove down Main Street and it felt achingly familiar, even after so much time. There was the Beach Bookstore, and Ocean Boutique where she'd once spent almost all her money on a white bikini with green spots. At the time it had seemed like a fortune for so little fabric, but it had the desired effect. She and Nate had made love for the first time the day she'd worn it.

Most people remembered the moment they met their first love. Joanna didn't. Not because it hadn't been memorable, but because there hadn't been a moment of her early life that hadn't had Nate in it. She remembered being four years old and digging in the sand with him, side by side. He'd helped her press sand into a bucket. She remembered taking surf lessons with him. At sixteen he'd held her head while she threw up the vodka she'd drunk. She couldn't pinpoint the moment when Nate had entered her life, because he'd always been there. She'd taken for granted that he always would be, but she'd been wrong about that. She'd been wrong about so many things.

She pulled into a parking space, resisted the urge to cram the hat back onto her head and headed to the Surf Café. The position hadn't changed, but everything else had. The outdoor tables that had once spilled onto the sand were now on a deck and shaded by palms. It was early, but already the place was humming with life. Small groups of young people nursing foamy coffees and sharing sugary treats before plunging into the waves. Tourists who wanted to start the day with the best view on this stretch of coastline. It was rustic, and yet refined. Upmarket beach chic.

Ignoring the curious gazes, Joanna walked across the terrace and in through the front.

She saw Mel first.

"She's in the back." She gestured, aware that Joanna would know where to go. "Greg wanted to keep her out of sight in case photographers show up."

Joanna headed for the door that led to the kitchen and the small office. Then she paused and turned to look at Mel, the girl she'd once shared every thought with. Her closest friend.

"Thank you," she said, and Mel gave a single nod.

"Of course."

Joanna felt a shaft of guilt. "We need to talk."

Mel smiled. "It can wait."

Joanna smiled back, grateful.

Maybe their friendship hadn't died. Maybe a friendship as strong as theirs never did.

She pushed open the door and walked into the kitchen. It was already frantically busy, as the staff handled the morning rush along with lunch prep. There was a clatter of plates, the sizzle of bacon frying, a chef shouting something to a girl balancing plates on her arm. No one spared her a glance. Here, she wasn't a person of interest, she was a person who was potentially getting in the way.

And then she noticed Greg, standing guard at the door of the office, arms folded, an immovable force.

A smile spread across his face. "Well, if it isn't Joanna Rafferty."

Rafferty. She hadn't been Joanna Rafferty in a long time. It felt good not to be Whitman. Good to not be linked to Cliff for once.

She should change her name. Why hadn't she thought of that before?

"Greg." She pulled off her glasses. "You look just the same." He'd been like a brother to her, but she had no idea how to bridge so much time and was surprised when he pulled her in for a hug. Even more surprised by how good it felt. "Are you allowed to do that when you're on duty?" She felt his rumble of laughter.

"I'm in charge. I can hug who I like."

When had she last been hugged? She couldn't remember. She'd missed it. She'd missed warmth and affection. She missed being with people who she trusted and who cared about her. There were other things she missed, too, like sex and excitement, but she tried not to think about that. These days she associated sex with anxiety. When she was with Cliff she hadn't been able to switch off the image of him with someone else. Even in those early days, when there was still hope for them, when they were both trying hard to make it work, the pictures had played in her head. She'd been unable to lose herself. She hadn't dated at all since the divorce.

There were lots of things she hadn't done.

Greg let her go. "You're back and you didn't call us? I should arrest you for that."

"I was hoping to stay unnoticed. I didn't want to cause trouble for anyone."

"I don't have a problem with trouble. Without trouble, I'd be out of a job." His smile faded. "You look tired. Like you have too many problems and no energy left to solve them. Maybe I can help with that."

She'd lived life for so long around the superficial and the selfish, she'd forgotten what it was like to be around good people who genuinely cared.

"You already have helped. Thank you for picking her up. I was worried sick."

"She's in the office." He gestured with his head. "Talk to her, and then we'll figure out where we go from here."

"We?"

He shrugged. "This is your hometown, Joanna. We're your people. If you're in trouble, then we help. It's as simple as that. You let us know what you need and we'll make it happen."

She felt hot tears sting. She was going to make a fool of herself right here in front of a man she hadn't seen for twenty years.

She'd hurt his wife, even though she knew there had been misunderstanding there.

But still his support was unwavering.

"I don't need anyone else to get involved. I can handle it on my own, Greg."

"I don't doubt it. But why would you want to deprive people of that good feeling that comes from helping someone?"

In her experience people helped as long as offering that help didn't impact on them.

"Greg—"

"You've been away a long time, so maybe you've forgotten." His gaze was steady. "You're back in Silver Point now, and you've got a whole bunch of people watching your back. You talk to her, and then let me know what you want to do next."

"Next? She comes home with me, that's what happens next." She told herself that it was his job to make her feel welcome, and to encourage her to open up. If trouble was coming, he needed to know about it. It didn't mean other people in Silver Point would feel the same way.

Greg was still watching her. "She seemed to think she was bringing you nothing but trouble. The sort of trouble that comes with cameras and maybe a TV crew."

The sort of trouble that would make the locals wish she'd never come home. The sort of trouble that would make them want to protect themselves.

But she'd be okay.

"It's nothing I haven't handled before. And none of it her fault."

He nodded. "You've read what's online today?"

She cringed at the thought of what her old friend might have read about her. What must he be thinking? She should be used to humiliation by now, but she wasn't used to looking old friends in the eye and talking about it.

"I haven't read it. But I can imagine what it says, and nothing is going to change the outcome. Ashley comes home with me." She put her hand on the door handle. "And you're right, they will come. Eventually they'll figure it out and track me down to Otter's Nest." And she was dreading that moment. After two weeks back in Silver Point, she was feeling more relaxed and at home than she had for decades. She didn't want them spoiling that.

Why? What was different this time?

The answer appeared with a clarity that surprised her.

She wanted to stay here. She wanted to make a home here. A life.

"It's my job to worry about that, not yours." Greg was calm. "The way I see it, Otter's Nest is private property and no one can set foot on that track without permission. And that's if they can even find the track. I'm not sure my directions would be that accurate. I've lost count of the number of times I missed that turn when we were growing up. I'm sure I'm not the only one in town who forgets where it is. All the sea air has a bad effect on our memory."

She'd forgotten what a good man he was. And because she'd known him her whole life, and he'd once rescued her from a group of bullies who had tried to steal her lunch at school, or maybe because he'd rescued Ashley, she rose on tiptoe and kissed his cheek. "Thanks, Greg. Always my hero."

"Whatever you need, Joanna, you let me know." He paused. "Nate's in there with her."

He was warning her. Giving her a heads-up? Anticipating more trouble?

"Thanks." She took a deep breath, stepped into the room and walked straight into Nate, who was guarding the door.

She felt his hands shoot out and steady her, and her body briefly brushed against his. *Nate.* She fought the instinct to sink against him, to wrap herself around him and pretend the last two decades had never happened. She glanced at his face, feeling a little dizzy. She'd imagined this moment, of course, so many times, but in her mind she'd been cool, calm and unaffected. She hadn't expected to feel anything after twenty years. But she did. She would have thought that her heart was too bruised, tired and wary to jump, but it did.

Everything about him was achingly familiar, from the strands of hair flopping toward his eyes to the way his mouth curved when he smiled. Feelings that she'd locked away and forgotten began flowing through her. Her imagination veered into forbidden territory, back to a time she tried never to revisit. He'd been everything to her. She'd believed it would always be that way, that what they shared was unbreakable. It was embarrassing to remember the intensity and depth of her feelings, and how childishly idealistic and unrealistic she'd been back then. How she'd thought one person could be everything she needed.

"Nate."

His gaze held hers for a long moment, as if he, too, couldn't look away. There was a flash of something in his eyes. A deep recognition. A connection that time hadn't managed to extinguish. It was unexpected and as unwelcome as the feelings that were swirling around unchecked inside her. She felt something close to desperation. *She didn't need this.* She needed to not care. To feel nothing. That was the secret of survival.

"Joanna." He released her and she stepped back and saw Ashley watching her from a chair. On the table in front of her was a cup of coffee she hadn't touched.

Her face was swollen and blotched from crying, her eyes red.

Joanna forgot about Nate. She rushed to Ashley and hugged her.

"You *scared* me! Don't ever do that to me again. If you're anxious about something, tell me." She held the girl tightly, and then realized she was probably being completely inappropriate. They weren't related. They'd only known each other for a short time and for most of that time they'd been polite, friendly even, but not tactile. Embarrassed, she tried to let her go but Ashley clung and hugged her back. Feeling those arms tighten around her brought a lump to her throat.

They held each other, and for a moment neither of them spoke.

"You're making me cry." Ashley's voice was muffled against Joanna's shoulder and Joanna gave the girl another hug and then eased away.

"You're making me cry, too."

Instead of taking the chair opposite, she crouched down. She was conscious of Nate hovering in the background, but he was no longer her focus. He was her past, and right now she was only interested in the present, and the future.

Ashley featured in both.

"So was it my cooking?"

Ashley scrubbed tears from her face with the flat of her hand. "What?"

"The reason you left. My cooking."

Ashley almost smiled but it was a poor effort. "Did you read it? What that woman wrote? It's *bad*. They wrote awful things about my mom, and they implied I was in the car because I was trying to blackmail him, and that the accident might have been my fault. It's horrible. I didn't mean to scare you by leaving but once they find out I'm with you it's going to make things a thousand times worse. They're going to come after you, too, and I know you hate that." Fresh tears bloomed and spilled. "I can't believe I'm crying. I can't believe I'm being this pathetic and emotional."

"You're pregnant—"

"Yeah, let's pretend it's that." Ashley sniffed. "It's kind of you to come after me, but it's going to be easier for you if I leave. Maybe we can stay in touch. If you'd like to. I could get a burner phone or something so they can't track me. Can they do that? Does that happen in real life? What even is a burner phone? I don't know. Can you order one online? Do you search 'burner phone'?"

Joanna felt a pressure in her chest as emotions overwhelmed her.

She'd gone from being numb to suddenly feeling everything. Why? Who was responsible for that? Ashley? Nate?

"You're not going to need a burner phone." Joanna took her hand and squeezed. "Remember what I said to you yesterday? It doesn't matter what they wrote, or what they write in the future. It doesn't change the truth. What happened was an accident, Ashley. You weren't responsible. And if there is blame, then it's Cliff's, for putting you in a position where that was the only way you could talk to him."

"But people think—"

"Strangers," Joanna said. "They're strangers."

Ashley eyed her. "They said stuff about you, too."

"I'm sure they did."

And she was so tired of it. She and Cliff had been divorced for a year before he'd died, and yet still they made her the story. They'd continued to hunt and she'd continued to hide. When was it going to end?

She rocked back on her heels.

It ended now. Right now.

What was it Ashley had said to her the day before?

Why do we have to hide?

It was a good question. She'd blamed Cliff for it. She'd blamed the press and the public. But *she* was the one who had chosen to live like this. And she could choose not to.

The idea rocked her.

Was it really that simple?

No, but how much harm could they do to her? What could they say that they hadn't already said? Over the past two decades they'd exposed her to scrutiny and publicly humiliated her in every way imaginable. Joanna had handled it by locking herself away, and locking her emotions away, exactly as she'd handled Denise. She hadn't fought back, she'd made herself small. She'd allowed Denise, and then the press, to chip away at her self-confidence. She'd allowed them to decide who she was, even though she didn't recognize the person they created.

But no more.

Maybe it was being back at Otter's Nest that had made her see things differently. Maybe it was Ashley, who was bold and brave and questioned things she hadn't had the courage to question herself. When she'd discovered that the intimate details of her life were about to be made public, her first instinct hadn't been to hide, as Joanna would have done, it had been to ignore it and carry on with her life.

And that, Joanna thought, was what they were both going to do.

"It only matters if we let it matter. For decades I let it matter. I don't want you to make the same mistake. But I understand that you're upset, and that's natural."

"Upset?" Ashley sniffed. "Yes, I'm upset, but mostly I'm really angry."

"Me, too."

"I'm not like you. You're so controlled and you never—" Ashley stopped. "What did you say?"

"I'm angry, too. Furious."

"You *are*?"

"Yes. Livid. Boiling with rage." But she also felt more in control than she had in her life before. She couldn't change what they did, but she could change what she did.

"Okay! I believe you." This time Ashley did manage to smile. "It's surprising. You never seemed to get that emotional about it. You were always so calm. I thought you were...kind of resigned."

"So did I, but it turns out I'm not." She stood up and rubbed her legs, which were slowly turning numb after so long in one position. "I have a suggestion of what we can do today."

"I won't hide." Ashley sat up straighter. "If a reporter had come along before that kind police chief—"

"Greg. He's married to Mel."

"The woman who called on you? She was the one who saw me in town. She called him, I think. It's good to have connections. I liked him. He stopped to check on me and we got talking. And I told him I'm not going to hide."

"I'm not going to hide, either. And I don't want to waste another moment of time, energy or emotion on thinking about them. It's a beautiful day out there. We're going to—" she searched her brain for the most public activity she could think of "—we're going to have breakfast right here at the Surf Café. Have you eaten? No, of course you haven't. You left before breakfast, and you barely ate anything last night. You're not eating enough, Ashley. We need you to stay healthy."

Ashley gave a funny smile. "No one has scolded me about eating since my mom died."

"I'm happy to take on that role. Not as a pseudo mom, you understand. As a friend."

"I think you'd be a great mom." Ashley sniffed. "You're also a great friend. I want to push you away and protect you from the vultures but I'm just so happy you're here. I want to be self-ish and say yes to breakfast."

"Then say yes." Joanna hugged her again. She'd forgotten just how good it felt to be needed, and connected, and important to someone. "It's not selfish. I'm doing it for me, too. I should have done it a long time ago. Maybe I would have if I'd had someone like you by my side. What's your favorite food?" She glanced at Nate and found him looking at her with an expression she couldn't interpret. Now those first shaky moments had passed, she was able to be a little more objective in her assessment.

Two decades, and he'd hardly changed at all. His shoulders had filled out, but his hair was still dark, his eyes still the same ocean blue and his body lean and fit. The world, their relationship, all of it, seemed so different now she was looking back on it with some perspective. And she knew now that it wasn't something they could just ignore. There were things they had to say to each other. Things she needed to say to him.

No more hiding.

She looked directly at him and ignored the bump of her heart. "Nate, do you still make those incredible pancakes?"

He smiled. "With bacon and maple syrup? Yeah, we make them."

"Great. We'll take a stack of those and anything else you think we'll enjoy. Maybe some fresh berries. Vitamin C." She reached out a hand and tugged Ashley to her feet. "I hope you're hungry, because unlike me Nate is a good cook."

Ashley looked at her. "If we're really going to eat here, then maybe we should have a quiet table."

"We don't want a quiet table. We want the best table, with the best view. Is there room on the deck?" It was like diving into the deep end of a pool.

"The *deck*?" Ashley's eyes flew wide. "Everyone would be able to see us."

Joanna's heart was thumping so hard she wondered if it was trying to knock sense into her.

"Let them see us. No more hiding." It wasn't enough to tell Ashley she wasn't going to hide anymore. She had to show her, even if it was a test of her acting skills.

"The deck?" Nate was watching her. "You're sure that's what you want? I can bring your order in here if you prefer or find you a table inside."

He knew. Even though they hadn't seen each other for twenty years, even though he couldn't possibly know how she felt about things now, he did somehow know.

"The deck would be perfect."

He nodded and eased away from the wall. "Give me a minute."

Ashley picked up her purse, and the backpack she'd had with her in the hospital. "You told me not to read what they'd written and I wish I hadn't. They said I look just like him. Cliff. That I *am* just like him. And now I'm scared I'm going to be a terrible parent, just like he was."

Joanna tried to imagine how it must feel to discover you were Cliff Whitman's daughter. It probably didn't feel like a moment to celebrate. Not something you were going to boast about with friends. She pushed aside her own hurt and heartache. "He let you down, there's no denying that. But Cliff wasn't a monster, Ashley. You only know one side of him—the side that treated you and your mother badly. The side the media writes about. But there was another side…" She paused. It was a side she hadn't thought about for a long time. A side that had been eclipsed by everything that had happened. "He had…qualities."

Ashley pulled a face. "You're kidding, right?"

"No. And I can talk more about him if that would help. Tell you more about the real Cliff." She was glad Nate wasn't in the room. Talking about Cliff in front of him would have been too awkward. "This isn't the right time to go into more detail, but

I will. For now, believe me when I say you're nothing like him. And you're not going to be a terrible parent, Ashley."

"I have his eyes."

"They're *your* eyes. Just as your decisions and choices are yours."

"I didn't make a great choice when I climbed into his car." Ashley blew her nose. "Maybe I've inherited all his worst traits."

"You were trying to do the best for your child. That already shows you're nothing like him. And I think you make great choices. Apart from creeping out in the early hours and leaving me a scary note." She gave a smile. "That wasn't a great choice. Promise me you won't make a habit of that. If you're concerned about something, talk to me."

"I will. I should have done that, I know. But I was worried that if I told you, you'd feel obliged to talk me out of it. I was trying to protect you."

Joanna felt a warm glow. Nessa, Ashley, Mel, Greg—maybe she wasn't as alone as she'd thought. "I appreciate the sentiment, I really do, but you don't have to do that. I'm good at protecting myself."

"I know. You're so…capable. I wish I was like you. I bounce between feeling panic and helplessness."

"You're not helpless. You've been through a lot, and you're having to come to terms with a lot of things. You have decisions to make, and I understand that feels overwhelming and stressful. But you don't have to make all those decisions at once. Take it a step at a time."

Ashley sat a little straighter. "I'm not going to do what he did. I'm going to take care of this baby, no matter what."

"I know you are."

"I would never abandon it."

"I know that, too."

Ashley drew in a breath. "I have no idea what I'm doing. No idea what I'm going to do. I've never been this scared in my life."

"It's okay to be scared. I'm scared, too. Do you have any idea how long it has been since I've walked around in public without looking over my shoulder? We'll do this together."

"They'll stake out the beach house."

Joanna's stomach rolled. "Probably, yes. And you're right, it does make me uncomfortable, but some of that is habit. Almost a reflex reaction. I've been doing this for so long I no longer even question it. But I'm questioning it now."

"Because of me."

"Yes, because of you. You've made me take another look at the way I'm living my life. You've made me ask myself some tough questions. And that's good."

"It is?"

"Yes. I'm tired of living like this." Saying the words aloud made her realize it was true. "I'm tired of having to restrict my life because of Cliff. I'm tired of still being associated with him even though we were divorced before he died. I'm tired of caring what people think of me. You talked a lot of sense yesterday. You said they shouldn't decide how we live. I agree with you. From now on we're going to do what we want to do, when we want to do it."

She glanced up as Nate walked back into the room.

"I've got you the best table in the house," he said. "And your order is on its way."

"Thank you." Who had he moved to get her that table? Whoever it was, no doubt he'd used that Nate smile, and that Nate charm, and they'd melted toward whatever alternative he'd offered without a word of protest.

"You're welcome." He paused. "It's good to see you, Jo."

His use of her name took her straight back to the past. He was the only one other than her father who had ever called her that and it was a name she associated with intimacy. *I love you, Jo.*

Was it good to see him? She didn't know. But she did know it felt good to have this first, awkward meeting over. The thought of bumping into him had been looming over her in a cloud of dread, as big a barrier to her strolling around town or along the beach as the worry of being spotted by the press. But now, thanks to Ashley, it was done. That first awkward moment was behind her and she'd survived.

And she realized she'd been wrong about two things. Firstly, that although two decades had passed, there was still a connection between them. And secondly, that he didn't feel like a stranger.

Later, she'd have to think about that but for now she directed her newfound courage into her smile. "It's good to see you, too, Nate."

She'd thought that seeing him might feel like closure, but it didn't. It felt like a beginning.

Unsettled by that, she took Ashley's hand and walked with her to the deck.

14

Ashley

"Those were the best pancakes." Ashley looked with some surprise at her empty plate. It was the first time since the accident that she'd eaten food and enjoyed it.

"It's good to see you eat. I was starting to worry." Joanna had barely touched her own food.

Was she finding it stressful?

Ashley knew all about stress. "I don't think there was room inside me for food, anxiety and the baby." The knot in her stomach that had been there since she'd climbed into the car with Cliff, maybe even before that, had gone. She felt—safe? No, it was more than that. She felt as if she mattered. As if people cared. Greg, Nate and Mel had cared, even though they were strangers. Most importantly of all, Joanna cared. Joanna had come after her. Joanna had been sick with worry. When had anyone last worried about her? "I couldn't believe it when you walked into that room. I didn't think I'd see you again. I thought you'd be relieved to find me gone."

"Relieved? Your note scared me to death. I kept imagining terrible things happening to you."

Ashley looked at her. Laughter bubbled up. "Joanna, my mom died, I got pregnant, I found out Cliff Whitman was my dad and whatever you say I'm sure I played a part in killing him, I was in a car wreck, the media think I'm a scheming blackmailer and on top of that I dragged you into my whole sorry life so now I have that on my conscience. How much worse could it be?" She saw Joanna's gaze flicker around the deck nervously. "Sorry. I should have used an indoor voice."

"Why? We're not hiding. And when you put it like that—" Joanna gave an awkward laugh. "You're right. It's been bad. But for what it's worth, you don't need to have me on your conscience. I'm happy fate brought us together."

"Seriously?"

"Yes, seriously. Where were you going, anyway?"

Ashley shrugged. Was it embarrassing to admit she hadn't even thought that far? "I was going to head back home and maybe crash with a friend for a while until I figure out what to do. I'm going to have to get a job. Find somewhere to live, try and pay off those hospital bills." Her insides tightened as anxiety returned. A mountain of problems and challenges lay ahead, and she wasn't sure how to tackle them.

"I really want to help. For now you're living here with me, so that's one problem solved." Joanna paused. "If that's what you want. Maybe it isn't. Maybe you'd rather go somewhere else, in which case I'll help you find somewhere safe and comfortable. And your hospital bills should be paid from Cliff's estate. After all, you were only there because of him. But leave that one with me. I'll talk to my lawyers and we'll decide the best way to move forward from here."

"You have lawyers?"

"I was married to Cliff for two decades." Joanna's tone was dry. "You'd better believe I have lawyers. Good ones, who charge me a fortune. Forget that for now. Are you happy to live with me in Otter's Nest? At least while we figure out what your best next steps are?"

Happy? Ashley thought longingly of the beach house. That big comfy bed. The breeze through the open doors. The fact that you could hear the ocean from every room in the house. Her own bathroom. Paradise. But the real appeal of the place, she realized now, had been Joanna herself. Joanna, who had been there for her from the moment she'd walked into that hospital room. Joanna, who had given her somewhere to recuperate after her accident. Joanna, who had put aside her natural urge to keep a low profile in order to come after Ashley. Joanna, who had treated her with compassion and kindness right from the start.

"Staying with you is the safest and most comfortable I've felt in a long time. I—you saved me. I don't know what I would have done without you." Ashley stumbled over the words, trying to express how she felt. "I'm grateful. That's partly why I left. I didn't want to make life tough for you."

"I'm the one grateful to you." Joanna sat back in her chair and closed her eyes. "Listen to that."

"What?" Ashley glanced around her. What was she missing? There was a couple laughing at a table near them, a clatter of crockery from inside the café, more laughter, the crash of waves on the beach just steps away. "What am I listening to?"

"Life." Joanna opened her eyes. She looked a little dazed. "Normal life. Do you have any idea how long it has been since I've felt normal? I've lived in a small protected world for as long as I can remember. My choice, but I didn't feel as if I had options. I didn't want the attention, and thanks to Cliff it was almost impossible for me to live normally *without* attention. That became my normal. I never questioned changing it. And then you came along and I pulled you into my world to protect you."

"And I feel guilty that—"

"Don't feel guilty. You forced me out of my comfort zone. I'm here because of you."

"And that's…good?"

Joanna watched as a toddler lifted her arms to her mother and was scooped into a hug. "It's good."

It made her feel better to know she'd helped Joanna, too.

"I hope you still think that when a bunch of reporters show up. They're going to carry on writing about you. Bad things, probably. Same about me."

"We'll handle it."

But they shouldn't have to "handle it," should they? She still burned with outrage at the injustice of it. She'd read the article in disbelief, overwhelmed by a sense of helplessness. "How can you be so calm? It makes me angry. It's none of their business if my mother slept with Cliff, or a whole basketball team for that matter, or the emperor of Sweden—"

Joanna blinked. "I don't think Sweden has an emperor..."

"Whatever—" Ashley shrugged "—they have no right to delve into my life. They can fuck right off." She slapped her hand over her mouth and her eyes went huge. "I didn't mean to say that. Do you think the baby heard?"

Joanna gave a choked laugh. "If it did, I'm sure it's impressed and reassured to know that its mother isn't going to be pushed around by anyone."

Ashley felt embarrassed at having lost control in front of Joanna, who never lost control. "I'm never going to swear in front of the baby. I want to set a good example. Be a good role model." She'd hardly been that so far, had she? She needed to grow up and take responsibility, which was one of the reasons she'd left even though the idea of it had scared her senseless.

"I think standing up for yourself, and having self-respect, is a good example. And it's an example I'm going to follow. Maybe next time a reporter approaches me I should tell them to—" she breathed "—to..."

"You're never going to say it. You're too polite." Ashley grinned at the thought of it. "But the main thing is that we're not going to let a bunch of people we don't even know force us to hide."

"No." Joanna's voice was stronger. "We're not."

"And yes, they wrote horrid things, but if we stay indoors, then they win."

"Yes."

Ashley looked at her. "And we don't want them to win."

"We definitely don't."

Resisting the temptation to punch the air, Ashley bit into a strawberry instead. She and Joanna were a team. On the same side. "So that's agreed, then? I am going to come back and stay in your amazing beach house, and in return I'm going to force you to hang out in cafés, and go shopping, and run on the beach and do all the stuff you've avoided doing. And if anyone so much as looks at you in a way you don't like, I'll give them a piece of my mind. I'll give them a statement."

"Do you intend to use anything other than four-letter words in your statement?"

"That depends on how they're behaving."

Joanna smiled. "I should have employed you to handle the media years ago. Or maybe as my bodyguard." She was more relaxed. She seemed to have forgotten that she was sitting on the deck in full view of anyone who happened to be passing. Ashley hoped a news van full of reporters wasn't about to speed into town and change all that. She didn't want Joanna fleeing back into her nest. It was good to see her sitting in the sunshine, a foamy coffee on the table in front of her. It made her feel good to know she'd played a part in it.

Joanna had protected and helped her, and now she was determined to protect and help Joanna.

"I'll handle the media. You don't need a bodyguard. You have Greg, Nate and Mel fighting in your corner. You should have seen them. They called a ton of people, spreading the word around town that if anyone saw anyone suspicious, anyone with cameras, they were to call." She saw Joanna's expression change.

"They did that?"

"Yes, I heard them. I had no idea you still had so many connections here. You said you hadn't been back in ages."

"I haven't."

Why not? Ashley couldn't figure that out. "I've always wanted to be part of a community. Where I grew up, everyone just minded their own business. I bet you knew everyone growing up here?"

"Yes." Joanna toyed with her cup. "Everyone."

"It must have been great. So now you're no longer hiding, there must be a ton of other people here you can reconnect with."

"Not really. Twenty years is a long time. We've all moved on."

And yet these people clearly cared for Joanna. Didn't she know that?

"I was a bit shaken when Greg pulled up next to me. He knew my name and who I was. Mel had seen me and called him. I bet he's a good cop." She saw Joanna take a breath.

"The best, I'm sure. Greg is kind. Even-tempered and patient. Mel can be like a walking explosion and Greg's been there to defuse it since we were kids."

She knew them well. And yet she hadn't intended to get in touch.

"So, anyway—" if she talked, maybe Joanna would talk too "—he brought me here, told Nate he needed to use the office. They obviously know each other well, too."

"Yes. They grew up together."

Ashley nodded. "That fits. We sat down and Greg said did I want to tell him what had happened and what I was doing standing on the street by myself, and I didn't intend to say anything but he had kind eyes and he was a good listener, so I told him everything. I didn't mean to, but I was angry and upset and scared and the words just sort of fell out. I told him about Cliff. About my mom. About how you tricked all those reporters outside your house in the middle of the night." She saw Joanna stiffen. "That was the only time I saw him react. When I said you'd disguised yourself and escaped through the woods in the dark and used a car that wasn't registered in your name."

"You told him that?"

"Yes. And his mouth went sort of tight. I think it was the whole dark woods at night thing. He was worried about you. And I pointed out that the real threat and menace was waiting in front of your house in full view, and in comparison walking through woodland at night was a piece of cake. I don't think he'd thought of it like that."

"I'm sure he hadn't." Joanna pushed her cup away. "What else did he say?"

"That it was wrong that you felt you had to live that way, and then I told him about the article and he read it, which was pretty uncomfortable. I was waiting for him to ask me if I was a blackmailer, but he didn't. He didn't pay much attention to the article, just asked me more questions about me, really. I told him I left without telling you where I was going because I didn't want to make things worse for you, and he said knowing you as he did you'd be worried sick. He asked if he could call you and if that was all right with me. I thought it was thoughtful of him to ask."

"Very thoughtful."

"Mel said she'd call you, and Greg said that I wasn't to worry about reporters coming here, because he'd handle everything. And then Nate came in with hot chocolate. But I was too sick with stress to drink it. Greg told him what had happened and asked him to stay with me while he went to talk to someone on his team and check no one that looked like press had shown up in town."

"He left you with Nate?" Joanna asked the question casually. A little too casually?

"Yes. I told him he could go back to work but he said it was all under control and that he always took a break about that time, anyway. Which I guess wasn't true, but it was nice of him." She watched Joanna's face. "He was kind, too."

"I—good."

"We talked." Ashley took another strawberry from the bowl in front of Joanna. "A lot."

"You did? What about?"

"You mostly." She saw Joanna's face change.

"Me?"

"Well, first I talked about me because I was upset about that article, and I needed someone to rant to. I used to live a normal life, but lately it's been nonstop drama. I'm not sure I'm built for drama—"

"Are any of us?"

"I don't know, but I'm definitely not. I have no idea why anyone wants to be a celebrity and have their life splashed around for public consumption. You've lived with this for two decades, which makes it all the more amazing that you're not more of a mess, frankly. Anyway, Nate wanted to know everything about you, and to begin with I clammed up and said nothing because I thought he might be about to call the press or something. I don't really trust people right now. But then he started talking about the past, about how you grew up together and knew each other well, and how he'd thought about you often. He said he'd been worried about you." Ashley eyed Joanna, wondering how carefully she had to tread. "He seemed very interested in you. He asked me a lot of questions about how you were and what you'd been doing."

"He did?"

"Yes. And he asked about Cliff, and said that whole thing must have been tough on you."

"And what did you tell him?" She said the words as if she wasn't too interested in the answer, but Ashley knew she was interested.

"I didn't tell him anything. I said if there was stuff he wanted to know, then he was going to have to ask you himself and he laughed and said that he intended to do that." She watched Joanna's face. "He's smoking hot. I mean, for someone older, obviously. It made me think—the way he talked about you…" She might as well say it, straight out. She and Joanna had already talked about so many personal things, why not this, too? "You were involved, right? When you lived here?"

Joanna tensed. "I don't know why you would think—"

"That the two of you have a connection? I have eyes in my head. The moment you saw each other—well, I'm good at sensing atmospheres."

"In this case you're wrong. There was no atmosphere."

"But last night when I was telling you about Jon, and how we were best friends and grew up together, you had this look on your face. That was you and Nate, wasn't it? You were best friends." She saw a soft pink flush slowly creep across Joanna's cheeks, and knew she was right. Should she drop the subject? Maybe, but the appeal of talking to someone who might understand the complexity of moving from friendship to romance was too great. "If you have any words of wisdom on that subject, it would be great to hear them. I need all the help I can get."

"Wisdom?" Joanna started to laugh and Ashley looked at her. "What? Why are you laughing?"

"It's the thought of anyone asking *me* for advice on romance."

Ashley grinned, too. "They say you learn from your mistakes."

"And you want to learn from mine?" Joanna shook her head. "I'm not sure what I can teach you, except don't do what I did."

"But Nate—tell me about Nate."

"There's nothing to tell." Joanna was evasive. "I haven't seen him in twenty years."

Conscious that there were people around them, Ashley leaned forward. "When you walked into that room it was like watching something out of a movie. You almost fell over, he caught you, you stared at each other. I have never seen two people look at each other the way you did. You were glued together. It was like—I don't know—an electric shock or something. I expected to hear a harp playing. I felt like saying, *Hello, I'm over here*, but I didn't because I knew neither of you was going to notice me."

"That's really not—" Joanna shifted in her chair, flustered. "I was worried about you. Thinking about you."

"I know, and I'm grateful for it, but right at that moment you weren't thinking about me, Joanna. You weren't thinking about anything but him, and I don't blame you." Ashley grinned at her. "Those blue eyes of his are a killer. And he has good shoulders. Between him and Greg, there was no way any reporters were coming through the door."

"Could you stop?" Joanna glanced nervously behind her. "Nate and I knew each other, yes. But it was twenty years ago. We grew up in this small town and we'd barely stepped outside it. I was friends with Greg, Nate and Mel. Close friends."

Ashley knew she'd been witnessing something far deeper than friendship. "Greg was with Mel. And you were with Nate."

Joanna knocked the spoon off the table and retrieved it, flustered. "Ashley—"

"That would explain a lot. You walked through that door and it was the first time you'd seen him in decades."

"Ashley—"

"You must have been *so* stressed about seeing him, but you did it, anyway." The pieces fell into place, and she realized just how stressful that meeting must have been for Joanna. "You put yourself through that for me. You did that for me." She felt a twinge of sympathy and guilt. "Was it something you'd been dreading? Seeing Nate again?"

"I hadn't thought much about it." Joanna fiddled with the spoon in her hand and then put it down on the table. "I've been dreading it ever since I arrived here. Otter's Nest—this whole place—is full of memories for me. It's like going back in time."

"Was Nate one of the reasons you weren't leaving the house?" She was talking in a low voice now and she glanced over Joanna's shoulder, but there was no sign of Nate.

"Maybe. Mostly I was avoiding the press, but I certainly wasn't in a hurry to run into anyone from my old life here, either. And then Mel showed up. That was unexpected."

"And you were close. She was your best friend. You told each other everything. You braided each other's hair. You did each other's makeup. And you were dating her brother." Ashley sat back in her chair. "When you saw Nate, you had to have been thinking about the past. It had to have been an awkward moment. I keep thinking about what I'm going to say and do when I see Jon again, because I guess it's got to happen sometime. And obviously I hope I'm looking my best and have some time to prepare so I don't just blurt something out and then spend the rest of my life regretting it, but even so the thought of it makes me feel a little sick. He's left loads of voice mails on my phone."

"What did he say?"

"I don't know. I haven't listened to them because I'm scared and cowardly and once I listen that will be it. Right now I can still dream that things might work out."

"He's probably worried about you."

"No. I did send him a message saying I was okay and that I'd call soon. I didn't want him to worry. I'm dreading seeing him again, though. I don't think I'll be as cool as you were with Nate. Were you nervous? It didn't show." She realized that however stressful the last twenty-four hours had been for her it had been equally, if not more, stressful for Joanna. "How did it feel, seeing him again?"

"I don't know. Do you want more food? You ate that quickly."

"No, thanks." Ashley wasn't thinking about food. "Had he changed much?"

"Twenty years is a long time. We've all changed."

"But you both still had feelings. That was obvious."

Joanna shifted position in her chair. "Do we have to talk about this?"

"Not if you don't want to, but the more I know, the less likely I am to say the wrong thing."

Joanna gave a faint smile. "Or you could say nothing?"

"I'm not really a 'say nothing' type of person."

"As I'm starting to discover." Joanna sighed. "I haven't seen Nate since the day he ended our relationship. The last time I saw him he was on the beach, kissing Whitney."

"Whitney?"

"She had blonde hair and was very beautiful."

Joanna was beautiful, Ashley thought. "I think you handled today brilliantly. And you looked great by the way, with your hair loose. Eat your heart out, Whitney, I say. You should wear it like that always. It suits you. Nate thought so, too. And he definitely wasn't thinking of Whitney when you walked into the room."

"You cannot possibly know what he was thinking."

"I saw the way he looked at you. It was the same way you looked at him."

"No!" Joanna gasped. "Did I? Oh, that's awful. I certainly didn't mean to. Do you think he noticed?"

"Not sure. Probably. Does it matter?"

"Yes, it matters. I don't want him to think—"

"That you're interested. Are you?"

"Definitely not."

"Why not? After two decades with Cliff, you deserve a little fun and romance. Why not Nate? He's not married. I heard Mel making a joke about him being single forever, so whatever happened with Whitney it didn't last. Oh, look—now you've spilled your coffee." She leaned across and mopped up pools of coffee with her napkin. "Keep your hands still. You have great taste in men, by the way."

"I married Cliff."

Ashley scrunched the napkin into a ball and shrugged. "We all mess up occasionally. We're going to get past that."

"We?"

"Yes. You said you were grateful to me for making you rethink the way you were living. Here we are, eating pancakes at a table overlooking the ocean. Next I'm going to help you with your love life."

"Really, I don't need you to—"

"You do, Joanna. You really do. You need my help. I'm good at fixing people up. I have an instinct about these things."

"Ashley, it's a kind thought but—"

"Have you ever tried online dating?"

Joanna looked at her as if she'd just suggested dancing naked down Main Street. "No. I've never tried any dating, online or in person. Why are you looking at me like that?"

Ashley leaned forward. "No dating *at all*?"

"No. Why so surprised? When would I? I was married to Cliff. I took my marriage vows seriously even if he didn't."

"But you divorced him a year ago—" She broke off, incredulity swamping tact. "You're saying you haven't dated *anyone* since your divorce?"

"That's right."

"You haven't been on a single date. Not even a bad date?"

"It was the anticipation of a bad date that stopped me dating again. After being married to Cliff, the last thing I wanted was another relationship. There were times when my marriage felt like one long bad date."

So why hadn't she left Cliff sooner?

No, she wasn't going to ask that. It was too personal a question for such a public place. Anyone could be listening.

"You've had a crap time with Cliff," Ashley said. "It's time you had some fun. You deserve it. I'm not talking about bad dates, I'm talking about fun dates." She reached across and stole another one of the strawberries that lay untouched in a bowl in front of Joanna.

"Ashley, stop!" Joanna sounded desperate. "The last thing I want at the moment is romance. I'm not interested."

"That's because you were married to Cliff for so long you've forgotten how to have a normal love life." Ashley pushed the strawberries toward Joanna. "These are delicious. You should try one."

"I'm not hungry."

"Because seeing Nate has made your stomach all churny?" Maybe they should postpone internet dating. Maybe Joanna's first date was right here in the café. "You felt something when you saw him. That's interesting, don't you think?"

"I don't find it interesting. I find it—" Joanna breathed. "I appreciate what you're trying to do, but I don't want to date. I'm happy to leave Otter's Nest, and not hide away—shop, do anything you want to do—but I don't want to date. I can't take it right now."

"I don't get it. You're forty. Half your life is still ahead of you and you're behaving as if it's over."

"Not over." Joanna frowned. "But I don't see dating playing a significant part in my future. I'm a failure in that direction."

Ashley stared at her. "A failure? Are you kidding? You're an inspiration."

"I made a lot of bad choices. And I've spent half my life so far being unhappy over a man. I plan to spend the next few years being happy without one. You're young. I don't expect you to understand. You still believe in sunsets and happy-ever-afters. You think romance happens the way it does in the movies."

Ashley looked at her. "Joanna, I'm pregnant by a man I'm not even officially dating. My father was a serial cheater and my mother had an affair with him while he was married to you. I think romance is misshapen. Bad things happen, I know that. But it doesn't mean good things can't happen, too. And dating doesn't have to be something serious. Dating can be light and fun."

"I haven't been on a date that was light and fun since I was sixteen."

She saw dating as a traumatic event. As something that would be more trouble than it was worth.

Right at that moment, Ashley felt older and more worldly-wise than Joanna. "In that case I'm going to share my rules with you. Eventually you'll probably want to make your own rules but for now you can borrow mine. I like to think they're foolproof."

"You have rules?"

"Sure. Although mostly I don't even think about them. It's instinctive."

"You have instinctive rules for dating."

"Yes. Rule number one—" Ashley held up a finger "—does he make you laugh? That's the single most important one. You are not going to have fun if your date doesn't make you laugh." It felt like an age since her life had been focused on simple things like her dating rules. An age since her priorities had been hanging out with her friends, and talking about fashion and music.

"Laugh. Right." Joanna nodded. "Rule number two?"

"Listening skills. I am not spending five minutes with someone who is more interested in looking at his phone or over his shoulder at the girl behind me when I'm right there in front of

him. Either I'm the most interesting thing in his life at that moment, or I'm gone."

"Does anyone take you on a date or are they too scared?"

Ashley grinned. "I demand respect, that's true. My mother
taught me that, which makes it all the more odd that she had
an affair with Cliff."

"Cliff could do those things," Joanna said. "Cliff could make
a woman laugh. He could listen and make her feel as if she was
the only woman in the world."

"But? There has to be a but."

"But he didn't mean it. It was all part of his play. Fake. I don't
know how to spot a fake. If I'd dated more when I was young
maybe I would have learned."

"How many men did you date before Cliff?"

"One."

"One? Are we talking about Nate?" It must have been even
more serious than she'd thought. "And was that fun?"

"It was fun until it wasn't fun."

"Why did you break up?"

Joanna leaned forward. "Ashley, we're sitting on the terrace
of his restaurant." Her voice was barely audible. "Things are
already awkward. If he overhears this conversation I will have
to go back to wearing a disguise. I'd like to talk about something else."

"Okay. We'll talk about your dating plans. Let's work up a
profile for you."

"No dating. For me, relationships aren't fun. They're stress."

Ashley thought about Jon, about their trips to the movies
where they shared popcorn and laughed. They weren't dating as such, but they'd had fun together. That was what Joanna
needed. Someone to have fun with. And share friendship. It
seemed to Ashley that was what Joanna lacked most in her life.
Good friends.

"Okay. I'll say no more." *For now.* Ashley reached across the table and gave her hand a squeeze. "You should eat something. If you don't eat what's on your plate, he's going to ask you what's put you off your food. Do you really want *that* conversation?"

Joanna sighed and picked up her fork. "Fine. I'll eat."

Ashley decided a change of subject was necessary. "Were you serious about not hiding? Because I'd love to take a look around this place. It's pretty, and I saw a cute dress in one of the stores." She wanted to do something about Joanna's "uniform" of jeans and white shirt, but one thing at a time.

"We can go shopping."

Ashley was about to reply when Mel appeared at the table.

"How are you both doing?" She was a little hesitant, as if she wasn't sure of her reception. "Can I fetch you more drinks? Anything?"

Joanna shook her head. "We're fine, thanks, Mel."

Was that all she was going to say? To a woman who had once been her best friend?

She was scared, Ashley realized. Scared of putting herself out there. Scared of being hurt again. Dates. Friendship. They all required the same thing—a willingness to make yourself vulnerable, and that required trust. Joanna had lost her trust in people.

Ashley took over. "Will you join us for a minute?" She saw Joanna tense but ignored it. "We want to go shopping. Where's the best place?"

"For clothes?" Mel sat down. "Ocean Boutique. It's owned and run by Rosa, who was at school with us. She has a good eye. Her stuff is great. You should start there. If you don't find what you need you could try Rags to Riches, but their stuff is a little more formal. I'm glad you're going to head into town. What else do you guys have planned?"

Joanna shook her head. "Nothing."

"In that case, you should come over. Greg and I live in one

of the houses down on Ocean. We're having a barbecue tomorrow. It would give us a chance to properly catch up, Joanna. I'd really like that." She paused, unsure, and Ashley realized Joanna wasn't the only one who was nervous.

Joanna frowned. "A barbecue?"

"Yes. You can meet our daughter, Eden." Mel smiled at Ashley. "It's family night, and she would be so pleased to be able to hang out with someone close to her age, instead of her parents and uncle."

Family night. Ashley felt a pang. It sounded wonderful to her, but Joanna was still frowning.

"Nate would be there, too?"

"Yes."

"I don't think—"

"It sounds brilliant," Ashley intervened before Joanna could wreck what sounded like a perfect evening. "We'll be there. What time? What should we bring?"

"Come at seven?" Mel stood up. "Bring yourselves, that's it. And maybe swimsuits, in case we swim."

"Seven. Swimsuits. Got it." Ashley beamed. "Thanks, Mel."

Mel disappeared back inside the café and Joanna stared at her in despair.

"Why did you say yes?"

"Because I'm a teenager and life has been far too heavy lately. I need light relief. I need entertaining and family night sounded like fun. Also because you weren't going to, and this is the perfect opportunity for you to spend time and relax with—" She almost said Nate, and then decided Joanna might refuse to go. "Your friends."

"I don't think it will be relaxing. It will be stressful."

"A barbecue overlooking the ocean? How is that stressful?"

"It's not the food that's stressful, it's the people. And the circumstances. You're behaving as if we're old friends, but we haven't talked properly in twenty years."

Ashley almost said, *Then it's beyond time*, but decided that would be rude. "It's just a barbecue. It might be fun, and if it isn't we can leave."

"You'd leave?"

"Yes. We can have a signal, like my friends and I do when we go on dates. We can press the emergency button." She had no intention of pressing that button. "But as this isn't a date, and there are going to be a few people, I don't think we're going to need to do that. It will be fun. But I need something to wear." *And so do you*, Ashley thought. "Let's try that boutique Mel suggested. We could go right now, before a bunch of report- ers show up." She should probably be saving what little money she had for the baby, but she'd worry about that later. The tiny amount she'd spend on clothes was hardly going to solve her problem, anyway. The panic that had haunted her since she'd stepped into the car with Cliff hovered close. She forced herself to breathe and ignore it.

Nate appeared at their table. "How were the pancakes?"

"Amazing, delicious, best ever." Ashley was grateful for the distraction. "Thank you for everything."

"Of course." Nate scooped up their plates. "What are your plans now?"

"We're going shopping," Ashley spoke quickly, before Joanna could say something different. "I need clothes."

"And no doubt Joanna needs books." Nate glanced at her and Ashley thought, *He knows her.*

"Yes, books."

"Greg has asked around, and there is no sign of any reporters or photographers in town. So you're good to wander around if you feel like it. Come back here for lunch if you get hungry. The shrimp salad is good." He paused. "No one is going to bother you, Jo. Not with Greg around, ready to uphold the law, and Mel with that temper of hers."

He called her Jo, Ashley thought. Not Joanna. Jo.

Joanna looked directly at him. "And what about you? What do you bring to this protection detail?"

"I don't know." Nate smiled. "Macadamia cookies?"

That *smile*.

Ashley decided that if Nate was just a little younger, and she wasn't secretly in love with Jon, she would have dated him herself.

The smile wasn't lost on Joanna, either, if the flush on her cheeks was anything to go by. She was normally so composed, but right now she looked like a flustered teenager.

So either that was because this was Nate, and she was finding it awkward, or because this was Nate, and she found him attractive.

It had to be weird, seeing someone you were once in love with. And it didn't seem as if they hated each other.

But Joanna had been loyal to Cliff for two decades.

Joanna thought relationships were too much trouble.

Joanna didn't want to date.

"We might be too busy shopping to make it for lunch," Ashley said, "but we'll be seeing you tomorrow evening for a barbecue. Mel invited us." And maybe, she thought, the best way to persuade Joanna to expand her social life was to ease her into it. A barbecue wasn't a date. But maybe it would turn into that?

What was the point of setting up a dating profile when a suitable candidate was right under your nose?

"Is that right?" Nate's gaze shifted to Joanna. "Then I look forward to catching up properly then." He waved away her offer of her card. "Breakfast is on the house. I'll see you tomorrow. Is a blue cheese burger still your favorite?"

"No," Joanna said. "I'm vegetarian."

Joanna wasn't vegetarian. Ashley had seen her eat meat. And fish.

"No problem. I make the best veggie burger you've ever tasted. See you tomorrow." He strolled to take an order from another table and Ashley gave Joanna a look.

"You're not vegetarian."

"I could be. I've been thinking about it."

"Well, that's good, because it looks as if you're eating a veggie burger tomorrow."

"Fine." Joanna gave Ashley an exasperated look. "Why are you smiling?"

"Because for the first time in months I don't feel totally crap. My tummy is full of pancakes, the sun is shining and I like your friends."

"Good. Because you'll be on your own with them tomorrow. I'm not going."

"Because of the veggie burger?"

"No! Not because of the veggie burger. Because…because—"

"Because you're scared. I know. I get it. But it's going to be great, Joanna. Once you get past that awkwardness, it's going to be fun."

"You don't know that."

"I do. These are good people. Whatever happened in the past, you used to enjoy being with them. I think you can enjoy being with them again. If I'm wrong, if you don't enjoy yourself, then you get to pick where we go next."

Joanna sighed. "All right."

Ashley smiled and finished the strawberries.

All she had to do now was make sure Joanna had fun.

15

Joanna

It felt strange to be back in Silver Point, walking along the pretty cobbled streets, gazing into shop windows, some familiar, some new. The old-fashioned candy store that Joanna had visited with her father had been replaced by a gallery, and there was a new coffee shop on the corner of Ocean Drive that hadn't been there when she left. But much of it was the same. There was the gift shop with its quirky window displays. Frozen Flavor, the ice cream parlor that she and Mel had frequented every week, still there and with the line stretching out of the door. Martinello's, the Italian bistro that had been in the same spot, run by the same family for three generations. People came and then fell in love with the area and stayed, and today it wasn't hard to see why. The early-morning mist had cleared, the sun shone and colorful blooms billowed from pots and window boxes. It was fairy-tale pretty, but Joanna found it almost impossible to relax.

When Ashley paused to admire a pair of earrings in a window, Joanna checked over her shoulder. It was a habit that was hard to break, particularly knowing the story that was brewing.

They'd come. She knew they'd come. But that wasn't the thought uppermost in her mind.

"Do you think the blue ones are pretty?" Ashley pointed at a pair of delicate earrings and Joanna tried to focus.

"Very pretty. You should have them." Was Nate feeling unsettled, too? Had he felt the same way she had? It was unnerving to feel anything at all after twenty years. Why would that happen? Was it nostalgia? Memories?

It had surprised her to see him there, running the place. He'd had plans. Ambitions. A lust for travel. She hadn't thought he'd end up running the family restaurant. She hadn't thought the Surf Café and Silver Point would be enough. She'd been even more surprised to discover that Mel was working there, too. When she was young, she'd had other plans.

But wasn't that true of all of them?

It was obvious now that Nate hadn't told his twin sister anything about the ending of their relationship. And maybe that wasn't such a surprise. Nate had always been protective of their relationship. *I just want you to know,* he'd told her once, *that what happens between us is between us. I'd never talk about it with anyone.* By "anyone," he'd meant Mel, his twin, and Joanna had liked that because it had made what they had special. It meant that there was a part of Nate that was hers and no one else's. But she could see now that by not being truthful about the breakup, he'd caused Mel pain.

"I'm going to look around first, in case I see something I like more. I have a strict budget, so I need to make sure I spend it well." Ashley glanced at her. "Are you okay?"

"I'm fine."

"You look a little freaked out. Are you stressing about someone seeing us and calling the press?"

"I'm not stressed." She didn't add that having sat on the deck in full view of the world for several hours, it was almost inevitable that someone would call the press. "Why don't I buy these for you? My treat."

"No, but thank you." Ashley gave a determined smile. "You're already giving me support and a place to stay. It's enough."

"Consider it a loan if that helps. When you're back on your feet, you can pay me back." She had no intention of asking for the money back, but if it made Ashley feel better, then it was worth saying.

"That's kind, but I still want to make sure I've seen everything." True to her word she proceeded to explore every store in town, lingering over sparkly earrings, trying on clothes, salivating over a pair of shoes.

Joanna hovered close by, looking out of the window and thinking about Nate.

She thought about the moment when she'd walked into the office and slammed straight into him.

The shock of that unexpected physical contact had almost had her running out of the door. Only the knowledge that Ashley needed her kept her from leaving.

She'd tried not to panic at the powerful response that engulfed her. She'd told herself it was shock, but she knew it wasn't shock. She told herself that it was anxiety or lack of food—but she knew it was neither of those things, either.

Sexual attraction.

It had been so long since she'd felt it that she was surprised she even recognized it. But it turned out it was a sensation that you didn't forget. Fortunately it was a sensation you could also hide and she was confident she'd made it through her first meeting with Nate without making a total fool of herself. It was normal that she'd think about the past, and what they'd once shared together. It meant nothing, and neither did the warmth of his smile.

Nate had always been an amiable, friendly guy. He smiled at everyone. Made everyone around him feel comfortable and important.

Yes, she'd felt something when she saw him again but she wouldn't be doing anything to encourage those feelings. She wouldn't be exploring where they might take her.

No matter how much Ashley tried to persuade her, she wouldn't be dating. She wouldn't be scanning photographs and bios on the internet, pondering over guys who claimed to like long walks in the country and movie nights. She wasn't going to be dreaming of romance. She didn't want romance. She'd be content with peace and quiet and a life that didn't involve being followed around by people with cameras.

"There it is—" Ashley grabbed her arm and pointed to the boutique Mel mentioned. "Can we go there?"

"Of course." Maybe Ashley's enthusiasm would distract her. And inside a store it was less likely that anyone would spot them.

Joanna pushed open the door and Ashley gave a murmur of appreciation as she saw the neatly stacked shelves and racks of clothes.

"Welcome!" A woman appeared from the back of the store. She was the epitome of style. She wore high heels, a fitted dress in a flattering shade of blue and her hair fell past her shoulders in carefully curated waves. "If you need any help, or you can't find something in your size, just let me know and I'll— Joanna?" She moved closer, scanned Joanna's face carefully and then smiled. "Joanna! It *is* you."

Joanna froze. It was inevitable that someone would recognize her, but she'd hoped it would be later rather than sooner. "Rosa. How are you?"

"I'm good! I had no idea you were in town."

"I haven't publicized it."

"Of course you haven't. Why would you?" Rosa rolled her eyes in acknowledgment of the challenges. "Well, I for one am glad you're home."

Home? Did Silver Point feel like home?

"Thank you, Rosa." Joanna remembered her manners. "This is Ashley. She's staying with me." She watched Rosa closely, waiting for her reaction, but Rosa's face didn't change.

"Good to meet you, Ashley. I hope you find something perfect. Are you looking for beachwear? Something more formal? I have some gorgeous pieces that came in just this morning. The fitting room is at the back if you'd like to try things." She turned back to Joanna. "So are you back here permanently? What you've done to Otter's Nest is astonishing. That living area with the glass—"

"You've been there?"

"Yes. A few times. A couple of people who rented it asked me to bring a selection of clothes up to the place."

Ashley made a sound. "They couldn't walk to the store?"

Rosa's smile widened. "Apparently not. They wanted the store to come to them. Anyway, you're welcome to browse and—" She broke off, her gaze fixed on the street outside. "Go into the fitting room. Now."

Joanna frowned. "But I don't—"

"Go." Rosa thrust two dresses into her hand and gave Joanna a push. "You, too, Ashley. Go! And don't come out until I tell you it's safe."

Safe?

Joanna opened her mouth to question her but then saw what Rosa had seen. A man with a camera, strolling down the street. She'd developed a sense for these things and knew he wasn't a tourist, so she followed Rosa's instructions and headed to the back of the store and into the fitting room. Ashley followed her.

"What's going on?"

Joanna pressed her fingers to her lips just as they heard the sound of the door opening and the bell rang out.

"Welcome!" Rosa's voice was clear and strong. "Can I help?"

"Maybe. Nice place you have here." The man's voice was deep and low.

Joanna's heart hammered harder. She recognized that voice. Mick Jennings. He worked as a freelance photographer and had sold his work to all the big newspapers and online sites. It was Mick who had taken that photo of her at Cliff's funeral. Mick who had once tailed her car so closely that she'd driven into a lamppost.

She hated him.

Had he seen her? Had he followed her into the store or was this just bad luck? Could it be a coincidence?

"I'm looking to buy something special for my wife." His voice carried and Joanna frowned.

Mick Jennings didn't have a wife.

"How thoughtful." Rosa was charming. Interested. "What's the occasion?"

"Anniversary."

"Oh, my favorite occasion of all. I love an anniversary," Rosa said. "So you're looking for a gift that is going to express your devotion. It's a gesture of love. Tell me about her and I can make some suggestions."

Mick cleared his throat. "What can I say? She has expensive tastes. But I guess you're used to that around here. You have some pretty notable residents in Silver Point."

Joanna closed her eyes. Notable residents. His presence wasn't a coincidence. He was here for her.

Why had she thought shopping was a good idea?

There was no rear entrance to this boutique, which basically meant she was trapped.

"Yes, we have notable residents," Rosa said. "Have you considered a new purse? You can't go wrong with that. Let me show you a selection—"

"Thanks. I'm interested in your most notable resident. I'm guessing you know who I mean."

"Of course. She's famous around here. A local celebrity. This one is jeweled—" there was a pause "—it's perfect for evening.

Not cheap, but you're celebrating an anniversary so presumably your message is that you love your wife?"

"I love her more than life. I'll take the purse. So tell me more about this resident."

"She was born here. Everyone knows her."

Joanna held her breath. This was what she'd been afraid of. She'd encountered this same situation before. Stories about her often cited "a source close to Joanna."

"You know where she lives?"

"Yes. Halfway down Ocean in the little cottage with the blue door. There was quite the fuss when she painted that door blue, but Elsa refused to budge. She went straight to the mayor's house and let the air out of his tires. You'll find the community divided on *that* particular incident."

"Elsa?"

Elsa? Joanna opened her eyes.

"Yes. Elsa Martin. One hundred and one years old. The oldest resident in Silver Point. Still does a yoga class on the beach most mornings. Did you know she's writing a novel? Is that why you're interested in her? Do you work in publishing? I happen to know she's partial to cheesecake if you wanted to charm her."

"It's not Elsa I was thinking of, although she sounds like a character. I was thinking of Joanna Whitman."

"Joanna—? Oh, *Joanna*. Right. Are you taking that bag?"

"Yes."

"Good choice. I know your wife's going to love it. That will be nine hundred and fifty dollars."

"How much?"

"It's a bargain, don't you think? I gave you a discount because you have a nice face and I like a man who knows how to spoil a woman. Your wife is going to know she's loved. Do you want it gift wrapped?"

"I—yes, I suppose so. Have you seen her in town?"

"Your wife? I don't know her, but I'm sure she's a woman with great taste."

"Joanna Whitman."

"Joanna? Here? Goodness, no. She moved on two decades ago. She's more the Hollywood type now, but I'm sure you know that. Red carpets. Paparazzi. I see her on TV. Does your wife like earrings? We had some beautiful ones in this morning and it's never too soon to start thinking about Christmas."

"I'm not thinking about Christmas. You grew up here and so did Joanna. You're about the same age. Did you know her? What was she like when she was young?"

"Did I know her? It depends how you define 'know.' I saw her around. She was a year older than me so we didn't hang with the same crowd. Silver Point isn't as small as you might think."

Joanna smiled. It was exactly as small as he probably thought.

Rosa was still talking. "Here's your purse. I hope your wife loves it."

"Her stepmother lives up the coast, I believe. Do you know where exactly? I might talk to her."

"Well, good luck with that. I'm told her memory has gone. That must be the cruelest thing, don't you think? Forgetting? Confusing facts? Are you sure I can't interest you in earrings? You'll be glad when it gets to December and you don't have to find something."

"I'll worry about that in December. Can you direct me to Otter's Nest?"

"Otter's Nest? It's decades since I went there. You head south. Take the third turn to the left. Or is it the fourth? I never remember. But if you head down the coast you can't miss it."

Joanna smiled. If he followed Rosa's directions, he was going to miss it.

"I enjoyed meeting you," Rosa said. "Come back soon."

"Here's my card. If you happen to see Joanna in town, will you call?"

There was a pause, presumably as Rosa read the card. "Mick. You're a photographer. Well, of course you are. I thought that the moment I saw that fancy camera hanging around your neck. Everyone else just uses their phones these days, don't they? I hate having my photo taken. I'm not sure I have a good side. Any tips?"

"If you see Joanna Whitman and give me a call, I'll give you a photo shoot for free."

"Thank you, Mick." There was a sound of rustling and then footsteps as Rosa guided her customer to the door. "I had an uncle called Mick. Died at fifty-two of a heart attack. His wife blamed the cheeseburgers. You take care now. Drive carefully. These roads are busy in the summer."

Joanna heard the door open and close and breathed again. She'd forgotten how clever Rosa was. She'd ripped the man off to the tune of almost a thousand dollars and she still hadn't told him anything.

She felt ashamed for having doubted her. Ashamed that she'd allowed herself to lose faith in people.

There was a tap on the door and when Joanna opened it Rosa was standing there smiling broadly.

"A temporary reprieve, but hopefully better than nothing. And once you head south there's no place to turn for ages. Let's hope he loses interest."

Joanna wanted to hug her. The reprieve might be brief, but she'd take anything. "I can't thank you enough."

"Hey, I still owe you for covering for me that time." She turned to Ashley. "I was sixteen. Drank my first vodka shots and was so sick and dizzy I couldn't walk straight. Joanna dragged me to a safe place on the beach, called my parents to say I was staying over with her and proceeded to take care of me until morning. Then she told everyone I'd eaten bad shellfish. No one was any the wiser."

Joanna remembered it. Remembered feeling envious at the concern in Rosa's dad's voice, his gratitude that she was safe with Joanna. Her stepmother hadn't cared where she was or who she was with. She hadn't even noticed that Joanna hadn't come home and had slept on the beach. "That was a long time ago."

"When someone helps you out, you remember it. You're still part of this community, Joanna. Don't you forget that."

She had forgotten it. Or maybe she hadn't truly been aware of it.

"Thank you."

Rosa grinned. "I'm the one who should be thanking you. That man just shelled out close to a thousand dollars on a gift for a woman who doesn't exist."

"You knew she didn't exist?"

Rosa pulled a face. "Who would marry a creep like him?"

Joanna looked at the woman who had once been a friend. "I married Cliff."

Rosa shrugged. "Hey, don't be so hard on yourself. Cliff was easy on the eye and he could cook. That's two damn good reasons to hang around with a guy." She stepped back and eyed Joanna. "While you're standing here, can I bring you a few things to try on? Not that I'm pushing for another sale, but seeing you in black and white the whole time seems like a wasted opportunity. With that hair of yours, you should be wearing bold colors."

"I agree," Ashley said. "My suggestions? Red. Green."

Joanna shook her head. "I prefer not to draw attention."

"You are an icon of strength and decency—we should attach a flashing light to your head." Rosa vanished and appeared a few moments later armed with clothes. "Try these."

It was an hour before they left the store, and when they did they were loaded down with purchases.

"Thanks again, Rosa." Joanna paused in the doorway as Rosa peered out and checked the street.

"The coast is clear. Hope we'll see you again soon, Joanna. You've seen Mel and Nate?"

"Yes."

Rosa met her gaze. "You take care. Come back soon."

"I like her," Ashley said as they left the store. "And that green dress she talked you into is gorgeous."

"It's going to have a very boring life because I don't go anywhere."

"You can wear it to the barbecue tomorrow. I can't believe you left this place. The people are so friendly."

Joanna thought about Nate. She thought about Cliff. "I wasn't in a good place when I left." She'd wanted to put it all behind her. She'd shared so much with Ashley, but she hadn't shared the detail of that day with her. With anyone.

"Because you'd broken up with Nate, and because you didn't have a good relationship with your stepmother. That's tough."

The three worst days of her life had been losing her baby, losing her father and the last time she'd seen her stepmother.

Was she going to visit Denise?

The question had been niggling in the back of her brain since she arrived here.

To take her mind off Denise she tried to imagine Cliff staying in Otter's Nest as it had been then. He was a man who had enjoyed his creature comforts. The sight of a rickety beach house would have had him booking a room at the nearest five-star hotel within minutes. "There wasn't a reason to come back."

"Well, everyone seems pleased that you have. Oh, look! The Beach Bookstore. Is that the place you wanted to work?" Ashley caught her arm. "It's so pretty. Like something out of a movie."

"Yes." Joanna felt a rush of nostalgia. "It was my favorite place when I was growing up. This place was a sanctuary for me. I used to come here after school and stay until they closed the doors." Anything rather than go home. "I stepped through those doors and all my stress fell away. I liked the way the books looked on the shelves, rows and rows of color and possibility. All those stories. All those worlds that weren't mine. I loved the way the place smelled. I loved the quietness and the way people looked when they browsed. I liked the way Vivian, the owner, would push a book into another person's hand and say, *Try this*. I used to watch her, and wonder how she knew exactly what a person would enjoy. It was a gift." She hadn't thought about those days in a while, but now she was remembering. "She let me read whatever I wanted to. She'd let me take them home. I was grateful, but at the time I didn't think much of it. It was only later that I realized how much money I must have been losing her."

"She sounds like a good person."

"She was. Is." And Mel had mentioned that she was struggling with arthritis. "I used to tell her that one day I was going to apply for a job at the store and work right beside her. It was my dream."

"And what did she say?"

"She said she'd give me a job anytime I wanted one." Joanna felt a lump in her throat. "She believed in me, at a time when I didn't believe in myself."

"So if it was your dream, why didn't you do it?"

"I left Silver Point."

"You could have got a job in a different bookstore?"

"I already had a full-time job. It was called Cliff." She'd fallen into the role by accident, without even questioning it. He'd needed her help, she'd helped. "I was his personal assistant, his performance coach, his psychologist and his own personal cheerleader. I had to taste all his new creations."

"At least that part must have been fun."

"It wasn't. I'd take a mouthful and he'd be watching my expression. There were times when I just wanted to eat a meal and not have to think about giving a full review." She'd never admitted it to anyone before. "With Cliff, everything was a performance. Theater."

"He's the reason you don't cook?"

Joanna frowned. "I don't cook because I'm not good at it. I burn things."

"Which means you have the heat too high. Anyone can cook basic food," Ashley said. "All it takes is practice and confidence."

"I have no confidence."

"Probably because you were married to a top chef. I'm sure I wouldn't be able to boil an egg in front of a celebrity chef."

Joanna thought about Denise. "I had no confidence before that, either."

Ashley looked at her thoughtfully. "Let's buy some food and we can cook together tonight."

"You want me to cook with you? You have a death wish?"

"No. I'm going to show you that cooking can be simple and fun."

"Cooking isn't fun. Cooking is torture and a way to make me feel really, *really* bad about myself." Thinking about it made her heart rate speed up. *Oh, this was ridiculous.* "We can't all be good at everything. I've accepted I'll never be a cook."

"You mean other people convinced you that you'll never be a cook. That makes me really snarly." Ashley sent her a pleading look. "Would you just try it with *me*?"

"Ashley—"

"I know you've always hated cooking, but you've never tried cooking with me."

"Who I do it with won't make a difference. It's the cooking part I hate."

Ashley tapped her chin thoughtfully. "You see, I don't think it is. I think it's the way people make you feel when you cook. And we are going to have fun. I promise."

Fun?

"Seriously, Ashley, I don't think—"

"Just one time," Ashley wheedled and coaxed. "If you don't smile once, I promise I will never ask you to cook again." She looked so hopeful that Joanna couldn't bring herself to say no.

"All right, fine. But don't blame me when it ruins a beautiful friendship."

Ashley smiled. "You're right. We do have a beautiful friendship and nothing is going to ruin that. Great. I'm excited. Not that I can cook anything fancy. My mom taught me. Basic stuff, but I was interested so I've learned a few things myself. I'm guessing your stepmother never taught you."

"No. She said I was a disaster in the kitchen."

"And then along came Cliff—no wonder you have no confidence." Ashley studied her. "What's your favorite food?"

"I don't know. I associate food with stress and tension."

"It's why you're so slim. Okay, let me think…" Ashley wrinkled her nose. "We're going to make a basic pasta sauce. Start there. Then tomorrow, we'll do something different."

"If I cook, there will be no tomorrow."

Ashley laughed. "I'll take the risk. Now we're going to go into the bookstore."

Joanna was about to resist but then she thought, *Why not?*

If she was going to revisit her past, she might as well revisit all of it.

16

Ashley

Ashley placed onion and garlic on the chopping board and handed Joanna the knife.

Joanna shook her head. "Cliff always said my knife skills are terrible. I'm slow, and everything is uneven."

"It's an onion, Joanna. You just need to chop it. It doesn't matter if you're slow, and it doesn't matter if the pieces are uneven. No one is going to be measuring them. The only thing that matters is that you don't chop your finger off."

Joanna picked up the knife with a glum expression. "Fine." She peeled the onion awkwardly and then cut it in half. "Cliff could chop an onion so fast you couldn't even see the knife moving."

If Cliff hadn't already been dead, Ashley would have said a few choice words to him. "That's a party trick. When you're watching a movie do you care how many takes a scene took? No. You just care about the end product. Food is the same. When we're eating this sauce, we're not going to care how quickly you chopped the onion. While you do that, I'm going to pick some oregano from the pots outside." Was it safe to leave Joanna? Just how bad was she with a knife?

Ashley lingered in the kitchen long enough to satisfy herself that Joanna wasn't going to chop her finger off and then walked onto the terrace to pick the herbs she wanted.

She paused for a moment. Breathed in the scent of flowers and salt air. Heard the crash of the waves on the rocks beyond the garden. Was there a more idyllic spot in the whole world?

Mindful that she shouldn't leave Joanna for too long, she picked a bunch of oregano and thyme and headed back into the kitchen.

Joanna was looking doubtfully at the small mound on the chopping board. "I've finished the onion but the pieces are too big."

"They're fine, but if you want them smaller just make a few more cuts with your knife." Ashley resisted the temptation to take over. "Maybe use a bigger knife."

Joanna selected a bigger knife and chopped gingerly. "Now what?"

"Heat the olive oil in the pan, and gently fry those onions until they start to soften and brown a little at the edges. While you're doing that, you can chop the garlic."

"I don't put the garlic in at the same time?"

"You can if you want to, just don't burn it. You have a good herb garden." She rinsed the herbs and handed the bunch to Joanna. "Pull the leaves off and we're going to add it to our sauce."

"If I don't watch the onion it will burn. Trust me."

"You have the heat too high. Turn it down."

Step by step, side by side, they made the sauce, adding herbs and garlic, chopping fresh tomatoes, letting the whole lot simmer.

Joanna stirred the sauce. "You did this with your mother?"

"Yes. She thought it was important that I learn to cook, and once I'd mastered the basics and a few recipes, we took it in turns."

"She sounds like a wise woman. You're lucky."

"It's generous of you to say that, considering everything. And it helps me to acknowledge the good stuff." Ashley thought about all the times she'd cooked side by side with her mother and was grateful for the positive memory. Lately all her memories of her mother had been linked with Cliff. "I've been feeling so angry with her, and pretty confused. And that makes me feel guilty."

"I don't think you should feel guilty. She kept a big secret from you. It's natural that you would feel hurt and upset about it. It doesn't mean you didn't love her. It doesn't mean she didn't have plenty of wonderful qualities."

"You said you'd tell me about Cliff—"

Joanna stopped stirring. "I will, but do you mind if we do that another time? If I think about Cliff now, I won't be able to cook."

"It can wait," Ashley said quickly. "We need to boil the water ready for the pasta now."

"I never know exactly when it's cooked."

"That's easy—I'll show you. Use a big pan—plenty of water." Ashley couldn't believe that no one had taught Joanna any of this. She'd been married to a top chef for two decades. "Did Cliff cook for you all the time?"

"Not all the time." Joanna measured the pasta carefully. "Whenever we had guests for dinner, because of course they all wanted him to cook. When he was experimenting with new recipes. The rest of the time we ate in restaurants."

"Didn't you ever just eat a grilled cheese sandwich?"

"No. But it sounds like heaven. Is it difficult to make?"

"No. That's going to be our next lesson. Let's make a salad to go alongside our pasta." She saw Joanna's tension and decided to change the subject. "I liked Mary-Lou. Did she really once put a frog in your stepmother's purse?"

"Yes." Joanna didn't take her eyes off the sauce. "But Denise thought I'd done it, so I didn't find it as funny as everyone else."

Ashley felt a pang. "It must have been hard. I'm so angry with my mom right now, but at least I felt loved."

"Some of it was my fault." Joanna tipped the pasta into the boiling water. "I grew up with just a dad until I was eight years old. It was the two of us against the world. I guess it was easier that I never knew my mother. He talked about her all the time, and I felt as if I knew her, but I'd never had her in my life. I missed the thought of her, rather than the actual person. And then he met Denise. I was young. Insecure. I'd never had to share my father with anyone. I guess she felt the same way. She wanted him all to herself." It was a raw, emotional confession and Ashley felt humbled hearing it. Joanna hid herself from everyone and yet here she was revealing herself to Ashley. Sharing her deepest secrets, exposing the layers of her life that no one saw.

She desperately wanted to say something wise and comforting, but she had no idea what that was.

"Denise was the adult." In the end she just said what she thought. "You were a child and being faced with a change like that must have been unsettling. She should have been more understanding."

"Maybe. He was going to divorce her. I heard them fighting about it—my father was a really mild, calm man, but he was yelling at her. Telling her that he couldn't be with someone who didn't love his daughter. That he'd made a mistake. That it was over. Is that boiling too fast?" Joanna stared at the pan while Ashley struggled to digest what she'd just heard.

This was *huge*. Had Joanna even told anyone that before?

"The water is fine." Ashley swallowed. "And what did she say?"

"That it wasn't her fault. That I was a difficult child."

Ashley forgot about the sauce and the pasta. She wrapped her arms around Joanna. "That's horrible. Unforgivable."

"My father thought so, too. He went kind of red in the face.

He put his hand on his chest. Made a funny sound. And then he collapsed. Fell to the floor." Joanna stared at the pan. "I once saw a tree being felled in the forest and it was exactly like that. I'm ruining the pasta. I told you I couldn't cook."

"You *can* cook. You *have* cooked." Ashley let go of her, turned off the sauce and turned down the pasta. Her hand was shaking. "What happened then?"

"He broke a chair." Joanna paused to breathe. "I rushed into the room. I was screaming, *Daddy, Daddy*, and Denise pushed me away. She shoved me, hard."

"I hate her." Ashley clenched her hands into fists. "I've never even met her, but I already hate her." And she was never, ever moaning about her life again. What she was handling was nothing compared to what Joanna had handled. Nothing.

"She said it was my fault. That he'd got into a state because of me."

Oh God, oh God, could it get any worse?

"But you knew that wasn't true, right? Tell me you knew that wasn't true."

"For years I thought it was. I carried that."

"It's like she…she—" Ashley floundered "—stabbed you with words. And that wound stayed with you."

"Yes, but at the time all I cared about was that my dad had collapsed. The one person I loved, heart and soul. The one person who loved me, heart and soul."

Ashley felt tears almost choke her, but she swallowed them down and blinked hard. If she sobbed into the pasta, as she wanted to, then Joanna would feel she had to comfort her and she was the one who needed to comfort Joanna.

"It wasn't your fault, Joanna. None of it was your fault." She echoed the words Joanna had said to her.

"I grabbed the phone and called for help, but by the time they came it was too late. He was gone."

He was gone.

So much emotion in just three words.

Ashley felt an ache in her chest. "I'm sorry. So sorry."

"I wouldn't let go of him. They had to peel me away. Should we drain the pasta now?"

Ashley had a clear image of young Joanna clinging to the body of her dead father. She couldn't think about pasta.

She had to think about pasta! It was important for this meal to be perfect.

"Sure." Her voice hardly worked. "Let's do that."

They drained the pasta, mixed it with the sauce and then served it into bowls.

"You can add fresh basil." It was surreal to be talking about basil and losing a loved one in the same breath. But maybe it was those small things that helped you endure the big. Cook another meal. Greet another morning. Add fresh basil to pasta. *One step at a time.* "Just tear the leaves."

Joanna reached for the pot. Her fingers shook a little as she shredded the leaves and scattered them. "It smells good. But that's because you made it."

"You made it, Joanna. I did nothing."

"You told me what to do." Joanna reached out and touched her arm. "You didn't run out on me even when I told you things that would make most people of your age dive for cover."

"I'm not diving for cover. Just as you didn't dive for cover when I was desperate." Crap, if she got through this meal without sobbing into her pasta it would be a miracle. "You can cook, Joanna, don't ever let anyone tell you otherwise."

"Because you stood next to me."

"And I'll stand next to you when you make a grilled cheese sandwich. And when I teach you to make my lemon risotto. You haven't lived until you taste my risotto. Shall we take this onto the terrace?" She scooped up the salad and a bowl of freshly grated parmesan, and took a deep breath of salty air. She'd felt guilty that Joanna was doing so much for her, sacrificing so much, and now she felt a warm feeling because she knew she was helping Joanna, too.

Joanna had trusted her enough to talk to her. Joanna had treated her like a friend.

She watched as Joanna placed a bowl of beautifully presented pasta in front of her.

"Wow. That looks incredible."

"It does, doesn't it?" Joanna stared at the food in front of her with surprise and something close to wonder. "I think it's possibly the first thing I've ever made that doesn't have charred edges. Thank you."

"You made it."

Ashley felt a warm glow spread all the way through her.

She was going to teach Joanna to cook. She was going to give her confidence.

Joanna sat down, but didn't touch her food. "She didn't even cry. My stepmother. She didn't cry. Not a tear. That made it worse somehow."

"Yes. It would."

"We should stop talking about this."

"Why? It's fine to talk about anything we want to talk about. Do you think she was in shock or something? When my mom died I felt so weird. A bit disconnected. It was nothing like I thought it would be."

"Maybe. You're right that grief doesn't always behave the way we think it will, but at the time I took it as confirmation that she didn't love him. And I still wonder sometimes whether she did. I don't know." Joanna poked at the pasta. "I told her I hated her. It was a cruel thing to say."

Ashley put her fork down. How could she possibly eat? "You'd just lost your dad and she was behaving like an evil b—" *language, Ashley* "—person. She wasn't helping you. It was an understandable thing to say."

"I thought things couldn't get worse, but they did. He'd changed his will a few weeks earlier, I suppose because he knew he was going to ask for a divorce. He left Otter's Nest to me. He left Denise a small amount of money, but it was the house she wanted. She blamed me for the fact that she didn't inherit the house."

"Which gave her more reasons to dislike you. But still, you lived there together."

"She was still married to my father when he died. We were family, even though neither of us wanted it." Joanna stared at her. "You're not eating. Is it my food?"

"No. It's the story you're telling me. It's actually making me feel a little sick."

"Me, too." Joanna gave a wan smile. "I shouldn't have mentioned it. I never have before."

"Not to anyone?"

"Mel and Nate. We were very close."

But then she'd lost them, too. Joanna had lost everyone.

No wonder she'd gone with Cliff.

"You can talk about it with me anytime. But you'd probably rather forget it."

"That's what I thought, but talking it out with you has helped. And I have decisions to make," Joanna said. "I need to decide whether to visit my stepmother, Denise."

Ashley was about to voice an opinion—*a strong opinion*—but then stopped herself. People should make their own decisions, shouldn't they? "Do you want to?"

"No. But I feel as if it might give me closure."

"If you go, I'll come with you. If you want me to, obviously."

"You'd do that?"

"Of course."

"Thank you." Joanna ate a little more pasta and so did Ashley.

"You didn't have her support or love, but you had the love of the community."

"Yes. I suppose I did." Joanna finished her pasta. "That's enough about me. Let's talk about you for a change."

"Let's do that another time. For now I suggest ice cream. Ice cream always helps, and then we need to plan what you're going to wear tomorrow." Distraction, she thought. That was the key. "I was thinking definitely the green dress with those silver earrings."

"I haven't been to a casual backyard barbecue in so long I have no idea what's appropriate."

"The green dress is appropriate."

Joanna sighed. "You want me to wear it for Nate."

"No." Ashley shook her head. "I want you to wear it for you. Because it made you smile when you saw your reflection in the mirror. Because you liked yourself in it—"

"That's true. I did."

"And because you haven't put yourself first, and done what you want to do, in a long time."

There was a long pause. "That could also be true."

"So you'll wear it?"

"Yes. I'll wear it."

Joanna wore the dress, although she kept fiddling with the fabric as they walked from the beach house to the car the following evening.

"I feel conspicuous. I don't know why I bought it. We were shopping for you, not me. I didn't need a dress."

Yes, you did. "Well, when you see something as perfect as that one, why not? That boutique had some cool stuff. And I loved Rosa." She'd bought some shorts for herself, a couple of sundresses that had room for expansion and a swimsuit. But she'd been more excited about joining forces with Rosa and nudging Joanna away from her usual clothing choice that blended into the background. As well as the green dress, they'd persuaded her to buy two more dresses, a pair of shorts, two tops and a bikini. "You said you hadn't been shopping in a while, so how do you buy clothes?" She slid into the car alongside Joanna.

"Online. Or I have someone deliver a selection to the house."

"Where's the fun in that?"

"I don't find shopping fun. It's a necessity. Clothes are worn for a purpose, to send a message."

What did her clothes say about her? "I've never thought of it like that. I choose clothes that are comfortable and make me feel good. Sometimes just because they make me feel good. What if you don't like what they bring?"

"I give them a brief."

And Ashley was in no doubt what the brief was. No color. Blend. "But then you miss out on surprise. Something catching your eye. Something that might be fun to wear."

Joanna drove toward town, turned off Main Street and followed the road toward the beach. "I don't think of clothes as fun."

"Be honest—once Rosa brought us all those clothes to try, you enjoyed yourself."

"It was a refreshing change to be out doing normal things." Joanna parked in front of a pretty cottage with colorful borders and fruit trees. "This is it."

"Cute." Ashley waited. "If this is it, why are we still sitting in the car?"

"It feels strange. This was Mel's dream house. We used to walk past it on the way to school and she'd say, *One day I'm going to live there with Greg.*"

"She's obviously a woman who knows what she wants."

"Unlike me." Joanna was still holding the wheel, her knuckles white. "I don't know what I'm doing here."

"You're spending an evening with old friends." And the next step was to peel Joanna from the safety of the car. She opened the door. "I've got the wine. Will you bring our swimming gear?"

She stepped out of the car as a golden ball of fur came bounding from the garden at the back of the house. It skidded to a halt, tail wagging so hard it was taking half its body with it, and Ashley grinned. "I guess you're friendly." She crouched down, held out her hand and then laughed when the dog leaped and knocked her over.

"Bess!" Nate was a few seconds behind the dog. "Remember your training? Any of it? All that fun we had with sit and stay? I'm sorry. She's friendly. Just likes to put her full body weight behind her greetings."

"I see that." Ashley, flat on her back under the dog, couldn't stop laughing. She hadn't laughed this hard since before her mother died.

"Also young. The family who owned her couldn't cope with her energy levels so I took her. Training is a work in progress. I'm telling myself it's because I didn't have her from a pup, and not because she's not trainable." Nate gave the dog a tug and a severe look. "Sit."

Bess gave him a piteous look, as if questioning why she would want to do anything so boring.

Ashley scrambled to her feet while Nate tried to persuade the dog to obey.

"Sit. I'm begging you."

Ashley grinned. "I'm not sure who is in charge, but I don't think it's you."

"She's covered your shorts in paw marks."

"I don't care. Back home I used to volunteer at the animal shelter. I came home with more fur on me than the dogs." She leaned down and fussed the dog. She wanted a dog of her own badly. Maybe one day. Did dogs and babies go together? She didn't know. There was so much she didn't know. So much to think about. "You're beautiful."

"Don't tell her that. She doesn't need more encouragement."

"Is she a Labrador?"

"There's some Lab in her, maybe a few other things—when she leaps I sometimes wonder if she's half kangaroo, perhaps a little goat even—but she's gentle, and smart. She had her own way in her last home but I'm hoping she'll learn to follow the rules with me." He held the dog tightly and then turned his head as Joanna emerged from the car.

Ashley was relieved to see her. She'd started to wonder if Joanna was going to wait for her to close the door and then head straight home.

"Hey there." Nate stood up and gave her an easy smile, keeping a tight hold on Bess's collar. "We were having some issues with the intensity of the greeting, but it's all under control now, which is good because I don't want her to think it's all right to knock visitors flat. Greg already has food on the grill. I hope you're hungry. It's simple stuff—" he glanced at Joanna, checking "—nothing gourmet."

"Sounds perfect."

They walked around to the back of the house and Ashley saw the pretty borders, a stretch of lawn and a gate with a path beyond that presumably led to the beach. She could hear the sounds of the waves in the distance and the shriek of children playing.

Her chest ached.

I want this, she thought. *One day I want this. A home of my own, by the sea.*

She was never going to have anything as breathtaking as Otter's Nest but this, or a smaller version of this, would be the dream.

Mel appeared. "Joanna! You look gorgeous." She hesitated briefly and then hugged Joanna first and then Ashley.

Ashley hugged her back, relieved. "Thanks for inviting me."

It could have been awkward, but it seemed Mel was putting the past behind them.

"I'm glad you both came. You already know Greg. Eden was supposed to be here, but she's been surfing and she's not back yet." She glanced over her shoulder, frustrated, and Ashley felt sympathy for Eden. How many times had her mother given her that exact same look? Adults forgot what it was like to be a teenager. They told you to grow up, but then they often treated you like a child, wanting to control your every movement.

Now, of course, she'd give anything for even one more day of being nagged at by her mother but at the time it had driven her to screaming pitch.

"I'm here!" A girl pushed her way through the gate and jogged across the grass. She was wearing a wet suit and her hair was damp around her shoulders. "Sorry. Lost track of time."

Mel let out a sigh. "You need to shower, change and—"

"I know I need to shower and change! I'm not six years old. On a good day I can even dress myself, Mom." The flash of irritation in Eden's eyes faded as she turned to Joanna. "Hi—" She gave Joanna a friendly smile and then glanced at Ashley. "I recognize you from the picture on TV. Also, there's loads of stuff about you today on the internet, and—"

"Eden!" Mel looked embarrassed. "Apologize."

"For what?" Eden rolled her eyes, but she looked embarrassed, too. "Sorry. I didn't know I wasn't supposed to mention it. It's everywhere, so I thought—sorry."

Ashley felt awkward. "It's totally fine. I mean, it's not fine, obviously, it's crap—" she sent Joanna an apologetic look "—but it is what it is."

Bess bounded over at that moment, followed by Nate.

"Drinks? What can I get you?"

Ashley decided that the friction between Eden and Mel wasn't going to make for a comfortable evening and she was desperate for this to work out. Joanna needed to spend time with Mel and Nate, didn't she?

She saw the surfboards propped against the wall and glanced at Eden. "You surf?"

"Since I was five years old. My dad taught me."

"That's cool. Can you get to the beach from here?"

"Through the gate." Eden hesitated. Met her gaze. "Do you want to take a look? I can show you."

"I'd love that, if it's okay with you."

"It's more than okay." Eden's tension eased. "Give me five minutes to shower and change."

She emerged exactly five minutes later. She was wearing shorts and a bright blue T-shirt, and her hair was still wet from the shower.

With Mel's request that they be back in time to eat ringing in their ears, they headed to the gate.

"Sorry about my mom." Eden pushed open the gate. "She can be a bit intense. Like everything has to be *exactly* the way she wants it. No one is allowed free will. At least, I'm not."

"I get it. That's a mother-daughter thing." Ashley glanced at Eden. "Your mom was kind to me yesterday. She was the one who helped me. Did she tell you?"

"She hasn't told me anything, but we didn't see each other yesterday." Eden closed the gate behind her. "Helped you how?"

"You saw the pictures. Read what they wrote about me. I was trying to leave Silver Point. I didn't want to make things worse for Joanna, so I thought that was best. I was feeling pretty low." She still couldn't believe she'd gone from there to here. "I was standing on Main Street trying to figure out what to do when Mel spotted me. She called your dad and he picked me up and took me to the Surf Café. Then they called Joanna."

"I didn't know that. But Mom and I don't talk much about anything at the moment."

"Your mom and Joanna were best friends once, did you know that?"

Eden shrugged. "She mentioned it sometimes whenever there was a new story on Joanna. Joanna used to date my uncle Nate, which is kind of weird to be honest. But it was a long time ago. They broke up. I don't know the details."

It was difficult, she knew, to see your parents as individual beings with a whole life history of their own.

They'd reached the sand and Ashley pulled off her shoes and lifted her face to the sun for a moment. She glanced at Eden. "Joanna was nervous about coming tonight."

"Because of Uncle Nate?"

"I don't know. Maybe." She curled her toes into the soft sand. "There was something yesterday—"

"Something?" Eden glanced at her and then shrugged. "You don't have to tell me. It's okay."

"I want to." She knew instinctively that she could trust Eden and it was bliss to talk to someone her own age. "Before I saw them together I had the sense it was a bad breakup. I mean, she doesn't like to talk about him. But then I saw them together and wham—it was like a movie."

Eden grinned. "I'm listening."

"It was probably nothing. Maybe twenty years is too long to hold on to bad feeling."

"Maybe. Or maybe it was something." Eden looked thoughtful. "My mom once told me she was really shocked when they broke up. Joanna went off with Cliff the same day—not that I'm an expert, but that seems like rebound to me."

"Me, too."

"But Joanna came tonight—so that must mean something, too. If she'd wanted to avoid him, she wouldn't be here, would she?"

Ashley gazed at the ocean. "She didn't want to accept, but your mom was persistent."

"That sounds like Mom." Eden pulled a face. "She has set ideas about what's best for everyone, and life's usually easier if you go along with it. If you don't—" she shrugged "—don't expect an easy life. She tells me it's time to be an adult, but then she tries to make all my decisions for me. It's only okay for me to make my own decisions if she approves of them. Is your mom the same?"

"My mom is dead."

"Crap." Eden raised her hand in a gesture of apology. "Me and my big mouth again. I'm sorry."

"It's okay. And I get it." Ashley thought about her own mother and all those years she'd kept the secret of Cliff. She'd said she'd done what she thought was best for Ashley, but was that really true or was she doing what was best for her? The question nagged at her. "I really do get it."

Eden frowned. "You do?"

"Yes. My mother made decisions that she thought were best for me, and I don't think they were. You know about Cliff Whitman. You know I'm his daughter." What was the point in holding back when Eden had probably already read it all online? "I always knew my dad wasn't my biological dad. My mother was straight about that. But whenever I asked for more details she just said it didn't matter, that it had meant nothing, just a wild moment on her part. But she'd never give me a name, which seemed odd to me because why not?" She was surprised by how much it all still hurt. "She thought it was best if I didn't know. And maybe she was right, but I don't think so."

"So if she didn't tell you, how did you find out?"

"She got sick. Money was tight…" Her stomach knotted. Money was almost nonexistent and that was something she still had to think about. But not yet. She couldn't do it yet. "She contacted Cliff again to try and make him take responsibility, although I don't know why she thought he would."

Eden made a derisive sound. "If he hadn't done it at the beginning, why do it at the end?"

"Right. She was desperate. And he didn't want to know, of course. And that was when she told me. Just before she died—" She broke off and felt Eden's hand on her arm.

"I'm sorry that happened to you. I'm sorry you're going through this now. It's total shit."

"Yeah." Her throat was clogged and for a horrible moment she thought she was going to cry in front of this girl she didn't even know, but then the tide of grief receded and she could breathe again. "I was pretty messed up."

"Of course. Anyone would be."

"And I was angry." Ashley breathed. "And confused. When she told me, I shouted at her." It killed her to remember it. "I actually shouted."

"My mom and I shout. It's a pretty normal thing, and you had reason to be upset." Eden paused. "Also, you were probably scared that she was so sick. That would make anyone shout."

She hadn't thought of it like that. "I was scared. Terrified. I wanted to know why she hadn't told me before, and she was crying and sobbing that she'd done what she thought was best, and I felt so bad I just said, *Forget it, let's forget it, it doesn't matter.*"

"But it did matter," the other girl said quietly. "And you couldn't forget it. That's why you went to LA?"

"Yes. At first I couldn't think of anything except the fact that my mom was dead, but eventually I went to find him. To confront him." And because Eden was the first person she'd talked to about it apart from Joanna, she spilled everything and Eden listened without interrupting, her eyes fixed on Ashley's face as she relived every moment of that night and the days that followed. And when she finally stopped talking, Eden took a breath.

"You climbed into his car. You confronted him. That's—"

"A risky thing to do?"

"I was going to say ballsy." Eden grinned. "Seriously ballsy."

Ashley hadn't felt the least bit like smiling, but now she was smiling, too. "You think so?"

"Oh, yes. You stood up. You didn't let him hide. I hope I would have had the courage to do the same. I'm just sorry it all turned out the way it did and he didn't help you. Is it true that you're pregnant?"

"Yes."

"Can you feel it?" Eden gave her a curious look and then blushed. "Sorry. That was rude. It's just that I've never known anyone pregnant before."

"Not rude. And no, I can't feel it. Not yet. The baby is another thing I have to figure out. I'm postponing the moment. I had all these plans, and now I have no plans."

"What were you going to do?"

"I had a college place. I wanted to do computer science. I wanted to design games." It seemed so far away now. "That was my dream, but when Mom got sick I couldn't leave her. And now I don't have the money, and also there's the baby—" It felt overwhelming and she took a deep breath. "Life doesn't turn out the way you plan it, but that doesn't mean it can't be good, does it? It's just a change in direction. And there's no law that says dreams can't change."

Eden gave her a long look, a strange expression on her face. "I guess."

"How about you?"

"I don't know. I don't know what I want." Eden paused. "Mom wants me to go to college, obviously."

"Which means you're tempted to do the opposite?" Ashley grinned and so did Eden.

"Sounds about right. And talking of my mother, we should get back or she'll have a heart attack. Also, Bess might eat our burgers." Eden took her arm and tugged her back toward the path.

They reached the gate.

Eden glanced across the garden to where Joanna was standing with Mel. "She's nothing like the stories make her out to be."

"I know. It's like the media invented this whole person. And because she never defends herself or says anything, people think she's weak, but she's the strongest person I've met. Quiet can be strong, that's something I've learned. And she's been kind to me."

"Is it weird? Knowing your mom—"

"Slept with her husband? Yes. At the beginning I kept wanting to apologize, but now..." Ashley shrugged. "It wasn't my fault. It wasn't Joanna's fault. That's why I left. I didn't want her to have more to deal with because of me. And I'm glad we're not leaving. She likes it here, I know she does. I just hope your parents, Nate and Joanna can fix things."

Eden tilted her head. "I guess it was complicated, with mom and Nate being twins. They're different, of course, but they're very close. Mom adores Nate, and Joanna just dumping him like that must have been hard."

Dumping him? Ashley frowned. "What?"

"Think about it—one minute they've been together their whole lives and then Joanna just leaves with a guy she only just met. Mom was pretty destroyed by it and you can see why. Her best friend ditches her brother in a pretty crappy way and doesn't even talk to her about it. Who do you support? How do you support both?" Eden shrugged. "Nightmare situation. I don't know what I would have done, do you?"

"But...that's not what happened. It was Nate who dumped Joanna. One minute they've been together forever and they're an item, and the next he's kissing some blonde in front of her." Ashley blurted out her defense of Joanna and then realized that this was Eden, and that Eden was Mel's daughter and she probably shouldn't have said anything.

Eden was staring at her. "He what?"

"Nothing. Forget it." Ashley felt her face burn. "I shouldn't have said anything."

"Yeah, you should. Kissing a blonde? That's the truth? He broke up with her?" Eden let out a puff of breath. "My mom thinks the fault was all Joanna's."

"Don't say anything."

"Maybe Joanna will tell her."

"Maybe."

Ashley watched as Joanna smiled at something Mel said. Whatever they were talking about, it didn't seem to be confrontational. It seemed Mel wasn't the only one who had decided to put the past behind them for tonight at least. "Do you think they'll get back together?"

"Joanna and Nate?" Eden frowned. "I doubt it. I mean, if it was going to work they would never have broken up, would they?"

"I don't know. People can change. I know Joanna is only here because Mel and I pushed her."

"Maybe Joanna would find it difficult to forgive Nate. And look, she and Nate aren't even chatting." Eden gazed across the lawn. "He's helping my dad with the food, and Joanna is talking to my mom."

Ashley watched. "Do you think we should—no. We shouldn't."

Eden considered. "Or maybe we should."

Ashley looked at her. "Engineer it so that they're together?"

"Why not?"

"Because we shouldn't interfere?"

"Adults interfere with our lives all the time. I don't see why we can't do the same in reverse. And we wouldn't exactly be interfering. We'd be creating an opportunity for them to talk. What they do with it is up to them."

Ashley grinned. "You're good."

"I wish my mom thought so." Eden pushed through the gate. "Let's do this."

17

Joanna

"That was about as subtle as a kick in the butt." Nate held open the gate that led to the beach. "I apologize for my family. I hope they didn't embarrass you."

"I have more experience with embarrassment than anyone in California. It would take more than a little well-meaning manipulation to embarrass me." Joanna picked her way along the sandy path that led from Mel and Greg's house to the beach.

She wasn't even sure how she'd got here. One minute she'd been talking to Eden and Ashley and the next they'd been suggesting a walk on the beach and now here she was. Alone with Nate. It should have felt awkward but it didn't, and that surprised her. It felt less awkward to be with him than it had with Mel. Her conversation with her old friend had been polite, but stilted. Was that Mel's fault or hers? Would that change if she shared the truth of her breakup with Nate? It seemed childish somehow, to be raking up the past. So much time had elapsed. Did the truth even matter anymore?

But she knew that the past was something they needed to address.

Long grass brushed at her bare thighs and she heard the constant roll and crash of surf on sand. When they were young they'd done this every day of their lives. Walked to the beach. Played on the sand. Swam in the sea. Laughed. It seemed so long ago.

"This brings back memories."

He glanced at her. "Good ones?"

"Of course." And then it occurred to her that although she wasn't feeling awkward, he might be. "I'm sorry they put you in this position. We can go back anytime you like."

"You mean being alone together? I'm not. I've been trying to figure out how we could get some time to talk privately, and they made it easy."

Talk? What was there to talk about?

He probably wanted to get the awkwardness out of the way so that they could coexist in Silver Point in relative harmony, but did she really want that conversation? She'd thought she did, but now she wasn't sure.

"You don't have to feel awkward about me being here, Nate. The thing between us was a long time ago." They'd promised each other forever, but it turned out that his idea of forever had been a lot shorter than hers.

And now with the benefit of time, age and experience, she saw how naive they'd both been. How different the world looked when you were an adult.

"Mind your step here, the path is uneven." He held out his hand but she ignored it and stepped carefully over the hole in the ground he'd indicated.

She didn't want to hold his hand. She'd made herself a few promises when she'd been smoothing color onto her cheeks in her bathroom and trying to create a "knockout effortless" look as Ashley called it. She'd promised herself that she wasn't going to talk about anything serious, and she definitely wasn't going to touch him.

It was harder than she'd thought it would be. This new Nate

was unfamiliar and yet at the same time achingly familiar. His eyes still crinkled at the corners when he smiled. He had the same way of laughing, the same way of looking at her when she was talking.

Unsettled, she kept her eyes fixed on the long blue horizon.

"Greg and Mel have a beautiful home. And Eden is so like Mel."

Nate laughed. "Don't tell either of them that if you want to stay alive."

"They clash?" She thought about what she knew about Mel, and the limited time she'd been able to observe Eden. "Yes, I can see how they would. They both say what they think."

"Fortunately they have Greg to step between them when it becomes necessary. Mel has strong views about what she should be doing with her life. She's raised Eden to think for herself and be independent—"

"And now she's doing that, and Mel doesn't like the outcome? It must be hard, worrying about your child who is no longer a child."

He glanced at her. "That's the funny thing about being on the edge of adulthood, isn't it? You think you know everything. You think you're sure and you have the whole world figured out. No one can tell you anything, and anyway, what do they know? And by the time you realize you didn't have it all figured out, and there was plenty you didn't know, it's too late to fix it and you just have to keep going and make the best of things."

Was he talking about his own life or hers? Or neither?

"I'm not sure I'll ever have life figured out. And maybe that's a good thing. If your life plan is too rigid it's harder to let it go." When did life ever go according to plan? Rarely. "Control is an illusion, isn't it?"

"Mostly, although we're human and part of being human is to believe that we get to control our destiny."

They'd reached the beach now and she slid off her shoes and left them by the path.

Would people recognize her? Hopefully not.

Joanna Whitman wore black and white and her hair and face were almost always partially shaded by a hat.

Joanna Rafferty wore her hair loose over a floaty, eye-catching green dress.

She didn't feel like herself, so maybe she didn't look like herself, either.

The setting sun glowed orange against a sky that was rose gold and red. She stared out across the ocean, past the plunge and tumble of the waves, past the sea spray and the sparkle, to the horizon.

"There's nothing more beautiful than a Californian sunset." She walked toward the water's edge and he walked next to her, just as they'd done so many times when they were young. It felt so familiar her fingers almost sneaked toward his.

He was obviously thinking the same thing because he stopped and looked at her, a strange expression in his eyes. "Joanna Rafferty."

She didn't correct him because that was how she felt.

Tonight, she was Joanna Rafferty.

Her heart was thudding. "Is this the point where you tell me I haven't changed?"

"You've changed. So have I. Life does that, doesn't it? It shapes you, the same way it shapes this coastline. You're the same, but different." He slid his hands into his pockets, as if he didn't trust himself not to touch her, and she felt a moment of disappointment closely followed by confusion because why would she want him to touch her? Didn't she already have enough complication in her life?

"How am I different?"

"You're wary. Guarded, although no one is going to blame

you for that. I'm guessing it's hard to know who to trust in your life."

She'd discovered that early on. She'd trusted, and been let down. She'd had expectations of people and been disappointed. "The safest and simplest way is to trust no one."

"Is that what you did?"

"Until recently, yes." She thought of Nessa, and now Ashley. She thought of Mel, Greg and Nate. Rosa handling the photographer. Mary-Lou in the Beach Bookstore treating her like a long-lost sister. Trust could be lost, but it could also be won again. "I didn't even question the way I was living. It became normal."

"No one should have to live like that."

"Thanks to Ashley, I'm rethinking." She told him about Rosa and the photographer and he listened carefully, the way Nate had always listened, as if every word she spoke was important. And when she finished he smiled.

"I heard about that. The guy was last seen heading south."

"You know?"

"This is Silver Point. Rosa put out the word so that people were aware. She said he was asking intrusive questions."

"He was," Joanna said. "It's his right, I suppose."

"Just as it's our right to refuse to answer them. We used to swim here. Do you remember?"

"Yes." She remembered all of it, including what had happened afterward.

His mouth. His hands. His body.

"Can I tempt you?"

"Excuse me?" Just four words—*can I tempt you*—and now her body felt hot and she couldn't breathe properly.

"Into the water for a swim."

Strip to her swimsuit, leave her dress on the sand and dip in the sea with him? Watch him strip off his shirt right next to her?

Something they'd done all the time growing up now took on new meaning.

"I don't think so."

It was obvious from the look he gave her that he knew exactly why she was refusing and the memories hovered right there between them, almost visible to the naked eye.

He smiled. "Let's walk, then."

They walked along the shoreline in the direction of Otter's Nest.

It was the first time she'd done this. "It feels strange. Being back. It feels like home, and yet not like home."

"I don't know how you stayed away for twenty years. You weren't tempted to come back sooner?"

"It was complicated." In some ways staying away had been easier than coming back. She paused and picked up a shell. "How about you? You stayed in Silver Point?"

"I went to college. Then I came back."

What had happened to his plans to travel and see the world? All those things he'd said he needed to do. She could have been hurt, but she wasn't.

Feelings were feelings. You either felt them or you didn't. She understood that now. Reasoning, excuses, desire—none of that was relevant.

"I thought you'd be married with kids." They'd talked about it once, when they were both too young to appreciate how complicated life could be.

"No kids. Married once—" he volunteered that freely "—took us four years to admit we'd both made a mistake."

She should have done the same, she knew that now. She should have admitted her mistake much earlier, instead of always trying to make excuses, make the best of things. She should have said, *I deserve more than this*, and set about getting it. But sometimes it was easier to accept what you had than take the steps needed to change things.

"I'm sorry it didn't work out for you. That's tough."

"Not as tough as it could have been. The feelings didn't run deep enough for either of us, which doesn't make for a great marriage but does make for an easier separation. We both felt the same way, untangled what we'd made, parted company and still speak occasionally." He stooped and picked up a shell. Its pearly surface gleamed. "Now it's your turn."

"Are you expecting me to reveal my own romantic past?" She stopped walking, too. "Because mine is in the public domain. I'm sure you've read all about it."

When things had first gone wrong with Cliff, she'd thought about Nate. When you were in a difficult situation, the mind played tricks. It showed you other images, options that seemed to have been a better choice, but Joanna had trained herself not to go there. She'd been careful not to polish and shine the past. But it was impossible not to think about it now. *What if?*

"I know what I've read. I'm sure I don't know the truth. I'd like to hear it, if you're willing to talk. If you'd rather not, that's fine, too." He walked away from the water and sat down on the sand.

She joined him.

"I've missed this. I've missed sitting on the sand early in the morning and late in the evening and just watching the ocean." She saw the light dance, the surface of the water change color.

"It's the best view there is. I couldn't live without it." Nate's arm brushed lightly against hers. "Someone who loves the ocean as much as you do must have struggled being in a city for two decades. Didn't you miss it?"

Joanna stared across the water. "I didn't mind it at first. It was a new life. We were building the business." She'd still believed that her relationship with Cliff was something solid and dependable. She'd still believed that they had a future.

"Were you in love?" His tone was raw and stripped away some of her own defenses.

She could have told him to mind his own business. That he had no right to ask her that question. But she didn't know how not to be honest with Nate.

"Was I in love? Not in the way I'd loved before—" she couldn't bring herself to say, *Not in the way I'd loved you* "—but I didn't expect that." *I didn't think I could have that.* It was hard to articulate just how low her self-esteem had been at that point, how her confidence had been eroded by everything that had gone before, from losing her father, to her difficult relationship with her stepmother and then Nate's rejection, and how all that had formed the foundation for her relationship with Cliff.

Looking back on it now, it all made so much sense. She'd been beating herself up for her decisions and the choices she'd made, but taken in context they weren't so hard to understand.

She'd spent so many hours believing that she'd made a bad choice, but the truth was that she'd made the right choice at the time. Cliff had been what she needed. Exactly what she'd needed.

In that instant she forgave herself and in doing so discovered that when you stopped beating yourself up for decisions you'd made when you were doing your best and trying to survive, you felt a lot better.

She felt a sense of peace and acceptance that she hadn't felt before. A certain sympathy for the woman she'd been then, and everything she'd had to face, and also pride because no matter what life had thrown at her she'd found a way through.

She thought about Ashley. *A failure? Are you kidding? You're a survivor. An inspiration.*

Her marriage to Cliff had been complicated, but in the beginning at least there had been friendship and hope. Love? She wasn't sure. Cliff had been there for her at the lowest point of her life, when she'd been bruised and vulnerable. She hadn't felt lovable, and yet he'd loved her in his own way. It hadn't been the kind of wild, romantic love she'd shared with Nate, but given the way that had ended, she'd been more than happy to consign that depth of emotion and all the emotional bruises that came with it to the past.

Cliff had been a friend to her, and in return she'd been a friend to him.

Nate rubbed sand from the surface of the shell and then glanced at her. "You're saying I put you off love?"

In a way he had. "I was young. I didn't know what to do with all those feelings when you—"

"When I ended it. I didn't mean for you to leave, Joanna. Not for one moment did I think you'd leave."

She remembered the way she'd felt when Nate had kissed Whitney. She'd decided right then that she didn't want to live her life watching Nate kiss his way through a succession of other women and pretending that she didn't care. Maybe if they'd lived in a city it would have been different. They could have led separate lives, their movements rarely intersecting, but here in Silver Point where everyone knew everyone, she'd be caught in a web of emotional connections.

She hadn't wanted to have to wear her brave face every day, and she hadn't wanted people feeling sorry for her. She'd wanted to start again. She'd wanted to wipe the past where she'd been Joanna-and-Nate and redesign herself as Joanna. She couldn't imagine how to do that. She hadn't known how to hear a joke and not laugh with him, how to see something beautiful and not share it with him. He'd been there for every one of the low points in her life, but then he'd become her low point and she'd had to find a way to get through it on her own.

"For me there was no other way. If Cliff hadn't come along when he did, I would have left, anyway." And maybe what she'd felt for Cliff wasn't love in the way she'd known love, but she'd been happier, felt safer, with the simpler friendship she and Cliff shared.

"I'm sorry you felt you needed a new life." He hesitated. "Joanna—"

"We don't need to talk about it, Nate." She turned her head and smiled at him. "It's all in the past."

"What if I want to? What if there are things I need to say? Would you listen?"

Would she? There had been a time when she'd dreamed about having the chance to have it out with him. *Whitney? Really, Nate?* How could she be everything to him one minute and nothing the next? So many questions and no answers, but eventually she'd realized that answers weren't going to change the facts.

"I don't see the point. It's been twenty years."

"Yes. And some people might decide that's a long time, too long to worry about what happened. But not me. I promised myself years ago that if I ever got the chance, then I'd say all the things I wished I'd said that night." Maturity had brought with it a quiet confidence. He was a man who knew what he wanted and wasn't afraid to go for it.

Her heart beat a little faster. "Friendships go wrong. It's a fact of life."

"We both know that what we had was so much more than friendship. And I wrecked it. That was down to me."

Twenty years ago she would have agreed, but now she knew life wasn't so simple.

"People change. Circumstances change. There's nothing to talk about. You wanted to end it. We didn't want the same thing, and at the time I struggled with that—" she'd been heartbroken "—but it's not a crime, Nate. Not loving someone enough isn't a crime."

"Maybe not, but I handled it in a crass, insensitive way. And it wasn't that I didn't love you enough. More that I didn't trust that love." He rubbed his fingers across his forehead and pulled a face. "I still can't think about what happened without wanting to crawl under a stone."

"At the time I would happily have pushed you under the stone myself, but time changes perspective." And it calmed inflamed emotions. "There probably wasn't a good way. Although seeing you kissing Whitney an hour after breaking up with me was a low point."

"Yes. For me, too. And for her—" He glanced at her. "She wasn't amused."

"No?"

"No. Because at first she thought I was cheating on you, and when I told her I'd just ended it she thought I was using her to send you a message. She was wrong about that—" he stared at the horizon "—it wasn't something I thought through. I was conflicted, miserable that I'd broken up with you, unsure I'd done the right thing, and I was trying to live this new life I'd chosen for myself. Trying it on for size to see how it felt."

"And how did it feel?"

"Empty. Strange." He paused. "If it helps, it was a year until I kissed another woman after Whitney."

That made her smile. "Nate, you were at college. Do you seriously expect me to believe you had no sex life?"

"For that first year? No. I threw myself into the work and the sport."

"And then?"

He smiled. "It's your turn. Tell me about you."

What was there to tell?

She'd only ever been with two men. One of them was dead, and the other was sitting close to her, his knee brushing up against hers.

"You know what happened to me. I met Cliff that same night."

"I blamed myself for that, too. You went with him because I'd broken your heart."

"Partly, but not entirely. There were reasons I went with him that night, and you were only one of them." It was her turn to tell the truth. "It wasn't a rebound affair, at least not at first. He was kind. He gave me a way out. I took it."

"There were other reasons?"

"Yes. I had—" what should she call it? "—an encounter with Denise after I saw you."

"You mean a fight?"

"No, not really. That requires two people, and she was the one who did the talking." She'd tried to put that episode out of her mind. "After I saw you with Whitney, I was upset. I was a mess. I had no one to turn to. Normally when something was wrong I turned to you, but in this case—"

"I was the problem."

"Yes. And I didn't feel it was fair to confide in Mel. It felt as if I'd be forcing her to pick sides. So I went home and I shut myself in my room. My stepmother came in. She wanted to know what was wrong. Normally I wouldn't have told her. We didn't have that kind of relationship. But I was upset, and she was there, so I told her and—" She paused, feeling the pain of it even after so many years.

"Knowing Denise, I'm guessing she wasn't sympathetic."

"Worse. She said she wasn't surprised you'd ended it with me. That I wasn't an easy person to love. *Unlovable*—she used the word over and over. She said that if I had been easier to love, then maybe her relationship with me would have been better. She accused me of destroying her relationship with my father. Without me, they'd still be together. She thought my broken heart was karma."

Nate threw the shell back into the ocean. "She was a cruel, vicious woman."

"Yes. But when you're feeling vulnerable it's easy to believe bad things. Her words soaked in. Unlovable—that's what I took from that day, and when I dragged myself to work in the café that night, it was how I felt." She'd wondered if people could see it in her as she walked around taking orders and clearing tables. She felt as if it was stamped on her forehead. *Unlovable.*

"And then there was Cliff, with all his money and charm."

"He paid me attention when I'd all but decided that I deserved none. He gave me a way out. I hadn't even known I wanted a way out at that point, but when he asked me to go with him it felt like a fresh start. The thought of staying in Silver Point and seeing you all the time—I couldn't do it. Nor did I want to go home. My stepmother was there and I didn't want to speak to her again. Living there with her was unbearable. I hated it as much as she did. I knew we couldn't share the same space."

"She had a responsibility toward you. You shouldn't have been the one to leave."

"I needed to." She watched as a couple walked hand in hand along the shoreline.

"Can I ask you a question?"

What could he ask that she hadn't already been asked by someone else, probably a stranger? "Yes."

"I know better than to believe everything I read, but—" He looked at her. "Did he make you happy?"

Once, she would have found that question difficult to answer, but talking it through with him had given her a clarity that had been missing for her over the years.

"He was what I needed," she said finally. "Were we happy all the time? No. But there were good times." It was easy to forget those and focus only on the bad. Easy to hold on to anger and hurt. Regret. Too easy, sometimes, to view her marriage through the eyes of others.

Cliff had been far from perfect, but she hadn't been perfect, either. She'd held part of herself back. She'd been afraid to give freely in case what she gave was rejected, afraid to be open in case that made her vulnerable.

"And now you're taking care of Ashley. Is that strange? Sorry—" He lifted his hand by way of apology. "None of my business."

She laughed and he looked at her again.

"What's funny?"

"You asking me if I'm taking care of Ashley. If anything, she's the one taking care of me."

"You mean because she left to protect you?"

"Not just that." She thought about Ashley teaching her to cook, patiently adjusting the heat to stop Joanna burning everything. She thought about Ashley urging her to try on dresses she wouldn't have touched had she been by herself. Ashley, offering her dating advice and offering to go with her to see Denise. "She makes me want more from my life. She makes me feel I could have more."

They sat quietly on the sand, side by side, watching the waves roll in and then retreat. Over and over again.

"You like her."

"Very much."

"She's lucky to have you in her corner. Lucky that you haven't lost your kindness, despite everything. What are your long-term plans?"

"We haven't figured that part out yet." In her head she had. The idea had been simmering for a few days but yesterday she'd been sure. She knew what she wanted. But what did Ashley want? They still hadn't talked about it. "We're taking this a day at a time. When she experiences firsthand the media feeding frenzy I attract, she might decide she doesn't want to be part of it."

"She didn't seem to care too much about that. Her feelings and concern were all for you."

Thinking about Ashley made her realize they'd been gone for too long. "We should get back." She scrambled to her feet and brushed sand from her legs. "They'll be wondering where we are."

"Wondering, maybe. But not worried. I'm glad we did this. It's good to finally get to talk."

"Yes." Her heart beat a little faster and she chose to ignore it.

"Can we do it again?"

"Do what again?"

"Spend time together." He paused. "Before anything else, we were friends. I'd like that again. Would you?"

"You want us to be friends?" Was that possible? She was feeling something, that was sure, but was it new or a shadow of the old? Of course, it was natural to look back and be curious about what might have been. But looking forward to what could be? When it came to Nate, she'd always have a weakness. But was that a problem?

"Right now I'm taking life a day at a time."

"As you're taking life a day at a time, what are your plans for tomorrow? It's my day off. Do you want to swim? I could bring a picnic."

They'd reached the path and he waited while she slid on her sandals, taking her time while she thought. Did she want to swim? Did she want to sit on a picnic rug and share food with this man who had once had her whole heart?

Maybe she did.

If she was going to stay here, live here, make the place her home, then she didn't want to hide from any part of it.

"I can't do tomorrow. I have plans with Ashley." She could see he didn't believe her. "She's teaching me to cook. Tomorrow is grilled cheese sandwich. The day after that is chicken—or maybe risotto. I can't remember. Ashley is in charge."

"Chicken? I thought you were vegetarian."

She smiled. "Sometimes."

"So…grilled cheese? Why?" He looked confused. "You've been married to a top chef for two decades."

"Precisely. I crave food that doesn't expect applause when it arrives at the table, and I want to learn to make it myself. Ashley is teaching me." An idea came to her. "Give me a few days to practice a few dishes, and then you can come to dinner. The question is, are you brave enough to say yes?"

"Yes." He didn't hesitate and she smiled.

"I'll let you know when. We can eat and swim from the beach, like we used to."

"Sounds good. Do you have your phone?"

"Yes. Why?"

"Because you're going to need my number for when you invite me to dinner."

She pulled out her phone, unlocked it and handed it over so that he could add himself to her contacts.

She had a feeling Ashley would be proud of her.

She was going to invite him on a date.

She was going to swim with him. She was going to cook for him. She was going to be his friend.

Did that make her brave or foolish?

She didn't know, but no doubt she'd find out soon enough.

18

Mel

"That was a success." Mel waved until Joanna's car was out of sight. "Nowhere near as awkward as I thought it would be. And Nate was warm and friendly. Can't have been easy. I'm sure a part of him is still hurt. Joanna ended their relationship very suddenly and then left with Cliff. You're probably thinking it was a long time ago, but when you're young these things can have a lasting impact. Why are you staring at me?"

"Er—maybe because that wasn't what happened?" Eden grabbed Bess to stop her chasing after the car.

"It happened." Mel tugged up a couple of weeds that had appeared on her front border. "I was here. I lived through it. But we're all putting it behind us, and that's good."

"Oh, for—" Eden shook her head in frustration. "You are always so convinced that your interpretation of everything is right, it doesn't enter your head that you could be wrong. Well, news flash. You're not always right, Mom!"

Mel glanced up and saw the fire in Eden's eyes and the lift of her chin. She wished, not for the first time, that her daughter was less like her. That rip of temper. That stubborn streak.

What had she done to attract Eden's anger this time? She had no idea.

"I don't always think I'm right, but I'm right about this." Mel tugged a weed out of the ground, harder than was necessary. She'd had a pleasant evening chatting with Joanna. It hadn't been as easy and comfortable as it had been growing up, but she'd enjoyed herself despite that. And now the evening was still warm. The scents from her border were intoxicating. She'd been feeling mellow, but that wasn't going to last if the conversation with Eden carried on.

"You see? You have to have the last word. You are *not* right. It wasn't Joanna who dumped Nate. It was the other way around."

"You know nothing about it, Eden." Mel gave up on the weeds. Mellow was giving way to irritable.

"No? Have you actually ever asked Joanna what happened?"

"I don't need to. I know what happened."

"You *think* you know. Ask her, Mom. Ask her what really happened, and then get ready to apologize."

A few years ago she'd been worried about how she'd handle Eden leaving the nest. Right now she was ready to push her out.

"Eden—"

"Uncle Nate dumped her. That's what happened. He dumped her." Her voice rose and Bess gave a little whine, not knowing what was wrong but sure that something was. "And she was so upset about the whole thing she left town with that guy. Cliff."

"That isn't true."

"Yeah, it's true. Ashley told me. She didn't mean to, but I'm glad she did because it reminded me again to always question what I think I know."

Mel ignored the less than subtle dig. Her heart thudded hard. Could it be true? No. Nate wouldn't have lied to her. But he hadn't actually talked about it, had he? He'd always refused. And if he was the one who had broken up with Joanna, it would explain why Joanna had looked so confused when Mel had demanded an apology. A hideous, uncomfortable feeling crawled through her insides. If Eden was right— "But if that's what happened, why wouldn't Joanna have called me?"

"I don't know." Eden rolled her eyes. "Maybe because you're so opinionated you're not that easy to talk to?"

Opinionated? Not easy to talk to?

She swallowed. Presumably, for Eden, this was no longer about Joanna.

"That's an unkind thing to say."

"Maybe." Eden had the grace to flush. "But it's the truth, even if it's difficult to hear."

It wasn't the truth. "If people are in trouble, I always listen."

"Yeah, but there are different types of listening."

"What's that supposed to mean?"

Eden shrugged. "There's the kind where you *actually* listen and hear, and then the kind where you listen and then rush in to offer solutions and judgment because you think you know what's best. You do the second sort. You have to fix things. It's like other people's problems are part of your to-do list and you want to tick them off."

Mel absorbed that blow. "If someone I love is in trouble, then yes, I'm going to try and help fix it. Is that a crime?"

"No, not a crime. But not helpful, either, because you can't fix someone else's life and sometimes all a person needs is to talk and express how they're feeling, but with you that's not allowed because you jump in with solutions."

But that was because she was trying to help. What was wrong with trying to help the people you loved?

"Joanna and I talked about everything. We were best friends." Her mouth felt dry. "If Nate had ended their relationship she would have told me."

"Well, she didn't. I can't explain that and I'm not going to try, because I'm not a mind reader and I have no idea what was in her head."

The implication being that Mel made assumptions.

Was that true?

She'd taken all the pieces and formed a picture in her head, but it was true that the pieces could also form a different picture.

Why hadn't that occurred to her before?

If Joanna hadn't already left she would have asked her straight out, but Joanna had gone, which left one other person who knew the truth.

Without saying anything else to Eden, Mel strode around the house to the garden at the back. Bess followed her, her tail wagging with a little less confidence than usual. Mel knew how she felt. She'd never felt so unsettled in her life. She felt shaky. A little beaten up by Eden's words. Later, she knew she'd need to indulge in some uncomfortable self-reflection but for now she just wanted to get to the truth.

Her husband and her brother were sprawled on the grass, beer in hand, deep in conversation.

"Greg?" The tone of her voice made him look up. "I need you to take a walk."

"A walk? Now?" He frowned and sat up. "I'm happy sitting here with—"

"You're going to take a walk on your own, and you're going to be gone for fifteen minutes."

"That's very specific. Why fifteen minutes?"

"Because that's how long it's going to take to say what I need to say to Nate and then calm down afterward."

Greg sighed and stood up.

"What?" Nate sat up. "You're seriously going to do what she says? What happened to brotherhood?"

"It takes second place to a little thing called marriage. Also, I call this de-escalation tactics."

"I call it cowardice," Nate muttered as he watched his friend retreat. Resigned to the inevitable, he turned his gaze onto his sister. "It seems you've got something to say."

"Too right I've got something to say. Several things. Stand up."

"Jeez, Mel—"

"Nate Monroe, you're going to stand up right now!"

He sighed and stood. "What?"

"I discovered an interesting fact tonight." She didn't say how or where she'd discovered it. She didn't want Eden in the middle of this. "About you and Joanna."

His expression turned wary. "Mel—"

"I never understood why she ghosted me. After everything we'd been through together, all those years, such a long friendship—I could never figure it out. She dumped you, but she also dumped *me*, and I couldn't make sense of that. Until today." She saw her brother's expression change. "You know what I'm going to say, don't you?"

"I can guess. Listen, Mel—"

"No, right now you're the one doing the listening." She stabbed him in the chest with her finger, then remembered that her hot temper was her downfall and reined it in. "And then you're going to be doing the explaining, but I'll let you know when we reach that part."

He backed away. "Mel—"

"*You* broke up with *her*? All these years you let me think she was the one who broke up with you, and it was the other way around, wasn't it?" She desperately wanted him to deny it, but he simply watched her and she wanted to groan and give herself a shake for not seeing the truth. "All these years I've been wondering what I'd done, and it turns out that I hadn't done anything—it was *all you*!" She was shaking with anger. "Why didn't you talk to me about it? Why didn't you tell me any of this?"

"Because it was my relationship. My business. Joanna's business. And you need to calm down. You're upsetting Bess—" He stooped, stroked and reassured the dog. "It's all right, girl. Your auntie Mel is angry, but you don't need to defend me."

"The way I feel right now, she may need to defend you. And normally I'd agree with you that your relationships are your business, but not on this occasion. Your relationship with Joanna was very much my business because she was my best friend, too. If I'd known the truth, I could have supported her but she pushed me away and I let her because I was so conflicted about the whole thing. I couldn't figure out how I could be friends with her, when she'd hurt you so badly. How could I sit and listen to her talking about you? It was complicated! But if I'd known the truth, it would have been straightforward. I would have been there for her."

Nate straightened. "I don't want to talk about this."

"But I want to, and you owe it to me. *Why*, Nate?"

Bess whined and he put his hand on her head.

"Why? Because I was eighteen and didn't know how to handle things." He glanced at something over her shoulder and Mel turned to see what had attracted his attention.

Greg stood there and she scowled. "I said fifteen minutes."

"They can hear you down on the beach, Mel. Possibly up in San Francisco if the wind is blowing in the right direction. You might want to take it down a notch." He sighed. "Ending a relationship is not a crime."

"No. But letting me throw my friendship under a bus because of it definitely should be. And you should stay out of this," Mel advised. "This is a twin thing."

"Actually, this is between Nate and Joanna," Greg said. "This isn't your problem, Mel."

"But that's just it—it *is* my problem." Why couldn't they both see that? They both had tunnel vision. "Joanna was my best friend. When she ended her relationship with Nate, she ended our friendship, too. I missed her. I missed her so much." She almost choked on the words. "But I lived with that because I thought she'd broken my brother's heart. I defended you, Nate! I was protective. Angry with her, and I've held on to some of that anger. A few days ago I yelled at her!"

Nate frowned. "You yelled at her?"

"Yes, and I *hate* myself for it. And I'm going to have to apologize for that and a lot of other things, but none of it would have happened if Nate had told me the truth from the beginning." She sank her hands into her hair, wishing desperately that she could wind the clock back. Wishing she could erase some of her worst character traits. "That was the night you kissed Whitney. I thought you were drowning your sorrows after Joanna ended it with you. You let me think that. Instead you wanted to let Joanna know it was over."

He winced visibly. "Kissing Whitney was a mistake."

"You think?" She looked at him in despair and frustration. "I always wondered why Joanna left with Cliff so suddenly and now I know. You made it impossible for her to stay—"

"That's not true. I never wanted her to leave. And I didn't know what was going to happen with Denise."

"Denise? What happened with Denise?"

"You don't know?"

"Why would I know? Thanks to you, Joanna doesn't confide in me anymore."

Nate ran his hand over the back of his neck. "Let's just say she wasn't supportive when she found out we'd broken up—"

"Stop, I can't hear this." Mel lifted her hands to her ears. "She had a fight with her stepmother and you didn't tell me that, either?"

"I only found that part out tonight."

Taken aback, Mel let her hands drop. "She told you? You talked about it tonight?"

"Yes, we talked about it."

"Well—good." Some of the fire vanished. "I hope she gave you hell."

"She didn't."

"She's too nice. She didn't have anyone, Nate. She was alone. She didn't talk to me because you were my brother and she thought I'd have divided loyalties." It killed her, thinking of how isolated Joanna must have felt. She'd been barely older than Eden.

Nate spread his hands. "What do you want me to say? You want to hear me admit that I screwed up? Yes, I screwed up. I knew that pretty much right away and I've known it for the past two decades."

"Why—why didn't you tell me the truth?"

He hesitated. "Because I was angry with myself, and I didn't want you to be angry with me, too. I didn't want to disappoint you. I'm your big brother, remember?"

"By four minutes."

"Also, you're so damn perfect and I wasn't sure you'd understand that even a person who means well can get it badly wrong."

"Perfect?" She almost choked on the word. "Me?"

"Yes, you. No matter what life throws at you, you cope. You always have the answers to everything. You never have doubts. You barrel through life with total confidence that you're right. You never screw up. I didn't need you to make me feel worse about it by telling me all the things I'd done wrong, and what I should do to fix it."

You're not that easy to talk to.

Mel felt her eyes fill. A lump settled in her throat. She flung herself at her brother and he raised his hands to defend himself and then realized it was a hug.

"I thought you were about to kill me on the spot." He pulled her closer. "Are you crying? Is drowning me your way of finishing me off? Don't, Mel—if you cry, then I'm never going to be able to forgive myself."

"I'm not perfect. I'm so far from perfect. I'm hot-tempered and impulsive and I think I know best about everything and I'm maddening and I'm a terrible listener, even though I try hard to listen, but you have to understand it's because I care so much and just can't bear anyone I love to be in trouble. I just want to fix things. And I know that seems controlling and it probably is but it comes from a place of love—"

"Hey, I know all this." He rubbed her back. "What is this all about? Are we still talking about Joanna?"

"I don't know." She pulled away and sniffed. "I'm sorry you felt you couldn't tell me. For the record, I love you even though you're flawed. Possibly more because of it."

He grinned and wiped her cheeks with the edge of his shirt. "Are we getting soppy now?"

"Maybe we are." She didn't feel able to smile back.

You're not that easy to talk to.

What if Eden found herself in trouble, as Joanna had? Who would she turn to?

Not Mel, if her comments had been anything to go on.

Did she know how much her mother cared? How much she loved her?

Obviously not, which meant she was a terrible mother.

Nate kept his hands on her shoulders. "So, are we good? Am I forgiven for totally messing up?"

This relationship at least she could fix.

"I'm glad you messed up. It makes you human and makes me feel slightly less bad about myself." She sniffed and Nate looked at Greg.

"Do you have the slightest idea what she's talking about?"

"No. But that's fine. I find it works sometimes to just accept things the way they are and not try and understand them." Greg held out his hand to Mel and she went straight to him.

The anger left her. Relationships ended, didn't they? It was a fact of life. And if the right feeling wasn't there, it wasn't there. But she'd thought that for Joanna and Nate it was.

"Maybe there never would have been an easy way," she conceded. "The four of us were so close it would have been difficult to find a way to recalibrate that. And it could have been us. Greg and me."

Greg pulled her closer. "No, it couldn't. I was gone from the moment I saw you do your first cartwheel on the beach. And you need me. You'd never get out of bed in the morning if I didn't rip the covers off."

"I hate that you rip the covers off."

"You sleep through the alarm if I don't."

"Does that annoy you?"

"No, it's adorable." His fingers stroked her arm. "I need you, too, by the way."

Mel felt a rush of gratitude. She'd never needed evidence of his love more than she did at that moment. "You don't think I'm a hot-tempered, interfering Miss Fix-it?"

"I do. And I love that about you."

"You do?" She kissed his cheek and Nate rolled his eyes.

"Not everyone has what you two have." He bent to give Bess a belly rub. "But for what it's worth, if I could change the way things happened, then I would. And I'm sorry it made things hard for you, Mel. I'm sorry that because of me you lost her, too."

Having confronted all her own flaws, she was ready to be forgiving about his.

"You were eighteen. Eighteen-year-old boys aren't known for their tact at handling delicate emotional situations." But now she was curious. "So you and Joanna talked about it? Did you apologize?"

Nate held up his hand. "Just because we discussed what happened twenty years ago doesn't mean I'm turning into a gossip. My conversations with Joanna are private."

She sighed. "I guess I love that about you, even if it is frustrating."

"Is everything okay here?" Eden appeared behind them and Mel turned.

How long had she been listening?

"Everything is fine. We've just been talking, that's all." And in a way she had Eden to thank for that. "Thank you for keeping Ashley company tonight."

"Of course. I like her." Eden looked wary. "We're going to hang out tomorrow. Can I borrow your car? She doesn't drive, and she doesn't want to bother Joanna because she's already done so much for her."

Mel's heart bumped. Not that she believed anything of what she'd read online, but Ashley *was* pregnant. Ashley wouldn't be going to college. Eden was so impressionable.

But she was also sensible. *Was she? Was she sensible?*

Either way, she couldn't protect her forever, could she? She was her mother, not her keeper. Her job was to support her, not control her.

It didn't matter whether her concern came from a place of love or not, she had to start trusting her daughter to make good choices.

"You can borrow my car," she said. "We'll drive up to Otter's Nest together and I can spend time with Joanna while you and Eden go wherever you want to go."

"Cool. Thanks, Mom." Eden seemed surprised that it had all been so easy, and sauntered off, ponytail swinging.

Mel wanted to call after her. She wanted to say, *Come and walk on the beach with me,* but she was afraid Eden might refuse and her confidence couldn't take another knock.

You're not that easy to talk to.

Eden had accused her of trying to fix everything, but how could she not try and fix this?

She needed her daughter to know that she could talk to her. She needed Eden to believe that her mother would listen. Properly listen.

How was she going to do that?

19

Ashley

"So did he kiss you?" Ashley passed the cheese to Joanna.

"No, he did not kiss me."

"Shame. I bet he's a good kisser. But you already know that, don't you? Don't slice that cheese too thickly. We're going to layer it."

"I haven't kissed him for more than twenty years. I don't even remember it."

"You're lying. But he's probably even better now." Ashley nudged Joanna. "Boy and man, right?"

The sun shone through the open doors and spilled light onto the kitchen counters as they chopped and sliced.

"We should not be having this conversation."

"Why not? I can tell you're loving it. You're smiling."

"I'm smiling because I like cheese."

"You're smiling because you like Nate. We were talking about kissing."

Joanna sighed. "I'm too old for this. If you want to talk about kissing boys, you can talk to Eden. I'm sure she knows a lot more about it than I do. Can I use any cheese to make this?" She sliced the cheese carefully, exactly as Ashley had taught her.

"See, that's your problem right there." Ashley leaned against the countertop and Joanna put the knife down and looked at her.

"Not knowing enough about cheese?"

"Thinking you're too old. You're forty, Joanna. Forty is young. You're in your prime! Stop acting like your life is over."

"Just because I'm not interested in romance, doesn't mean I'm treating my life as if it's over. You were going to tell me about cheese."

"In a minute. You're scared, I get it. Love is the biggest risk you take, isn't it?" She thought about all the missed calls and messages waiting on her phone from Jon and the thought of it stressed her out so much she leaned across, cut some cheese and ate it. "I mean, it's your heart, and your trust, and giving all that to someone is a big deal because you're basically giving them the most vulnerable part of you. What if you ruin everything?" She stared at Joanna. "Okay, maybe this whole love thing is over-rated. Maybe we should just live here, make grilled cheese and grow old together. That sounds safer."

"Are we talking about me or you? I've lost track."

"Both of us. I have feelings for Jon." She wouldn't have admitted that to anyone but Joanna. "I always have. But he's been a good friend to me, and I guess I'm afraid of losing that. Everything is going to change."

"You haven't listened to the messages?"

"No. Haven't had the courage. Because the moment I listen to those messages I'm going to have to respond, and I still haven't figured out the best way to tell him about the baby." And now she felt embarrassed, because she'd nudged Joanna out of her comfort zone but was staying firmly within her own. But this was different. Wasn't it?

"Maybe he saw the news and he already knows."

"Maybe. All the more reason to figure out what I want before we talk. When you and Nate went from friends to something more than friends, were you nervous?"

Joanna put the knife down. "No. Nate was always in my life.

Friend, then lover—it seemed a natural progression. I didn't think about it ruining our friendship because I didn't think that would happen. It didn't cross my mind." She glanced at Ashley. "That was pretty naive of me, wasn't it?"

"No. Did it feel strange seeing him again?"

"Surprisingly, no. It felt natural and easy. Which is why I'm going to do it again." Joanna picked the knife up again. "When you've taught me three courses, I'm going to invite him to dinner."

"You—" Ashley gaped at her. "You're inviting him to dinner?"

"Yes. But everyone in this town knows I'm a terrible cook, so I'm going to need some practice first. I need you to help me pick a menu. I want it to be about the conversation, but I don't want to poison him with one of my usual charred offerings."

"You haven't burned anything while we've been doing this together." Ashley's head was reeling. Joanna was going to invite Nate to dinner. She wanted to punch the air. "I'm proud of you. Is this just dinner, or dinner and something more?"

"I don't know. Best to see if he survives dinner first. Do you cook for Jon?"

"Yes, but he cooks, too. He's always hungry. It's kind of a joke. And I fix his computer. I'm more practical, and he's arty." *She missed him so much.* "He's a brilliant musician. He plays five different instruments, and he writes songs and plays the guitar— I'm sure he's going to be big one day. And he draws. Funny little sketches that look exactly like the person he's drawing. I can't draw, and I can't sing. But I can fix his car, so I guess that's something."

"He sounds special, and you obviously have a good relationship. Maybe you should stop worrying about what to say to Jon and just call him."

"It's not that easy. What do I say? Do I just tell him I'm pregnant? Or do I tell him I love him and I'm pregnant? That's double the pressure, right?" The thought of it made her feel ill. She was putting off listening to those messages because she was afraid of the outcome. Once she listened, it would be real. Whatever he said would be fact, and then she'd know, and she could no longer lie there at night dreaming and imagining.

She was scared. She was so damn scared.

"You're assuming it's going to be bad." Joanna ate a slice of cheese, too. "He might be thrilled and you'll both ride off into the sunset and live in a cottage by the sea with roses around the door."

Ashley felt an ache in her chest. "There won't be a cottage with roses around the door. Right now a roof over my head is the dream. Whether I can afford walls, too, remains to be seen." A wave of gloom engulfed her. "I don't know why I'm worrying about love, when what I really need to worry about is how I'm going to afford to live. And then there's medical care, as you said before. I ought to see someone."

"I'll talk to Mel. Find out who she recommends. She knows everyone. Are we going to cook this or just eat the cheese and then the bread?"

"We're going to cook it. Layer the cheese."

Joanna put thin slices of cheese onto the bread the way Ashley had taught her. "Talking of being able to afford to live, I called my lawyer this morning."

"Right. Hope he was helpful. You're going to need slightly more cheese than that. This is comfort food, and the amount you've put in there wouldn't comfort anyone. If you're going to sin, sin big, I always say."

"My lawyer is a she, and she was helpful. I wanted to ask her the best way to give money to you and the baby." Joanna finished constructing the sandwich and slid it carefully into the pan. "Now watch me burn this."

"Money?" Ashley stared at her. "You can't give me money."

"It's my money. I can do what I like with it. And what I'd like to do," Joanna said, "is what Cliff should have done in the first place. Is the heat too high?"

"It's fine." Ashley barely glanced at the sandwich. "You mean a loan, right?"

"No, I don't mean a loan. You don't need that hanging over you. You have enough to deal with, Ashley." Joanna wiped her hands on her apron. "I can't help with most of your worries, but at least I can help with the practical side and also pay for proper medical care. I'll be giving you money, and I'd like you to live here with me for a while. You can figure out what you want to do before making any big decisions. I should probably tell you the amount, so you can plan." Joanna named a figure and Ashley assumed she'd misheard.

"How much?" She listened as Joanna repeated it and then held the countertop because it was that or faint. "You're kidding."

"I'm not kidding." Joanna carefully turned the sandwich. "Now, don't distract me because I'm *not* going to burn this."

"I can't accept."

"Ashley, this is what Cliff should have done when you were a baby. The heat is too high. No matter what you say, I know this is too high." Joanna lowered the heat slightly. "If he'd done the right thing, you and your mom would have lived in comfort, her medical bills would have been covered, you wouldn't have lost your home and you wouldn't now be worried about how to go to college and support a baby. I want that for you now."

"Joanna—"

"Don't make a decision now. Think about it for a while. And then say yes."

"But…" Emotion rushed through her, filled her throat and made her eyes sting. "It's the thing I've been struggling with most. How I'm going to afford to work, and still look after my baby."

"Well, now you have choices."

"Why? Why would you do that?"

"Why wouldn't I? I have what I need. The rest of the money is just going to sit around while I figure out which charities to support. I was never lucky enough to have kids…" Joanna paused, focused on the sandwich. "But if I ever had a daughter I would have wanted her to be just like you. Not that I'm pretending to be your mother or anything weird. From the sounds of it, you were lucky enough to have a caring and wonderful mother, but I hope I can be a friend."

Ashley looked at her, this woman who had every reason to hate her. Certainly had reason to resent her mother. "How can you say that? You should be so angry with her. I'm angry with her. And embarrassed."

"Why? Her choices aren't yours." Joanna lifted the pan from the heat for a moment. "Was I angry with her? Yes, of course. I was angry with her and angry with Cliff. But doing a bad thing, making a bad choice, doesn't make you a bad person. There was plenty your mother did right."

"You never met her. You didn't know her."

"But I know you. She raised you to be independent and have self-respect. She taught you to be courageous and stand up for what you thought was right—that's why you climbed into the car with Cliff. She loved you, and made sure you knew you were loved. I've never been a parent, but I've been a child and I'm pretty sure that feeling loved, knowing you're loved and accepted no matter what, is the most important thing." Joanna paused and then smiled at her. "And she taught you to cook, which is always a bonus."

I've never been a parent.

Ashley was sure Joanna would have been a wonderful mother, but she didn't say so. That might upset her. She didn't want to upset Joanna.

"How do I forgive my mom for not telling me the truth about my real dad? How do I stop being so angry?"

"I don't know. I'm not a psychologist." Joanna frowned. "But honestly, I think your mother wanted the best for you, and she probably knew that Cliff wasn't the best. And I think she was probably right. Even if he had taken responsibility, he probably would have let you down. That's who he was. I'm guessing your mother was trying to protect you from that. Also, she might have been trying to protect you from the media attention."

Why hadn't any of that occurred to her? "That actually makes sense. You said that there was good stuff about him, too. You said you'd tell me." Even though she struggled to think of Cliff as her father, she needed some good to dilute the bad.

"The good stuff?" Joanna leaned against the counter and kept one eye on the pan. "He had more charisma than anyone I've ever met. When he talked to you he made you feel as if you were the only person in the room. He was a good listener, and he was a born entertainer."

"He liked the attention."

"A little too much." Joanna paused. "But he had his reasons for that. Cliff had a tough childhood. He never talked about it much, he tried to put it behind him, but I know his father was abusive. It was just the two of them, and Cliff had to fight his way out of that situation. He cooked because if he didn't, then they didn't eat. And he discovered he was good at it. He drove himself hard, and some of that was because of his childhood. It was survival. But it was also about proving something to himself. And he never felt as if he'd done enough. Never felt secure. He was running from his past, but he never felt he could stop running. He needed constant reassurance, adulation—love."

She'd seen Cliff as this remote, public figure. It was strange to think of him as a human being with a whole life she knew nothing about.

"You think that was why he had affairs?"

"I think it contributed. People do things for a reason. The past shapes all of us."

She thought about her own experiences. "I guess it does. You think that was why he wasn't interested in me? Because of his own childhood?"

Joanna thought for a moment. "I suspect he was scared. Scared that he might have some of his own father in him. Scared that he might mess you up the way he'd been messed up. But he was also selfish. He'd had to look after himself for so long he wasn't used to putting anyone else first."

"Right." Her image of Cliff had shifted and changed in her head, and her feelings had shifted, too. Her anger and hurt were blunted by the reminder that he'd been human, that he'd been dealing with things just like everyone else. "Thanks for telling me that. It helps."

"Good." Joanna smiled. "Now can we talk about cheese? I'm still waiting for you to tell me about cheese. Whether I can make this with any cheese." Joanna glanced at her. "You're crying! Why are you crying?"

"Because you—" Ashley flung her arms around her and after a moment felt Joanna hug her back.

"Is this a test?" Her voice was thickened. "Are you trying to see what it takes to make me burn the food?"

"No." Ashley clung for a moment and then stepped back. "You're right. Concentrate. And no, you can't use any cheese. It needs to have good melting properties. Jarlsberg is my favorite, but you can use others. My mom used Monterey Jack and Gruyère." Ashley pointed to the bread they'd picked up in the market. "This artisan white bread is perfect, but my mom always used sourdough and it was delicious." Her mind flashed back to the hours she'd spent in the kitchen with her mother, learning to make bread. The fun times they'd had. Joanna was right. The affair with Cliff was just one part of her mother's life, and who she was.

"I like this artisan bread. I'll keep using that."

"What are you going to make for Nate?" Ashley dried her cheeks with the flat of her hand. "How about chicken with olives? It's easy. You can serve it with a green salad."

"Sounds perfect. Do lots of things have to happen at the same time?"

"No. You can make it in advance and then it can sit there and wait until you're ready to eat it. When are you inviting him to dinner?"

"As soon as you've taught me the dishes and I've practiced them once, I'll call him."

"We'll practice tonight. I'll pick up what we need when I'm out with Eden."

Joanna carefully transferred the grilled cheese, now golden brown, to the plates. "You're getting along well?"

"Yes, she's great. You don't mind me going out?"

"Of course not. You don't have to ask permission, Ashley. This is your home." Joanna handed her a plate. "Shall we take this onto the terrace?"

"Yes, let's." *Home.* "Are you serious about me staying here with you for a while?"

"As long as you like. I assume you'll want your independence eventually, but if you don't that's fine."

Ashley was floored by the generosity. "It doesn't seem right somehow."

"Well, I'm not offering you charity." Joanna sat down and ate her first mouthful of grilled cheese sandwich. She closed her eyes and savored it. "I'd expect something in return."

"What?"

"You cook sometimes, and carry on teaching me to cook. You can brush the sand out of the living room because I hate that job." Joanna opened her eyes and stared down at her plate. "This is delicious. Better than anything I've tasted."

Ashley laughed. "Joanna, it's grilled cheese."

"I know. And it's perfect." Joanna savored another mouthful. "Maybe you do have some of Cliff in you, after all."

Ashley tensed. "You said I wasn't like him."

"Well, you can cook—" Joanna finished the sandwich "—so you have that in common. Cliff was a natural in the kitchen. He did it all by instinct, and his instincts were good. You seem to have inherited that."

Ashley pondered on that. Had her mother encouraged her to cook because of her heritage? Was that her nod to Cliff being her father? "As long as that's all I've inherited. I do love cooking, but more as a hobby. I'm a nerd at heart. Maybe, one day, I'll go to college."

"Why 'one day'? Why not now?"

"Well, there's a small thing called a baby..." Ashley put her hand on her belly. "At the moment it's a small thing, but soon it will be a big thing. And that's the thing I've been struggling with most."

"You can study when you're pregnant."

"But what about when the baby comes? I can hardly take it to classes with me, can I?"

"Some colleges are child-friendly. They have childcare programs." There was a pause. "Or I could look after it. I promise not to teach it to cook. I'll leave that part to you."

"You'd help care for the baby?" She couldn't believe Joanna would offer something like that. "Would you...want to?"

"Be Auntie Joanna? Oh, yes. I'd love it. This grilled cheese is so delicious. What are you teaching me to cook next?"

She heard the buzzer on the gate. They'd been talking and hadn't noticed the time. "That must be Mel and Eden. You'll be okay with Mel?"

Joanna stood up and picked up their empty plates. "Yes. Last night seemed all right, unless she was waiting for us to be alone together again to yell at me."

"Er—I have a confession to make about that."

"A confession?"

"I might have accidentally told Eden that it was Nate who broke up with you."

"Oh." She'd been worrying about it ever since, and wondering if Joanna would be upset. Was she? She couldn't tell. "I was defending you. That's one of my jobs, alongside teaching you to cook and sweeping sand from the living room. I'm not going to apologize for any of that. I do apologize for spilling a secret. I'm not generally a gossip."

"I—right." Joanna breathed. "It wasn't a secret exactly. I didn't even know that was what she thought until she turned up here. And we haven't discussed it, because it never felt like the right time."

The buzzer went again, more insistent this time, and Ashley shrugged.

"Maybe the right time is now."

20

Mel

They took towels to the beach as they had when they were children, along with a cooler Joanna had filled with drinks and snacks.

Mel stripped off her top and shorts, sprawled on a towel in her swimsuit and examined her legs and arms. "Remember when we used to count freckles?"

"Yes." Joanna settled down next to her, the brim of her hat almost concealing her features. "But I always won that game."

Mel looped her arms around her bent legs and rested her chin on her arms. "I missed this view—" She almost said, *And I missed you*, but maybe that was too much too soon. She had other more pressing things to say first.

"The view is almost the same from the Surf Café."

"Not really. My view is full of people. Here, you have the ocean to yourself. Just you and the water and the wildlife." As teenage girls they'd lain on the sand, simmering in a soup of teenage hormones, exchanging thoughts and experiences, their agile minds bloated with questions. *What? Did he—? Would you ever—?* Mel had spent the night planning how best to apologize, but now the moment was here she just plunged right in. "I owe you an apology. I didn't know Nate was the one who ended the relationship. I only found out last night." And had a sleepless night because of it.

"Ashley told you."

"She told Eden, but I'm glad she did so don't be angry. You must have wondered why I came up here yelling that first time." She was mortified to remember it, and it was no good telling herself that she hadn't had the facts. She should have considered other options. Taken a more balanced view, as Greg always did.

"I'm not blaming you for that, Mel."

"I am. I need to fix myself. I'm a horrible person."

"What?" Joanna turned to her, horrified. "Nate not telling you what happened doesn't make you a horrible person."

"But I should have thought there might be more to it. I should have asked myself more questions about why he would never talk about it. I'm forty. You'd think by now I would have learned to be a better human being."

"You're a wonderful human being, always have been." Joanna brushed sand from her legs. "If you were perfect, I'd have to hate you."

"Yeah, well, you have every right to do that." She was not going to cry. She was not going to get all emotional. She was going to own her mistakes and try and learn from them.

Joanna reached across and touched her arm. "Mel, stop it. Stop beating yourself up when none of this is your fault. If there's blame, then maybe it lies with me for not talking to you about it, and Nate for not telling you the truth. But he never talked about our relationship and frankly I liked that. I liked the fact that we had something he didn't share with anyone else. It made it feel special."

"I was so angry with him last night. When I found out the truth. Aren't *you* angry with him?"

"For the fact that he ended our relationship? No. Was I upset?

Yes, of course. Devastated." Joanna paused. "But he did the right thing."

"What?" Mel whipped her glasses off her nose. "You don't mean that."

"I do. And I admit that it took me a long time to see it, but I see it clearly now. I was a mess, Mel. I was barely holding it together living with Denise, who stripped away my confidence and sense of self-worth layer by layer. The last time I saw her was something I've never forgotten."

"I can imagine, but—"

"I loved Nate. I really did love him, but the truth is I also depended on him. I used him as support, and that wasn't healthy."

"He was everything to you."

"Exactly. And that's not healthy, either. No one can be everything." Joanna stared out to sea. "I'm not surprised Nate felt uncomfortable with the pressure. It wasn't fair on him. I'm not surprised that he questioned what our love might have looked like had I not been so dependent on him. I'm not surprised that he didn't trust it. Breaking up was a difficult thing to do for him, and hideous for me, but it was brave. And he did the right thing. Apart from kissing Whitney, of course. That part was... clumsy. Unfortunate."

Mel sat cross-legged on her towel. "Whitney has been married to Richard Kelly for the past fifteen years. We were on the school committee together for a while. She's ferociously organized."

"She always was."

"She hasn't changed. It's exhausting, although useful if you want something done. Her daughter was in Eden's diving class."

"I remember Richard. Not sure I would have pictured him with Whitney."

"I would never have pictured Whitney with Nate."

"I think it was just a kiss."

"I'm relieved about that, because a lifetime of spending Thanksgiving with Whitney telling me where I was going wrong and providing me with a spreadsheet so that I could do better next time would have made me move to Hawaii."

Joanna laughed. "I've missed talking like this."

"Me, too."

"What else has been going on in my absence?"

Mel smoothed sunscreen onto her arms. "Ellen Grey and Linda Merrick bought the guest house on the corner of Ocean and Sunset."

"Oh! I loved that place. It was falling down."

"It's not falling down now. They've turned it into an up-market boutique B and B. Their breakfasts are to die for. We should go. The view from the terrace is great. They adopted a little girl a while back. Eden babysits sometimes. Did you hear about Dan Little?"

"No? What happened?" Joanna rolled onto her stomach, chin on her palm as she listened, and Mel thought back to all the times they'd done this, to a time when sharing everything with Joanna had been part of her life. One of the best parts.

She talked, telling Joanna everything that she could recall, from small scandals to big changes, and when she finally paused for breath Joanna smiled.

"Does anything happen in Silver Point that you don't know about?"

"Greg has his finger on the pulse, obviously, not that I repeat anything he tells me. But this is a small town so if you're arrested people are going to find out. Also, I'm an interfering busybody so I volunteer everywhere, not because I'm a caring person but because it means I know everything that's happening."

"You're a caring person, Mel. You always have been." Joanna pulled her hat off and Mel thought that without makeup, or newly styled hair, she looked more like the Joanna she'd grown up with. The Joanna she knew.

"My life here must seem pretty boring compared to yours. All those fancy events you attended. All those famous people you mixed with." And now she was curious. "Was it exciting?"

Joanna sat up. "Sometimes. And sometimes it was lonely."

"Did you have good friends?"

"I spent time with people. But there was no one I was close to."

"Hey, are you saying you never replaced me?"

Joanna laughed. "You were irreplaceable." She looked at Mel. "I should probably be apologizing to you, for leaving town without getting in touch. But I was crushed by breaking up with Nate, and my stepmother was vile, and it was all too raw and I didn't want to put you in the middle of it. I knew you'd be angry with him. I didn't want to be the cause of a rift between you, and I didn't want you to try and persuade him to change his mind."

"If Cliff hadn't charmed you that night, what would you have done?" It was something she'd often wondered. How big a part had fate played in Joanna's departure? If Cliff hadn't shown up, would she have stayed in Silver Point?

Joanna lay back on the towel and stared up at the sky. "He didn't charm me that night. That wasn't what happened."

"But that's the story that he always told when anyone asked him."

"I guess he thought it sounded better than *This girl was crying into my chowder so I took her for a walk on the beach*."

"He took you for a walk? I thought it was an amazing whirlwind seduction. Sexy older man and all that."

"It was nothing like that. He saw that I was upset. He waited until the end of my shift and then we went for a walk. I told him everything. Cliff was a really good listener when he wanted to

280 • SARAH MORGAN

be, and I was in a bad place. I told him I was going to leave. I'd already decided I wasn't going home to Otter's Nest that night. I'd packed a bag and stowed it in the back of the café. I didn't want to spend another night under the same roof as Denise."

"You could have come to me. You could have stayed with me."

"When Nate had just broken up with me?"

Mel had to admit it would have been complicated. "Damn it. I hate that you were in that position. I hate that you felt you had to leave, and that you didn't talk to me about it. I was a bad friend."

Joanna reached across and touched her arm. "You were a great friend. The best. None of this was about you."

"If I'd been the best I would have known all this." Mel couldn't forgive herself so easily. "I would have been there blocking the road when you tried to leave Silver Point. I wouldn't have let you leave."

"You wouldn't have been able to stop me. I was desperate to put Silver Point behind me."

Mel sat up. Enough. Enough regrets and self-punishment. "So what happened with Cliff?"

"He loaded my small bag into his car and we drove down the coast with the top down, listening to music and breathing in the air, and the farther we got from Silver Point, the more I thought I might actually survive. We spent two weeks in a beach cottage somewhere north of San Diego."

"Are you telling me that Cliff Whitman saved you? Because I've been hating him for treating you badly for years and I'm not sure I can make that mental readjustment, too." It was hard to accept that she'd got it all so wrong.

"I suppose you could say he helped me save myself. At least at the beginning. And I'm not even sure I regret it. What would the alternative have been? Staying with Denise? Allowing her to erode my confidence layer by layer? No. I did the right thing. I know that for sure now." Joanna pulled off her hat and secured her hair in a twist. "Let's not talk about Denise. Or Cliff. He's my past and right now I'm enjoying my present. Let's swim."

Swimming. Wasn't that exactly what they would have done in the days when their friendship was simple and uncomplicated?

"Good plan. As long as you're prepared to be outclassed." Mel scooped her hair up into a ponytail. "I was always way better than you. And hardly surprising. Your dad taught me, and he was the best."

Joanna smiled. "He was such a great swimmer."

"He really was. The best of all of us. But I'm second best—" Mel jumped to her feet and raced to the water, ponytail swinging as it had when she was a child.

Joanna followed and they plunged into the ocean as they had as children, swimming out beyond the rocks and letting the waves draw them back to the sand. Then they lay, wet and cold from the water, panting for breath.

Joanna stared up at the sky and then laughed. "Thank you."

Mel grabbed a towel and wrapped it around herself. "For what? Swimming was your idea."

"For being you." Joanna sat up. "For coming out here to see me that first day—"

"Any time you want to be yelled at for no reason, I'm your woman."

Joanna squeezed water out of her hair. "You thought you had a reason to yell."

"Turned out I should have been yelling at Nate. I did that, too, by the way."

"You did? How did he take it?"

"Like Nate. Calmly. Although he did admit he messed up, so I took that as a win. My perfect brother isn't so perfect, which obviously means I can be smug and superior for a while, which is always fun." Mel sat up and scrubbed salt water from her face. "So you don't think I should kill Nate?"

"I do not think you should kill Nate."

"You want to do it yourself?" Mel opened the cooler and helped herself to a drink.

"Me? No." Joanna reached for a drink, too. "I have other plans."

"Plans?"

"I'm going to cook him dinner."

Mel choked on her drink. "So you *are* going to kill him."

"No." Joanna was laughing, too. "I'm going to enjoy an evening with him with no pressure. Thanks to Ashley, I have new skills."

"What kind of skills?"

"Inside that cooler you'll find cookies."

"What's that got to do with your skills?" Mel helped herself to a cookie. She bit into it, and caught it in her palm as it crumbled. "Oh, wow. This is delicious. I don't recognize the flavor. Not one of Nate's?"

"Pistachio and Greek honey."

"Mmm." Mel finished the cookie and helped herself to another. "Who made them?"

"I did. With Ashley's help. She's teaching me to cook."

"If I'm still alive in five minutes I'll give you both a gold star." Mel chewed. "These are good. So she's like her father?"

"She's nothing like her father. Cliff didn't have the patience to teach anyone, least of all me. And Ashley cooks real food."

Mel finished the cookie and brushed the crumbs from her legs. "I've never eaten in one of Cliff's restaurants. Greg and I were in LA a few years back and we looked at the menu. Too expensive for us. And—" she eyed Joanna "—dare I say pretentious?"

"Totally pretentious."

"And…overpriced?"

"Hideously overpriced. When they served my food I wanted to invest it, not eat it. And don't start me on the wine." Joanna started to laugh again and Mel laughed, too, and the next minute they were both giggling uncontrollably as they had so many times as children.

Mel wiped her eyes. "I'm trying to imagine you with expensive wine."

"I dropped a bottle once. There were only a few hundred bottles of this vintage left in the world, and I dropped one. The wine in his cellar was worth more than the house." Joanna rubbed her ribs. "I missed laughing like this."

"Me, too. I missed *you*. I missed you so much."

"I missed you, too. So much."

Mel felt her throat thicken. "What happened to the wine? Who owns it now?"

"I do." That part of her life felt so distant now. "He left it to me, and I have no idea what to do with it because I don't drink much."

"Well, you can do one of two things." Mel gathered up her things. "You can sell it, or you could have a massive party and invite everyone from Silver Point. Whitney could organize it and then you are guaranteed to have all the guests and invitations color-coded. Alternatively, just invite Greg and Nate. I'm sure they'd be more than happy to help with your wine problem. What about your job? What happens to that?"

"That's something I'm still figuring out." Joanna put her hat back on and knotted her towel around herself. "Without Cliff, the company is going to change, obviously. Maybe even go bust, although I don't think so. But do I want to be part of whatever is left? I'm not sure. I came here on impulse, but now I'm here I don't want to go back."

"Then don't. Sell the wine! Live off the money."

Joanna looked at her for a long moment. "Maybe I'll do that."

"What about Ashley? What is she going to do? She is his daughter, I assume? The media didn't make that part up?"

"No, they didn't make it up."

Mel listened while Joanna told her everything, from start to finish. She told her about the happy times and about the bad. She told her about the miscarriage, about the affairs, about Cliff denying his daughter and about where she'd been when she'd seen the news that his car had come off the road.

When Joanna finally finished, Mel let out a long breath.

"I'll give you this, Joanna Whitman, your life certainly hasn't been boring."

"Rafferty." Joanna picked up her flip-flops. "I'm changing my name back to Rafferty. I'm tired of linking my life with Cliff's. I'm tired of talking about Cliff! Tell me about Eden. She seems great. You must be very proud."

"Worried and anxious mostly. I guess that's being a parent." Remembering the miscarriage, Mel shook her head. "I'm sorry—"

"Don't be. And I'm sure being a parent is very anxiety inducing. I'm worried about Ashley and she isn't even mine. What's your biggest worry?"

Mel hesitated. "You don't want to hear about this."

"I do. I want to know everything."

And that was friendship, wasn't it? Listening, when listening was hard. Being there, when it might have been more comfortable to walk away.

"Sometimes I feel as if she does the opposite of what I want her to do."

"To make a point?" Joanna slid the bag over her shoulder and they walked up the steps to Otter's Nest.

"Yes. As if she's throwing down a challenge. At the moment she doesn't want to go to college, she wants to stay home and hang out on the beach because life is short, and surfing is her dream, and we should all live our dreams, which I wouldn't yada yada."

"And you have a problem with that?"

"Yes. A big problem." Mel stopped. "Or maybe I don't. It's more that I'm worried she hasn't thought it through. That it isn't what she really wants at all, but she's just choosing that path to flex her independence."

"You mean she wants to do the opposite of what you want her to do?"

"Feels that way. I'm worried she's going to make bad choices. Do something she'll regret."

"What if she does? Isn't that life? A bad choice often doesn't seem bad at the time. And I speak from experience."

Mel tried to imagine how she'd feel if Eden did what Joanna had done. But that wouldn't happen, because Joanna had no support at home, but Eden knew she was loved and supported. Didn't she? She felt a moment of panic. What if she didn't know? What if she felt she couldn't talk to her mother?

"So what would you tell your younger self?"

Joanna thought about it. "Relax. Forgive yourself when you make mistakes. Understand that decisions aren't always simple and the best path isn't always clear. Know that it's never too late to switch direction. That the most important thing in life is having people who love you. That grilled cheese is more satisfying than a poached quail's egg served with foam. Be kind to yourself even when other people are cruel, remember that you made the choices you made for a reason, even if that reason isn't clear anymore." She stopped, realizing that Mel was staring.

"Wow."

Joanna shrugged. "I guess I've had a lot of practice at making bad choices."

"But you came home," Mel said, "and that was a good choice."

"Yes."

"And you picked me as a friend when you were four years old so that was a good choice, too."

"True."

They walked across the terrace, showered off the sand and salt and then wrapped themselves in towels and walked into the kitchen.

Joanna filled two glasses with ice and topped them up with lemonade from the fridge.

Mel was still thinking about Eden. "What did you need when you were Eden's age? What would have helped?"

"You mean from an adult?" Joanna handed her a glass of lemonade. "I'm not a parent so I'm no expert, but I think the best thing you can do is listen. Listen to what she wants."

"I'm scared that if she doesn't go to college, she'll regret it."

"And if that happens, then she can go to college later."

Mel took a sip of lemonade and then put the glass down. "This is delicious."

"I made it." Joanna felt a flash of pride. "Cookies, lemonade, and so far you're still alive."

"It's a miracle. But the real miracle is spending time with you again." Mel put her glass down and hugged her old friend, feeling the warmth of a lifetime flow through her. "It's so, so good to have you back, Joanna Rafferty."

Joanna hugged her back. "It's good to be back."

21

Joanna

"Right, I'm off." Ashley walked onto the terrace and whistled when she saw the table with the flickering candles and the gleam of silverware. "That's romantic."

Joanna panicked. "Is it too much?"

"No. It's perfect." Ashley straightened a napkin. "Don't forget to toast those pine nuts and add them warm to the salad at the last minute."

"Got it."

"And remove dessert from the fridge thirty minutes before you eat it."

"I know. I've made a list and set alarms on my phone. Anything else?"

"Er—remember to have fun?"

Joanna hugged her. "You, too, although pizza, ice cream and a movie are a pretty unbeatable combination. What movie are you watching?"

"Something with zombies where everyone dies a grizzly death. Eden's choice. I'm going to cover the baby's eyes and use subtitles so it doesn't hear screaming. I won't be home tonight, by the way." Ashley said it casually. "I'm staying over at Eden's.

That way no one has to drive me, and everyone can have a drink while I nurse my sparkling water."

"Are you sure? I don't mind coming to get you."

"I'm hoping you will have your mind on other things." Ashley waggled her eyebrows. "Also, Eden and I are going to eat pancakes at the Surf Café for breakfast so don't feel you have to rush to get dressed in the morning."

"What exactly are you implying?"

"That if you and Nate want to have sex in every room in the house, you don't need to worry you'll find me in any of them. You'll have the place to yourself."

"Ashley!" Joanna felt her color rise. "We won't be having sex."

"Oh. That's disappointing. Why not?"

Was she serious? "For a start because we barely know each other."

"Okay, I'm going to give you the benefit of my considerable life experience in these matters. Three things. First, number one—" Ashley held up a finger "—you've known him your whole life and you've already had plenty of sex with him. Just because you had a gap, doesn't mean you don't know him. Two, sex is a really good way of getting to know someone."

"I hardly dare ask about number three."

"Number three is that sex doesn't have to be serious. It doesn't have to come with a bucketload of emotions. It can be fun. A hookup."

"A hookup?"

Ashley shook her head. "Stop taking life so seriously. Live in the moment. When did you last have really good sex?"

Joanna stared at her.

"Ha!" Ashley pointed a finger. "That's what I mean. You can't remember."

"Maybe I can. Maybe I just don't want to talk about it." *Nate*, she thought. Nate was the last time she'd had really good sex.

When love, at least, had seemed simple and uncomplicated. Not that her sex life with Cliff had been bad exactly, at least not at the beginning, but romance, excitement, intimacy had all been missing from her life for a long time.

Ashley nodded. "Give yourself a gift, Joanna. Enjoy yourself."

"I'm twice your age. How come you're the one who is so sure about everything?"

"I'm not. I'm still a teenager, with all the associated insecurities. I'm always comparing myself to other people. I think I'm not clever enough, or funny enough, or thin enough. Do people even like me? Do I even like myself? Most days I feel as if someone threw my emotions into a blender. I'm not sure of anything at all, except that it's okay for sex to be fun. But you, Joanna—" Ashley smiled "—you are serene and dignified in the most trying of situations. You've never thrown a rotten egg at a reporter, or sworn at a photographer."

"Yet."

"You are always in control, and…" She shrugged and waved a hand toward Joanna. "Look at you! You're gorgeous. Your skin, your hair—I mean, talk about serious hair goals. Basically Joanna, you are the *boss*."

"I'm the boss?"

"You are. Every morning when I look in the mirror I tell myself, *Be more Joanna.*" Ashley hugged her. "I'm going now. And whatever happens, I hope you have fun."

Fun? Caution had been her priority for a long time. But maybe she needed to throw that away, along with all the other elements of her life that were linked with Cliff.

She gave Ashley a ride to Mel's house and was back at Otter's Nest in plenty of time to shower and change.

She told herself she wasn't nervous, but she changed her dress three times. She blamed Ashley for persuading her to buy new clothes and extend her color scheme. Now she had a choice and she was struggling with it. Why hadn't she asked Ashley's advice?

On the other hand it was a bit sad that a woman of forty didn't have the confidence to pick something to wear.

Pull yourself together, Joanna.

She glanced at the clothes again.

Definitely not the blue. It was too showy for a casual supper on the terrace with a friend. Friend? Ex-lover?

She stared at the clothes and in the end selected a white sundress that looked cool, summery and appropriate for the weather.

She was sliding a pair of silver hoops into her ears when the buzzer sounded.

She pressed the button to open the gates and walked to the front door, her dress feeling light and cool against her bare legs.

It was just dinner.

She opened the door and felt her heart jump in her chest, not just because of the smile or the way he was looking at her, but because he was holding flowers.

She hadn't expected him to bring flowers. And not any flowers. Seaside daisies. Her favorite.

Her knees shook a little. She lifted her gaze to his face. "You didn't have to—"

"My mother would have something to say to me if I didn't take flowers and wine when I've been invited to dinner."

He was implying the gesture was good manners. If he'd brought roses, or tulips, maybe. But seaside daisies—these daisies had meaning, and he knew it. By bringing them he'd tugged the past and the present closer together.

She took the bunch, buried her face in them and felt her heart ache a little at all the memories that came with them. "My father grew these."

"I remember. They reminded him of you, because they have to be protected from hot afternoon sun."

She had her mother's coloring—her real mother—with fair skin that burned easily. She wore hats with wide brims and was generous with sunscreen, but still she had to be careful.

Nate knew that, too.

Daisies.

"Thank you. Come in. I'll put these in water." She took them through to the kitchen and found a vase. Being practical helped steady her.

He followed her and glanced around the kitchen. "This is a fantastic room." He gazed across the terrace to the sea. "I remember when your kitchen was at the back of the house, with a small window looking onto trees."

She filled the vase with water. "It seemed a waste of the view."

"Yes." He strolled from the kitchen to the terrace, and his gaze lingered on the table. "It looks great."

She put the daisies in water and carried them to the table. "I thought the first time I cooked a proper dinner for someone it should be an occasion."

His gaze slid to hers. "I'm the first person you've cooked dinner for?"

"If you don't count Ashley, then yes. But if you're nervous and you want to leave I'll understand."

"I don't want to leave. But I confess I'm intrigued. You were married to a top chef for two decades. What does Ashley have that Cliff didn't?"

"Patience," Joanna said. "And a generosity of spirit that Cliff lacked. Cliff hated anyone else being in the kitchen so he couldn't see the point of teaching me to cook, particularly when I had no aptitude."

Nate shook his head. "But he had a TV series teaching people how to cook."

"That was all about him. He was the star. He was doing the

cooking. Whatever people then did in the privacy of their own homes wasn't his problem."

Nate laughed and glanced back at Otter's Nest. "I can't believe what you've done with this place. Remember when we used to get splinters just from sitting on the deck?"

"Oh, yes."

He turned, a gleam in his eyes. "Can I look around? Is that rude?"

"Go ahead. I'll pour us a drink. Wine or beer?" She thought of Ashley. *Have fun.* "Or... I have champagne?"

"Champagne sounds good." His gaze held hers for a few seconds longer than necessary. "But give me the tour first."

"Sure. We'll start upstairs and work our way down." She carried her phone with her because she didn't want to miss any of the reminders she'd set as part of her dinner planning. She was determined that the food was going to be perfect and she, Joanna, would have cooked it.

She pushed open doors, gestured to glass, soaring ceilings, bookshelves, cozy reading nooks.

"I can tell you had a hand in design." He wandered into the guest suite that Ashley was using. "Is there a room in the house without a dedicated reading corner?"

"No."

She hadn't bothered with shoes, and the floor was cool against her bare feet.

It was only when she entered her bedroom at the far end of the house that she remembered she hadn't made the bed. The sheets were rumpled, evidence of a restless night punctuated by vivid dreams. Nate had played a leading role in those dreams.

She felt her cheeks warm.

The tour of her house had somehow become personal. Revealing.

"We should go downstairs. Open that champagne." She turned

to leave and slammed up against him because he'd been standing right behind her.

There was a moment of exquisite tension and then they were kissing, her mouth on his, his on hers. She felt his fingers in her hair, tracing her jaw, holding her head, as if he didn't know which part of her to touch first, and then his arms came around her and he pulled her in. His body was hard against hers, familiar and yet unfamiliar.

She clutched his shoulders, then wrapped her arms around his neck needing to get closer, *closer*. The thud of her heart against her ribs was almost painful. There was an ache low in her pelvis. She felt his hands slide her sundress from her shoulders and she tore at his shirt, as impatient as he was. Had she ever felt this way before? Been this desperate? If she had, she couldn't remember. With him, maybe, but years and experience had sharpened the excitement or maybe it was just that now she knew. She could have waited. Taken her time. Protected herself and her heart. The old version of herself would have done that, but right now, right here in her bedroom with the sound of the surf in her ears and the sea breeze cooling her skin, she was the new version. Different. Or maybe it was just that her emotions had been locked away and controlled for so long that they'd been waiting for a moment like this to make their escape. She didn't know about the future, and she didn't need to know. All that mattered was now, and right now he was all she wanted. He was everything.

The bed was a few short steps away but they never made it that far because her foot tangled with his and she lost her balance and, in trying to save her, he lost his balance, too. They tumbled to the floor and he broke her fall, smacking his head and his elbow in the process.

She gasped. "Are you—?"

"I'm okay, I'm fine." His mouth was back on hers and he

kissed her fiercely, desperately, which suited her fine because it mirrored the way she was feeling.

She heard a noise in the distance, a faint buzzing, but she ignored it until he lifted his head.

"Maybe I'm not fine. I hear buzzing—"

"I hear it, too…" And then she remembered. "It's my phone. It's my reminder to toast the pine nuts."

His mouth was a breath away from hers, his gaze unfocused. "Toast the pine nuts?"

"Never mind." Neither of them could hold the thought for long enough to follow through and she pulled him back to her, feeling the heavy weight of him pressing her into the floor, the slide of his hand between her legs.

She felt hot, so hot, and she lifted herself against him as they made love with frantic, urgent, furious haste until the whole world exploded and she clung to him and he clung to her, both of them panting for air as they came back down to earth.

They lay there breathless, locked together, and then the alarm went again.

Nate lifted his head. "You obviously had a desperate need to toast pine nuts."

She started to giggle. She was lying here naked with Nate, on a hard, uncomfortable floor, like teenagers. And they were talking about pine nuts.

"That's not the pine nuts. That moment has passed." She slid her hand over his bare chest. "This is the reminder to turn the heat up under the Mediterranean chicken."

He raised himself on his elbow, studying her face. "You've set alarms for every stage?"

"Yes. I was determined to get it right and produce a perfect meal. I wanted to impress you. And now it's all messed up."

"I'm already impressed." He reached out and stroked her hair away from her face. "I haven't had sex on the floor since I was seventeen. And that was with you."

"Was it more comfortable back then? I can't remember."

"Probably not, but we didn't have a massive bed as an option." He pulled her closer. "You're beautiful, Jo. So beautiful."

"So are you. We should make the most of it, because tomorrow we're both going to be covered in bruises."

He winced. "That could be true. Do you want to take an icy shower?"

She laughed. "No. Do you?"

"No. But we could swim in the sea. That would have the same effect."

"That requires standing up, finding a swimsuit, putting it on and walking to the beach and I don't have that in me."

He kissed her and then stood up and scooped her up.

"Nate! What are you doing?"

"We're going for a swim."

"Naked?"

"Why not? We're the only ones here and the beach is secluded."

By the time she thought of reasons to argue he was on the terrace and heading down the steps to the beach.

"Are you seriously going to throw me into cold water?"

"We're going in together." He strode into the waves and she gasped as the freezing spray hit her bare skin.

"Nate! This is—"

"Fantastic?" Grinning, he dropped her into the water and she clung to him as they both went under, the ocean muffling sound.

When she finally surfaced he was right next to her.

"Remember when we used to swim here?" He pulled her against him and she wrapped her arms and legs around him. His eyes were a smoky blue, his lashes clumped together and droplets of water clung to his jaw. She'd never seen a sexier man in her whole life.

"I remember." She kissed him, unable to keep her mouth away from his for more than a few minutes at a time. "But we never did it naked."

"We must have been boring back then." He smoothed her wet hair away from her face and then they were kissing again and the kissing led to other things and she stopped thinking, her senses swamped. All she could do was feel—the intimate stroke of his fingers, the warmth of his mouth. The hard heat of him. The sea, ice cold. The smoothness of her skin against the roughness of his. The contrasts were dizzying. She clung to his shoulders, digging fingers into hard muscle. Sound was muffled—soft gasps, the call of a gull, the rush of the ocean as it hit the sand.

Afterward he carried her to the beach, set her down on the sand and kissed her again. "I missed you, Joanna."

It was a simple declaration but it slid inside her and warmed her body from head to toe. "I missed you, too."

He grinned. "I'm starving. All that sex and swimming. Is the food ruined?"

"No. But I haven't done any of my preparation because I ignored all the alarms."

"No worries. We'll do it together."

They headed back to the house, showered and retrieved their clothes and then made their way to the kitchen.

"Pine nuts." She grabbed them and sprinkled them in the pan. "Starter is a salad. Citrus salad with toasted seeds and pine nuts. Why don't you open the champagne?" She was conscious of him standing close to her, but she focused on the pan, kept the heat low as Ashley had taught her, gave the pan a shake halfway through.

She checked the list she'd made. Pine nuts, check. Next was

plate up the salad and turn the heat on under the casserole she'd made earlier.

She walked to the fridge and retrieved the orange she'd sliced earlier and the watercress.

She arranged both on the plates and then added the warm pine nuts and dressed it. She switched on the heat under the casserole, making sure it wasn't too high.

"Voilà." She handed him a plate and he handed her a glass of champagne.

"To friendship, long but no longer lost."

She tapped her glass lightly against his and they carried their plates to the table.

"This place is stunning." He glanced back at the house. "You used an architect from LA?"

"San Francisco. He understood my vision for the place. I wanted to make the most of all that was good about it—the old beach house didn't make the most of the view."

"I remember. I wondered if you'd sell the place."

"I thought about it. But then I thought Grandfather Rafferty might come back to haunt me if I gave away the land he'd worked so hard to get."

He grinned. "Good call. He was one scary guy according to my grandmother." He picked up his glass and drank. "I think he'd approve."

"Probably not. My father always said he had no interest in the house, only the land. The views. The ocean. The garden. Those are the things he loved. That's why I didn't feel guilty knocking the original beach house down and starting again. I think my father would have approved, though."

"I'm sure he would." Nate ate his salad. "He'd be glad to see you back here, that's for sure."

"What about you? You took over the family business. You weren't going to do that. You had so many plans." It was one of the things he'd said to her when he'd ended their relationship. *I want more than this, Joanna. More than Silver Point.*

He put his fork down. "I grew up seeing how hard my parents worked in that place. How much they sacrificed. I didn't want that. I didn't want to spend my life serving food and drink to people I didn't know. It seemed like a small life to me, when there was a whole world out there. I wanted a piece of that."

Joanna listened and waited. This wasn't the end of the story. It couldn't be, because here he was running the Surf Café.

He glanced at her. "You haven't changed, have you?"

"What do you mean?"

"Anyone else would have been hammering me with questions about now."

She frowned. "I assumed you'd tell me what you wanted me to know. I believe in respecting a person's privacy. People aren't public property. They shouldn't have to reveal everything."

"Right." His gaze held hers for a long moment. "It must have been so hard for you. Being married to Cliff. All that attention."

"I handled it. We were talking about you."

"Yes. Sorry." He pushed his empty plate away. "You make plans when you're a teenager. That's what people do. But no one tells you that sometimes things just happen that are outside your control, that some decisions can be hard and sometimes plans need to change." His gaze met hers. "I'm not going to pretend it doesn't unsettle me, talking about this with you. It's as if time has jumped backward."

She reached across the table and took his hand. "What happened, Nate?"

"My dad had a heart attack."

She felt a thud of shock, quickly followed by compassion. "I'm sorry. I didn't know. Mel didn't—"

"She didn't tell you? She was probably trying to be sensitive.

Worried that it might be all too raw given what happened to your dad."

"It hurts. It will always hurt, but you find a way to live alongside it. But we were talking about *your* dad."

"His heart stopped—SCA, sudden cardiac arrest—while he was helping the athletics team at the school. He'd complained of feeling breathless earlier in the day, but otherwise there was no warning. He dropped, right there on the track, but fortunately they had a defibrillator and they used it."

Joanna could smell the chicken. It was ready to serve. The heat needed to be turned off now. But listening to Nate was more important than producing a perfect meal. "He survived?"

"Yes. It was Greg who saved him. Greg who was standing next to him when it happened. He said my father was chatting away one minute and the next he was on the floor with no pulse, not breathing. He grabbed the AED—"

"The defibrillator?"

"Yes. Used it. Had to shock him twice. But he got him back. That doesn't always happen. We were lucky. Lucky Dad collapsed right there, where there was help to be had. Lucky that Greg was—is—so calm and steady."

"How awful for you, and for your mom and Mel." She kept hold of his hand. Tight hold.

"He was in the hospital for a while, and when he came home he was focused on eating well and exercising—doing all the things the hospital had told him to do. Reduce stress was one of them. No more long hours in the café. Mom couldn't handle the extra load, and anyway, she wanted to care for him. I was working as a surf instructor in Europe. It was a way to travel and earn money. I came back."

"Of course you did. That's what family does." She felt a pang, because she had no family who would drop everything for her, and no one who needed her to drop everything for them.

Ashley, she thought. She'd drop everything for Ashley, and she had a feeling Ashley would drop everything for her.

"Did your stepmother ever get in touch?" He'd obviously read her thoughts. "When things started going wrong with Cliff? When the press were hounding you?"

"No. Why would she?"

His mouth tightened. "Some might say it was because you were family."

"Not all families are like yours, Nate." She thought of him, getting that phone call about his father, flying across the country to get home. Then staying home. Family loyalty. Love. "She didn't feel any responsibility for me. She thought I wasn't her business, and maybe she was right about that."

"She wasn't right about that. When you marry someone, you marry everything about them. Their likes, their dislikes, their present, their past—their family. All of it."

"She didn't see it that way. And if he had lived, he would have divorced her. She knew that. And she was angry that my father left this place to me."

"Your father was a wise man, although—" He stopped and she glanced at him.

"You were going to say that if he'd been that wise he wouldn't have married her. You're not wrong. But when it comes to relationships, we're not always wise, are we?" Her father must have felt that marrying Denise was the right decision at the time, even if later he'd regretted it. She, of all people, could understand that relationship decisions were influenced by a number of factors. That those decisions weren't always straightforward.

"No." Nate spoke quietly. "We're not always wise. That's because decisions aren't always clear. I hated the way she treated you. Spoke to you. After your father died you were hurting badly. She should have been your main source of comfort, but instead she made everything hurt more. She rejected you when you needed support."

"And you were the one who was there for me. You and Mel, and your parents, who were always so kind and generous. I preferred being in your home than mine. I slid into your world because I didn't much like my own." And she could see now how that feeling had developed and grown as the years passed. "You and your family were my whole world, and when our friendship shifted to something more, you became my whole world. You were everything." She saw it so clearly now. "And I scared you. I'm sorry for it, Nate. For the way I was back then. For the way I shared all my problems with you."

"Are you kidding? I loved that you were so open and honest with me. That you felt you could tell me anything and everything. It made me feel special. It was what made *us* special. We shared without either of us holding back and what's intimacy if it isn't that?" He ran his hand over the back of his neck. "I'm the one who should apologize to you."

"For what? For not being able to handle all the issues I was carrying? For not loving me enough? Neither of those things is a crime."

"I loved you enough." He let his hand drop. "I loved you, but I was scared. You trusted me with yourself, and I was afraid I'd let you down. You'd had so much hurt in your life, and I was scared of the responsibility. Afraid that I couldn't be what you wanted and needed me to be. I suppose I was a bit in awe of what we had. Maybe I knew it was rare. I was afraid of ruining everything, and in the end that's exactly what I did."

"We were both young. A relationship shouldn't come with so much baggage at the start. I don't blame you at all for ending it."

"I blame myself. For handling it badly. For being insensitive."

She shook her head. "You were direct and honest, the way you were right the way through our relationship." She paused, thinking of Cliff. "It took me a few years to appreciate how brave you were. How tough it must have been for you. A few years of living with a man who lied to me because that was easier, who dodged any and all conflict, who didn't respect me or himself, taught me that."

"Jo—" He paused and turned his head. Sniffed. "Do I smell burning?"

"The chicken!" She shot to her feet and he gathered up plates and followed.

"I take full responsibility. I kept you busy through all the reminder alerts."

She turned off the heat, gingerly checked the casserole. "If I tell Ashley I burned it, I will never hear the last of it."

"So don't tell her." He peered over her shoulder. "Looks delicious."

She poked it with a spoon. "The bottom is stuck to the pan."

"We won't eat the bottom part." He grabbed the plates and served two portions.

"The pan is ruined."

"I'll buy you a new one." He carried their plates back to the terrace and this time they sat next to each other instead of facing each other. Her thigh brushed against his. He had that same easy way about him that had always drawn her. Being with him was relaxing, except that right now she didn't feel relaxed. Her pulse was fast. She was acutely aware of him so close to her.

"This is the first time I've cooked anyone dinner."

"I have never enjoyed a dinner more."

She smiled, because she knew he wasn't talking about the food. "I was supposed to remove the dessert from the fridge thirty minutes before we ate it."

"Go and do it now," he said, "because I have a good idea of how we can spend the next thirty minutes."

22

Mel

Mel served pancakes to the couple at the front of the deck. Her head ached. Ashley had spent the night on the spare bed in Eden's room and the two girls had giggled and talked all night.

Mel had grumbled to Greg, who had reminded her that she and Joanna had done the same. So she'd stopped grumbling because it was true that they had, and also true that it had been an important part of their lives and their friendship. That intimate exchange of thoughts, those confidences shared in the darkness. It was all part of figuring out life, wasn't it? And one of the best parts of friendship.

And if the price was Mel's headache, then it was probably worth paying.

The day before she'd loaned Eden her car again, and the two girls had driven up the coast to Carmel. They'd returned with overstuffed bags and smiling faces so Mel assumed the trip had been a success.

Now they were seated at a table in the shade, heads together, still talking as if they had too much to say and no time to say it.

Nate appeared with a tray loaded with coffee.

She watched as he served a group of women with a smile and a few friendly words, and then followed him back into the café.

"I'm not going to ask you how your evening was because I know you won't tell me. But judging from the fact you were late to work, and you're never late to work, and the fact that you've been smiling constantly, even when that woman complained that her *pain au chocolat* was dark chocolate not milk, I'm guessing you had a good evening."

"I had a good evening." He grabbed two plates and started making up shrimp salad. "And thanks for stepping in this morning."

"Of course. I was awake, anyway."

"You?" He glanced at her. "You're never awake early."

"I am when I don't go to sleep, which is what happened last night. Eden and Ashley were 'whispering' half the night. I'm still figuring out whether a muffled giggle actually penetrates the walls more effectively than a normal one."

Nate smiled. "They seemed to be enjoying themselves when I saw them a moment ago."

"Pancakes do that to a person." She watched her brother assemble the perfect salad. "You're happy. And I'm pleased."

"So I'm forgiven?"

"I was more angry with myself than you." Through the open doors she saw Ashley stand up, give Eden a quick wave and then walk lightly across the deck and down the steps.

Presumably Joanna had arrived, which meant that Eden would be heading home, and then to the surf school.

Later, she was meeting up with friends in town so it was now or never.

"Nate—" she turned to her brother "—will you cover me for ten minutes? There's something I need to do."

"After you did the same for me this morning I can hardly say no, can I?" He picked up the salads and piled them on a tray along with crusty bread warm from the oven and a jug of iced water. "You're not interrogating Joanna, are you?"

"No." She paused. "I want to talk to Eden."

He met her gaze and nodded. "Go for it."

She flashed him a grateful smile and headed back onto the deck in time to see Eden taking the steps to the beach.

"Eden! Wait!"

Eden turned, ponytail swinging. "What?"

Mel felt suddenly nervous. Nervous around her own child. "Do you want to walk on the beach with me?"

"When?" Eden frowned. "You mean right now?"

"Yes, now. I thought we could...talk."

Eden's gaze was shuttered. "You mean, you want to lecture me on all the reasons I should go to college."

"No. Not that." But she couldn't blame Eden for thinking that, could she? She took a deep breath. "If you decide you don't want to go to college, then that's fine with me. Us. Your dad and me."

"We both know it's not fine with you, Mom. Don't lie."

"It's true that I'll worry, but I'll worry whatever you do. It's part of being a parent. I want what you want, Eden. And most of all I want you to be happy. That's all. And only you know what that's going to take."

Eden stared. "Have you been drinking?"

"No, of course not. Can we walk on the beach? I don't really want to have this conversation in full view of everyone."

"I don't—"

"You said I didn't listen. I want to listen to you. I want to do it now."

Eden didn't move. "I didn't say it to upset you."

"I know that, and I'm not going to pretend it didn't upset me because of course it did." She managed a weak smile. "Despite what you may think, I'm trying to be the perfect mother here and you providing plenty of evidence to the contrary didn't make me feel good, but I did listen, Eden. And you were right, that I always try and control and fix things."

Eden sighed. "I probably shouldn't have said it. I was out of line—"

"No, you weren't. You were honest, and that's good." It didn't feel good, but it *was* good. "I do try and control and fix things, and the fact that I do it because I love you doesn't change the facts. It's just scary being a mom sometimes, that's all. I want the best for you. I want your life to be perfect, I don't want you ever to be unhappy, but that's ridiculous because of course no one's life is perfect and no one can be happy all the time."

"Mom—"

"Can we walk? Just for five minutes."

Eden took a breath. "Sure. I'm not due in surf school for another hour."

"We'll walk back along the beach to the house. That way you won't be late." Mel pulled off her shoes and they walked across the sand to the water's edge. "Remember when we used to do this? Jump in the waves?"

"We haven't done that since I was twelve."

"Let's do it again, right now." Mel stopped and grabbed her daughter's hand, but Eden tugged it away, sending a mortified glance around her.

"What are you doing? What is wrong with you? I'm too old to be jumping in the waves with my mother."

"Right. Yes, of course you are." She was doing this all wrong and she had no idea what right looked like. "Family has always been the most important thing to me. It's been the driving force behind most of the decisions I've made in my life. And I know that those decisions wouldn't be for everyone, but it was what I wanted. You once told me that I'd sold out—"

Eden looked uncomfortable. "Do we have to talk about this?"

"I want to talk about this. I want to share my thinking, and then I hope you'll share yours." She was simply going to tell her story, and hope that Eden would listen. "I can't remember when I fell in love with your dad, but it feels as if I've been in love with him my whole life. We went off to college, and it was a really happy time, and maybe for a while I did wonder if it would be fun to travel, and get a job on the East Coast, New York or somewhere buzzy and exciting. Your uncle Nate was in Europe and I didn't see myself working in the Surf Café, except maybe during holidays when I was home from my glitzy life. I wanted more than that, or so I thought. And then I found out I was pregnant."

"So I ruined your fun?"

"Having you was the most exciting thing that happened to me. And I didn't see it changing my life. Your dad and I decided New York could wait. And then Grandpa had a heart attack, and Uncle Nate came home. We all helped in the café so that Grandpa didn't have to, and that was fine. I used to bring you to the café and you'd sit—"

"With Grandma, I remember."

"Yes. Or any number of my friends from town. Mary-Lou. Rosa. Whenever I needed help, there was someone I could turn to. Life was easy here. Did I occasionally think about New York City, and how it might have felt to stride down Fifth Avenue with my heels tapping, wear a smart suit and maybe work in a fancy glass office with a view of the Empire State Building? Yes, I thought about it. I even interviewed for a job."

Eden's face changed. "I—you went to Manhattan? When? How old was I?"

"You would have been eighteen months old. I saw a job advertised—an entry-level position in a big creative agency. I didn't even want to apply, but Nate insisted. He knew that living in New York was my dream. He wanted me to have my dream. He said he'd handle the café. Your grandparents took care of you for a few nights, Nate covered the café and Greg and I flew to New York. We stayed in a fancy hotel, we went to a show and had a romantic dinner in one of those restaurants that have a view of the city. And the next morning I wore my high heels, brand new, and a smart suit, also brand new, and I took a cab to the company offices on Seventh Avenue and I was interviewed in a glass office, so high in the building I felt as if I was looking down on the world. I'd never felt anything like it, the excitement and adrenaline."

"But you didn't get the job. I'm sorry, Mom."

"What makes you think I didn't get the job?"

Eden frowned. "Because we never lived in New York. You never worked there."

"That's right, we didn't. I didn't. But not because I didn't get the job. They offered me the job right there and then, along with more money than I'd ever seen, although of course this was Manhattan so between accommodation and childcare the money would have been eaten up in a New York minute."

"They offered you the job?" Eden looked confused. "So what happened?"

"I turned it down."

"You—*Mom?*"

"That's right. Was it an easy decision? Yes and no. Like most decisions, there were arguments to support both sides. I always wanted to live in New York for a while, and it was everything I thought it would be. Glitzy and exciting." She could still remember the breathless feeling of just being there.

"What happened?"

"I was in the hotel with your dad, and then you called me with a little help from your grandmother and you were laughing, and having fun, and you'd learned to put two words together for the first time. You said, 'Mommy gone,' and I realized that wasn't what I wanted. I didn't want someone else to witness all your milestones. I didn't want to be 'gone.' I could hear the ocean in the background and I looked out of the window at the city and I thought, *What am I doing here?* And Greg and I arrived home and there was live music in the café, the sun was setting over the ocean and Rosa kissed Adam that night—which had been coming for a long time—and Nate was dancing with you and I remember standing there thinking, *I'm home. This is my place. This is where I want to be.* And did it feel glitzy and glamorous? No, but it was other things, and those other things eclipsed what New York would have offered me." She still remembered the feeling, how sure she'd been. "I know you think I sold out, Eden. I can see how it might look that way, but that isn't what happened. Grandpa wanted us to take over the café, that's true, but Nate made it clear that I didn't have to be part of that. I could have left anytime, but I made a choice to stay and live my life here in Silver Point. I've never regretted that choice, even though I'm sure plenty of people questioned my decision at the time. And I suppose what I'm saying is that I made that choice. No one made it for me. If it had turned out to be a mistake, it would have been my mistake and up to me to fix it. But somehow, with you, I've forgotten all that. I guess when you're a parent you want to spare your child pain, but pain is how we learn." She smiled at her daughter. "Make your choice, Eden, whatever it is. Make mistakes, because that's what life is all about. Live your life the way you want to live it. And I'm here to cheer you on and support you whatever you do—oh!" She gasped as Eden flung her arms around her, almost knocking her onto the sand.

"I'm sorry." Eden's face was buried in Mel's neck. "I've been a moody, horrible—"

"No." Mel hugged her back. "No apologies and no blaming. That's behind us."

"I love you, Mom."

I love you, Mom.

Mel felt her eyes fill. Damn it. Now? Here? On the beach in public? "I love you, too. Always."

Eden sniffed and pulled away. "I must look like crap."

"Don't say 'crap.'"

"I thought I was allowed to make my own choices?"

"Not when it comes to language on a public beach with small children around."

"But—"

"We may have a new relationship, but I'm still your mother."

Eden grinned. "Are you sure you meant all those things you just said?"

"Absolutely. Try me."

"All right. There's something I want to do right now. I want to jump in the waves, like we used to."

Mel started to laugh. "Now? Aren't you too old to jump in the waves with your mother?"

"I don't know." Eden grabbed her hand and tugged her into the water. "Let's find out."

They plunged together, gasping as the cold water splashed at their legs and soaked their shorts, and as Mel laughed with her daughter she caught sight of the Surf Café in the distance and she thought, *I didn't settle, I made a choice. And it was a good choice.*

23

Joanna

Joanna pushed open the door of the Beach Bookstore. The sun shone, her head ached slightly from lack of sleep and she couldn't remember when she last felt this happy.

Mary-Lou was handing a book to a customer. "You come back and let me know what you think. I have my own opinion about the ending, but no spoilers. You have a great day now."

Joanna smiled at her and headed straight for the children's section.

Mary-Lou waited for the door to close behind the customer and then wandered over to join her. "I'm waiting for the day someone comes in and demands a refund because they didn't enjoy the ending. You're smiling. You look different. Has something happened?"

Nate, she thought. *Nate had happened.*

A wonderful evening had turned into a wonderful night.

"I'm enjoying being back in Silver Point, that's all."

"Mmm." Mary-Lou's expression suggested she didn't believe her. "Does this enjoyment have anything to do with the fact that Nate Monroe bought a bunch of daisies from Glenda's Flower Shop yesterday afternoon?"

"You saw that?"

"Carly saw it, and she told Letitia in the bakery, and Letitia told me when I picked up some of those delicious warm French pastries this morning. We all remembered you used to be partial to them."

Joanna laughed. "This place never changes."

"Thank the Lord, no, it doesn't. But I won't be the only one pleased to see the two of you together again." Mary-Lou eyed her. "Some things are meant to be."

"It was just two old friends spending an evening together, Mary-Lou. I'm not looking for a relationship, and I doubt he is, either." And that, she thought, was just one of the many reasons the evening had been so perfect. Neither of them had expected anything of the other. There was no pressure. They'd simply enjoyed each other's company in the moment and this morning he'd returned to his place.

Where was he now? Probably serving customers with a smile that might be just a little less wide this morning on account of the fact he'd had less than three hours sleep, something he'd pointed out when he'd pulled her into the shower with him that morning.

Was he thinking about her?

Mary-Lou raised an eyebrow. "Seeing an old friend doesn't usually make me glow the way you're glowing, but sure, let's pretend that's what this is if it makes you more comfortable. We'll see how that works out. Now what can I help you with this morning? You're looking for books on relationships? One just came in yesterday, *First Love, Second Chance*."

"Seriously?"

"No, I was kidding." Mary-Lou raised her hands. "Sorry. You came in here for something, and probably not to give me the chance to tease you."

Joanna smiled. It had been so long since anyone had teased her in a friendly fashion. So long since she'd felt this comfortable with the people around her. "I want to buy books for Ashley's baby."

Mary-Lou stared at her. "The baby she's carrying? Not that I know much about child development, but it will be a while before it's reading."

"My earliest memory was of my dad reading to me. I was on his lap on the porch of Otter's Nest and I remember the sound of his voice, and the excitement as he turned the pages, and the feeling that this was an adventure we were taking together."

Mary-Lou sniffed. "He was a good man, your dad. We all miss him. Now let's find you some books."

"I want to make her a library. It's my gift to her." She was going to clear the bookshelves in the second guest bedroom and turn it into a nursery. Even if Ashley wanted to move to a place of her own, it would be somewhere that could be hers and the baby's when they came to visit.

"She's lucky to have you in her corner."

Joanna thought about Ashley's spirit and patience. "I'm the lucky one."

"Maybe. She was out with Eden last night. The two of them laughing so hard into their ice cream sundaes that everyone in the place was smiling, too. Do you know which books you want, or are you browsing?"

Joanna pulled out her list. "I have ideas, but suggestions are always welcome."

"With a list as long as that, you're the one who is welcome. If you want to spend your money here, I'm not going to stop you. Take all the time you need."

Joanna caught the anxiety in her voice. "How are things, Mary-Lou?"

"The store is busy enough." Mary-Lou rearranged a few of the books that people had put back randomly. "The most frustrating thing is that people come in here to browse, and then they go buy it online. I could do with hiring someone to help out here so I can spend more time at home—my mother's arthritis is worse, and there are weeks when she can't walk across the room—but I only need someone part time and I can't find anyone who wants to do it." She paused as her phone rang. "It's Mom—I need to get this."

Joanna waved a hand. "Go ahead—I'm fine here."

"Thanks. Mom?" Mary-Lou turned away and then stopped. "You *fell*? No! Did you call 911?… Well, of course you should!… No, it isn't bothering anyone—well, maybe they are busy, but you're as important as everyone else. More important, in my opinion. Stay there. I'm on my way—what?… It doesn't matter about the store. I'll close up. I'm coming with you to the hospital, and that's the end of it." She dropped the phone. Cursed. Fumbled for it. "Sorry, Joanna, I'm going to have to—"

"Close the store. I heard." Joanna rescued the phone and pressed it back into Mary-Lou's hand. "Give me the keys. I'll lock up for you. Just go. Call me later and let me know how she is. Send my best wishes to your mother, and if there is anything I can do, let me know."

"You'd lock up? That's kind. My mother is already worrying about how much money we'll lose. You know how she loves this place—I swear it's like a second child to her. But the store is the least of our worries right now." Mary-Lou glanced around the store, distracted.

"You need your purse." Joanna grabbed it from behind the counter. An idea formed, so momentous that she almost dismissed it. But these days she wasn't dismissing anything. "And unless you particularly want me to close, why don't I keep this place open? I worked a few shifts in Cliff's Cookstore when I was getting experience of the business. Enough that I can figure this out. And if people have questions, I can make a note of their details and you can deal with it when you're back."

Mary-Lou shook her head. "I can't ask you to do that."

"You're not asking, I'm offering. I'd really like to."

"But why? It's not like you need the money or a job—" Mary-Lou clamped her mouth shut. "That was rude. I'm sorry."

"Don't be. I'm not doing it for money, Mary-Lou, I'm doing it for you. For your mom. And for myself, because I can't think of a better way to spend a few hours than with a store full of books."

"Are you sure?"

"Positive. I haven't forgotten how kind your mother was to me when I was young, or her generosity. This is my chance to do something in return. Hopefully she will worry less if you reassure her that the store is still open for business. Now go. Call me when you have news on her."

"Well, in that case—thank you. You're a lifesaver." Mary-Lou pressed the keys into her hand and sped out of the door.

Joanna stood for a moment. She wasn't a lifesaver, but it was good to be able to help in a small way.

Moments later the door flew open. It was Rosa, from the boutique.

"Joanna! I just heard about Vivian. Thought Mary-Lou might need help with the store. I can watch both—or close mine for the day. Whatever works."

Community, Joanna thought. Here, everything and everyone were interconnected. They knew each other. They cared. She hadn't even realized how much she'd missed it until now.

"I've got this, Rosa, but I'll let you know as soon as we have news of Vivian."

"Mary-Lou will message me, I'm sure." Rosa grinned at her. "I hear you wore the white dress last night. How did that turn out for you?"

Thinking of exactly how it had turned out made Joanna's cheeks heat. "How did you—?"

"Ashley mentioned it. She and Eden were trying on half the

clothes in the store yesterday. I'm going to track down a few maternity pieces for her, for later on. Of course, right now you wouldn't even know she was pregnant." Rosa winked at her. "And look at you. Spending an evening with Nate. It's like time rewound."

In fact, it wasn't, and that was one of the things Joanna had enjoyed most about it. It hadn't felt like an extension of the old. It had felt new. Fresh.

"It was just dinner. I cooked it."

"And he survived. I know that because I saw him on the deck of the Surf Café a few moments ago. Smiling that smile of his, very much alive."

"I make it a point to try not to kill my dates."

"It's good to see both of you happy." Rosa folded her arms and narrowed her eyes. "Look at you. Joanna Rafferty. You always were the bookworm, and now you're in charge of a bookstore. This is your dream, right?"

Joanna laughed. "It is, although not under these circumstances, obviously." She thought of Vivian, and all the books she'd given Joanna over the years. "I owe Vivian a lot."

If there was a way to help, then she was going to help. And it wasn't as if they were likely to be busy.

Turned out she was wrong about that. By the time Mary-Lou reappeared at the end of the day, Joanna had served an endless stream of customers and hadn't had time to use the bathroom.

"You come back when you're ready for the sequel," she told a girl of seven who had just bought the first in a series of ballet books. "I'll keep it right here for you."

"Will you put my name on it?"

"I'll do that right now." Joanna pulled the book off the shelf, tucked a note inside and slid it behind the counter. "There. It's waiting for you."

The girl's mother smiled. "Thank you. This was fun."

Joanna waited for them to leave and then turned to Mary-Lou. "How is Vivian?"

"Nothing broken, thank goodness. She's going to have bruises, and she needs to take it easy for a while, but it could have been a lot worse. She sent her love to you. Said she hoped you'd stop by and see her soon."

"I'd like that. Mary-Lou, you look exhausted."

"Just worried. I'm going to have to close this place for the next few days so that I can stay close and help her." Mary-Lou rubbed her hand over her back. "Thanks for stepping in today."

"Don't close. I can cover this, although I've made a list of things I need help with so I don't lose you money." Joanna grabbed the notepad and quickly ran through her questions.

Mary-Lou hesitated. "If you're doing this, then I'm paying you."

"I don't—" Joanna was about to say she didn't want payment but then she saw the stubborn set of Mary-Lou's jaw. Independence, she thought. She knew all about the need for that. "Sure. Pay me whatever you feel is fair."

"It will be a meaningless amount to you."

"Money is never meaningless," Joanna said. "And this is my dream job."

Mary-Lou laughed. "Well, in that case, you're hired. You start at eight tomorrow. Unpack any new stock and shelve it. Clean the place. It's time to change the window display—we have a signing next week, so if you feel like flexing your artistic talents you can work on that."

She told Nate about it later as they strolled along the sand from the Surf Café. "I landed my dream job today. At forty. Can you believe that?" She pulled off her shoes and carried them, loving the feel of the sand on her bare feet. "I'm excited about going to work tomorrow, and I have never felt like that before."

"Are you sure you're not just going to sit there and read all the books?"

"That, too. Perks of the job, right? I've put together a few ideas for the window display. Do you think it would be interfering or forward of me to suggest doing a few events for children? I thought we could start with dressing up and reading." The ideas kept popping in her head and she couldn't wait to discuss some of them with Mary-Lou.

"I think Mary-Lou and Vivian will be glad for anything that attracts business."

"I don't want to overstep." But she couldn't stop herself planning. "I was thinking that in the future we could hold book club evenings at the Surf Café. That way we'd be combining—"

"Books, food and drink." He smiled and pulled her closer.

"You like the idea?"

"Yes. I also like the fact that your plans for the future involve being here for a while."

She thought about Mel and Greg. About Mary-Lou and Rosa. Ashley lying by the pool. Otter's Nest. Nate. "I didn't come here planning to stay, but now I can't imagine leaving. I spoke to the lawyers this morning. I'm selling my shares in Cliff's company." She'd made up her mind after their night together, when she'd realized that being with Nate hadn't been a trip back to the past, but a step into the future. The phone call had been the final severing of her old life from the new.

"You won't be part of it in the future?"

"No." The relief was enormous. "I don't know why I didn't do it before. I should have, but I suppose throwing out your entire life in one go is daunting."

"So what is this? A fresh start?"

They'd walked to the water's edge and she let the waves wash over her feet. The setting sun sent fingers of gold across the ocean and she'd never seen anything more beautiful in her life.

"Yes," she said. "It is a fresh start. I want to put the past behind me and just start again." She felt his arms come around her and he pulled her close.

"Are there any aspects of your old life you might want to keep? I'm asking for a friend."

"I don't want the old version of us." She slid her arms around his neck. "But I'm excited to explore the new version. Whatever that looks like."

"It looks good from where I'm standing." He kissed her and then finally lifted his head. "If we're going to do some exploring, we'd better find somewhere more private."

"Otter's Nest?"

"My place is closer."

They all but ran there, laughing when she dropped her shoes, stumbling through the side entrance of the Surf Café and up the wooden steps that led to his apartment.

It was breezy and light, the furnishings all white and ocean blue.

They washed the sand off their feet in the bathroom and then kissed their way to his bedroom, with its large bed overlooking the sea.

She awoke later feeling the chill of sea air on her skin.

Nate was sleeping deeply, one arm flung over her naked body.

She snuggled closer and tugged the covers over them, smiling and content as she relived the evening before.

She dozed again, and next time she woke the light was trickling through the windows. She picked up her phone to check the time, and saw that Nessa had returned her call from the day before.

The only thing she would miss about her old life was Nessa.

She slid out of bed and walked to the window. Today a low sea mist clung to the shore, blurring detail.

She gazed at the view for a moment and was about to go back

to bed when a couple of people caught her eye. It wasn't unusual to see people on the beach this early, but these two didn't seem interested in the beach. They were interested in the Surf Café.

She spotted the camera and stepped out of sight, heart racing.

Tourists? She so badly wanted it to be tourists, but there was no reason for a tourist to be interested in the Surf Café when it was closed.

It was all too familiar.

She scooped up her phone and walked quietly out of the bedroom into the living room.

It could be coincidence.

It didn't take her long to find out that it wasn't. The story was right there, along with a photograph of her and Nate kissing on the beach the evening before. The way he was holding her meant that her white dress was rucked up around her thighs. She was standing slightly on her toes, her arms locked around his neck. Her hair tumbled down her back. She was pressed so close to him that there wasn't a chink of light to be seen. *Is that how they'd looked?* She'd experienced that kiss from the inside, and now she was seeing it from the outside.

Nate was going to see that picture. Everyone in Silver Point, everyone he worked with, served, spoke to, were all going to see that picture. She no longer had any doubt that the people outside on the beach were watching the apartment. Because of her, his whole life would be exposed. It had been fun, and light and dizzyingly new, but now it felt tarnished. It was red wine spilled on a white dress. And to make it worse, they'd tracked down Denise and extracted a comment from her.

Serious? I doubt it. She isn't easy to love. If she was, then Cliff Whitman wouldn't have had all those affairs, would he?

Her hands shook on the phone. No matter what she did, who she saw, this was never going to stop. They'd carry on pointing their cameras, and pressing their noses up against her life.

Who needed that? Who wanted that?

She didn't.

Nate wouldn't.

She turned off her phone, not wanting to read anymore.

She took a few deep breaths and glanced longingly at the bedroom door, to the room where Nate still slept, oblivious.

She wanted to climb back into the bed and pretend this hadn't happened. She wanted to hold him for a bit longer. She wanted to walk on the beach with him, make dinner, make love, maybe make a life, but he was going to wake up, see the photographs and realize that life with her would always be complicated. And he was going to decide he didn't want that. And she would have to deal with the fact that he didn't want that.

Or maybe he'd pretend he was fine with it all, that it didn't bother him, and they'd carry on seeing each other, having fun, enjoying themselves, and she would fall deeper and deeper and—and what? What happened then?

One day he'd wake up and decide he wasn't fine with it and he'd reject her a second time.

Instead of a fun hookup, it would be heartbreak.

Caring had made her vulnerable.

There was sweat on her brow and the back of her neck. She felt sick. She kept remembering that day he'd ended it. It had almost broken her. She'd have to be a fool to let herself be broken by the same man twice, wouldn't she?

She retrieved her clothes and dressed quickly. Should she leave a note? No. Their relationship was still casual. Best to keep it that way.

She grabbed her car keys and quietly left the apartment. There was no sign of the photographers. Presumably they still had their cameras pointed at the window of the apartment, not expecting her to leave this early.

Without pausing, she slid into the car and drove back to Otter's Nest.

She half expected to see people gathering at her gates, but there was no one. But they would come. Her whereabouts had been plastered all over the internet.

And now she needed to stop thinking about Nate, and think about how she could best protect Ashley.

She'd imagined a future where their lives were intertwined, where she spent her days caring for the baby. She'd imagined them as a family.

It wasn't only Nate who would be exposed to this; Ashley would be, too. And Ashley's baby. And Rosa, Vivian, Mary-Lou, Mel, Greg—the list was endless.

She'd been lonely for so long, loneliness had become normal. If you did something for long enough, you forgot there was another way. Somewhere along the way she'd lost the ability to imagine an alternative, but now she was living the alternative and the thought of giving that up and going back to the lean, emotionally sparse life she'd led before made her want to cry. For the first time in ages she felt as if she was part of something. Connected. She didn't want to lose that.

But what could she do? She loved these people, and when you loved someone you wanted to protect them.

She didn't want this for any of them, but she especially didn't want it for the baby.

Maybe the best thing she could do for Ashley wasn't to babysit, but to set her up somewhere far from Joanna.

Maybe the best thing she could do for this community was leave it again.

The gates closed behind her. She felt a thickening in her throat and the hot burn of tears behind her eyes.

That short, sweet taste of freedom had made it harder to go back to her old way of life.

She'd started to make connections, and now she was going to have to cut them again.

She'd turn up at the Beach Bookstore in the morning because she'd promised Mary-Lou that she would and she would never break a promise to a friend. She'd help for as long as Mary-Lou and Vivian needed her, but she knew that it would be a temporary thing. Who would want Joanna Whitman and all her baggage working for them permanently?

She couldn't, wouldn't, pull anyone else into this.

24

Ashley

Ashley woke suddenly, and heard the sound of Joanna's bedroom door closing.

Half-asleep, she checked the time and saw that it was a little after six.

What was Joanna doing coming home at this hour when she'd stayed the night with Nate?

That wasn't good, was it?

Maybe they'd had a fight.

Or maybe Joanna didn't want to be seen leaving his apartment in the morning, wearing the same clothes she'd worn the night before. She'd texted Ashley to say she'd be helping out at the bookstore, so Ashley had assumed she'd go straight there.

Ashley opened the door of her own bedroom and stared at Joanna's closed door.

Should she check on her?

She was just debating the merits of that when the door opened and Joanna emerged.

Back to wearing jeans and the crisp white shirt, Ashley noted. Hair scooped into a twist on the back of her head. It was Joanna's "dealing with the world" uniform. Which could only mean one thing.

Trouble.

Something to do with Nate?

Joanna saw Ashley and paused. "I'm sorry. I didn't mean to wake you."

"I was already awake," Ashley lied. Something was wrong, and she intended to find out what. "I'm starving. Do you want to make pancakes?"

"Now?"

"Why not? We can eat them on the terrace. Perfect start to the day."

"I don't know how to make pancakes." Whatever the problem was, it had left Joanna looking pale and drawn. Ashley had been expecting secretive smiles and a happy glow.

"I'll teach you."

"Ashley, I'm not sure that—"

"The great thing about pancakes is that they're quick. Which makes them the perfect snack, any time of the day or night. I have the best recipe. Let me show you. You'll thank me." She headed to the kitchen and was relieved when Joanna followed. "You fetch the milk. I'll measure the flour. Does maple syrup work for you?"

"I—"

"My mother always thought maple syrup was the best. My dad—not Cliff, my real always-there-for-me dad—liked melted chocolate. Which turns pancakes into dessert, I always think, but each to his own."

Joanna removed the milk from the fridge. "How much?"

"Depends on how hungry you are. How was your evening?"

"Fine, thank you."

Fine?

Ashley handed her the rest of the ingredients and the whisk. "If you want to invite him to dinner again, I have another recipe to teach you."

"You can teach me the recipe because I enjoy cooking with you, but he won't be coming to dinner again."

"Any particular reason?"

"Yes." Joanna put the whisk down. "And this affects you, too."

"Me?"

"I woke up this morning and saw a couple of photographers on the beach."

"I assume you don't mean the tourist variety. Outside Nate's place?" So it had finally happened. The fact that they'd expected it didn't make it any less outrageous. "Did they see you?"

"Not then, but earlier." Joanna sighed and picked up the whisk. "You can see for yourself. Check your phone."

It took her seconds to find the photographs, and a few more seconds to scan the words that went with them.

"Lucky in Love—Has Cliff Whitman's Widow Finally Found Happiness?" she read the headline. "Well, the answer to that is a big fat yes. You should tell them that what you've really found is good sex and that they should mind their own business." She was relieved to see Joanna smile. "I like this headline. Jojo Finds Her Mojo. Do you know what this does?"

"Ruins my life again?"

"It gives women hope. This photo says that you can find happiness after you've been royally messed around by a lying, cheating man. And the fact that you're able, and willing, to trust again sends a powerful message."

Joanna took the phone from her and stared at it. "This photo says that whenever you find happiness, you can guarantee the press will try and ruin it. Everyone will see it. Everyone will read it."

"And everyone will know that this is nothing to do with you." Ashley removed the phone from Joanna's fingers and put it down. "You're upset because they photographed you with Nate."

"I was enjoying being in his world, and now I've dragged him into mine."

"Not exactly. What did Nate say about it?"

"Nothing. He doesn't know. I left before he woke up."

"Because of this?" Ashley glanced up. "So you don't know how he feels? It might not bother him at all."

"I know how *I* feel, and it bothers me. I don't want this for someone I…care about."

Love, Ashley thought. *She'd been about to say love.*

She thought about Nate, always so calm and relaxed. "At least you ought to hear what he has to say." She paused. "What are you afraid of, Joanna? Really?"

"There's only so much people can take."

Ashley swallowed. "Are you saying you don't think you're worth it? That people won't put themselves through a little press intrusion for you?"

"I guess I'm saying they shouldn't have to."

"Really? Why did you bring me here, Joanna? You disrupted your whole life for me, and to begin with, it was because you felt real empathy for my situation, I get that. But what about afterward? By linking our stories, and not distancing yourself, you've made it worse for yourself. You didn't have to keep me here in your home. You didn't have to include me in your life. You didn't have to stop me leaving."

"I care about you. I didn't want you to leave. I would never abandon you."

"I know. And that part was hard for me to accept. I didn't dare trust it. Why would you risk putting yourself through even more? Why would you do that? And then I realized that you were doing it because you really did care about me. And caring for someone means sticking by them not only when things are easy, but when things are tough. It's easy enough to lie on the beach in the sun with someone, but what about when the wind howls and the storm hits? Do you run for cover?"

"Ashley—"

"You didn't run for cover. You did the opposite. You were

right there for me, in the middle of the storm. And the fact that you were willing to do that, the fact that you cared that much…" She swallowed. "You don't think people love you like that, Joanna? You don't think these people care about you enough to stay by your side when the wind howls and the storm hits? You think Nate, Mel, Greg, Mary-Lou, Rosa are going to turn their backs on you because of a few photos?"

"I don't know. I really don't know. They shouldn't have to—"

"It takes real courage to accept that people care, and love you. It's easier to push them away, because then you can't be hurt. Easier to protect yourself and not allow yourself to be vulnerable. Not allow yourself to be disappointed in people. But there's a price to pay for that, and the price is loneliness. Is that really the life you want to live? At least give them a chance, Joanna. Let them decide whether this is too much or not. Don't decide for them, the way I did when I walked away from here. I should have just said to you, *Joanna, is this too much*, but I was scared and I made the decision for both of us. Don't do that. Deep down you know these people care. *You know that.*"

Did she? Did she know that?

There was a long silence.

Ashley felt a rush of anxiety. Maybe she didn't know that. Maybe it was impossible to truly understand how it must feel to be Joanna. After all, she'd had years of this. Decades.

She put her hand on Joanna's arm. "I'm sorry to push you. If you want to hide out here, then we can. I'll hang out with you. We'll—"

"No." Joanna finally spoke. "We won't be hiding. And everything you said is true. It does take courage to trust that people care about you. And people should make their own decisions on what they can handle, and what they can't. I suppose that's about to be put to the test."

"So you'll stay?"

"Yes."

It felt as if the sun had broken through the clouds. Ashley picked up the phone again. "You know what I see when I look at that photo? I see a happy ending. The press hate happy endings. They're boring. Maybe they will leave us alone now."

Joanna looked at her. "Or maybe they won't. They're going to focus on you, too."

"That's my problem."

Joanna straightened. "No. It's our problem."

Ashley felt a rush of warmth. "We'll handle it. I'm not sure I even care." She paused. There was one other thing neither of them had mentioned. "What are you going to do about Denise?"

"Denise?"

"You were deciding whether you wanted to talk to her or not. Whether it would give you closure. Are we going to go and see her?"

Joanna glanced toward the phone. "That quote of hers has given me closure. We're done."

And that, Ashley thought, was a giant step in the right direction.

"Good. Now let's make these pancakes and then you can go to work. We can meet for lunch at the Surf Café, just as we planned. Twelve thirty?"

"If Mary-Lou can take over the store for an hour."

"And are you going to talk to Nate?"

Joanna raised an eyebrow. "This, from someone who still has to listen to her messages from Jon?"

"Ouch. Point taken. I'm going to do that today. Maybe when we get home tonight." Ashley watched as Joanna heated the pan and added a dollop of mixture. "Will you listen to them with me?"

"Of course." Joanna put the spoon down and hugged her. "We'll do it tonight, when we're home. And I can show you the books I bought yesterday, for the baby. I was thinking maybe we could turn the small guest room into a nursery. If you decide to stay for a while, obviously. We need to research the best place for you to have the baby. We need to find you a good doctor. I'm going to ask Mel today."

Ashley felt a ripple of anxiety. Talk of books, and nurseries, and doctors made it all seem alarmingly real. "You're probably right." It was so much easier to focus on Joanna's problems than her own. "You changed the subject. What are you going to do about Nate?"

Joanna flipped the pancakes. "I'm not going to do anything about Nate."

Ashley tried to hide her disappointment. She so badly wanted Joanna to be happy, and with Nate she'd seemed happy. But it was her decision, of course.

They ate their pancakes on the terrace and then Joanna stood up.

"I'm going to change."

"Change?"

"I thought I'd wear a dress. If they're going to take my photo, then I want to look my best."

Ashley grinned. "Good plan."

Ashley took a shower and they headed into Silver Point.

"You can come to the bookstore with me if you like." Joanna pulled into the parking area behind the store. "It won't be easy for photographers to hide themselves in there."

"Thanks, but I'm fine." Ashley grabbed her bag and stepped out of the car. "I'm meeting Eden on the beach. She's giving me a surf lesson. I'm going to catch my first wave, and if they want to photograph me making a total fool of myself in the water, they can go right ahead."

"If you're sure." Joanna locked the car. "You know where I am if you need me. I'll see you later for lunch."

Ashley headed to the beach and spent a happy morning with

Eden. By the time she walked up the steps of the Surf Café, she was starving.

Joanna was already there, seated at a table at the back of the deck.

There was no sign of Nate.

Ashley slid into the chair facing the beach. She ordered a burger and fries, and Joanna ordered a salad.

"So it turns out that learning to surf starts with standing on your board on dry land—" She bit into her burger and paused, her attention caught by the small group of people who had gathered at the base of the steps. One of the men had his camera trained right on her.

The people at the table closest to them turned to stare.

Ashley lowered the burger.

"What—?" Joanna followed her gaze and saw the cameras. "Here we go."

One of them took the steps and would have walked right to the table but Greg appeared from nowhere and blocked their path.

Who had called him? Maybe it was Mel. Or maybe it was one of the other inhabitants of Silver Point.

Greg stood, rock steady, legs spread. "Do you have a reservation?"

The man frowned. "No, Officer, but—"

"If you call for a reservation, I'm sure the team would be glad to find you a table sometime."

"I don't want a table." The man's gaze flickered to Ashley and Joanna. "I just wanted to have a few words—"

"A person deserves to be able to eat their lunch in peace."

Everyone was looking at them now. Food was ignored. Drinks were untouched.

Ashley felt guilty for encouraging Joanna to expose herself like this. "Let's leave," she muttered. "We could head out the back."

"We are not leaving. And when we do, we'll be using the front entrance." Joanna put her fork down and stood up. She walked to Greg and put her hand on his arm. "Thank you. I'm sorry to disrupt the peace of Silver Point."

"You're not the one disrupting anything."

"I don't want this to take up your time or impact you in any way. You have more important things to do in your job."

"I'm not doing this because it's my job," Greg said. "I'm doing this for a friend. A good friend."

Joanna squeezed his arm. "I'll deal with this, Greg."

Ashley swallowed. She stood up, too. What was Joanna doing? It looked as if she was going to talk to the press. But that couldn't be right. She never talked to the press. She never gave interviews.

She saw Joanna smile at the other people on the terrace.

"I apologize for the disturbance. I hope you enjoy your lunch." With that, she walked down the steps onto the beach, and stood directly in front of the group with their cameras and their microphones.

Ashley grabbed her purse and followed. If Joanna was doing this, then so was she.

She followed Joanna down the steps and stood next to her.

There was no doubt as to who was in control, and it wasn't the crowd with the cameras and the microphones. She aspired to have half Joanna's poise and dignity.

"Joanna! Joanna Whitman—"

"It's Rafferty." Joanna was cool and calm.

"You changed your name? Why?"

"I stopped sharing my life with Cliff a long time ago. It seemed wrong to keep sharing his name." The way she said it made it sound entirely logical.

"Is it true that you're leaving the company?"

"Yes, that's true."

"Are you going to be staying in Silver Point? What will you be doing?"

"I'll be staying. This is my home, and I'll be building a life here. That's what I want. I hope you'll agree that I deserve it."

"When did you discover that Cliff had a child?"

"Is it true that Ashley is living with you?"

The questions came in a flood but this time Joanna simply lifted a hand. "I won't be answering any more questions."

The reporters turned their attention to Ashley.

They yelled her name and pointed microphones. "How does it feel to know you're Cliff Whitman's daughter? How do you feel now you know who you are?"

How did she feel? She felt like a zoo exhibit.

How did anyone put up with this? It was so intrusive. So personal. All your mess strewn right there for everyone to witness, like someone looking inside your bedroom before you'd had a chance to tidy it. Yes, her life was a mess, but it was her mess and hers alone. She didn't want to share it with the world. She didn't want strangers picking through the pieces of her life and judging her.

She felt vulnerable and alone and then Joanna stepped in front of her.

"That's enough." Her voice was firm. "We've said all we intend to say."

Ashley felt shaky with relief and gratitude.

She wasn't alone.

She had Joanna. Joanna, who had coped with this for years on her own.

Ashley grabbed Joanna's hand and stood by her side. "Yes, Cliff Whitman was my father," she said, "but that's my business and not anyone else's. And frankly you can all—" She stopped as she felt Joanna's fingers bite into her arm.

"Enjoy the beach," Joanna said calmly. "Ashley and I both want you to enjoy what Silver Point has to offer, but we're not included. Now we'd be grateful if you'd leave us alone."

But it seemed there was no chance of that.

"Who is the father of your baby? Now we know it wasn't Cliff, are you going to tell us who it is?"

"No, I'm not. That is none of your—"

"I am." A male voice came from the back of the crowd, clear and strong. "I'm the father. And now I'd like you to all move on and stop stressing the mother of my child."

Ashley felt her knees wobble. Her purse slid from her fingers. She couldn't see the face, but she knew that voice.

"Jon?"

"That's Jon? Dark hair at the back?" Joanna spoke under her breath. "You forgot to mention that he's *seriously* cute."

"Did I? I—he is cute. And kind. And smart. I don't know what he's doing here."

"Well, given that he just announced his presence to the world, I think we can safely say he's looking for you." Joanna gave her hand another squeeze and then let go. "You should talk to him."

"I don't know what to say." But she'd run out of time to plan a strategy because he was pushing his way through to the front of the crowd.

"Just say what comes into your head." Joanna stepped to one side and smiled at the photographers and reporters who were still snapping away. "I'm sure you'll want to give them privacy."

"All right, enough." Greg appeared and moved the crowd away.

Ashley didn't even notice. She'd ceased to worry about the audience. All she could think about was the fact that Jon was here.

She could handle the press, but she couldn't handle this. Facing Jon. Losing Jon. Worse, losing him in public.

She'd been too terrified to listen to his messages and because of that she was going to have to hear him tell her in person all the reasons why their night together had been a mistake. If she'd listened to the messages she would have had time to nurse her misery in private, before facing him now.

She'd thought she'd already lived through some horrible moments, but this was going to be the worst.

His shirt was rumpled and his eyes were tired. He looked as if he'd driven through the night.

She felt a stab of guilt. "I was going to contact you."

"When?" He picked up the purse she'd dropped. "When our baby is off to college?"

"No, of course not." She felt a sting in her throat and then flung her arms around him. "It's so, so good to see you. You have no idea. And I'm sorry for everything. This is all my fault."

"I don't know how you figure that." His hand was on her back, rubbing gently. "I seem to remember having a lot to do with it. Why the hell didn't you call, Ash? I've been out of my mind with worry. I saw your photo on TV and I called the hospital but they wouldn't tell me anything and no one seemed to know where you were. And then you sent me one message. That was it. One message, saying you'd call soon only you never did. Why not?"

"Because I thought this was something I had to handle on my own. It was my mess. And—" she swallowed "—I was scared."

"Scared?" He pulled away so that he could see her face. "I said something that scared you?"

"No. I don't know what you said."

"Neither do I. I left so many messages I lost count."

She squirmed. "I haven't listened to them yet."

"You—" He stared at her. "You haven't listened to my messages?"

"No. I didn't dare. I didn't know how to handle the situation. I didn't know how you felt."

He let out a long breath. "Right. If you'd listen to your messages or answer your phone once in a while, you'd know how I feel." He smoothed her hair back. "Were you ever going to call me?"

"Yes, when I'd figured out what to say. I didn't want you to feel pressured. I actually was going to listen to your messages tonight. Joanna was going to do it with me."

"Good thing I kept them clean, but I hate the idea you thought you needed moral support to listen to a message from me." He held out his hand. "Give me your phone."

"But—"

"Phone."

She handed it over and he accessed her voice mail.

"Listen." He put the phone to her ear.

Ash, it's Jon. I'm worried about you. Please call.

Ashley, it's Jon again. Please pick up the phone.

Ashley, it's Jon.

It's Jon. If you don't want to see me, that's fine, but at least tell me you're safe.

She listened to the messages one by one. They grew more and more urgent.

Ashley, I just saw your photo on TV. I know about the accident. I know you're messed up about Cliff Whitman being your dad and your mom not telling you, but we'll figure it out. I know about the baby and I know it's mine. We really need to talk. I miss you.

She looked up at him. "You...missed me?"

"Of course I missed you. My laptop broke again and there was no one to fix it."

She grinned. "That's it? That's why you missed me? Because I can fix your laptop."

"There might have been a few other things about you that I missed."

"Like what?"

He pretended to think about it. "I miss your singing."

"Jon, I'm a really bad singer."

"I know. But I love the way you do it, anyway. And I missed the way you dance around the room even when there's no music playing. The way you eat peanut butter with a spoon. The way your hair is so wild and curly in the mornings you can hardly see through it. The way you suddenly have a great idea and you burst if you don't immediately tell me. Also, the way you put things off when you absolutely don't want to do them. Talking of which—" He pointed to the phone. "There's another message."

He loved those things about her?

She played the last message.

Ashley, I love you. And it feels weird saying this to a machine, but you haven't called and I don't know where you are so there's no other way to tell you how I feel. I love you.

She couldn't breathe. She wanted to play it again to be sure she'd heard it correctly. "You love me?"

"Do you really need to ask me that? We've been friends for a decade, Ash. You know I love you."

"I know you love me as a friend, but—"

"We spent the night together."

"I know. But I was upset, and—"

"You think it was pity sex? Tell me you don't think that." He raked his fingers through his hair. "Did it *feel* like pity sex?"

"No." She felt her face turn hot. "And I don't think that. Not really. But I was upset, and I did wonder if I took advantage of you."

"Any time you want to take advantage of me, go ahead." He pulled her back into his arms. "I love you."

She hadn't known those words could make her feel the way she did. "Do you mean that? Really?"

"Yes, I mean that."

"And you don't care that Cliff Whitman was my dad?"

"Why would I? How is that relevant?" He studied her face for a moment and then held out his hand. "Give me your phone again."

"Why?"

He waggled his fingers. "Just give it to me."

She handed it over and he unlocked it, because he knew her

code just as she knew his, and then he scrolled back through her photos.

"What are you looking for?"

"Give me a minute." He scrolled, and then grinned. "This." He turned the phone and showed her a photo of her and David learning to rollerblade. They were clutching each other and laughing so hard their faces were contorted.

She remembered that day, and the fun they'd had, and felt a pang. "We were so bad at it. And that's a terrible photo. I don't know why I keep it."

"You keep it because it's an important memory. And look." He flipped through her photos and found another one. "Here's one of the two of you at that festival."

"He was trying to be cool. He bought a new shirt specially because he didn't want to embarrass me by wearing his usual shirt." She sniffed. "I miss him so much. I wish he was here now. But I'm pleased I have those photos. And you're right, they're perfect. They're not staged, or edited, but they're real."

"And David was real. Your real dad. Cliff wasn't your dad, Ash." Jon handed the phone back. "Not in any real sense of the word."

He was right. She knew it. Why was she worrying so much about Cliff, when he'd never played even a small part in her life? When he'd made it clear he didn't want to be in her life?

He'd never been a part of her life in the past, and he didn't need to be a part of it in the future.

"It's just embarrassing, that's all."

"So? Who doesn't have an embarrassing family member? Wait until you meet my aunt Maud. She makes Cliff look respectable."

He made her laugh. He always made her laugh, and feel better about everything. Even Cliff.

"I can't believe you're here. I can't believe you love me."

"What will it take to convince you?"

"Well, you're here, so that's pretty convincing." She leaned

BEACH HOUSE SUMMER • 339

her head against his shoulder. "But if you wanted to tell me a few more times, that wouldn't hurt." She felt his arms tighten.

"I love you. I love you, I love you, I love you. Are you tired of hearing it yet?"

She knew she'd never get tired of hearing it. "I love you, too."

"That's good to know, because we're having a baby."

"Oh." She sniffed and hugged him back. He smelled good. He *felt* good. "That photographer is taking photographs."

"I don't care. I'm happy to share my feelings with the whole world if that's what it takes."

"You're going to college. You have plans. Your life is all mapped out."

"Plans change, Ash. We'll make new ones. We'll figure this out together. My mom sends her love by the way."

Ashley groaned. "She probably thinks I ruined your life."

"No. She's pretty cool, my mom. She thinks that you don't choose when love comes along, but if you're lucky enough that it does, then you have to grab it. College, jobs—all those other things can be figured out, but love is too precious to lose. She'll give us all the support we need. And talking of support, you still haven't told me where you've been staying."

"With Joanna." Joanna! How could she have forgotten Joanna? Ashley pulled away and saw Joanna talking to Greg.

Where was Nate? Why was there no sign of Nate?

She'd been sure that once he woke and found Joanna gone, he'd be in touch.

She felt guilty feeling so happy when Joanna must be miserable.

Joanna waved at her and gestured that she was going back to the bookstore. She looked fine, but Ashley knew that was probably an act. No one hid her feelings as well as Joanna.

Ashley felt a desperate urge to talk to her but she was already walking away and Jon was standing in front of her and she hadn't seen him in so long. And they still had so much to talk about.

"Wait—" Jon looked confused. "You've been living with Joanna Whitman?"

"Rafferty." Ashley watched Joanna walk away from the beach, Greg by her side. "She's not Whitman anymore. And yes, I've been living with her. She's amazing, and I can't wait for you to meet her properly. I have so much to tell you."

"I can't wait to hear it. Any chance you could tell me over some food?" Jon glanced at the Surf Café. "I've been traveling for hours and I'm starving."

She started to laugh because it was so, so Jon. "You're always hungry."

"I know. And I haven't changed in the short time you had your phone turned off. Maybe it's because we're pregnant."

"I'm the one who is pregnant."

"I have sympathy hunger. What's the burger like here?"

"Er—the best I've eaten anywhere?"

"Then what are we waiting for?"

She hesitated. "You don't want to go somewhere more private?"

"Later. But for now this seems like a good place to celebrate this new chapter in our lives." He grabbed her hand and they headed back to the table she and Joanna had vacated earlier.

Ashley held his hand tightly, because only by touching him did this whole thing feel real. He was here. Jon. Her best friend. The person she loved most in the world. The father of her baby. Her past and now, it seemed, her future.

It was definitely something to celebrate.

25

Joanna

Mary-Lou was waiting for her when Joanna arrived back at the store.

"I hear Silver Point is suddenly a popular destination."

"Seems that way, and I'm sorry for my part in it." Joanna felt nerves hop around in her stomach. She kept waiting for people to tell her they didn't need this. "Is it too much for you?"

"What?"

"Having me here. Attracting attention."

"Nothing wrong with attention. It never hurts to have the spotlight shone on our little corner of the world. If it brings in business, we'll all be thanking you." Mary-Lou narrowed her eyes. "Why would you think it's too much for me? You think I can't handle myself if I need to?"

"I know you can, but—"

"But why would I want to? Is that what you're asking?" Mary-Lou's mouth tightened. "Let me ask *you* something, Joanna Rafferty. Why are you here today?"

"Because you needed help. Because Vivian was always so kind to me when I was young, because you're a friend and because I love books and this bookstore in particular and frankly I don't need an excuse to work here."

Mary-Lou nodded. "We needed help. And here you are. That's what friends do. And that goes both ways, Joanna." She picked up her purse. "If one of those photographers sticks their camera inside this store, they'd better buy a book is all I can say. And you can tell Nate from me that if I'd known he kissed as well as it seemed he did in that photo, I would have snatched him away from you when I was sixteen."

Joanna laughed, ignoring the tug of emotion. She couldn't tell Nate anything because he hadn't been in touch.

But despite that, she felt better. "Thank you, Mary-Lou. How is Vivian?"

"Bruised and aching, but well enough to make sure I know how much pain she's in. She loved the flowers. That was thoughtful. Thank you."

"You're welcome. You should go. She'll be waiting for you."

"Are you sure?" Mary-Lou hesitated. "You're not going to change your mind about helping? You'll be sticking around? No matter what?"

Joanna understood the question. Mary-Lou had seen the photos, along with everyone else. She was probably wondering what happened next. She knew that last time Joanna's relationship with Nate had ended, she'd left town.

"I took this job, Mary-Lou. I won't let you down." She was relieved when the door opened, and the bell rang. "Customers."

The "customer" turned out to be Mel. She exchanged a few words with Mary-Lou as she walked through the door, and then joined Joanna.

"I finished the book I was reading."

"Was it good?"

"Thriller. Quite the body count. Might need something a bit more uplifting this time around." Mel leaned on the counter. "I was thinking maybe a romance."

"You? A romance? You don't read anything that doesn't include blood and gore."

"I'm trying to expand my reading taste. If you're going to be working here, I'm guessing you can help me with that."

"You heard about my job?"

"Yes. And I punched the air. Finally one of Joanna's dreams has come true—she's working in a bookstore. Now we just need to work on the other one."

"The other one?" Joanna picked up a box of books that had been delivered that morning, and carried them to the back. She'd shelve them later, when the store was closed.

"They were good photos." Mel flashed her a smile and waggled her eyebrows. "Anything you want to tell me?"

"Nothing at all. Why don't you try this one?" Joanna pulled a book from the shelf nearest to her. She couldn't, wouldn't, talk about Nate. "It's the first in a series."

"Which means that if I enjoy it, I won't have to make any reading decisions for the foreseeable future." Mel flipped the book over and read the back. "Sounds good. I'm sold." She handed over the book and her credit card. "I hear Jon appeared at the crucial moment. I'm sorry I missed the drama."

"You know about Jon?"

"Ashley mentioned him when she and Eden had their movie night. Eden's talked to me more since Ashley arrived on the scene than she has in the past two years."

"I'm glad things are better between you."

"So am I. I'm sure Ashley is part of the reason. I saw her and Jon just now, heads close together, holding hands under the table. Not that I know much about young love, but I'd say the signs were hopeful." She slipped the book into her bag. "It's Rosa's birthday next week, did you know? We're organizing a surprise birthday party for her at the Surf Café. One of those occasions where we all jump out from behind a door or something. Although half the town is likely to be there so how we're all fitting behind a door I have no idea. It was Mary-Lou's idea. I said to her, *If Rosa has a heart attack, I'm holding you responsible.* But I think she might like it."

"I think so, too."

"Will you come? You and Ashley? And Jon, of course. We want the whole community there. All her friends."

She was Rosa's friend. She was part of a community. They were going to celebrate a birthday. "Yes. Thank you. What can I bring?"

"A bigger door?" Mel laughed. "Just yourself. Fancy an early-morning swim tomorrow? Like we used to?"

Joanna looked at her old friend. "Yes, I really do."

Mel nodded. "It's a date. I'll see you on the beach at seven." She left the store and Joanna watched her go and thought what a luxury it was to be part of something, to belong, to be surrounded by people who cared.

She went into the storeroom to sort through the books that had arrived.

She'd only managed to open one box when she heard the sound of the bell.

Her heart rate increased and she stood up and smoothed her hair.

Nate?

She stepped back into the store and stopped dead. "Nessa?"

"Hi, boss." Nessa grinned. "Why is it that when I'm not around to help you always get yourself into a mess?"

"What are you *doing* here?"

"I'm still officially your assistant." Nessa swung her backpack off her shoulder. "I thought you might be able to use some help now those photographers are starting to swarm again, but it seems you have everything under control. You look great, by the way."

"Thank you. It's good to see you." Joanna gave Nessa a big hug. "I'm so grateful for all you did. The car. Handling the media. All of it. The car!" She stepped back with a flash of guilt. "I need to return the car. How could I have forgotten?"

"Judging from the latest set of photos, you had other things on your mind." Nessa winked at her. "No hurry. Dan doesn't need the car."

"Do you have some time off? Can you spend a few days here?"

"I can spend as long as I like. I'm no longer working for the company, either."

"What? That can't be right. Your job was secure. I made sure of it." She felt a flash of anger. "I'll make a call right now."

"Don't. They didn't want me to leave. It was my choice."

"You chose to leave?"

"Yes. I worked for you. If you don't need an assistant, I'll figure something else out."

Joanna thought about everything Nessa had done. How she'd been a friend to her when everyone else had turned away. "I need an assistant. We can figure out the details later. Do you have somewhere to stay? I have room at Otter's Nest."

Nessa tilted her head. "Do you have a pool?"

"A pool and a beach."

"In that case say hello to your newest houseguest. I don't expect you to cook for me, obviously—"

"I can cook for you. Ashley has been teaching me."

"Ashley—?" Nessa turned as the door opened and Ashley walked in, tugging Jon with her.

"Joanna! Are you okay? You were amazing back there."

"I'm fine. And this must be Jon." Joanna held out her hand and then dispensed with formality and hugged him. "We're so very pleased you're here."

"Thanks." Jon's face turned pink. "And thanks for everything you've done for Ashley."

"I should be thanking her for everything she has done for me."

"Did she fix your laptop? She's great at that. And cooking.

And if your car won't start, she'll get it going. She's great at everything. Well, maybe not singing." He grinned at Ashley, who poked her tongue out.

He was so proud of her. She could see it in his eyes, the way he looked at her.

"Joanna?" Now it was Ashley who was turning pink. "Can Jon stay at Otter's Nest for a few days?"

"He can stay as long as he likes. You both can. Nessa will be staying, too."

And it would be fine, she realized. Whatever happened, she was going to be fine. Because her life was different now. She belonged here. She was part of something. Or maybe she was older and wiser. It wasn't that she didn't want things to work out with Nate, because she did. *Oh, yes, she did.* But her life wasn't going to fall apart if that didn't happen. And whatever did or didn't happen, she wouldn't be leaving this place.

Nessa stepped forward. "Good to meet you, Ashley. I just saw your romantic moment live streamed on the internet. Best thing I've seen all year and I watch a *lot* of movies. I'm happy for you both."

They laughed and chatted and Joanna served a couple of customers, taking time to choose exactly the right book for the little girl who loved dinosaurs.

"We'll see you later, Joanna." Ashley edged up to her when she finished. "We're taking Nessa to Frozen Flavor because I keep telling her she hasn't lived until she's tried their mint chocolate chip, and then we're going to pick up food for tonight and she's giving us a ride back to Otter's Nest. We're going to make you dinner."

"That sounds perfect."

Almost perfect. Of course, she would have loved Nate to be there. She was human, wasn't she? She wasn't going to pretend to herself that she didn't care. But she understood.

She didn't blame him for not showing.

She walked back into the storeroom and took another glance at her phone, cringing as she saw the intimacy of those photos. Who would voluntarily sign up for that? Who needed it? Not her and, apparently, not him. It had felt good to stand up in front of those photographers for once. Good to stand her ground. But she was never going to enjoy it, or embrace it.

Fame, whether positive or negative, was something she could happily live without.

She put her phone away and was lifting books out of boxes when she heard the door open again.

At least they were busy. Mary-Lou would be happy about that.

She walked through to the front of the store, a smile on her face. "How may I—?"

Nate stood there.

"Help me?" He smiled and closed the door. "How long have you got? I can think of a million ways so this might take a while."

All morning she'd waited for him to call her, or show up, and he hadn't. She'd resigned herself to the fact that he was staying away. Forced herself to be okay with that.

And now here he was.

And he was smiling at her.

"Nate—"

"I woke up and found you gone. Why did you leave?"

"Isn't it obvious?"

"Not to me. You had to get to work? You had to go home and change first? Why not wake me?" He searched her face. "What am I missing?"

"You…don't know?"

"Don't know what?"

"The photographs. All over the internet. You haven't seen them?"

"What photographs? I had a meeting with a supplier this

morning. I haven't even looked at my phone. I almost called you on my way home, but I'm more of a face-to-face guy than a phone guy. Half the time I forget to switch the thing on. Mel says it's one of my most irritating features."

He hadn't looked at his phone.

He hadn't seen the photos. All morning she'd been stressing out and he didn't even know. Was that good or bad?

"They took photographs. On the beach last night."

"Photographs of us?" He held out his hand. "Show me."

She opened up her phone, found the page and handed it over. She felt like taking a long walk, but that would mean leaving the bookstore unattended and she wasn't doing that.

Nate studied her phone. "You look good. I look good, too. A bit like a romantic hero, but that's probably because it was evening light and I look good in the dark." He glanced at her and shrugged. "Are you telling me that they're going to point cameras into my bedroom? Because if so, I am definitely going to have to tidy up."

She wanted to be able to laugh. She wanted to joke about it and roll her eyes and say, *This doesn't matter at all,* but she hadn't yet reached the point where she could do that.

He glanced back at the photos, and this time he was presumably reading what they'd written because his mouth tightened. "I see Denise hasn't mellowed with age."

"Doesn't seem like it."

He handed the phone back. "This is why you left without waking me up?"

"I was up early and I saw them on the beach outside the Surf Café. Photographers. I saw what they'd already posted. I didn't want you to have to deal with that. It's part of my life and it's possible it's always going to be part of my life, but it doesn't have to be part of yours."

He was silent for a moment and then walked to the door and locked it. Then he flipped the sign to Closed.

She frowned. "What are you doing?"

"Guaranteeing us five minutes' privacy. If they want to take photos through the window, they can go right ahead." He walked back to her. "Did you really think I'd care about any of that, Jo? Did you really think I give a damn about what a bunch of strangers, or Denise, or anyone that isn't you or I, think about our relationship?"

"It's intrusive, and personal and—"

"It feels personal, I get that, but it isn't really personal, is it? They don't know you, or me, any more than we know them. Intrusive? Yes, maybe that, but I don't care. I don't care if they want to spend their day hiding out and taking photographs. It seems like a weird way to make a living to me, but who am I to judge? I make shrimp salad and macadamia cookies and I spend my life surfing so I'm hardly changing the world. That doesn't matter. The only thing that matters is you and me. Us." He took her face in his hands. "I don't know where this thing between us is going, but I want to find out."

She wanted to find out, too. But it wasn't that simple, was it? "What if they don't leave us alone?"

"What exactly are you afraid of? What is this really about?" His voice was gentle. "You think they're going to publish something that will influence the way I feel? That isn't going to happen. Firstly, because I don't check my phone that often so I'm probably not going to see it, anyway, and secondly, because I like to make up my own mind about things. I know you, Joanna. I know who you are."

She'd expected him to distance himself. She'd thought his response would be the same as other people who had come and gone from her life. But this was Nate.

"You really don't care?"

"If you have to ask me that, then you definitely don't know me as well as you should. We need to work on that." He kissed her, long and slow, and then he lifted his head. "Dinner tonight?"

It would have been easy to be swept away by the romance of it all, by the dizzy excitement that came from being this close to him. Once, she would have been, but she was a different person now. Her childhood had been saturated by wild emotions—grief, insecurity, anxiety—as she'd struggled to shape a life in the absence of a loving adult. She'd brought all her insecurities to her relationship with Nate. But now she was free of them. All she was bringing was herself.

And she realized that this wasn't really about the media, it was about *her*.

She eased away. "I need to be clear about something. I love being with you, Nate. The time I've spent with you is the happiest I've been in a long time. But my life is more than my relationship with you. Last time—" she forced herself to remember it "—last time you were everything and I couldn't picture a life without you. Now, it's different. I want to carry on seeing you. I want to find out where this leads. But if it doesn't work out, for either one of us, I know I'll be fine. I don't want you to feel pressure or obligation. I don't want you to feel responsible. I'll be okay. And I won't be leaving town, no matter what happens. I won't run again. I'm building a new life, and I'm going to carry on building it."

"And what if I want to build that life with you?"

"It's too soon to—" She felt his fingers cover her lips.

"I'm forty years old, Joanna. I know exactly what I want. And what I want is to carry on seeing you. I want to find out where this leads. But if it doesn't work out, for either one of us, I know you'll be fine. And I wouldn't want you to leave." He let his hand drop. "I lost you once before, and I'm not losing you again. We can talk about the past, but the past is done. Those four decades behind us—finished. I care about the decades we have ahead. The future. Our future. And we can make this complicated, but really it's easy because it comes down to one thing. You make me happy. Being with you makes me happy. It always did."

"Being with you makes me happy, too."

Was it really that easy?

Could it be that easy?

He kissed her again, more urgently this time, and she felt her past melt away and thought, *Maybe it can be this easy. Maybe all I have to do is let it be easy.*

They kissed until her heart was racing and she almost forgot where she was. But not quite.

Reluctantly, she pulled away. "We shouldn't be doing this. I need to open the store again. I'm working. I have responsibilities. I need to serve customers."

His gaze was fixed on her mouth, as if he wasn't quite sure if he was ready to give it up.

"Working. Right. So, Joanna Rafferty…" He cleared his throat, plunged his hands into his pockets and glanced at the shelves. "Do you have any books on second chances?"

The question made her heart lift. Right now her whole life felt like a series of second chances.

The beach house, the bookstore, Ashley, her friends, *Nate.*

Nate. Always Nate.

Happiness spilled through her. "You have a particular interest in that?"

He turned to her and smiled. "It so happens that I do."

★ ★ ★ ★ ★

ACKNOWLEDGMENTS

My editor told me recently that I've sold almost 22 million copies of my books since I started writing, a figure that made me feel vaguely dizzy but also immensely grateful. It's a testament to the skill and hard work of my publishing teams that my stories have reached such a wide global audience. Seeing my books on the shelves is a continuing thrill, and the result of a herculean effort on the part of sales, marketing, publicity, editorial and the art teams who design my beautiful covers (do you ever choose a book by its cover? I know I do!).

I'm grateful to everyone at HQ Stories in the UK, particularly Manpreet Grewal and Lisa Milton. Your energy, passion and support for my books is humbling and I feel lucky to work with you. Also to the brilliant Margaret Marbury, Susan Swinwood and the rest of the wonderful team at HQN in the US. It's been so long since we traveled anywhere, but I can't wait for the chance to thank you in person again. What a celebration that will be.

My talented editor, Flo Nicoll, read the manuscript multiple times and offered insight and endless encouragement. She deserves a medal (as far as I'm concerned, it's a gold, Flo!).

My agent, Susan Ginsburg, is the best of the best, and I'm grateful for her support and wisdom. Thank you also to Catherine Bradshaw and the rest of the team at Writers House.

I write about families, and I'm extremely lucky with my own who tolerate my moments of writerly panic and self-doubt with patience and humour.

Finally thank you to you, the reader, for continuing to buy my books, for chatting with me on social media and for always being so encouraging. I'm lucky to be writing for such a receptive and special audience.

Turn the page for an excerpt of
USA TODAY *bestselling author Sarah Morgan's*
captivating new book.

SNOWED IN FOR CHRISTMAS

Coming soon!

1

Lucy Clarke pushed through the revolving glass doors and sprinted to the reception desk, stripping off her coat and scarf as she ran. She was late for the most important meeting of her life.

'There you are! I've been calling you. I'll take that.' Rhea, the receptionist, rose from her chair and grabbed the coat from her. 'Wow. You look stunning. You're the only person I know who can look good in a Christmas sweater. Where did you find that one?'

'My grandmother knitted it. She said the sparkly yarn was a nightmare to work with. Feels weird wearing it today of all days, but Arnie insisted that we look festive so here I am, bringing the sparkle. They've started?' She'd hoped she might just make it, but the desks around her were all empty.

'Yes. Get in there.'

Lucy replaced her running shoes with suede boots, hopping around as she pulled them on. Her fingers were so cold she fumbled. 'Sorry. Forgot my gloves.' She thrust her bag towards Rhea, who stowed it under the desk.

'What was it? Trains not running?'

'Signal failure. I walked.'

'You *walked*? You couldn't have grabbed a cab?'

'Everyone else had the same idea, so there wasn't one to be had.' She dropped her scarf on Rhea's desk. 'How is the mood?'

'Dismally lacking in festive joy, given that we're all waiting for Arnie to make us redundant. Even the Christmas sweaters aren't raising a smile, and there are some truly terrible ones. Ellis from Accounts is wearing what looks like a woolly Christmas tree and it's making him itch. I've given him an antihistamine.'

'Arnie is *not* going to make us redundant.'

'You don't know that,' Rhea said. 'We've lost two big accounts in the last month. Not our fault, I know, but the end result is the same.'

'So we need to replace them.'

'Usually I admire your optimism, but I don't want to raise my hopes and then have them crash around me. I love my job. Companies always say *We're a family*, and it's usually a load of rubbish, but this one really does feel like a family. But it's not as if *you* really need to worry. You're brilliant at what you do. You'll get another job easily.'

Lucy didn't want another job. She wanted this job.

She thought about the fun they all had in the office. The laughter. Late-night pizza when they were preparing a pitch. Friday fizz when they had something to celebrate. The camaraderie and the friendship. She knew she'd never forget the support her colleagues had given her during what had undoubtedly been the worst couple of years of her life.

And then there was Arnie himself. She owed him everything. He'd given her back all the confidence that had been sucked from her in her first job, and he'd been there for her at her lowest moment. She'd worked for Arnie for six years, and she still learned something new from him every day. She had a feeling she always would, because the company was small, and nimble, and everyone was encouraged to contribute, whatever their level of seniority. That wouldn't happen if she moved to one of the major players.

'Do I look okay?'

Rhea reached out and smoothed a strand of hair out of Lucy's eyes. 'You look calmer than the rest of us. We're all in a state of panic. Maya has just bought her first flat. Ted's wife is expecting their first baby any day.'

'Stop! If you keep reminding me of the stakes I'll be waving goodbye to calm.' Lucy pressed her hands to her burning cheeks. 'I ran the last mile. Tell me honestly—does my face look like a tomato?'

'It's a seasonal colour.'

'You mean green like holly, or red like Santa?'

'Get in there.'

Rhea gave her a push and Lucy sprinted towards the meeting room.

She could see all of them gathered around the table. Arnie was standing at the head, wearing the same red sweater he'd worn for the past five 'Christmas Jumper' days.

Arnie, who had set up this company over thirty years ago.

Arnie, who had left his family's Christmas celebrations to be by her side in the hospital when her grandmother had died two years earlier.

Lucy pushed open the door and thirty heads turned towards her.

'Sorry I'm late.'

'Don't worry. We've only just started.'

Arnie's smile was warm, but she could see the dark shadows under his eyes. The situation was hard for all of them, but particularly him. He never fired anyone, preferring instead to work with someone to develop their strengths. But this unexpected blow to their bottom line meant he had difficult decisions to make. The thought of it was obviously giving him sleepless nights.

She'd seen him working until midnight at his desk, staring at numbers as if will-power alone could change them. It was no wonder he was tired.

She sat down in an empty seat and tried to ignore the horrible burn of anxiety.

'It's a Christmas campaign...' Arnie returned to the subject they'd been discussing before she'd interrupted. 'Think festive sparkle, think Christmas trees, think snow. We want photographs of log fires, luxurious throws, candles, mugs of hot chocolate heaped with marshmallows. And fairy lights. Fairy lights everywhere. The images need to be so festive and appealing that people who think they hate Christmas suddenly fall in love with Christmas. Most of all they need to feel that their Christmas will not be complete unless they buy themselves and everyone they know a—' Arnie looked blank. 'What's the product called again?'

Lucy's gaze slid to the box in the centre of the table. 'The Fingersnug, Arnie.'

'Fingersnug. Right.' Arnie dragged his hand through his hair, leaving it standing upright. It was one of his many endearing habits. 'The person who advised them on that product name should rethink his job, but that's not our problem. Our problem is how to make it *the* must-have product for Christmas—despite the name and the lack of time to build a heavyweight campaign. And we're going to do that with social media. It's instant. It's impactful. Show people looking warm and cosy... Has anyone tried the damn thing? Lucy, as you were the last one in through the door and you always forget to wear gloves you can take one for the team and thank me later.'

Lucy dutifully slipped her hand inside the Fingersnug and activated it.

They all watched her expectantly.

Arnie spread his hands. 'Anything? Are you feeling a warm glow? Is this life-changing?'

She felt depressed, and a little sick, but neither of those things had anything to do with the Fingersnug. 'I think it takes a minute to warm up, Arnie.'

Ted looked puzzled. 'It's basically a glove.'

'Maybe.' Arnie planted his hands on the table and leaned forward. 'But running shoes are running shoes until we persuade the public that *this* particular pair will change their lives. There are few original products out there—only original campaigns.'

The comment was so Arnie. He was a relentless optimist.

Lucy felt the lump in her throat grow. Arnie had so many bigger things to deal with, but the client was still his priority. Even a client as small as this one.

'It's warming up,' she said. 'It may even cure my frostbite.'

Arnie grabbed one from the box. 'It would be the perfect stocking-filler. I can see it now…keeping hands warm on frosty winter nights. Does it come in smaller sizes? Can kids use it? Is it safe? We don't want to damage a child.'

'Children can use it, and it comes in different sizes.' Lucy felt her fingers growing steadily warmer. 'This might be the first time in my life I've had warm hands. It might be my new favourite thing.'

'We need photographs that appeal to kids—or more specifically to parents of kids. All those activities parents do at Christmas…ice-skating, seeing reindeer—the client specifically mentioned reindeer…' He floundered and glanced around for inspiration. 'Reindeer doing what? I have no idea. Where does one even *find* a reindeer—apart from on the front of Alison's sweater, obviously? And what do you do when you find one? Maybe someone could ride it. Yes! I love that idea.'

One of the reasons Arnie was such a legend in the creative agency world was because he let nothing get in the way of his imagination. Sometimes that approach led to spectacular success, but at other times…

There was an exchange of glances.

A few people shifted in their chairs.

A few people sneaked glances at Lucy.

She looked straight at him. 'I think using reindeer is an inspired idea, Arnie. Gives us the potential for some great creative shots. Maybe a child clutching a stack of prettily wrapped parcels next to a reindeer…capturing that look of wonder on its face. A patch of snow, warm fingers…' She let her mind drift. 'Aspirational Christmas photos. But make them relatable.'

'You don't think someone should ride it?'

She didn't hesitate. 'No, Arnie, I don't.'

'Why not? Santa does.'

'Santa is a special case. And he's generally in his sleigh.'

Were they seriously having this conversation?

There was a moment of tense silence, and then Arnie laughed and the tension in the room eased.

'Right. Well…' Arnie waved a hand dismissively. 'Get creative. Whatever you think will add that extra festive touch, you're to do it, Lucy. And I won't tell you to impress me because you always do.'

'You want *me* to take on the account?' Lucy glanced around the room. There were twenty-nine other people in the meeting. 'Maybe someone else should—'

'No. I want you on this. Getting influencers on board at this late stage is going to be next to impossible, and you're the one who can make the impossible happen.'

He rubbed his chest and Lucy felt a flash of concern.

'Are you feeling all right, Arnie?'

'Not brilliant. I had dinner with one of our competitors last night—Martin Cooper, CEO of Fitzwilliam Cooper. He was boasting about having too much business to handle, which was enough to give me indigestion. Or maybe it was the lamb. It was very spicy…and I'm not good with spicy food.' He stopped rubbing his chest and scowled. 'Do you know he had the gall to ask if I could give him your contacts list, Lucy? I told him it would do him no good, because it's *your* relationship with those contacts that adds the magic. The whole thing works because of you. You have a way of persuading people to do things they don't want to do and definitely don't have time for.'

Lucy chose not to mention the fact that a recruiter for Fitzwilliam Cooper had approached her twice in the last month about a job.

She thought it wise to change the subject. 'Finding a reindeer in the middle of London might be—'

'There are reindeer in Finland and Norway…but we don't have the time or the budget for that. Wait!' Arnie lifted a hand. 'Scotland! There are reindeer in Scotland. I read about it recently. I'm going to ask Rhea to track down the article and send it to you. Scotland. Perfect. I love this job. Don't you all love this job?'

Everyone grinned nervously, because almost without exception they *did* love this job, and they were all wondering how much longer they'd be doing it.

Lucy was focused on a more immediate problem. How was she supposed to fit a trip to Scotland into her schedule?

'It's only two weeks until Christmas, Arnie.'

'And you know what I always say. Nothing…' He put his hand to his ear and waited.

'Nothing focuses the mind like a deadline,' they all chorused, and he beamed like a conductor whose orchestra had just given a virtuoso performance.

'Exactly. You'll handle it, Lucy, I know you will. You're the one who always swoops in and saves the day, and you're always great with everything Christmas.' Arnie waved a hand as if he'd just gifted her something special. 'The job is yours. Pick your team.'

Lucy managed a weak smile. As usual, his enthusiasm and warmth had swept her along. She couldn't say no to him even if she wanted to.

And what would she say, anyway?

Christmas isn't really my thing any more.

No, she couldn't say that. She'd leaned on Arnie hard at the beginning, when the grief had been so raw and sharp it had been agony to live with. But time had passed and she couldn't keep being a misery, no matter how tough she found this time of year. She needed to pull herself together, but she hadn't yet figured out how to do that. There were days when she felt as if she hadn't moved forward at all.

But her priority right now was the company—which meant she would have to go to Scotland. Unless she could find reindeer closer to home. The zoo? Or maybe she could persuade the client to switch the reindeer for a llama. An alpaca? A large sheep?

Her mind wandered and then someone's phone pinged.

Ted jumped to his feet in a panic, sending papers flying. He checked his phone and turned pale. 'This is it! It's coming. The baby, I mean. The baby is coming. My baby. Our baby. I have to go to the hospital. Right now.' He dropped his phone on the floor, bent to retrieve it, and banged his head on the table.

Lucy winced. 'Ouch! Ted—'

'I'm fine!' He rubbed his forehead and gave a goofy smile. 'I'm going to be a dad.'

Maya grinned. 'We got that part, Ted. Way to go.'

'Sophie needs me. I—' Ted dropped his phone again.

This time Alison was the one who bent and retrieved it. 'Breathe, Ted.'

'Yes. Good advice. Breathe. We've done lots of practice. I mean, obviously it's Sophie who's meant to be doing that part, but no reason why I can't do it too.' Ted pushed his glasses back up his nose and cast an agonised and apologetic look at Arnie. 'I'm—'

'Go!' Arnie waved him towards the door. 'And keep us updated.'

Ted looked torn. 'But this is an important meeting, and—'

'Family first.' Arnie's voice was rough. 'Go and be with Sophie. Call us when you have news.'

Ted rushed out of the room, then rushed back in a moment later to collect the coat he'd forgotten, and back again a moment after that because he'd left his laptop.

'Also…' He paused by the door, breathless. 'I have a train set arriving here today. Can someone take delivery?'

Maya raised her perfectly sculpted eyebrows. 'A train set?'

'Yes. It's a Christmas present for my son—' His voice cracked, and Arnie walked around the table and put his hand on Ted's shoulder.

'A train set is a great choice. We'll take delivery. Now, go. Ask Rhea to call you a cab. You need to get to the hospital as fast as possible.'

'Yes. Thank you.' Ted rushed out of the room, knocking into the door frame on his way out.

Maya winced. 'Can't they give him a sedative or something? And is a cab really going to be quicker than taking the train?'

'It's going to be quicker than Ted getting flustered and lost,' Arnie said. 'At least the cab will deliver him to the hospital door—hopefully in one piece and with all his belongings still about his person.'

'A train set?' Ryan, the intern, grinned. 'He does realise that newborn babies can't play with train sets, doesn't he?'

'I suspect it will be Ted playing with the train set,' Arnie said. 'Now, exciting though this is, we should return to business. Where were we? Fingersnug… Lucy? Are you on it?'

'I'm on it, Arnie.'

She'd find a way to show it at its most appealing. She'd put together a last-minute Christmas campaign. She'd find a reindeer from somewhere. She'd pull in favours from her contacts—content creators with high profiles and engaged followings that she'd worked with before. She'd find a way to handle it all and try not to think about the fact that her job was occasionally ridiculous.

Arnie cleared his throat and Lucy glanced at him. It was obvious from the look on his face that they'd reached that point in the meeting everyone had been dreading.

'Now for the tough stuff. You all know we lost two big accounts last month. Not our fault. One company is downsizing because they've lost so much business lately, and the other is trying to cut costs and has decided to go with someone cheaper. I tried telling them that you get what you pay for, but they weren't listening. It's a significant blow,' he said. 'I'm not going to pretend otherwise.'

'Just give us the bad news, Arnie. Have you made a decision about who you're going to let go?' Maya, always direct, was the one to voice what they were all wondering.

'I don't want to let anyone go.' He let out a long breath. 'And not just because you're a fun bunch of people when you're not being annoying.'

They all tried to grin and there was a chorus of *'Thanks Arnie.'*

'The truth is that to win accounts we need good people. To staff accounts we need good people. But I also need to be able to pay those people—and unless we bring in a significant piece of business soon we're in trouble.' He rested his hands on the table and looked round at them. 'I've never lied to you and I'm not going to start now. This is the most challenging time we have faced since I started the company thirty years ago. But all is not lost. I have a few new business leads, and I'm going to be following those up personally. And there's something else we're going to try—speculative, but worth a shot. It's major. If we could land that, then we'd be fine.'

But what if they weren't fine?

Lucy thought about Ted and his new baby. She thought about Maya and her new flat, and how scared she'd been taking on the responsibility of a mortgage. She thought about herself— about how much she loved this job and how badly she needed to keep doing it.

In the early days, after she'd lost her grandmother, her job had given her a reason to get out of bed in the morning. Her job was her source of security—both financial and emotional.

It was the most important thing in her life.

She felt her chest grow tight.

She couldn't handle more change. More loss.

She gazed through the glass wall of the meeting room, forcing herself to breathe steadily. From her vantage point twenty floors up she had an aerial view of London. She could see the dome of St Paul's Cathedral and the River Thames winding its way under Tower Bridge. Three red London buses nosed their way through traffic, and people scurried along, heads down, looking at their phones, all of them in a hurry.

A lump formed in her throat.

If she had to leave the company would it mean moving?

She didn't want to move. She'd been raised here, by her grandmother, who had loved everything about London and had been keen to share its joys and its history with her granddaughter.

'Do you see this, Lucy? Pudding Lane—where The Great Fire of London started in 1666.'

They'd visited the Tower of London—Lucy's favourite place. They'd strolled through the parks hand in hand, picnicked on damp grass, fed ducks, rowed a boat on the Serpentine. Her annual Christmas treat had been a visit to the Royal Opera House to watch a performance of *The Nutcracker*. Every street and every landmark, famous and not so famous, were tangled up with memories of her grandmother.

She loved London. She belonged here.

Sometimes it felt as if the city had wrapped its arms around her—as her grandmother had in those early days after her parents had died.

This time of year was particularly tough. It was impossible not to think about her grandmother at Christmas. Impossible not to wish for one more day with her...walking through the city looking at the sparkling window displays, sipping hot chocolate in a warm café. They'd talked about everything. There wasn't a single thing that Lucy had held back from her grandmother, and she desperately missed that. She missed being able to talk freely, without worrying that she was a burden.

Unconditional love. Love that could be depended on. That was what she missed. That gift had been ripped away from her, leaving her feeling cold, exposed and alone.

She sat there, made miserable by memories, and then caught sight of Arnie's face and felt guilty for being selfish and thinking about herself when he was going through hell. He was worrying about everyone's futures.

They had to win a big account. They *had* to.

He was still talking. 'Let's start by looking at the positive. We're harnessing the power of social media and changing the way brands reach their customers. We're experts in influencer marketing. We're changing consumer habits...'

Lucy made a few notes on the pad in front of her.

In less than a minute she had a list of about ten people to call who might be able to help her with Fingersnug. People she'd built relationships with. People who would be only too happy to do her a favour, knowing that they'd be able to reclaim it in the future.

'We're raising our profile. And on that note, a special shout out to Lucy—our cover girl.' Arnie gestured to the latest edition of a glossy marketing magazine on the table. '"*The Face of Modern Marketing*". Looking good, Lucy. Great interview. Great publicity for the company. If any of you still haven't read it then you should. Lucy, we're proud of you. And as for the rest of you— let's have more of this. Let's get ourselves noticed.'

There was a chorus of '*Go Lucy!*' and a few claps.

Lucy gave a self-conscious smile and glanced at the cover. She barely recognised her own image. She'd spent an hour in hair and make-up before the photoshoot and had felt completely unlike herself. On the other hand, feeling unlike herself hadn't been a bad thing. The Lucy in the picture looked as if she had her life together. The Lucy in the picture didn't stand in front of the bathroom mirror in the morning hyperventilating, worrying that her control was going to shatter and she was going to lose it in public. She didn't stand there feeling as if her emotions were a ticking time bomb, ready to explode without warning.

Anxiety had plagued her since she'd lost her grandmother. She felt as if she was on the edge, navigating life with no safety net.

And now it was almost Christmas. And if ever there was a time designed to emphasise the lack of family it was now. The worst thing was that she'd always *adored* Christmas. It had been her absolute favourite time of the year. Until that horrible Christmas two years before, when she'd spent Christmas Eve and Christmas Day in a vigil by her grandmother's hospital bed.

Now Christmas wasn't tinsel and fir trees and wrapping up warm to listen to carol singers. It was beeping machines and doctors with serious faces and her grandmother's frail, bruised hand in hers. *'Massive stroke,'* they'd said, but she'd hung on until December the thirty-first before finally leaving Lucy to face the New Year, and all the years ahead, without the person she loved most. The person who had taken on the role of both parent and grandparent. The one person who had known her and loved her unconditionally.

The previous year she'd forced herself to celebrate Christmas—although maybe 'celebrate' was the wrong word. She'd bought herself a tree, and decorated it with all the ornaments she and her grandmother had collected over the years.

I'm doing this, Gran. You'd be proud of me.

But it had been hard work—the emotional equivalent of running a marathon uphill in bare feet. Christmas had always been a magical time for her, but now the magic was gone and she didn't know how to get it back. The truth was she was dreading it. And given the choice she would have cancelled Christmas.

Panic rose, digging its claws into her skin.

'This is the point where I'm going to challenge you all,' Arnie was saying. 'Do I believe in miracles? Maybe I do. Because I have my eye on the one of the biggest prizes of all. One piece of new business in particular that would solve all our problems. The biggest fish in the pond. Any guesses?' He glanced around expectantly. 'Think sportswear brands. Think fitness and gyms.'

And now Lucy had a whole new reason to panic.

Not sports. Anything but that.

She was intimidated by gyms and she had no reason to wear sportswear. Her exercise regime involved racing round London meeting clients and influencers and scoping out new cool places to include in their visual campaigns.

Wishing Ted was here, because this was right up his street, Lucy scrolled through the big brands in her mind, discarding the ones she knew were already locked in with other agencies.

One stood out.

'Are you talking about Miller Active? The CEO is Ross Miller?'

'You know him?'

'Only by reputation. His family own Glen Shortbread.' Her grandmother had described it as 'comfort in a tin' and it had been her favourite treat at Christmas.

'Is Glen Shortbread the one in the pretty tin?' Maya chewed the end of her pen. 'The one that changes every year? Last year it was snowy mountains and a loch? I love it. Delicious. I buy it for my mum every year. Just looking at it makes me feel Christmassy.'

'That's the one.'

Lucy still had three of the empty tins in her apartment, even though she didn't have room for them. She couldn't bear to throw them away, so she used them as storage. Two were full of old photographs, and the third held the letters her grandmother had written during Lucy's first year of college, when she'd been homesick and tempted to throw it all in.

'Same Millers—different business.' Arnie rubbed his chest again. 'The son Ross went a different route.'

'Rebel Ross...' Lucy murmured, and saw Arnie glance at her with a question in his eyes. 'I read an article—last year, I think. That was the title. *"Rebel Ross"*. It was all about how he was the first not to go into the family business. He wanted to strike out on his own. The implication was that he and his father were like two stags, fighting over their territory—although given the way Miller Active has grown, I'm assuming he's proved himself by now. There was a lot about the family. His grandmother—can't remember her name... Jane, maybe? No, it was Jean. His father is Douglas, still at the helm of Glen Shortbread. His mother is Glenda. She's been involved with the business from time to time, although I'm not sure she still is. There are three children—Ross, obviously. He's the eldest. Then Alice, who's a doctor, and Clemmie who... I don't know what she does.'

Maya was staring. 'How do you remember all that?'

'I have a good memory for useless facts.'

She wasn't going to tell them the truth. That the article had stuck in her mind because she'd had serious family envy. There had been photographs of the family estate in the Scottish Highlands, showing ancient trees and herds of deer and their baronial home, Miller Lodge, with its gardens sloping down to a deep loch. There had been a glossy shot of the whole family gathered around a roaring log fire, their world-famous shortbread piled on an antique plate on a table in front of them.

Who had been in that photo? She couldn't remember. She'd been too busy gazing at the big, perfect family and envying their perfect life. They'd all been smiling. Even the dogs had looked contented. The message of that picture was that no matter what happened in life they had each other and their gorgeous home.

After she'd salivated over the picture she'd ripped out those pages and thrown them away, because no good ever came from wanting what you couldn't have. Now she wished she'd kept them. It would have been a good place to start with her research.

'I'm impressed.' Arnie sounded more cheerful. 'Background is important—we all know that. And context. Where does a client come from? What does he need? These are the questions we must ask ourselves. And they're the questions you're going to be asking yourselves when you come up with ideas for a campaign. That's the challenge. I'm hearing a rumour that Ross Miller has reached out to a few agencies. He wants to shake things up.'

Lucy felt her spirits lift. 'He's invited us to pitch?'

'Not exactly...' Arnie shuffled some papers. 'But he would if he knew how good we are? We need to grab his attention. It's up to us to give him what he needs.'

Lucy thought back to that article. It seemed to her that Ross Miller already had everything he needed.

'Don't Miller Active use Fitzwilliam Cooper?'

'Yes, but their last campaign was uninspired. That's just my opinion, obviously, but that doesn't mean I'm not right. Miller Active has a strong customer base, but they seem unable to expand beyond that. They're going to be shopping around in the new year. They need *us*. And it's our job to persuade them of that fact.' Arnie waved a hand at the team seated around the table. 'Over the next few weeks I want you to come up with some ideas that will blow them away. Then we need to find a way to get those ideas in front of Ross Miller. It will be our number one priority for the New Year.'

'This is one for Ted,' Lucy said. 'He lives at the gym.'

Maya leaned back in her chair. 'He's not going to be going to the gym for a while, or Sophie will kill him.'

'We have to assume that Ted will be out of the picture, but we can handle this without him.' Arnie gathered up his papers and his laptop. 'The timing is good. Everyone thinks about fitness in January, right? We've all stuffed ourselves over the festive period. Turkey...multiple family meals...'

If only...

Lucy kept her expression neutral. 'It's true that there is a focus on health and fitness in January.'

'All we have to do is find a unique angle, and that's what we're good at.'

Maybe... But a *sports* client? Why did it have to be a sports client? If gym membership was what it was going to take to save Arnie's company she was doomed.

Unless...

An idea exploded into her head out of nowhere. Maybe the perfect idea.

She opened her mouth and closed it again.

Maybe it wasn't a perfect idea. She needed to think about it... work it through in her head. But still...

She was definitely on to something...

Ross Miller hadn't built a successful business in a competitive space by being predictable. When he'd started out there had been no way he could outspend the big brands, so he'd chosen to outsmart them, and that approach had seen his business grow faster than all predictions.

Arnie was right. Whatever they came up with had to be creative. Different. And the idea bubbling in her brain was certainly a little different.

People started to file out of the meeting room. Except for Arnie, who was checking his phone.

Lucy stood up and headed to the coffee machine. She poured two cups and took one to him. Now that she was closer, she could see that his face had a greyish tinge. 'Have you taken something for that indigestion? Maybe I shouldn't give you this coffee.'

'Give me the coffee. The indigestion will pass, I'm sure.' He took the coffee and caught her eye. 'What?'

'I'm worried about you.'

'Why? I'm fine. Never better.'

It was tough, Lucy thought, keeping up an act. No one knew that better than she did.

'Everyone has gone. It's just you and me. You can be honest.'

His shoulders sagged. 'There's no fooling you, is there? I'm worried, that's true. But all we can do is our best. I'm going to reach out to a few more contacts this afternoon. It will be all right… I'm sure it will. Next year will be better. It *has* to be better.'

'About Ross Miller…'

'Don't worry. I know sport isn't your thing,' Arnie said. 'It was just an idea. Grasping at straws. Even if we come up with an idea that's a game-changer, Ross Miller is a tough cookie. I doubt he's going to even give us a meeting or agree to hear our pitch. He's always used the big names. We're not on his approved agency list.'

'Then we need to get ourselves on that list.'

She was not going to give up. And she wasn't going to let him give up either.

'We can do this, Arnie.'

'That's the spirit.' He managed a smile. 'But you're not to worry. If the worst happens I can make some calls and you'll be in another job before the day is out.'

'I don't want another job.'

'I know.' He put the coffee down untouched. 'You and I go back a long way, Lucy. And frankly that makes me feel worse. We have so many loyal and wonderful people in this company and I've let you down. We should have spread our net wider. We relied on a few big accounts instead of taking on multiple small ones. It's left us vulnerable, and that's on me.'

It was typical of Arnie to take full responsibility. Typical of him to blame himself and not others.

'You're not responsible for the economy and world events, Arnie. You're brilliant.'

'Not so brilliant.' He gave a tired smile. 'Anyway, enough of that. How are you doing, Lucy? I know this is a difficult enough time of year for you, without all these additional worries.'

'I'm doing fine, thanks.' Now she was the one putting on an act, but that was fine. The last thing he needed was to listen to her problems on top of everything else. 'You've been working too hard. Maybe you should go home.'

'Too much to do.' He rubbed his hand across his chest again. 'I need to make some calls…start putting together some ideas ready for January.'

'Right.'

But she knew that if major agencies were going to be pitching to Miller Active in the New Year they needed to get in front of Ross Miller before that. He was known to be a workaholic. Surely he wasn't going to be wasting time partying around the Christmas tree?

She left the room, and when she glanced back she saw Arnie slumped in a chair at the head of the long empty table, his head in his hands.

Feeling sick for him, she headed to the water cooler. She was going to do whatever she could to fix this—and not only because this job was the one thing in her life that was good and stable.

Maya was leaning against the wall, swallowing down an entire cup of water. 'Sorry.' She stood to one side when she saw Lucy. 'Fear makes me thirsty. I'm pretending this is gin. What are you going to do?'

'I'm going to go after new accounts—starting with Miller Active. What I'm *not* going to do is panic.'

At least not outwardly. She was keeping all her panic carefully locked inside.

'If you're serious about Miller Active then you should panic. Ross Miller has a black belt in three different martial arts. He can ski. He's a killer in the boxing ring. He sailed across the Atlantic. He has muscles in all the right places.'

'When have *you* ever seen his muscles?'

'In photos.' Maya put her cup down. 'He did some fitness

challenge for charity last summer. Trust me, I would have handed over my credit card happily.'

'You have nothing but debt on your credit card. And what does any of that have to do with going after Miller Active as a client?'

'I love you to bits, but your exercise programme is couch to kitchen. Any chance I can turn you into an exercise fanatic before January so you can increase your credibility? Or give you any credibility at all?'

'I don't need to be an exercise fanatic.'

Maya frowned. 'This is a fitness account. Sportswear. The brief is to expand their customer base. No offence, Lucy, but do you even own yoga pants?'

'No. But in this case that's going to work to my advantage.' Lucy helped herself to water. 'Think about it... Ross Miller wants new customers. What is the profile of a new customer? Not someone like Ted, who's already a convert. It's people like me, who would normally never go near a gym. What would it take to make me buy a pair of sexy workout leggings and show up for a morning weights session?'

'I honestly can't answer that,' Maya said. 'Knowing you, I'm guessing it would take something major.'

'The Miller Active account is major.'

'Lucy, I'm your biggest admirer, but be realistic. The major agencies are pitching. This is the big time. How would you even begin to compete?'

'By being smarter than they are, and by getting ahead of them.'

'But it's Christmas.'

'Exactly. It's the perfect time to work.'

'For you, maybe, but not for most people. And probably not for Ross Miller.' Maya hesitated. 'Look, about Christmas... I've already told you, you can come and spend it with Jenny and me.

It's our first Christmas in the new place. Jenny's mother is joining us, and her brother. Not her dad, because he still can't bear seeing the two of us together and I don't want to spend Christmas with a knot in my stomach.'

'I'm sorry.'

'Don't be. I've never been happier, that's the truth, and if some family tension is the price I have to pay then I'll gladly pay it. And we'd love to have you.'

'It's a kind offer, and I appreciate it, but no, thanks.' She knew Christmas would be rough. She didn't want to inflict her misery on anyone else. And pretending to be fine when you weren't fine became exhausting after a while. Her Christmas gift to herself would be to give herself permission to feel horrible.

Maya sighed. 'Lucy…'

'I'll be fine, honestly. I'm going to be busy with work.'

She didn't mention her conversation with Arnie. If the team knew how worried he was they'd worry even more than they already were. What was the point of ruining everyone's Christmas? It would be better for the team to return from their holiday well rested and optimistic.

'I'm going to come up with a plan to get us in front of Ross Miller.' It would be just the distraction she needed.

'I can't bear to think of you on your own and working over Christmas.'

'I'm thrilled to be working. It will make the whole thing so much easier.'

This would be her second Christmas alone. Third, if you counted the one she'd spent with her grandmother in hospital. Although Arnie had been by her side for that one. She'd survived the others. She'd survive this one.

'Lucy—'

'Christmas is just one day, Maya. This year I'm going to be too busy even to notice it.' She'd been dreading Christmas, but at least now she had a purpose. 'I'm going to find out everything there is to know about the Miller family, and Ross Miller in particular, and I'm going to secure a meeting with him before the other agencies have even swallowed their first helping of turkey. And then in the New Year we are going to knock him dead with our collective brilliance.'

'I'm assuming you don't mean that literally?' Maya didn't look convinced. 'The competition are big players. They're motivated.'

Lucy thought about Arnie, sitting with his head in his hands. She thought about Ted and his new baby. About Maya spending her first Christmas in her new flat. She thought about her own situation.

'I'm one step further on than motivated. I'm desperate.'

Desperate for Arnie. Desperate for her colleagues. Desperate for herself.

'That's all very well,' Maya said, 'but how are you going to get yourself in front of Ross Miller?'

'That's something I'm—' Lucy stopped as she heard Rhea shout her name. She turned. 'What—?'

'Come quickly!' Rhea was breathless and pale. 'Arnie has collapsed. The paramedics are on their way. Oh, Lucy, this is terrible.'